COLLECTING HIS DUE

His finger touched the side of her neck. She shivered and unconsciously tilted her head. The gesture allowed Billie to look anywhere but at him. She wasn't sure she wanted him to know that she liked the way he touched her, that she wanted him to do it again, or that she might combust if she looked into those wickedly colorful eyes.

Craig chuckled. His breath teased the nape of her neck. She started and straightened her back. Too late, she realized the movement brought her almost nose to nose with the irresistible man.

He traced the outline of her lips. "I've been waiting."

"Waiting?" She frowned, but he smoothed the wrinkles from her brow.

"You were going to welcome me back one night, but I didn't make it." His voice was deep and husky.

Her breath caught. She trembled all over. Lightning crackled and thunder boomed. Billie felt her heart stop.

"Thought I'd better collect what's due me."

Her lips parted. Craig hadn't forgotten. *The kiss.*

JUDITH STEEL

ANGEL'S KISS

ZEBRA BOOKS
KENSINGTON PUBLISHING CORP.

ZEBRA BOOKS are published by

Kensington Publishing Corp.
850 Third Avenue
New York, NY 10022

First Printing: August, 1994

Printed in the United States of America

For Susie, my little black dog who for fifteen years—she's older than my one hundred-and-one-year-old grandpa in doggie years—has traveled every mile and taken every step with me. With bright eyes and a wagging tail, she's lain at my feet since I first picked up a pen and decided I wanted to try to write a romance. Ten published historicals later, her eyes are dimming and I'm afraid she won't make number eleven.

So, while I'm still able, I want her to know. "This one's for you, pooky."

Chapter One

June 1863. Alder Gulch, in the Territory soon to be known as Montana

"You can get down now, lady."

Old Buck Benson pulled the team of mules to a stop in front of the Alder Gulch Freight Office. He puffed one last time on the pipe nearly hidden amidst the bushy hair of his gray-streaked beard, then directed a wary glance toward his lone passenger.

She sat as still as a wart on a toad, eyes downcast, hands folded daintily in her lap. Her rich green evening gown and lustrous emerald necklace were coated with dust. To soften the hard wooden bench, she sat on a lightweight cloak that was as valuable as tits on a boar during the cool mountain nights.

Buck heaved a disgruntled sigh and reverted to the commanding tone he'd had to use the entire trip if he wanted her to do anything but just sit. "Scoot over here, lady. I'll help you down."

She obeyed without a flicker of emotion. He shook his head and held her icy fingers as she clambered from the wagon box to the ground.

"This here's the end of the line. If you wanna go farther, you'll haveta check with the boss." Buck ruefully eyed her tall, slender form, then scanned the rough, tough mining community. He couldn't help but worry about the poor woman. She'd ridden with him for almost two weeks and he'd taken care of her like she'd been his own daughter.

Yet, during all that time, she'd never spoken a word. Who was she? Where had she come from? He'd never seen a fancy woman like her in Denver before, and had been shocked as a tom cat stepping in dirty water when the freight agent there had led him to this passenger.

She'd had no luggage. Just paid to ride until the fare ran out. And her money had taken her to Alder Gulch, of all places.

A small blur suddenly darted past Buck and latched on to the woman's skirt. Grubby hands felt the rich, soft taffeta. "Got a penny, ma'am? Or mebbe a nickel?" begged the child who greedily eyed the ornate jewels the lady wore.

Buck quickly grabbed the boy by the scruff of his collar. "G'on, kid. Yore ma'd whup yore hiney if she saw you botherin' the lady." He nodded toward the shabbily dressed woman making suggestive gestures to a disinterested miner down the street. The woman and boy had been a fixture in Alder Gulch during his last several trips. And though he might feel sorry for them, he couldn't allow the youngster to harass the customers.

Not the least intimidated, the boy looked up at the lady's expressionless face. "What's the matter with 'er, mister?"

Before Buck could answer, gunshots reverberated along the dusty street. He turned to take his passenger in hand, expecting to find her in hysterics. Instead, she stood still as death, barely blinking when another shot was fired.

Buck grabbed the arms of both the lady and the boy and pulled them to the rear of the wagon. "Durn fools. Don't have the sense God gave horny toads."

A collective gasp from the gathered crowd drew Buck's attention back to the street. A pair of swinging rattan doors opened and a man staggered through, clutching his bloodstained chest.

The *thwop, thwop* of the doors echoed loudly. Suddenly, the injured man's eyes locked on the back end of Buck's wagon. He looked to see what caught the poor fellow's attention at such a time.

The lady. For the first time in weeks, she was looking at something. She was looking at the man who'd just collapsed into the dust. Looking at him as if she really saw him. Buck shook his head. Her eyes were wide as saucers, her face like chiseled stone. It was as if she'd been mesmerized, so intently was she staring at the man in the street.

The gunshot victim's eyes rolled, then closed. His body jerked once. Buck heard the lady suck in her breath, but when he looked toward her, her eyes were once again locked on the ground. Other than the whiteness of her knuckles where her fingers entwined, the event might never have happened.

But he'd seen. Somewhere, deep down inside, the lady had felt *something*.

The droning buzz of voices replaced the silence. He once again took hold of her elbow. "C'mon, lady. Let's get you inside the office where it's safe."

The little boy saw his mother heading in their direction and whispered, "Uh-oh. Gotta go." He turned big brown eyes on the quiet lady and said, "I'll hit ya up fer that pen—nickel, some other time."

Buck growled and swatted at the kid, but the boy was already off and running. Buck started to turn back toward the lady when she suddenly careened into him.

"Sorry, ma'am. Didn't see . . . Buck? I heard shots. What's going on out here?" Craig Rawlins, the owner of the freight depot, steadied the woman he'd bumped into and stared at his driver.

Buck gulped and looked up at the man who'd rushed from behind the freight office. "Uh, I was just comin' to fetch you." He nodded over his shoulder toward the street. "It's Bobby. Would've done somethin' fer him myself, but had this passenger . . ." His words trailed off when he realized no one was listening.

The instant he'd heard the shots, Craig had had a sick premonition that something horrible would happen—something more tragic than the all-too-frequent gunfights the town had come to expect. Now Buck mentioned Bobby. *Something had happened to Bobby?*

Craig automatically walked toward the tight knot of people in the center of the street. The group parted and moved away. Then he saw his cousin's sprawled body. His stomach clenched like he'd swallowed a thousand-pound lead weight. He knelt next to Bob Rawlins and felt for a pulse. There was none. A chill unlike any he'd known before gripped him. Bobby was dead.

Damn it, why Bobby?

Craig gently patted the dead man's shoulder. It was partly his fault. If he hadn't buried himself in his other businesses, purposely avoiding the saloon, he might have been there today. He might have been able to protect his best friend and favorite relative. Hell, his *only* relative.

His chest expanded on a long, inhaled breath. He released the air with a loud, *whoosh. Why had this happened?*

He glanced toward the Empty Barrel Saloon. He tensed. Had he seen a shadowy movement?

In less than a heartbeat, Craig bolted. The swinging doors slammed open, then crashed behind him. He stopped. The room was empty. He tilted his head and listened. Nothing. No sound. No movement. Damn. Always the same. Whoever it was disappeared as if into thin air.

Bobby had been Craig's partner in the Empty Barrel. Now Bobby was dead, just like Big John Turnbow, Craig's first partner. Why had both men been killed? Were the deaths connected?

Poor Bob had shrugged off his predecessor's murder as just one of the risks they all took in a wild, fast-growing gold camp. But Craig hadn't been that easily convinced. Was even less so now.

A shudder shook his tall form as he gazed around the room. Who else had been in here with his cousin? Taking a deep breath, he inhaled the woodsy aroma of newly hewn tables and chairs mixed with the pungent odor of spilled whiskey.

Memories of a dozen such saloons—some shabbier, some larger, all grotesque and exciting to the small boy he'd once been—swept over him. His breathing became labored. He riffled long, calloused fingers through his thick, collar-length hair. As if driven by a will of their own, his feet moved. In a few long strides he was outside again, gulping in crisp, clean air.

Craig leaned against one of the tall double doors, folded back against the outer wall, that would replace the swinging rattan doors of summer during the winter months. Frustration wedged into his chest as he looked around. Most of those residents who'd taken enough interest to poke their heads out at the sound of gunfire had disappeared. Only a few curious souls loitered in the street. And the undertaker was already bringing his rig up to retrieve the body.

It was the "business as usual" attitude that allowed killers to hide here. But he'd find this one, if it was the last thing he ever did.

With a heart as hard and dry as the ground over which he walked, he went back to kneel beside the man he'd loved. "I'll get him, Bobby," he whispered. "That's a promise."

Shoe leather scuffed over gravel. He glanced up to see the woman, the stiff stranger he'd bumped into earlier, hesitantly approaching. For the first time, he was able to take a good, long look at her.

Her movements were more unconscious than careful as she picked her way through dirt and manure droppings in lightweight slippers. Slippers? He snorted. What kind of fool would wear such flimsy footwear into this rough terrain?

Yet, as he watched her, he realized she wasn't what she seemed. Shoulders, stooped under the weight of an unseen burden, belied her natural height. Her gown . . . What in the hell was she doing wearing an evening gown at this time of day? He frowned. The rich, deep green material looked expensive and was wrinkled and dusty enough to appear as though she'd been living in the thing. And a hardly serviceable cloak was thrown over one arm.

Curious now, his gaze traveled upward, noting how the flare of her hips narrowed to a tiny waist. She filled out her bodice very nicely, displaying a hint of ripe swells above the scalloped neckline. His eyes reluctantly moved on. He sucked in his breath. A huge emerald necklace spanned her breastbone. He'd never seen such a wondrous piece of jewelry. But from the little caution she displayed, she hardly seemed to remember she wore the thing. And she wouldn't have it much longer. There were too many in Alder Gulch who'd slit that delicate throat for such a trophy.

He took back his original assessment. She wasn't a fool. She was an idiot.

His gaze continued upward as he prepared to deliver a good lecture. He froze. Lord, once a man saw those arresting hazel eyes and the pale perfection of her heart-shaped face and those shimmering locks of strawberry-blond hair . . . who'd notice whether or not she was wearing jewelry?

He mentally shook himself. From her clothing to the way she handled herself, she appeared to be a lady. A lady whose complexion was much too pale for the Montana sunshine and altitude. A somewhat bedraggled lady whose hat didn't even match her gown.

What was she doing in Alder Gulch?

Then he noticed her intense gaze was directed to the body on the ground. Guilt spasmed within him. For just a moment, he'd forgotten the horror of his cousin's death. For just that moment, puzzling over this perplexing lady, he'd pushed reality aside.

But now it came gushing back like Alder Creek after a sudden storm. He glared from the prone figure to the shocked lady. That woman did not belong in Alder Gulch! His jaws clenched. Rage at her stupidity and fear for her safety battled within him.

Buck chose that moment to hesitantly approach. "Lady? C'mon, now. Let's git you out of the street afore you git hurt." He looked helplessly at his boss.

Craig's anger suddenly dissipated. The woman didn't act as if she'd heard a word Buck said. In fact, when Buck turned her slowly around, she gave no appearance of feeling any emotion at all. She followed him like a child, obeying when he shouted at her to stop and wait for a wagon to pass, only moving again when he told her to walk.

Now Craig was really curious. As soon as he and the undertaker had dealt with Bobby, he'd hunt up Buck and find out more about the woman.

An hour later, Buck had unloaded the wagon and stood scratching his head at the sight of the woman still standing where he'd left her just inside the freight-office door. Several miners had stopped and looked in, gawking at the pretty new addition to Alder Gulch. All had asked him questions for which he had no answers. She was one cargo he wouldn't mind turning over to his boss.

Where had Craig Rawlins disappeared to, anyway? He'd hoped the boss would be able to decide what should be done with her.

Surely she had family, or a man, or someone here, or she wouldn't have come this far into the wilderness. So, why hadn't someone come to claim her?

Buck stood helplessly by after he'd finished his chores.

He had other things to do, friends to meet. Craig had yet to show up and it was time to close the office. He walked over to the woman and bent his creaking back as far as he could to look into her eyes.

"Lady, you have to leave. You hear me?" Though he was certain she was looking at him, he saw no acknowledgment to his question, or even a hint that she'd heard him speak at all.

Finally, he took a deep breath and ordered, "Go on now. Find whoever you came here to meet. Git."

He stepped back when she straightened away from the wall. His conscience nagged at him as he watched her walk slowly down the street. Her eyes were still downcast. She never noticed the men who smiled or waved or called a greeting. Several followed her a ways, awed by the presence of a mysterious "lady" in Alder Gulch.

Buck shoved his sweat-stained hat to one side and scratched his head again. At least it appeared she was on her way to *somewhere*. She was no longer his responsibility. But while he hurried to the nearest bar, he kept looking over his shoulder.

Craig Rawlins stepped out of the mercantile and paused to roll a cigarette. Striking a match down the seam of his trousers, he cupped the flame in his palms, drew in several breaths, and ignited the tobacco.

He exhaled slowly, taking time to gaze around the crowded main street. Two-foot ruts from the last rain, stacked crates, and piled garbage did little to impede the progress of men. Beggars, thieves, businessmen, and those made wealthy beyond their wildest dreams by the precious metal, all walked the street with little to distinguish one from the other.

The booming gold camp was a rough, dangerous community, but Craig loved the uncertainty and challenge—the freedom to use his knowledge and strength to the best of his ability. So far, he'd done well in Alder Gulch. He was finally making something of himself, rising to prominence as a man whose opinion was sought after and whose word meant something.

His eyes shuttered. People in Alder Gulch had never heard of Craig Rawlins, didn't know his background and probably wouldn't care. Here, a man was judged for what he did with his life each and every day. The past was irrelevant, the future precarious.

A spiral of smoke escaped his lips. He watched it dissipate into the thin mountain air and was about to go across the street to the freight office when he noticed a woman ambling dangerously close to passing wagons. A team of mules, startled by a gust of wind whipping her skirt, would have turned the wagon into her if not for the alert actions of the cursing driver.

Craig frowned. It was the woman Buck had brought into town. The one with such an odd expression. If you could call that blank stare on her lovely face when she looked at Bobby an expression.

What on earth was she doing wandering the streets? Couldn't she see it was dangerous?

He sucked in his breath when a burly miner didn't see her coming, turned, and almost knocked her down. As Craig started across the street, he saw her body tense. His eyes narrowed when she shied away from the man's awkward but helpful hands. This time Craig recognized her expression. Terror. And the more the man tried to help her by touching her, the more frightened she became.

Craig was about to intervene when the scene was interrupted by a very unlikely source. A young girl whom Craig knew only by the name of Molly, rushed around a corner and stumbled over the miner's foot.

"Dangnab it, ya son of a sow, watch where the hell yore goin'." The girl put her hands on her hips and sized up the miner, then batted her lashes. "Say, ya

wouldn't wanna go behind that barn over there, would
ya? Just charge ya two bits."

Craig thought he'd burst out laughing at the wild-
eyed miner. The man threw up his hands in wonder
over one woman who fought off every move he made to
help her, then another who came along and cursed him,
then asked if he wanted to give her a roll in the hay.
Poor fella. Wasn't a man alive who'd ever understand a
female.

He sobered quickly, though, when Molly's attention
turned to the strange newcomer.

The girl splayed her hands on her hips and circled
the shaking lady. "See what ya gone an' done," she announced loudly. "The sucker would've paid me two bits
if'n ya hadn't gone an' run 'im off."

Craig had to wait for a wagon to pass before he could
finish crossing the street. By the time he reached the
other side, he could hear Molly asking, "Yore new in
town, ain't ya?"

He watched the lady look from side to side, then duck
her head. She had no answer for Molly.

Molly looked behind the woman and saw Craig
Rawlins approaching with a hard glint in his eyes. She
backed away, but gave one last parting jibe. "Stay outta
my way, hear?"

Craig came up even with the lady, but she didn't appear to notice him and moved forward again with jerky,
unsteady steps. He was tempted to reach out and take
her arm, but remembered her reaction to the miner.

He felt a jerk on his pantleg and glanced down. The
little boy who'd been with Buck and the lady beside the
wagon earlier was looking up at him with wide, questioning eyes.

"You know what's the matter with 'er, mister? She
acts kinda loony, don't she?"

Craig had to admit the boy had a point, but didn't
think the woman was crazy at all. She acted like someone who'd suffered a tremendous shock, or experienced

a pain too great to deal with. "I don't know what the matter is, Danny. I think she just needs someone to watch out for her."

The boy eyed him warily. "Hey, how'd ya know my name?"

Craig arched a brow. "I know a lot of things about a lot of folks around here."

Danny's mouth opened wide. "You must be purty smart, huh, mister?"

"I like to think so."

"Ya know my ma's name, too?"

Craig sighed and had to admit, "No." But he'd seen the pair around town. They appeared on the verge of starvation, but the woman always seemed to keep them going. Like Molly, he'd seen her soliciting men. Once he'd offered her money for food, but she'd bristled like a mother grizzly and informed him she didn't take charity.

The grubby hand tugged at his trousers again. "Then ya ain't smart, atall."

The little fellow looked so disappointed that Craig grinned and reached into his pocket. Finding a penny, he bent over and held it out. "Bet I know a boy who likes licorice."

"Wow, yore durned sure right 'bout that." Danny snatched the penny before the big man could change his mind and darted down the street.

Craig straightened, feeling pretty proud of himself. Of course, he'd never tell the boy that the dark smudges around his mouth made his love of the candy obvious.

A commotion down the street suddenly reminded Craig of the woman. Searching her out, he wasn't surprised to find that she was the cause of the ruckus. Inhaling deeply, he hitched up his gunbelt and headed to her rescue.

"C'mon, little lady, give us a kiss. Just one kiss."

"Yeah, ain't been anyone as pretty as you around here in a coon's age."

Doors swung open and a burly barkeeper emerged, wiping his hands on a dirty towel. "What you find, boys?"

The first man grinned. "Ain't she somethin', Les? She were just wanderin' the street an' happened to bump inta ole Mike. It were her lucky day, eh, gal?"

Craig arrived just in time to knock the man's hand away when he reached for the woman.

"Hey, jest who da ya think ya are? We saw the woman first. She's ours."

The barkeep looked quickly to the woman, noting immediately the expensive piece of jewelry hanging around her throat. "Whatta ya say, little lady? Ya like to come inside an' let me show ya around? I pay the best rates in town and'll even throw in a room with clean sheets."

Craig growled and stepped forward to stop her, but found his path blocked by the other two. The woman's glazed eyes desperately sought a path of escape, but the bartender had a hold of her arm.

"Take your hands off—"

A fist bigger than a hamhock smashed into Craig's cheek. Falling backward, his pain was nothing compared to the woman's anguished whisper. It reverberated over and over in his throbbing head.

"Plee-e-e-ease, help . . ."

Chapter Two

The woman's haunting plea galvanized Craig Rawlins. The man who'd hit him must've had confidence in his one swing, for he'd turned his back and playfully slapped his partner. The two men then followed the bartender, who was pulling the lady into the saloon.

They were both trying to go through the doorway together when Craig rammed them from behind. He kicked the backs of the smaller one's knees, knocking him onto the disreputable establishment's dirt floor. Craig grabbed the larger one's shoulder and swung him around.

The fellow swiped at Craig with the back of his hand, but Craig ducked and hit him in the gut. The man roared and came at Craig with both arms spread in an effort to trap him in a vicious bear hug. Craig sidestepped and kicked him in the shin as he lumbered by.

Worried about the woman, Craig waited until the big man turned back to face him, then waded in swinging both fists, hitting him first on the chin and then the lower belly. Air hissed through the man's teeth in a giant gust. He sagged to the floor and didn't get up.

Craig spun to face the smaller man. He threw up his hands and backed away. "I ain't got no argument with ya, mister."

Shifting his gaze over the startled patrons, Craig finally found the woman. She was backed into a corner, her huge eyes flashing green and gold. Though she was taller than the average woman, he sensed her fragility.

The bartender attempted to thwart Craig's approach by stepping between him and the lady. He reached for the woman, but she slapped at his hand and flattened herself against the wall.

Craig mentally applauded her, noting that she at least seemed to be more aware now of what was happening around her. But while he watched her from the corner of his eye, he was also keeping close tabs on the saloonkeeper. When the man made another grab at the woman, Craig lunged forward and caught his hand. Spinning the man around, Craig bent his arm behind his back.

"Stop!" Les yowled. "You're breakin' my arm."

"It's no more than you deserve, manhandling the lady like that."

Les snorted. "She ain't no lady. Jest look at them clothes. She ain't nuthin' but a fancy whore."

Craig growled and jerked the man's arm up higher. Other men in the saloon nodded their approval. Women were a rarity in the gold camps, and most men treated them like precious treasures, to be appreciated, maybe even plundered, but never damaged.

A miner Craig had met before by the name of Lucky stepped forward and took the bartender in hand. "Go ahead, Mr. Rawlins. Take the lady out of here."

Craig glanced around and found that other miners had disarmed the two men who'd sided with the barkeep and had them sitting quietly on the floor. His gaze encompassed the room as he nodded his thanks.

Then, taking a long, deep breath, he turned to the woman. She looked like a trapped fawn. His heart lurched painfully in his chest. Someone had hurt this beautiful woman. Hurt her badly.

"Hello," he whispered. "No one's going to hurt you now." He pointed to the bartender and the other two who'd waylaid her, so she could see they were securely under guard. "They won't bother you again."

He eased closer. She cringed. He sighed and backed up again. Panic glazed her eyes, warning him that she wasn't thinking rationally and might do something foolish. The thought of her hurting herself sparked another idea.

He backed up to where Lucky was standing. The miner had forced the bartender down with the other two men and then come up to watch Craig deal with the woman.

"Lucky, don't try to get up to her, but keep her where she is. I think I have an idea on how to get her out."

Lucky nodded.

Craig strode quickly from the saloon. His eyes scanned the street. He spied the person he needed, looking in the mercantile window.

The little boy jumped when Craig reached down and touched his thin shoulder. He turned his smudged, sticky face up to Craig and pouted. 'The door's locked. Didn't git my lic'rish."

"Tell you what, Son. If you'll come and help me, I'll be here bright and early in the morning to buy you a whole pound of candy."

"Wow." Then he tilted his head and eyed Craig suspiciously. "What's I gotta do?"

Craig put a hand behind the boy's back and prodded him down the street as they talked.

"Remember that pretty lady we thought someone needed to watch out for?"

Danny solemnly nodded.

"Well, she's gone and gotten herself in a little trouble and is too afraid to get out of it by herself."

"And she needs me to help?"

Craig squeezed the boy's shoulder. "Think you can do it?"

"Yep." Danny swaggered importantly when Craig pointed to where they were going.

Just outside the swinging doors, Danny stopped. Hiding in front of Craig's legs, he peered up and down the street. "My ma'll whup me if'n I go in there."

"I'll explain to your mother." Craig bent down and looked the boy in the eyes. "This is very important, Danny. She's real scared. You have to talk firm to her, but show her you're not going to hurt her." Craig closed his eyes, hoping his instincts were right, that she'd be more apt to accept help from a child than grown men.

Danny's little chest puffed out, but he stammered, "I—I'll try my bestest."

"That's all anyone can do." Craig stood and looked through the door. The woman still cowered in the corner. The men inside still watched her closely.

"Wait out here a minute, Son," he told Danny, then pushed through the doors. Once inside, he talked quietly to the men. "Fellas, let's all go outside. Maybe if there aren't so many of us watching her, she'll feel less frightened."

Everyone agreed Craig might be right and filed out, keeping the three troublemakers corraled in the middle of the group.

Craig smiled encouragingly at Danny. "All right, Son, see what you can do."

Danny gulped and walked beneath the doors, looking as if he expected a monster to jump at him any moment.

Seeing the woman scrunched in the corner, he cautiously glanced around the room to make sure nothing else was there to take him by surprise. Then he tiptoed toward her.

"Hey, lady. About that penny I ast ya fer . . . Just fergit it, huh?" Edging closer, he hunkered down in front of the woman and gazed up into her wide, wild eyes. He grasped the leg of a chair, just in case he'd need to protect himself.

"Uh, Mr. Rawlins, he got all them men outta here so you wouldn't feel so 'fraid." He glanced nervously toward the door. "Ya ain't 'fraid o' me, is ya?" He shifted his eyes back to hers and fell back onto his bottom when she lowered her eyes to him. It was the first time she'd actually looked at him. It was the same kind of look a hound dog had given him once when he'd held out a piece of jerky. All of a sudden, she wasn't quite so frightening.

He got up on his knees and crawled close enough that he could almost reach out and touch her.

"I won't hurt ya, lady. Cross my heart."

"And hope to die?" Her voice was a reedy whisper.

His eyes widened, but he nodded.

Danny stood up. "Please come out with me, lady." He puffed out his chest and offered proudly, "I'll protect ya."

To Danny's estimation, the woman seemed to shrink two feet. He held out his hand. "C'mon." Her fingers were cold and rough when they wrapped around his. He gulped, but tugged and said, "Jest foller me."

A chorus of murmured questions and comments greeted Danny and the woman. He felt her pull on his hand, but refused to release her. He'd promised Mr. Rawlins, and was within a foot of a whole pound of licorice.

When the doors closed behind them, Danny led the lady toward Mr. Rawlins. Holding on to her for dear life, he darted his eyes to the man and asked, "Now what're we gonna do with 'er?"

Craig hadn't thought that far ahead. The speculations of several of the men convinced him she needed someone with her. He motioned for the boy to bring the woman and moved down the street and around the corner away from the crowd of men—those who'd been inside the saloon when the commotion started and others who'd stopped to see what was going on.

Glancing worriedly at the silent, frightened woman, he wished there was a doctor he could take her to. And there probably was, somewhere along the gulch, up to his knees in cold water and mounds of mud. No, someone else would have to provide for her. Someone she could trust. Someone who . . .

Rubbing the tip of his chin, Craig eyed Danny keenly. "Why don't you take her to the barn."

Danny blinked and suddenly found a beetle to stare at. "What barn?" he muttered.

Craig folded his arms across his chest. "My barn. You know, where you spend so much time hiding from your mother."

"How'd ya know . . ." Danny's Adam's apple bobbed precariously.

Shrugging, Craig informed the boy again, "I know everything that goes on in Alder Gulch."

"But—"

"Tell you what . . ." Craig pulled a handful of coins from his pocket and handed them to the boy. "This is for you if you'll feed and water my paint horse tonight and . . ." He bent to look the boy in the eye. "And if you'll watch after the woman a while."

"Goshes, Mr. Rawlins, how'm I gonna do that? I don't know nuthin' 'bout *wimmen.*" He said the word with distaste.

Craig smiled and mussed the boy's already mussed hair. "Amen," he said sarcastically, then asked. "Think maybe your mother would help?"

Danny chewed his lower lip. His mother would be grateful to be able to stay in a nice warm barn for a change. But he darted a wary glance at the tall man. "Reckon. What would it cost us?"

Craig's brows slashed together. What a cynical question from such a little boy. He and his mother must have had it pretty rough.

"All it will cost is the time you spend." Scooting his hat forward, he rubbed the back of his neck. "Look, do we have a deal or not?"

"Reckon." Danny switched hands with the woman and stuck out his right one.

Craig barely suppressed a chuckle as he shook with the boy. "Come over to the freight office after you get settled. I'll see if I can't rustle you up something for supper."

"Ma, too?"

"Absolutely."

"Wow. I mean . . . s'right." Danny could hardly stand still. He held on to the woman's hand like she was an angel from heaven.

He looked up at the pretty woman and urged, "C'mon, lady. Foller me agin." They hadn't gone three yards before he looked back and announced, "Hot damn, jest wait'll we tell my ma."

Craig watched them walk away, worried about whether he'd done the right thing. But had he really had a choice? The woman was an easy target for the men in this town. He'd had to do *something* with her. At least she'd be in a warm, dry place and have the boy and his mother for company. He'd done all he could do being as how he was a bachelor and there was no hotel.

Spinning on his heel, he set off to find the food he'd promised. From all he'd seen of the odd trio he'd put together, they hadn't had too many good meals.

Then he'd hunt up Buck and find out what the driver knew about the woman and Bobby's murder. His eyes narrowed. For that matter, he'd like to question the woman if she ever snapped out of whatever was bothering her. She very well might have seen or heard something important.

He wondered, too, if he shouldn't do something to find the woman's family, or husband, or whatever. Surely she'd come to Alder Gulch to meet someone. However, he rationalized, enough people knew of her presence in town to spread the word. If someone had been expecting her, they would soon know she was here and come to claim her.

A scowl deepened the lines between his eyes. How

come the thought of her being taken from his charge didn't make him feel more relieved?

Danny led the lady between a gambling "house" hastily set up in a tent and a wagon with a broken wheel. Skirting a pile of garbage and an odorous privy, he guided her down a lane that paralleled the main street.

He urged her toward a sturdy wood barn behind one of the few wooden buildings in town. Just behind the two-story building was another privy. This one didn't stink to high heaven and actually stood square without giving the appearance it would topple over with the next gust of wind.

Danny pointed toward the small building and said, "That one's ourn." Then he turned to the left and stopped in front of the barn door. Tilting his head, he looked up at the woman and asked, "Ya ain't gonna run off if'n I let go yore hand, are ya?"

Satisfied at a shake of her head, he released her and struggled to lift the bar. Suddenly, it raised easily and a huge grin split his mouth when he looked at the lady, who handed him the long piece of wood.

"Gee, thanks. My ma says I'm growin' faster'n a baby chick mothered by two hens, but I ain't got as tall as I'd like." He opened the door and motioned her to follow him inside. "One o' these days, I'm gonna be as big as Mr. Rawlins. Yessiree, ya just watch."

A big paint horse in the first stall whickered and shook his mane as the boy approached. "This here's Spot. Don't know what 'is real name be, but that's what I call 'im."

After scratching the animal's neck, he grabbed the woman's hand again and dragged her to the stall opposite the horse.

"This here's where I stay." He glanced guiltily around. "I mean . . . when I'm not out workin' with my ma, an' all." He dug beneath the straw and pulled out a handful of treasures. "See my marble? An' this here purty rock? An' one o' ma's friends carved this pony fer me."

He glanced up to see if the woman was looking. She was. "You kin play with 'em if'n ya want."

When the lady sank down to sit beside him, he handed her the wooden horse.

"Danny? Danny, you in there?"

The boy's eyes widened. "Uh-oh." Snatching up all of his toys, he quickly replaced them beneath the straw. He glanced conspiratorially at the woman. "That's my ma. We can't tell her this is where I come an' hide."

The door slowly creaked further open. "Danny, I know you're in here. Some man stopped me on the street and said I should come an' find ya."

"I'm over here, Ma." He stood and waited until she saw him.

Danny's mother, a short, small-boned woman with mousy brown hair and faded blue eyes, peered across the shadowed interior of the barn and moved cautiously across the floor.

"What're ya doin' in here, Danny? Haven't I done told ya, folks don't 'preciate our trespassin' on their property?"

"But I ain't," he said, skipping over to her. "I done got us a job," he waved a grubby hand around in a circle, "taking care o' Spot an'," he indicated the woman sitting quietly in the straw, "an' my new friend."

His mother gazed at the other woman with suspicion. As she placed her hands on her hips, her face registered curiosity, then caution. Then walking slowly forward, she held out her hand. "My name's Anna Corbett. I reckon ya've already met my son, Danny."

Danny jerked on his mother's skirt. "She don't talk, Ma. Mr. Rawlins an' me, we jest decided we should look after her, since it didn't 'pear no one else was."

Anna's eyes narrowed. "I kin hardly keep food in our

own bellies. Cain't be lookin' after some fancy man's light lady."

"But, Ma, it ain't like that. Mr. Rawlins don't 'spect us to feed 'er."

"This Mr. Rawlins . . . Is he real tall, kinda thin, with reddish-colored hair, wearin' a black suit an' hat?"

Danny nodded vigorously. "Yep. He's real nice."

"Yeah, real nice. Look what he done to her."

Too young to recognize his mother's cynicism for what it was, Danny blithely continued. "Yeah, he he'ped her a bunch. An' me, too. She come in with the freight an' got in all sorts o' trouble. Reckon she's all alone an' needs us. He's gonna pay me . . ." Suddenly, his eyes rounded. "I gotta go, Ma. Will ya watch the lady fer me?"

"But . . . where . . ." She was speaking to empty space. Danny had already disappeared out the door.

Anna cocked her head and studiously regarded the woman sitting silently in the straw. Her eyes were downcast, as if intently interested in the creases her fingers were making in the folds of her taffeta gown.

Remembering that her son had said the lady didn't talk, Anna wondered if she was deaf and dumb. What a shame. She was so pretty, with that strawberry-blond hair and flawless complexion. Beneath the dirt and grime, Anna could now see the woman was *quality*.

Sitting on a pile of straw, Anna leaned over and tried to look into the woman's eyes. "Hello. I'm Anna, remember?" When there was no response, Anna looked helplessly about the barn. Spying a bucket of water, she asked, "Are you thirsty?"

Anna almost fell backward when the woman looked up quickly and focused dull, faded hazel eyes on her. "Yore thirsty?"

The woman nodded.

Scrambling to her feet, Anna fetched the pail and handed over a ladle of water. She watched, amazed, as the woman greedily gulped the tepid liquid, then shyly handed back the dipper.

"Th-thank you."

Anna bent her head over, unsure she'd ever heard the raspy whisper. But there was a slight flicker in the woman's green-brown eyes as she nodded. Anna swallowed. "Yore welcome."

A loud scrape, high-pitched mutters, and shuffling sounds announced Danny's return. When Anna saw him stumble into the barn with his thin arms filled with packages, she hurried over to help. "What's all this, son?"

His bright brown eyes gleamed with pride over his accomplishment. "It's grub, Ma. An' I brunged it all by my lonesome."

Anna smiled and took several parcels. "So you did. Yore gonna be a growed man fore we know it."

He grinned impishly and ran over to plunk himself down by the lady. "See what I brung? We got crackers an' pickles an' cheese an' canned peaches an' jerky an' all sorts o' stuff."

"Danny? Where'd you get all this?" Anna's concern was evident. She was afraid she hadn't kept a close enough eye on her son lately.

"Mr. Rawlins said we could have it as part o' my wages."

She frowned, but said for Danny's benefit, "Well, that were mighty nice of the man."

Assuming the role of provider, Danny divided the jerky and cheese and set the crackers in the middle of a horseblanket Anna had spread between them. Before either he or Anna could take a bite, they stared, stunned, as the woman ravenously tore into her food.

"My goodness."

"Wow. She really must've been hungry." Danny dug in, too, never taking his wide eyes off the woman.

Anna leaned over and squeezed the woman's knee.

After getting her attention, Anna said softly, "Slow down, dear. Yore gonna make yourself sick."

The woman did as ordered and ate more slowly.

Since Anna and Danny were every bit as hungry, it didn't take them long to finish their meal. Anna was rewrapping the few leftovers when she asked Danny, "Does yore friend have a name?"

"Don't know."

Gazing steadily at the woman, she asked, "What's yore name, dear?"

No response. Then thinking back, she remembered that whenever she or Danny had said something in the form of a command, the woman had obeyed. It was strange, but if it worked . . .

"Excuse me." She smiled encouragingly when the woman looked up. "Tell us yore name."

For a minute, Anna figured her hunch had been wrong, but then the woman blinked.

"W-Wi . . ." The woman's hand jerked up. Her fingers encircled an emerald. "B-Bi-Billie."

"Billie . . . Well, what a pretty name."

"Aw, Billy's a man's name," Danny piped up.

"Shush yore mouth, Danny. I've heard of girls named Billie afore. It's short for another name. Kinda like a nickname."

"Short fer what? I ain't never hard of it afore."

"Dan-n-ny . . . Yore gonna hurt the . . . Billie's feelings."

Danny's cheeks turned even redder than usual. He ducked his head. "I didn't mean to."

"I know." Billie's voice was getting stronger.

Anna glanced covertly at the woman and noticed there was more life in her eyes now. It was a good sign.

The paint horse snorted. Danny started, then jumped up. "Damn, I almost fergot to feed Spot."

"Danny," Anna scolded. "What've I told ya about cursin'? I'll wash yore mouth out if'n I hear ya say that agin."

"Yes'm." But he didn't seem very worried about the threat as he skipped over to the barrel where Mr. Rawlins had told him the oats were stored. It had been a long time since his mother'd had a sliver of soap.

"That boy," Anna huffed. She tilted her head as she looked over to Billie. "Do you have children?"

Billie seemed lost in thought, then shook her head.

"Well, I'm sure you will someday, a woman purty as you. They're a trial, but pure joy, too." She gazed fondly at her son.

When Danny returned, he grinned and pointed to the woman. Billie was nodding slowly. Anna smiled.

Danny yawned and Anna took one of the blankets Mr. Rawlins had sent over. After spreading it on top of the straw for herself and Danny, she wrapped the second blanket around Billie's shoulders.

"I'm sleepy, too. First time we've gone to bed with a full stomach in a long time, eh, Danny?"

The boy grinned and curled up next to his mother. "I'm gonna take care o' us from now on, Ma. I got us a job. Mebbe I'll even take care o' the nice lady. I think she likes us."

" 'Pears so, son." But Anna frowned. "Jest don't go countin' yore chickens 'fore the eggs hatch."

A rooster crowed. The inhabitants of the barn slowly began to stir. Anna sat up carefully, so as not to awaken Danny. She glanced over to where Billie had fallen asleep and started. The woman was gone.

Close to panicking for fear Billie would come to harm, Anna clambered to her feet and started toward the door. She came to a sudden stop when she saw Billie silhouetted in the narrow opening.

Anna strode purposefully forward, making as much noise as possible to keep from frightening the woman. When she was directly behind Billie, she asked, "Billie? Are you all right?"

Billie turned her head, looked at Anna, and nodded.

"Oh, good," Anna sighed. "It scared me when I saw you were gone. This is a dangerous town for a woman alone."

The curious look Billie shot her made Anna blush. "I'm not alone. I have Danny," she added defensively.

Billie started out the door. Anna rushed forward. "Where are ya goin'? Ya aren't leavin', are ya?"

Billie shook her head and pointed across the way to the privy.

Anna's cheeks burned. "Oh. Well, all right, I s'pose."

Anna watched Billie cross the street and enter the outhouse. Then she went over to wake Danny. "C'mon, son, time to get up. After Billie gets back an' ya feed the horse, we'll hunt us up something ta go with what we had left last night fer breakfast."

Danny rubbed his eyes with the backs of his knuckles. "Don't worry 'bout breakfast. Me'n Mr. Rawlins done took care o' that."

"Oh? I wanna know some more about this Mr. Rawlins, young man. Seems you two been cookin' up a mess where there ain't no grease."

Craig Rawlins was coming out of the only restaurant in town holding two heaped, covered plates, when someone called to him. He grimaced and waited, knowing there was no way to escape the confrontation.

"Craig Rawlins," drawled a southern, very feminine voice. "Where were you last night? Justin and I waited supper for over an hour."

Forcing a contrite look of guilt, he turned to face the petite, black-haired woman. "I'm really sorry, Sunny. Something came up and I couldn't get away."

"I keep tellin' you, you work too hard, darlin'. You could've come on up after you were through," she purred, running her palm down his smooth cheek.

"It was too late. Justin would've already been in bed.

You, too, probably." He turned his head from her caress.

"I'd have gotten up for you, and you know it."

"Ahem, yes, you . . . ah . . ." He wished he had a free hand to tug at his constricting collar. He felt like he was going to choke.

Sunny looked at the plates. "You have a big appetite this mornin'." Her eyes narrowed. "Are you sure all you did was work last night?"

Craig didn't remember telling her exactly what he'd been doing, but if that was what she wanted to think . . .

"Maybe I could join you—"

"Not this morning, Sunny. I'm sharing this with some of the . . . boys." Craig felt heat spread up his neck. He didn't know why he was being so secretive about his "guests," but for some reason, he wasn't ready yet to tell Sunny about the woman.

"Then you'll come to supper tonight, won't you?" Seeing the indecision in his eyes, she hurriedly added, "I won't take no for an answer. You disappointed us last night, and can make up for it tonight." She pouted prettily and flounced away before he had a chance to give her a reply.

He heaved a sigh of relief. Sunny was the widow of his first partner, Big John Turnbow, who'd also been killed in the saloon. He'd felt it his responsibility to look after Sunny and her seventeen-year-old son, Justin. But *she* seemed to be getting other ideas. Ideas he didn't care for at all.

He was approaching the back of the saloon, walking past the privy, when the door suddenly swung open. A woman walked out, turned, and landed directly between his arms.

The plates tilted. Balancing them precariously, he begged, "Don't move, ma'am. Please don't move."

Chapter Three

Craig felt the woman tense. Gradually, she started to tremble. Her eyes locked on his chest.

"Ma'am, I'm not going to hurt you," he promised softly. His brows slanted together when she lifted a shaking hand to clutch at her necklace.

"Ma'am, I've brought breakfast. See these plates? If you move too quickly, you're going to make me spill them. You wouldn't want that, would you?" he coaxed. "Little Danny wouldn't have anything to eat."

"Danny?" Her voice sounded thick, unintentionally sultry.

His heart nearly dived to his stomach when she raised her head and looked at him for the first time. Flecks of green and gold swam in luminous brown eyes that brimmed with confusion and distrust.

"My hands. Look at my hands."

Billie blinked, then looked at the man's hands. Vaguely, she realized that his arms stretched out awkwardly, his muscles quivered. She swallowed the knot of fear lodged in her throat. Warmth from his body, the comforting aromas of bacon and biscuits, lessened her terror.

"Step back!" he ordered. "Back away slowly."

She took a deep breath and moved out of his unwieldy embrace. Standing dead still, she cocked her head and stared at the tall, well-dressed man.

Uncomfortable under her intense scrutiny, he shifted from one foot to the other and asked, "Ma'am, are you all right?" He didn't like the faraway look that had glazed her eyes again. At least when she'd gazed at him a minute ago, even with her panic clearly evident, she'd seemed aware of him.

"Would you mind taking one of these plates? My arms are about to give out."

Billie continued to regard the man. He was tall and lean with huge, broad shoulders, narrow hips, and long, muscular legs. He looked as if he could hold those plates forever and not get tired!

"Take a plate, please."

She took the one tilting the most precariously.

"Thanks." He started walking toward the barn, looked back over his shoulder, and called, "Are you coming?"

She blinked at the sound of his voice.

Craig sighed and commanded, "Bring the plate and follow me."

Trudging after him, Billie gratefully realized she was becoming more alert. If only she could figure out why her memory was fuzzy, who these people were, and where in the West she was. But her mind seemed to fade in and out. And at odd moments terror seized her.

Inside the barn, Craig handed a plate to the boy. The woman sat down on a blanket in the corner of the empty stall and stared with huge green eyes at her surroundings, ignoring the plate on her lap. He shook his head and went over to retrieve the plate. He handed her a biscuit and urged her to eat a portion of the food he'd brought for them to share.

Then he and Anna and Danny watched, amazed, as she ravenously attacked the biscuits and bacon.

The cold sensation of being watched quaked down Billie's spine. Her hand stopped halfway to her mouth and she looked up. They were staring. All three of them. The biscuit crumbled from her fingers. Embarrassment flooded her cheeks when she realized that somewhere, somehow, she'd completely abandoned her manners.

She reached daintily into her lap, picked up a piece of bacon, and chewed it very slowly.

Craig finished his breakfast quickly, retrieved the plates, and was about to leave when Danny stopped him.

"What're we gonna do with Billie t'day, Mr. Rawlins?"

"Billie?"

"That's 'er name. She told us."

"You mean she's been talking?"

Anna nodded. "A little."

He crossed his arms. He hadn't thought any further than getting her off the streets for the night. Danny had a good point. What were they going to do with her now?

Realizing they were all looking at her again, Billie stood up and shook out her skirt. Though these people all seemed friendly enough—even the big man—their long, considering looks made her uneasy. She knew they were talking about her. Her mind was hazy. She'd probably acted a little dazed. But she wasn't deaf.

Craig glanced around the barn, at the beds they'd made in the straw, the few possessions piled in a corner. The building was well constructed. It was dry and fairly clean, but still no place for people to live.

Anna, her hands clasped tightly before her, said timidly, "Mr. Rawlins, Danny and I appreciate what ya've done an' all, givin' him a job takin' care of yore horse and . . ." She darted a look toward the other woman. "But we cain't stay here no more. I got things to do, an'—"

"But, Ma—"

"Shush, son. You heard me. We cain't keep takin' this man's charity." She lifted her pointed chin and gazed defiantly at Craig Rawlins. "I've always managed to take care of me an' mine jest fine."

Though he sincerely ached to do so, Craig knew better than to argue. She was a proud woman, and he could not take her dignity away, even if it was for her own good.

"Then could I ask a favor of you and Danny?"

"F-favor?"

"Would you please stay around for a few hours? Give me time to see what I can come up with for . . . Billie?"

Anna darted a glance from the man to Billie. The consternation seen in the woman's eyes just before lowered lashes hid them from view convinced Anna she couldn't run off and leave without granting Mr. Rawlins his request.

"What ya got in mind to do with 'er?"

Craig felt the accusation behind her words. He straightened but said evenly, "Find a safe place for her. See to it nobody forces her into something she's not willing to do."

Anna nodded. "I reckon we got nuthin' so important that we cain't stay. But jest fer a while, mind ya."

Later that afternoon, Billie stood in the barn doorway, staring at . . . nothing. Her eyes burned. She blinked. She was beginning to feel again. But wasn't sure she wanted to.

Listening to everyone talking about her that morning, wondering what they were going to do with her . . . A shiver raced down her spine. She wasn't their responsibility. *She* had to snap out of this indistinguishable blur of pain and heartache and take care of herself.

Leaning against the doorjamb, she rubbed her hands up and down her upper arms. Bits and pieces of the past day and night flashed through her mind, but before that, only one thing was clear.

She didn't recall how she'd gotten to wherever she was, or what had brought her here. Numbly, she turned and walked back into the barn. Emptiness settled around her like fog on a cold fall morning. Anna and

Danny Corbett were gone. Had left hours ago. She had watched them leave, barely summoning the energy to wave goodbye.

She sniffed and sighed. The sweet smell of hay and straw, even the pungent aroma of manure, was a balm to her senses. She closed her eyes. The scents filling her head reminded her of . . . St. Louis.

Her eyes snapped open. St. Louis. It had popped into her mind so easily, so naturally. She struggled to recall more, but only grew frustrated. What connection did she have with St. Louis?

Shaking her pounding head, she decided to quit trying to remember the past. She needed to concentrate on what she was going to do now—this minute.

She paced back to the door and took several steps into the lane. Her nose wrinkled. Strange, she didn't remember the town smelling so foul yesterday, or looking so . . . It was hard to describe what it looked like. Some of the establishments were constructed only of canvas. Some had log sides with canvas or dirt roofs. Only one or two businesses were like the one in front of the barn—built solidly of wood.

As if thinking about construction of buildings conjured the act, she heard someone hammering alongside the structure at which she'd just been staring. The noise stopped. A tall, ruddy-complected man wearing a black broadcloth suit and string tie sauntered around the back corner.

She recognized him immediately. Mr. Rawlins. The man who was under the mistaken impression he had permission to control her life. She backed up a step when he saw her and changed direction. Her mouth suddenly went dry even as her palms perspired.

"Afternoon, ma'am. Everything all right?"

Of course not. How could he ask such a thing? She nodded.

"Good. Soon as I finish boarding up this back window, I'd like to have a talk with you." Talk? What was he saying? He mentally shook his head. The woman didn't know the meaning of the word. He'd talk. She'd stare with that blank expression on her delicate features.

Good, Billie thought. She had a thing or two to tell him, too.

Gritting his teeth, he drove the last nail with one stroke of the hammer. Then he backed off, gave the saloon one final glance, and turned to take care of a chore he'd put off as long as possible.

The woman was still standing in the lane, still staring at the saloon. He had no idea what she found so fascinating about it.

He walked toward her. She backed off. He frowned when her body went rigid and she looked at him as if he were something less than human.

He stopped a few yards away and spread his hands. "Look, ma'am, I have no intention of hurting you. I just want to put this hammer in the barn and then talk. That's all."

She backed inside ahead of him. She still had the appearance of a frightened doe ready to bound off at the slightest threat of danger, but at least that dazed look was gone from her eyes.

Billie stood by the horse's stall, stroking its velvety nose. She waited while Mr. Rawlins put the tool on a shelf, then sucked in her breath when he turned to face her.

"I won't be staying here tonight. I'm leaving." The words came out in a rush as she released the air she'd been holding.

Craig stopped abruptly at the sound of her hoarsely spoken but determined words. He tilted his head and stared at her for a long moment before calmly agreeing, "I know."

Her brows slashed together.

"This is no place for a lady." He still hadn't quite made up his mind where to take her. Mrs. Timms's boardinghouse was full. There was no hotel. But he'd

have to think more about her lodgings later. There were
other things he wanted to discuss with her first. He'd already spoken with Buck about his cousin's death and
was going to meet with another witness Buck had mentioned later that evening after supper.

Supper. He quickly pulled out his watch.

Billie tensed when his strangely colored eyes shot to
her. Green, blue, and brown seemed to war for dominance, but at that moment, blue and green combined
into aqua as he gave her a thorough once-over. She
stiffened and lifted her chin.

"Grab your things," he ordered. "We'll eat and talk."
His eyes widened when she didn't immediately follow
his instructions. Always before she'd meekly obeyed.

She almost worked up the courage to give him a
piece of her mind. Eat and talk? Without even asking
her consent? The man had gall. But the rumbling in her
stomach from the mention of a real honest-to-goodness
meal decided her against rebelling at that particular moment. There'd be time to tell him exactly what she
thought *after* they ate. And she'd also inform him that
somehow she'd repay him for dinner tonight and for the
other food. She would never allow herself to be beholden to a man.

She darted a glance his direction. He was tapping his
foot and opening and closing his watch. Oh, she'd forgotten. He wanted her to get her belongings.

Her throat closed. She went to the stall where she'd
slept and picked up her spring cloak. There was also a
small straw hat. She'd removed it herself, but it didn't
match her gown and she knew it wasn't hers. Where
had she gotten it?

And her gown. The beautiful gown. Sadly, she
smoothed her free hand down a wrinkled panel of taffeta. She remembered how elegant and light-hearted
she'd felt when she'd first put it on. Now it was tattered
and filthy. Tattered. Filthy. Like her very soul.

"Are you ready? We're late."

His voice rumbled so close to her ear, she started. Something brushed the top of her head. She jerked away and found Mr. Rawlins holding a piece of straw. Heat crawled up her neck and suffused her face.

Sensing her embarrassment, he soothed, "That's the only piece. Don't worry. You look fine."

Of course, she silently muttered. A cow in a top hat looked "fine," too. She shook out her cloak, slid one arm in a sleeve, and was fishing for the other when he gently took it from her.

She felt the heat from his body. Smelled the scent of leather and spice and man. Heard his indrawn breath. He was close. So close. Too close. She couldn't breathe. She jerked to get away. Her flailing hand smacked his wrist.

"Hold on, now," Craig insisted. Grabbing her hand, he literally stuffed it into the empty sleeve and quickly yanked the cloak up and over her shoulders. "See? It just takes a little patience." He'd immediately stepped back and watched as she swallowed, ducked her head, and breathed deeply until the color began to seep back into her cheeks.

"Shall we?" He held out his hand, indicating she should precede him to the door.

Billie stood still for another minute, until she was certain she could walk without stumbling. What was wrong with her? Why couldn't she control her reactions? The man had been nothing but helpful. But he was young and handsome and virile. Just like . . .

She lost the thought. A numbness filled her and she walked out the door. He closed up the barn, then offered his arm, but she couldn't make herself take it. She couldn't touch the man.

Sliding his hands into his pockets, Craig started walking along the lane. Looking back over his shoulder, he called to the woman rooted insecurely to the ground. "Coming?"

Her stomach churned its excitement. Food. He was

taking her to eat. She didn't need to be told to follow him.

Craig hid a grin as she hurried to catch up. She stepped gingerly, then began to limp. He remembered the slippers she wore and cursed under his breath. If she planned to stay here long—which if he had his way, she wouldn't—she'd have to have something more serviceable.

Billie bit back an oath when she stubbed her toe on a root. The soles of her slippers were worn through in several places and provided no protection. She stumbled over a ridge of dirt and nearly slid into the hole on the other side.

Craig stopped and extended his elbow once again. "Changed your mind?"

She shook her head. If it wasn't getting so dark, she'd be able to see where she was going. Suddenly, she stopped and peered through the encroaching darkness. What had happened to the lights of the town?

"Wh—where are you t-taking me?"

"To a friend's house. I was invited to dinner—" He saw the stricken look in her eyes. "There's always enough on the table to feed an army. It'll be good to see the food appreciated for a change."

"No." She stopped. No, she wouldn't go to his friend's house uninvited. No, she wouldn't be made a spectacle again. She'd been hungry at breakfast. It seemed she'd been hungry forever, though the driver who'd brought her had done his best to see she had something to eat. She just hadn't had an appetite. Until now.

Craig inched closer. He cocked his head and peered into hazel eyes darkened by the shadows. Or was it from shadows? She became more mysterious every minute.

When it appeared she'd decided to turn and run, he grabbed one of her hands. She jerked, but he kept a firm hold. He crooked his right arm and determinedly flattened her fingers on his forearm and anchored them there with his left hand.

"Hold on. The going gets a little rough."

"But . . ." The path steepened. She clawed her fingers into his arm to keep from stumbling. Once when the path leveled, she glanced up and saw the outline of a huge, gaily lit house. Her jaw clenched. Surely they weren't going there.

When it appeared that was exactly where they were headed, she balked. She couldn't. Not dressed as she was. Grimy and rumpled and with straw sticking out from who-knew-where.

Feeling her hesitation, Craig looked down at the top of her head. "Come on. We're almost there."

"I—I can't."

He followed her eyes as she looked down at her torn, dirty gown and then to the big, fancy house. Evidently her condition was improving. She seemed worried over her appearance. It was the first time she'd given a damn about anything so normal, so female. That was good.

With the hope of reassuring her, he swatted dust from the back of her cloak. His hand brushed the feminine curves of her derriere. "Ahem. You've nothing to be ashamed of. Believe me, the folks inside that home have experienced lean times, too. If it hadn't been for a gold strike . . . No one's going to think a thing about the way you look."

Unaware of his sudden discomfort, Billie did some hasty brushing of her own. His acknowledgment that she must look pretty awful didn't help matters. She tugged, but couldn't free her hand.

The door swung open. Too late to run. Mortified, Billie stood in the beam of light that spilled out.

"Craig, darlin', there you are. I was worried that somethin' had happened . . . Who's that?"

Craig literally dragged the reluctant woman on his arm into the foyer. "This is . . ." Uh-oh. Danny had told him her name that morning, but it slipped his mind. He swallowed heavily and looked down at the woman. "Uh . . . what was your name again?"

Billie wished a hole would open up and completely engulf her. Yet, how could he know her name? He'd never asked, and she'd certainly never volunteered it.

"B-Billie."

Craig hesitated, thinking she might say her last name, then grinned sardonically. "Billie, this is Sunny Turnbow."

Billie noted the narrowing of the buxom woman's dark eyes, but stood tall beneath Sunny's wary regard.

"Well," Sunny smiled at Craig, "don't just stand there. Come on in. And bring your . . . friend."

Billie could have sworn she heard an "if you must" hissed under the woman's breath as she passed by, but saw no evidence of the slight in the hospitable countenance the olive-complected Mrs. Turnbow bestowed on them.

The exotic-looking beauty fawned over Mr. Rawlins to an extent that embarrassed Billie, shooting strange little pangs through her stomach. Evidently, she was hungrier than she realized.

Sunny Turnbow's long curls brushed Craig's sleeve as she bent forward, and Billie swore that more than silky black soft hair touched him when the woman's breasts appeared to nearly burst from their low-cut, loosely laced confinement.

Sunny ushered them into a small parlor. A slight frown puckered her dark brows when Billie's dirty cloak swished against an elegant brocade chair, but she recovered swiftly when she saw Craig was watching. Parting her full, rouged lips, she seductively purred, "How did you and Craig meet, Billie? You don't mind if I call you Billie, do you?"

Billie shook her head, thinking it wouldn't be mannerly to do otherwise. The fat little woman had already taken the liberty. Billie blinked at her catty thought.

What in the world had gotten into her? Even when she'd been in her right mind, she'd never acted like this.

Before Billie could answer, Craig offered, "We didn't actually *meet* until this morning. She'd just come into town when Bobby was murdered." Which reminded him that he still needed to question her, just in case she might have seen or heard something, *anything*.

"Oh!" Sunny gasped. "How horrible for you."

Billie stood silently, engulfed in the memory of standing over that poor dead man. He'd looked so young and vital. What could he have done to deserve such a brutal death? What did *anyone* do to deserve being treated abominably by another human being?

She closed her eyes and shuddered. The sensation of cold hands choking . . . gouging . . . hurting . . . An involuntary chill mercifully numbed her.

"Ma'am? Billie?" a deep voice rumbled. "Are you all right?"

Billie swayed. She had an overwhelming urge to sink back into oblivion. No. She took one deep breath, then another. No. She would not allow herself to take that route of escape. Not again.

"Hello, Mother. Good evening, Mr. Rawlins."

The shrill voice succeeded in jarring Billie fully into the present. All three of the people in the parlor turned toward a gangling young man standing in the hallway. Billie thought he looked to be in his late teens. He was lighter complected than his mother, with a long, thin face and cropped brown hair that stuck out over slightly protruding ears.

He glanced briefly at Billie, then centered his attention on Craig. "You're late. Mother was terribly worried. You shouldn't worry her like that." He absently took Billie's cloak.

Craig walked over and shook the boy's hand. "Don't worry, Justin. I was, er . . . unavoidably detained." He darted a meaningful look at Billie.

Billie shivered when Justin's pale-brown eyes turned

fully on her and seemed to scour her messy gown. Then she felt rather small when he gave her a buck-toothed grin.

She swallowed and croaked, "Hello. My name's Billie."

After the removal of Billie's cloak, Sunny's eyes took in the damaged gown, judging it and her unwanted guest harshly but silently. Then her gaze locked on the necklace. "What a gorgeous bauble. Where'd you get it?"

Billie immediately clutched one of the stones. "I—It was a . . . gift." Her stomach churned. Perspiration beaded her brow.

"And someone's going to cut your throat for it, if you don't quit flaunting it in front of everyone." Craig felt better after voicing his opinion. Those damned emeralds were going to be her downfall.

"Fl-flaunting?" Billie gasped. "I'm not. I—I just can't t-take it off." They'd been clasped around her neck by . . . Samuel. Whispered words echoed through her head like a litany. *They will keep you safe. They will keep you safe.* She hadn't taken them off. Not once. The name *Samuel* rang through her again. She shivered even as a protective cocoon enfolded her.

Sunny waved her own splendidly bejeweled hand in front of Billie's face. "That's all right by my thinking. Never hurts a woman to have a few added *enhancements,* don't you think, darlin'?"

Completely ignoring Sunny, Craig scowled. Why had Billie used the word *can't?* What made her think she couldn't take it off?

Justin suddenly burst out, "No one would steal from a lady like Billie. Why, with a necklace like that, everyone would know who it belonged to."

Billie gazed gratefully at the boy.

Sunny's eyes glittered as she glared at her son.

Craig squeezed the youngster's shoulder. "I think you've got a point, Justin."

Soft, pattering footsteps sounded in the hallway. A middle-aged Bannock Indian woman nodded deferentially to Sunny.

Sunny smiled and took Craig's arm. "Ah, dinner must be ready."

The servant nodded.

"Thank you, Lucy." She gazed meaningfully into Craig's eyes, then glanced to Justin and purred, "Justin honey, why don't you take Billie to the dinin' room. There's somethin' I want to show Mr. Rawlins, then we'll be right along."

Justin's thin features drooped, but he obediently turned to Billie. "C'mon. It's this way." But he kept looking over his shoulder.

Billie didn't know what to say or do. Sunny had put her in the awkward situation of not being able to politely refuse. Of not being able to stay close to the one person she knew, Craig Rawlins. Justin walked agitatedly out of the room and she followed.

"Wait till you see the dining room, Billie. You'll love it," Sunny called after them.

"I live here and I don't even love it," Justin mumbled.

"H-how long have you l-lived here?" Billie asked, struggling to be a polite guest and reminding herself she needed to meet situations and people head on.

"Not long." He shoved his hands in his pockets. "That Mr. Turnbow was having it built special for my mother. Wasn't finished till a month ago."

"You didn't like your father?" She thought it strange he would call the man "that" Mr. Turnbow.

"Wasn't my father," he said vehemently, then shot startled eyes to Billie. "He and my mother only been married about six months before . . ."

"Before?" she prodded. Her throat ached from the unaccustomed use.

"Someone killed him."

"K-killed him?"

"Yeah. Just like Bob. Down at the Empty Barrel. That's the saloon Mr. Rawlins owns."

"How awful." She disregarded the pleased note in his voice, thinking instead of how terrible that must have been for Mr. Rawlins. The poor man. That was two people, that she knew of, who'd been murdered at the saloon. Had there been others?

Justin suddenly stopped and pointed into a room whose entire length was taken up by a long, long table with chairs down each side and at either end. Four crystal chandeliers were spaced evenly above the gleaming cherry wood furniture. Pale-green lace covered the table. Deep-green drapes hung in front of the windows. An Oriental carpet woven in hues of green graced the floor, accented by green brocade wallpaper.

She closed her eyes and reopened them slowly, but everything was still *green*.

At that moment, Sunny and Craig joined them. Billie noted Sunny's furrowed brows and Craig's evident look of relief. What had the two of them been up to?

Clapping her hands together, Sunny invited with a strained voice, "Shall we sit down? Cook doesn't like to be kept waiting."

Justin held out a chair for Billie. She nodded, thinking Sunny Turnbow had done a good job teaching her son manners. Billie only hoped her own upbringing didn't abandon her again as had happened in the barn.

Silence seemed to drag on forever. Billie looked up to see the other two adults casting surreptitious glances in her direction. When the Indian woman hurried over with an extra place setting, Billie tucked her napkin into her lap and pleated it with her fingers. Finally, she cleared her throat.

"Excuse me," Sunny said. "Did you say something?" When Billie only stared back and shook her head, Sunny forged ahead. "So, what do you think of the room?"

The older woman brightened, waiting for a response.

"I did it myself. John allowed me to decorate the entire house anyway I pleased."

Billie looked around, at a loss for words, confused about how to sound sincerely appreciative.

Sunny frowned at her, then turned away. "Craig darlin', don't you think it's nice?"

Craig was sipping a spoonful of the soup Lucy had placed in front of him. He nearly choked when Sunny spoke directly to him. "Uh . . . it's real . . . green."

Billie covered her chuckle with the kelly-green napkin.

Craig caught Billie's eye and smiled, encouraged to see her react to humor.

"Silly man," Sunny gushed. "You know it's my favorite color."

Billie, under Sunny's watchful eye, touched a hand to the emeralds at her throat. "It's a comforting color."

Once Sunny got started on her house, she dominated the conversation, which certainly suited Billie and, evidently, the men, as they devoured the elk chops, boiled potatoes and onions and baby peas. Butter melted on bread fresh from the oven and Billie thought she'd been transported to heaven.

Dessert was bread pudding with raisins. Billie was the first to finish. Worried she'd eaten too fast, she sat in embarrassed silence until the others consumed theirs.

"My goodness, Billie, how do you stay so slim when you eat like a field hand?"

Justin frowned at his mother.

Craig cleared his throat.

Billie paled. Even if she had made a spectacle of herself, she couldn't let it defeat her. Summoning all of her nerve, she looked Sunny calmly in the eye. "I guess I'm still young enough not to have to worry about extra weight."

Sunny choked on her coffee.

Craig placed his folded napkin on the table and pushed his chair back.

Sighing gratefully, Billie did the same. "Thank you for the dinner, Mrs. Turnbow." Darting a glance to Craig, she informed him, "I'll be going now, Mr. Rawlins."

Sunny arched her dark brow at Billie's formal tone.

Craig placed his hand on Billie's to stay her. When the young woman yanked her hand away, a smug smile slipped across Sunny's features, although the gesture was made to appear quite unobtrusive.

"Well," Craig tugged at his collar. "Ah, you don't need to rush." He swallowed. There was a long pause, during which he shifted nervously in his chair.

"Tell her why, darlin'," Sunny suggested.

Craig cleared his throat. "In fact, I insist you stay here."

"What?" Billie said softly. Too softly.

Chapter Four

Billie rose slowly from her chair and turned to face Craig Rawlins. Remembering her decision to face things straight on, her fingers fisted in the folds of her skirt.

"What do you mean?" She enunciated each word carefully, for her own benefit as well as his. "I'm staying . . ." she choked, "here?"

Craig slipped from his seat and smiled reassuringly. He was proud of himself. The woman should be grateful for his thoughtfulness. His lashes flickered, though, at the look in her green eyes. It was a look he'd never seen before and it shot a dart of apprehension into his gut.

"I've made arrangements with Sunny for you to stay here with Sunny and Justin until I have a wagon going to Salt Lake. Then, I'll give you a ticket home." A one-way ticket, he added silently, so he wouldn't have an added burden to worry about.

Billie blinked and gazed from the pleased-as-punch Craig Rawlins, to the surprised Justin, to the resigned Sunny Turnbow. So, that was what the two had been discussing. A weird fluttering assailed her. Annoyed by the reaction, she concentrated on Justin.

"Would you p-please fetch my cloak?"

Craig speared the boy with a sharp glance and shook his head. Justin sank back in his seat. With deceptive calm, Craig asked, "Where are your manners? Sunny graciously opened her home to you, a complete stranger, and you up and leave without even thanking her?"

"Stray cats have been known to bite the hand that takes them home," she told him.

Inside, his blood was boiling. What had happened to the gracious outpouring of gratitude he'd expected? How dare she act as if he'd affronted her dignity. It wasn't as if she had another choice.

Billie sighed, despising the fact that she'd had to be reminded, again, of her upbringing. The man was right. She'd been terribly rude. But then, so had he. How dare he take it upon himself to act in her behalf.

She gazed apologetically at Sunny Turnbow. "I beg your pardon. But," she emphasized, "I feel uncomfortable imposing . . ."

Finally, after a veiled glare from Craig, Sunny spoke up. "It's not an imposition." She let out a long-suffering breath. "This is a huge house. And you'll be my first overnight guest." Her eyes widened as she added, "You'll also be right here to attend my party tomorrow night. There's a shortage of women to invite in this town." She smiled at Craig. "You're going to be here, aren't you, *darlin'*?"

Craig had been planning on it, out of loyalty to Big John. As he nodded his agreement, he watched Billie . . . Whoever. He wished she'd tell him her last name. With his connections, he might be able to find her family and send her home.

Billie mentally railed at being put in this position. To leave now would be the height of indecency. And even if she did leave, where would she go? No doubt, if she refused his kind arrangement for her shelter with Sunny Turnbow, he would deny her the use of his barn.

She glanced at Sunny. The thought enticed her. A clean bed. Perhaps a bath. Breakfast. And for a reason she couldn't yet define, she really needed this generous, but slightly tacky, woman to see her as a proper lady worthy of the invitation.

She'd already acknowledged that it would be rude to refuse. Hadn't she taught her students that one's manners and deportment, the knowledge of etiquette, not only determined in large part one's social standing, but also made a public statement of one's estimate of her own worth?

Billie froze. She had taught? She had taught manners and deportment? She *had!* To whom? Girls. Her students had been young girls at a finishing school in St. Louis. The warmth of familiarity filled her even as a chill raced over her skin.

Bits and pieces. Pieces of her past—or maybe her present. It felt good to have memories to cling to. What was the name of the school? She struggled to hang on to the fragments as she fingered her necklace. But like wisps of smoke, what had seemed so substantial suddenly faded and vanished.

Details eluded her, but she was certain she had been a teacher in a finishing school in St. Louis.

Her lips curved with encouraging personal discovery as she looked around the very green room and decided this house just might be good for her after all. Finally, her glance landed on Sunny. "If you truly don't mind, I'd be pleased to stay."

Craig, momentarily transfixed by the apricot glow in Billie's cheeks and the first hint of a smile he'd seen on her lovely features, suddenly realized where he was and what he was doing and heaved a visible sigh. Thank heavens, she'd come to her senses. Other than physically subduing the woman, he'd had no other plan to keep her here. Before either woman could recant their decisions, he quickly shook hands with Justin and bid them good night.

With mixed emotions, Billie watched him leave. On the one hand, she felt he'd betrayed her. On the other, he'd gone out of his way to do something nice for her, a total stranger.

When her eyes sought Sunny and her son, Justin was

calmly eating another slice of bread, with his own gaze glued to his mother. A sorrowful expression turned down Sunny's lips; it didn't alter when she turned to stare at Billie.

"Well, here we are." Sunny eyed the younger woman with speculation. "You didn't bring any baggage."

It wasn't stated as a question, but Billie shook her head.

"Is *that* all you have?" She made a dismissive gesture toward Billie's soiled gown.

Billie bristled. It galled her to take Sunny's charity in the first place. She didn't have to be belittled—

"Now don't go and get all huffy on me," Sunny scolded as she led the way from the dining room. "I've been in your situation, maybe worse, more times than I care to remember." She started up the stairs. "In fact, if it hadn't been for Big John . . . John Turnbow," she explained, "I'd still be workin' in a crib."

Billie's eyes rounded. "Excuse me? A . . . crib?"

Sunny sighed. Her eyes suddenly studied the floor as they walked. "I worked in a saloon. You know, as a lady of the evening?"

Billie blinked. This beautiful, elegantly dressed woman, a prostitute? It couldn't be true.

"I'm sorry about your husband. Justin told me."

"Yeah . . . Poor Craig. He just can't seem to keep a partner."

"Your husband . . . He was Craig . . . Mr. Rawlins's partner in the saloon?"

"Yep." Sunny opened the door to a huge guest room. "Somethin' about that saloon must be jinxed, huh?"

Billie was too absorbed by the opulence of the room to answer. Again done in shades of green, the room contained an armoire, a delicate desk and chair, a dressing table with mirror and stool, a fireplace, and a large cherry-wood bed with a feather mattress.

"This is lovely, Mrs. Turnbow."

The older woman snorted. "Name's Sunny. Thanks. Like I told ya, I done it all myself."

Billie heard the woman's cultured voice revert to a more natural way of speaking. Probably letting down her guard now that Mr. Rawlins wasn't around.

"You got yore eye on Craig?"

The question hit Billie broadside. She blinked rapidly. "Of course not." There *was* something that caused him to pop into her mind now and then. But he was, after all, a man. That was something she wanted no part of. She added more definitely, "No."

Sunny's eyes slitted. "You don't think he's handsome?"

"I suppose." Billie sat on the edge of the soft bed. She spread her arms and entreated, "Look, I didn't come to Alder Gulch to find a man. There are . . . other reasons . . . for my staying."

Sunny eyed the jewels around Billie's neck. " 'Cause of the gent what gave you them emeralds?"

Billie's hands trembled as she clasped the stones together. She felt chilled from the inside out. "Yes." Because of *him* . . . She unconsciously rubbed her fingers over the emeralds. Because of Samuel, she had been . . . safe. She couldn't remember . . . but knew that for him, she must continue to protect herself.

"You sit right there for a minute," Sunny said, suddenly much more friendly. "I think I've got a night dress that will fit you. And how about a bath? Would you like a bath first?"

"Please." There wasn't much she wouldn't do for a long soak in a tub of hot water, except—

"I'll get Lucy right away."

"Thank you." Billie stopped Sunny on her way out the door. "I don't know how I'll ever repay you."

Sunny laughed. "Don't even think about it. Big John left me more'n I could spend in two lifetimes. Might as well share a little. S'posed to make you a better person, eh?"

"Well . . ."

"Don't go nowhere. Be right back."

Billie shook her head. Sunny Turnbow changed colors more often than a chameleon. The next few days were going to be interesting.

Billie's eyes shot open at the tap on her door. For a moment, she thought she was home in St. Louis. Terror filled her. Until she realized only the color green surrounded her. Feeling safer, she sighed and snuggled her nose under the blanket.

The rap came again.

She covered her head, wishing she could sleep another twenty-four hours.

Tap.

"Yes-s-s-s," she sighed.

"Miss Billie?"

It was Justin's squeaky voice. "Yes, Justin."

"You awake?"

"I think so," she replied, with a quirk of her lips.

"Mother said to tell you breakfast'll be served in half an hour. Or if you prefer, you can eat in your room."

Another few minutes to lounge on the feather mattress. It was tempting. But she inhaled deeply and called, "I'll be down in twenty minutes."

His footsteps clomped down the hall.

She arose and remembered all she had to wear was the night dress. The Indian servant had taken her gown while she'd bathed, promising to return it after it had been cleaned.

To her surprise, hanging in the open armoire, she found a gingham day dress and clean underclothes. On the dressing table lay a hairbrush and comb.

By the time she reached the dining room, Billie felt like a new woman. A bath. A good night's sleep. Clean clothing . . . The smell of bacon started her mouth watering before she even saw the lavish buffet.

"Morning, Billie," Sunny called, stepping up to take a plate. "Help yourself." She picked up one muffin, sniffed, put it down, and picked up another. With a slight tilt of her head, she eyed Billie from head to toe. "I'm glad the gingham fits. It's yours to keep."

"But . . . I can't," Billie gasped.

"Of course you can. You can't parade around town in a ball gown the rest of your life. Now quit fussin' and grab some food."

Justin stood back and indicated Billie should precede him. She inclined her head and followed Sunny down the line of covered dishes set atop candles to keep the substances within hot. Soon her own plate was heaped with scrambled eggs, bacon, corn cakes, and hashed potatoes. As soon as she sat down, Lucy set a glass of cold milk and a cup of steaming coffee at her place.

She didn't realize she'd spoken aloud when she wondered, "How did they get all these lovely things to Alder Gulch?"

Sunny swallowed a mouthful of corn cake. "I'll tell you, it wasn't easy. Everything except for the wood for the foundation and siding had to be freighted in." Her eyes gleamed. "You'd be surprised what you can do if you have the time and the money."

Billie nodded and glanced around at the opulent furnishings. "I never expected anything so fancy."

Justin's Adam's apple bobbed as he hurriedly cleared his mouth of food. "It's the fanciest, all right, but there's two more big places in town. Both built by miners that made a rich strike." He waved his fork importantly. "They had to build them houses quick when their wives showed up."

"Is Mr. Rawlins a miner?" Billie pursed her lips. Now what had brought him to mind?

Sunny wiped her mouth on her napkin. "He was one of the first to arrive, and I believe he found gold. But he already owned most of his freight equipment and livestock."

"So he runs the freight company?" Billie lowered her eyes and moved the potatoes around the plate with her fork. "He must be doing quite well."

"I'd say so." Sunny beamed.

"May I be excused?" Justin suddenly asked.

"Sure. Just let me know if you decide to leave the house." Sunny favored her son with a benevolent smile.

After Justin left the room, Billie broke a long, uncomfortable silence. "Your son's very polite and well-mannered."

Sunny leaned closer. "He's a good boy, but I can't get him interested in doing anything but helping me. And when he isn't underfoot, he's got his nose stuck in a book. Don't know if it's natural," she whispered.

Billie shrugged. "He's young. Something will catch his attention."

"Yeah. Hopefully she'll be five foot two and have long blond hair."

Billie smiled. She was beginning to like Sunny Turnbow.

Looking in the mirror later that evening, Billie was drawn back to the night the jewels were placed around her neck. When was it? A month ago? Longer? As she stared at the emerald necklace, an icy chill rioted down her spine.

Her hands clenched. Emotions assailed her. Black shadows with no definite shape threatened her. She closed her eyes. Anger budded and blossomed within her until its heat chased away the cold. The anger had no source or target, but with it came a measure of comfort. If it hadn't been for that life-sustaining emotion, she might not have made it this far.

Gazing at her reflection, she was horrified by dark smudges beneath her eyes and the unfamiliar paleness of her complexion. She felt a vague sense of having been raised amidst luxury and privilege, that her shabby appearance was a rarity, not her normal state. And she suspected she'd known nothing about the hardships of traveling through the wilds of the West. It was probably a blessing she remembered so little of her journey here. But she'd survived. She had survived.

Then her eyes touched on the emeralds. The necklace, and all the lost memories and loving people it represented, would provide the courage she'd desperately need in the days to come. For whatever reason she'd landed in Alder Gulch, it looked like a good place to stay. For one thing, no one had pried into her past. It was as good a reason as any to call the mining community home.

Pain knifed through her heart. Home.

"There you are. Folks'll be coming soon," Sunny bubbled. "Aw, now, don't you look fine. That dress cleaned up real nice. You know, that's one of my favorite shades of green."

Billie gulped, fighting to find her voice as she turned to face the dark-haired woman.

"Thank Lucy for me. It's good as new. But . . . I'm not so sure about going to your . . . party."

"What? You've got to be joking. Aren't you?"

Billie shook her head. "No. I appreciate everything you've done . . . your hospitality, and all. But—"

Hand splayed on her rounded hips, Sunny's almond-shaped eyes glared down her nose toward her guest. "If you're so appreciative then, you'll come to my party."

"I . . . there'll be so many people. I just don't know—"

Softly, almost apologetically, Sunny said, "That's why I need you to come. Another woman, especially someone new, will make my party the talk of the town."

Realizing Sunny had just left her with no excuses, Billie sighed and shrugged her shoulders. Besides, she was already dressed.

Sunny smiled briefly at Billie's capitulation. But as she studied the younger woman, she scratched her chin and her eyes hooded. "Can't help wonderin' what a lady like you is doing in Alder Gulch, with nothing to her name but an expensive evening gown and jewels that'd drown a duck."

Billie's eyes turned furtive. She backed away from the mirror.

Sunny had already headed toward the door. "Don't matter. Guess the ole code of the West goes for a woman same's a man."

Billie's shoulders sagged. "Code of the West? What's that?"

Justin rushed through the doorway. "There's some folks at the door, Mother."

"Well, Justin, open it and let them in." She darted a glance at Billie and lifted her arms as if to say, "What's a mother to do?", then squared her shoulders and sailed gracefully from the room.

Billie shook her head, marveling at the woman's ability to change back into the cultured lady at a moment's notice. Sunny Turnbow could make a fortune in the theater.

Billie jumped when Sunny reappeared and called, "Shall we, my dear?"

Billie took one last look in the mirror. Her heart hammered with anticipation and trepidation. She hated being in a crowded room, especially one full of men. Praying she'd be able to manage her fear, she curtsied to Sunny and said, "If we must, my lady."

As they swept down the hall, Billie admired the way Sunny's pale-green dress complemented her dark features. "You look stunning."

"I know." Sunny tugged her already low-cut bodice down even lower, then curved her lips into an impish grin.

Craig Rawlins stood in front of Sunny Turnbow's door. He hesitated to knock, almost afraid of facing the two women inside, yet also angered that he allowed them to intimidate him. So what if they would both be unhappy with his news. There was nothing he could do and they'd have to accept that for the time being.

His hand was completely steady when he rapped sharply. Justin opened the door. Craig felt a traitorous leap of relief in his stomach and sneered at his own brand of cowardice.

"Evening, Justin. That's a nice suit."

"Thanks." The young man ran his finger under his collar and smiled uncomfortably. "I'm glad Mother doesn't give these things very often, though."

Sunny floated into the room and pouted prettily. "Craig darlin'," she drawled. "I was beginnin' to think you were goin' to stand me up again."

Trailing behind her was an astonishingly beautiful strawberry blonde wearing a familiar green gown. Stunned, he realized the gorgeous person was the same ragged, dust-covered woman he'd rescued from the street.

The change was remarkable. *She* was remarkable. It was plain the gown had been cleaned and mended, and the fresh color matched the flecks of green shimmering in her bright hazel eyes. Her hair had been brushed until it shone, and instead of braided coils, was swept up and pinned in a riot of glorious curls. And her face, clean and glowing with no trace of makeup, was artless in its simple beauty. He literally couldn't catch his breath.

Sunny grabbed his arm and led him, a little dazed, into the huge living room that had been cleared of everything but a few chairs along the walls. The wood floor had been swept and polished until it looked slicker than new ice on a pond.

At the far end of the room, four men were tuning instruments on a raised dais. Only a few merchants had brought their wives into the wilds of Montana, but those who had were there, filling punch glasses and chatting

with the miners who sported freshly trimmed beards
and the cleanest clothes they could find. The men appeared to have gone to a lot of effort to spruce up for
the affair, and mingled as if they were neighbors from
the best families in New York—which they very well
could be, for all anyone knew.

Craig looked over his shoulder for Billie, but she was
almost obliterated from view amidst a horde of gaping
admirers. A pang of something he might have called
"jealousy" under other circumstances shot through his
chest. She was a beautiful, classy lady. He just enjoyed
watching her, even if she did look as skittish as a fawn
with a coyote prowling nearby.

A few minutes later, Billie wished her tall height
served her better. She'd lost sight of Craig Rawlins and
needed to be sure her eyes hadn't deceived her. She
hadn't remembered him being so attractive before. But
in that dapper black suit, crisp white shirt, string tie, and
shiny black boots, he'd be the rescuing knight for any
damsel in distress. And she certainly felt like a damsel in
distress.

The large crowd literally crushed her. Her ears
burned from the noise of a thousand questions she
couldn't answer. She wanted to hide from all of the curious glances. Instead, she self-consciously swiped beads
of perspiration from her brow.

A bow slid across the strings of a fiddle. Conversation
hushed. Sunny, still holding on to Craig, announced,
"Thank you all for coming. You all know my son, Justin.
Tonight, we're celebrating his seventeenth birthday. Everyone, please enjoy yourselves." She smiled and nodded toward the motley group of men composing the
orchestra.

The first tune was fast and lively. Sunny tugged a reluctant Craig onto the dance floor. Billie found herself
the center of a discussion between three men as to
whom would get to dance with her first. Just as their
words were about to lead to fisticuffs, she shifted nerv-

ously and found Justin Turnbow shyly reaching for her hand.

"Do me the honor, Miss Billie? After all, I'm the birthday boy."

She eagerly stepped from the midst of the bickering men. "Thank you, Justin."

He flushed and ushered her to the edge of the dancers.

She flinched when he touched her. Her skin crawled when their bodies met. She gulped deep breaths and concentrated on the rhythm of the music rather than the nausea churning in her stomach. She reminded herself that this boy was the son of her hostess. With effort, she even managed to keep from grimacing too often when he trounced on her toes.

When the music ended and another song began, another man claimed her and she suffered the same terrifying feelings of being held and controlled. Moisture slicked her flesh. She breathed in short gasps. *Please, Lord. Please don't let me panic. Don't let me make a fool of myself.*

The miner named Lucky smiled and grasped her hand tightly. Awkward and stiff, he didn't hold her too close. Thankfully, the space allowed her to get through the dance, though her heart thudded frightfully by the time the song ended. She had to get away from the crush of men. Fresh air. She needed fresh air.

Spinning, she ran directly into Craig Rawlins.

Caught off guard by the speed with which she barreled into him, Craig grasped her arms and gazed down into wide, terrified eyes. He noted the perspiration beading her upper lip and how she glanced suspiciously over her shoulder. Damn! Hadn't Sunny known better than to release this frightened little kitten in a room full of wolves?

"What is it?" he demanded, glaring at the puzzled men behind her. "One of those galoots hurt you?"

"No. Oh, no," she gasped, desperately wanting to run and hide from everyone.

"Then why're you . . ." Deciding it would be foolish to upset her further by asking questions, he inhaled deeply and said, "Perhaps you just need some air. Would you be my guest for a stroll around the porch?"

Huge, grateful eyes turned up to look at him. "Thank you," she whispered, never relaxing her biting hold on his arm.

Craig nodded toward the disappointed men. "Excuse us, gentlemen. The lady is feeling a bit indisposed. Hopefully, she'll be able to return in a little while."

He guided her across the room, through a side door, and stopped in the middle of a large patio. "There, is that better?"

She swallowed and nodded.

Craig felt a movement on his arm and realized she still clung to him. For the first time, she was touching him of her own volition. It was then he realized the actual depth of her fear. His chest constricted and he was glad—very glad—he'd been there for her tonight.

"Billie, I—"

"Craig, what are you doin' . . . Oh. I hope I'm not interruptin' anything," Sunny lied as she glared at the couple standing much too close to each other.

Craig glowered back at the dark-haired woman. Before he could open his mouth, he was shocked to hear Billie speak up.

"I'm sorry to have taken Mr. Rawlins away from the party. I wasn't feeling too well and he offered to escort me outside for some fresh air." Billie reluctantly released her hold on Craig's arm and stepped away.

"Well, I was worried when I noticed Cra—you all . . . were gone." Sunny sniffed and batted her lashes at Craig. "You are feelin' better now, I presume?"

Billie nodded.

"Good. Then you won't mind if I whisk Craig back

inside for the next dance. Will you?" She smiled too sweetly.

Billie blanched. But when she saw Craig looking at her questioningly, she said, "Go ahead. I'm fine now. Really."

Craig hesitated, but saw no reason to protest further as Sunny dragged him back to the dance floor. He couldn't very well stay with Billie if she didn't want him to.

Following after Sunny and Craig until she could peer inside through large double-paned windows, Billie sucked in her breath when she saw them dancing. They looked good together—Sunny and her petite, dark good looks, Craig and his tall, fair handsomeness.

When Sunny smiled seductively, Billie frowned. Then she scolded herself. For heaven's sake, one would think she was jealous or something. But she wasn't. She hardly even knew the man. And who knew what sinister motives he might have for all of his kindnesses. Her eyes narrowed. What had caused her to think something so terrible? Everything Craig Rawlins had done had been to her benefit. So far.

Flustered, she turned and automatically walked down a few steps into a stand of tall alders. A sturdy tree provided much-needed support as she gazed down on the lamplit city. The men in the streets looked small and harmless until every once in a while the breeze carried harsh sounds of arguing and drunken laughter.

Gunshots blasted. She jerked, then closed her eyes. Would she ever feel safe anywhere ever again?

"Oh, darlin'," drifted through the growth of trees to her right. Immediately she recognized Sunny Turnbow's voice. "Darlin'," the woman cooed, "there isn't a thing you can do down there. Stay and enjoy the party. Your being here means so much to Justin."

Billie heard a beleaguered sigh. A familiar male voice regretfully agreed. "I guess you're right. There isn't much one man can do."

Craig Rawlins. Billie heard the impatience and frustration in his words and could almost picture the way he would shove his hands in his pockets and hunch his shoulders.

There was a soft rustling sound and Billie ashamedly found herself straining to hear more.

"About the woman, Billie," Sunny purred.

"What about her?"

Billie chafed at the indifference in his voice.

"Just who is she?"

"I have no idea." He sounded chagrined. "Just another woman down on her luck, I guess."

"Think she's a prostitute?" Sunny sounded smugly certain.

"Absolutely not."

Billie's eyes closed as tears of gratitude escaped. Tree bark gouged her arm, she pressed against it so hard to keep from rushing through the brush to thank him for believing in her. Craig didn't *know* her. Had no idea what had brought her to Alder Gulch. Still, he was willing to see something good in her.

"She seems tarnished to me," Sunny insisted.

Billie trapped an anguished sob, holding it inside by clamping her hands to her mouth. Another tear—this time a tear of pain—leaked through her tightly closed lashes. Sunny, who'd been so nice, thought the worst of her.

"So you really don't have any interest in her?" Sunny persisted. "She is kind of pretty, in a pathetic sort of way."

Craig grunted.

Billie's heart ached worse than ever.

"I'm not interested. At least not in the way you mean."

Billie was too busy gathering her scattered emotions to pay much attention to the halting rhythm of his words. He'd better not be interested. She'd sooner be associated with a three-legged wart toad than any man . . . that way.

"Justin seems taken with her, don't you think?"

The sultry voice turned Billie's stomach. Justin? For pity's sake. He was just a boy. She was ten years his senior. What could his mother be thinking?

"Was he?"

Billie cocked her head. He sounded distracted. Those little rustling noises were driving her crazy. What were they doing over there?

"Well, it doesn't matter. How long does she have to stay here?"

Billie had known she was an imposition, but hadn't realized Sunny considered her a burden.

"I can't send a wagon to Salt Lake until next week."

He assumed she would leave whenever he decided she should? Billie seethed. As if he had the right to dictate her life! It was just like a man.

Well, come tomorrow morning, she'd no longer be a concern to either Mrs. Sunny Turnbow, or the overbearing Mr. Craig Rawlins.

"I wonder where my *guest* has gotten to? After all I've done for her, and to even invite her, a stranger, to my party, she has the nerve to only dance two dances. I swear, darlin', it's just not fair."

Sunny's voice sounded almost faint. Billie imagined how she must be swooning into Craig's supportive embrace.

There was an eagerness in Craig's words Billie hadn't noticed before when he urged Sunny to go back inside. "I'll see if I can't find her for you."

"But, darlin'—"

"I insist. Now, go on and see to the other guests."

Billie waited until their footsteps faded before stepping out of the trees. She slid her damp palms down her skirt. If she was very careful, perhaps she could slip back into the house and up the stairs without being noticed.

Feeling hopeful, she'd just stepped onto the patio when a husky voice froze her in her tracks.

"There you are. Still taking in the fresh evening air?"

A thread of amusement slithered through his voice. Her eyes narrowed. He couldn't know she'd been eavesdropping. No . . . She gulped, and without looking up, said, "I—I was just going—"

"To dance with me," he declared, leading her into the house.

"N-no, please, I-I . . ."

He looked into her agitated features and frowned. When he placed his hand on her shoulder and she flinched, he became concerned. "What's wrong? You danced with Justin and Lucky." Of course, he rationalized, she'd acted strangely since the first moment he'd seen her. Why should he expect her to behave differently now?

Billie opened her mouth, but what could she say? How could she tell him the truth, or explain what she didn't understand herself? There was something so earnest and appealing about the man that it made her doubt her own reactions. For that reason, he was all the more dangerous and frightening.

"Am I ugly? Do I smell bad?"

"Ooh-h-h, no." She inhaled his masculine scent. In a way, it reminded her of her stepbrother, Samuel. The thought made her feel strange, yet . . . safe. "You smell wonderful." Gazing into his bluish eyes, and over his chiseled cheekbones and square chin, she sighed.

Suddenly, she realized she was being swung deftly around the floor, that she was swaying gracefully along with him and had been so preoccupied that she hadn't been afraid when their bodies brushed together.

"Then why are you scared of me?" he questioned softly. He was amazed by how soft and fragile she felt in his arms despite her height. And he was becoming more and more irritated at his body's juvenile responses every time their hips touched or her breast nudged his arm.

He had no interest in involving himself with a woman. Especially a woman who'd been nothing but trouble.

Damn it, he wished he didn't have to wait a week to send the next wagon to Salt Lake.

He felt her push against him and realized he'd pulled her even closer. Why was he holding his head so he could smell the fresh, womanly scent of her? He *wasn't* enjoying the sensual smoothness of her movements. He *wasn't*. Her skin couldn't feel like spun silk.

He blinked and mentally chided himself for behaving like a fool. He had a weak spot for strays. It was possibly his worst shortcoming.

They danced beneath a crystal chandelier. Light glanced off her hair, giving it a golden glow. With her heart-shaped face, huge beguiling eyes, and aura of innocence, she was an . . . angel.

The music stopped just as he abruptly halted his steps.

The jarring movement caused Billie to trip, but, luckily, he still gripped her hand and shoulder. Glancing into his scowling features, she stiffened.

Then, suddenly, he dropped his arms from around her and stalked away. Her jaw dropped and she followed his progress across the room with puzzlement. From the way he'd looked at her, one would think she was some precious cargo for his freight company.

Chapter Five

Early the next morning Billie made up her bed, tidied up the things she'd used, and walked into the hall, all the while looking longingly around the warm, comfortable room. Braving the unknown again was scary. She hoped she wouldn't have cause to regret her decision to leave.

Justin called to her as she descended the stairs. She approached the dining room hesitantly, then when she discovered the boy was alone, entered with more confidence. Maybe she'd be able to get away without having to explain herself to Sunny.

"Cook made cinnamon rolls this morning," Justin mumbled around a mouthful of gooey hot bread. "Specially for our guest."

Billie blinked and sighed. Cinnamon rolls. Her favorite. Perhaps she did have enough time to eat breakfast. Besides, she didn't want to appear unappreciative. The Turnbows had treated her kindly, despite the fact her presence had been forced upon them.

Taking a roll and a cup of coffee, she sat down opposite Justin. "Did you enjoy your birthday?"

He swallowed and shrugged. "It was just an excuse for Mother to throw a party."

She opened her mouth to tell him he had to be mistaken but took a bite of yeasty bread, cinnamon, and sugar instead. As far as she knew, Sunny's motives could have been every bit as selfish as he indicated.

Glancing toward the doorway, she fiddled with the handle on her cup. "Uhm . . . where is your mother?"

He picked up a piece of bacon and moved it from one side of his plate to the other. "Aw, she won't be down till lunch or after. She likes to get a lot of sleep."

The tension in Billie's muscles began to ease. She thoroughly enjoyed the rest of her sticky roll.

"You like Mr. Rawlins?"

She choked and took a quick drink to clear her throat. She cast Justin a wary glance. Although his expression was intense, it seemed innocent enough. Which it would be. He was just a boy.

"I . . . suppose. Why?"

Justin picked up the bacon, crunched it between his teeth, and licked his fingers. "Don't know. My mother seems to think he's better than chocolate candy."

Billie blinked. Even felt a slight urge to grin. "Well, he seems nice enough. He likes you." In fact, from what she remembered, whenever Justin was around Craig made a special effort to include the boy in the conversation or activity.

"Yeah." He pushed back his plate. "You gonna stay in Alder Gulch?"

Billie's hand stopped halfway to her mouth. She set the forkful of food down on her plate before answering. "I—I don't know."

While he continued to watch her, Billie hurried and finished her breakfast. She was tempted to wrap a roll and take it with her, but didn't want to field more questions from Justin.

Rising from her chair, she was about to clear her place when Lucy materialized and shooed her away. Feeling as guilty as a thief stealing the silver, she nervously inhaled and glanced at Justin.

"Please tell your mother how much I appreciated her hospitality."

Seemingly lost in thought, Justin just shrugged.

Billie shook her head and made a swift getaway. Someday soon she'd see Sunny and tell her in person. Right now, she needed to go into town and figure out what to do next.

Billie smoothed a wrinkle from the day dress, wishing she hadn't been so proud and left the taffeta gown in exchange. If only she hadn't forgotten her cloak . . . But to go back, she'd risk running into Sunny and having to come up with a believable explanation for leaving. She wasn't ready for that. So, she swallowed, drew herself up to her full five feet and seven inches and started up the main street of Alder Gulch. On the way down the hill, she'd taken inventory of her situation. She was in a strange and dangerous town. She had no money. No place to stay. She needed clothing, work, and food.

Her hand stole up to the large emerald stones draped about her neck. Her fingers tightened on a gold setting until her knuckles ached.

She stumbled over a rut and nearly fell into a man sitting dejectedly at the side of the street. Excusing herself, she hurried on, taking more notice of what was happening around her. She'd learned last night from snippets of conversation that there had been some healthy gold strikes around Alder Gulch. The town was filled with people, mostly men. Eager miners in a big rush bought supplies and loaded wagons. Unlucky prospectors lounged in front of the various businesses, most of which seemed to be saloons or gambling dens. The undertaker hitched horses to his wagon, on which rested a new coffin.

Ducking her head, she continued on, glancing timidly from side to side, wishing someone would rush from a decent establishment and offer her work.

"Hey, sweetie, ya new in town?"

Billie started, turned slowly, and stared at a little man

sporting a goatee and handlebar mustache. He stood in an open doorway, wiping his hands on a once-white towel now smudged dirty brown.

She looked around and behind her. His eyes were definitely trained on her. She frowned, but nodded.

He took a step toward her. She backed up.

He cocked his head. "You be lookin' for a job?"

Her pulse accelerated. Dare she hope? Again she nodded and stood her ground when he came another step closer.

"Hot damn, I knowed it. Ya just had that look about ya." He grinned, exposing brown front teeth.

She looked down her slender form. What *look* was he talking about? "Wh-what kind of work would I be required to do?" She fought down the urge to run away as he walked around her, speculatively regarding her from head to toe.

"Hey now, boys," he called to several miners pushing past him through the door. "Listen to this, would ya. We're gonna have a right fancy whore workin' tanight."

Billie choked. Whore? When the man reached toward her, she screamed. "No! N-no-o!"

The little man scowled. "Look, missy. Make up yore mind. You workin' tanight, or not?" He scratched his whiskered chin. "Gal with yore looks'll make us both good money."

She continued to back away as if he carried the plague. "No. I won't . . . Ohhh!" She spun and ran, tripping over her hem until she finally reached down and lifted her skirt. Her face flamed when she heard the laughter following her flight.

Shame and embarrassment knotted her insides until she almost doubled over. It was as if he'd looked into her soul and found her as tarnished as Sunny had. If she had that look . . .

Get off the street. She had to hide from suspicious eyes.

Slipping between the next two buildings on her left, she came out on the familiar narrow lane. As if uncon-

sciously putting off thinking about what just happened,
she focused on the deep ruts and the small lean-tos and
shacks so hurriedly thrown together that one could
hardly call them shelters—even for animals.

She stopped and leaned against a tent support to rub
her aching arch. Another day and she'd walk right out
of what was left of her slippers. No wonder people were
jumping to conclusions about her—what with the opera
slippers she wore with common gingham and incredible
emeralds.

She tugged at her bodice but couldn't raise it. Her
face flamed anew. A tear sizzled down her cheek. She
must look like a harlot. It was no wonder they treated
her like one.

But, for the time being, she had no other choice.
Hopefully, there would be someone running an honest,
respectable business in this town who was more understanding and would offer her work.

She sighed and started walking down the lane. As
soon as she gathered her courage, she'd head toward the
main thoroughfare again.

Watching where she was treading to keep from stepping on more sharp stones, she didn't see the man coming from between the buildings.

"Ooommpph! Damn it, watch—"

"I beg—You—"

"Well, if it's not Miss . . . Billie," Craig Rawlins
drawled. "Thought I left you safe and sound on the
hill."

Billie realized she'd come all the way down to the
barn where she'd spent that one night. How on earth
could she have been so stupid? She knew there was a
good chance *he*'d be in the area.

Craig was irritated to see the woman out on the street
and flaunting her jewels again, but in a way it was as if
he'd conjured her out of thin air. He'd been thinking
about her all morning and was about to go up to Sunny's. She'd saved him the trip.

He slipped his hands into his pockets and searched her face. He'd tried to broach the subject before, but always seemed to get distracted. "I've been wanting to talk to you. Do you have a few minutes?"

She rubbed her shoulder where it still tingled from their hard, but brief, encounter. Her lashes lowered warily. "About what?" she asked suspiciously. If he was going to tell her he was sending her out of town, he could just save his breath. Or if it had to do with their dance—

"Would you mind telling me just what you saw or heard the day you arrived?"

Relieved, she exhaled softly and thought back. It all seemed so long ago, yet had been only a few days. *Oh.* "You mean about the shooting?"

He nodded curtly.

"I—I didn't . . ." She shivered, reacting now to the sounds of gunfire and people running for their lives. Most of that afternoon was a vague blur, but she did recall the sight of the injured man stumbling helplessly into the street. It had jarred her momentarily from the haze that had been her constant companion.

"There must have been something," Craig pleaded. "You were right there."

She closed her eyes and scrubbed her hands up and down her upper arms. The manufactured friction didn't help. She felt chilled to the core. Just before he fell, the man had looked directly at her. His lips had moved, almost like he'd been trying to tell her something . . . But he'd been too far away. She hadn't heard anything.

She shook her head and opened her eyes. They locked with Craig's, which seemed to change from intense blue to penetrating greenish brown.

"I'm sorry."

His shoulders hunched. "So'm I."

"Was he a very good friend?" She had an overwhelming urge to reach out and touch him, to offer comfort of some kind. Instead, she twined her fingers in the folds of her skirt.

"The best." He removed his hat and dropped his head back to gaze into the cloud-filled sky. "He was also my cousin."

"Oh."

Recovering his composure quickly, he slapped the dust from his hat and replaced it, then once again scanned her apricot-hued features. "Do you at least know if he was shot inside the saloon or in the street?"

"Yes," she said with more enthusiasm. "I heard the doors batting. He staggered . . . came through them, clutching his chest."

"So he had to have been shot inside?" he said more to himself than as a question. "That was old Buck's feeling, too."

She nodded anyway.

It wasn't much to go on, but it was something, he thought, slowly shaking his head.

"You never did say what you're doing in town—alone?" he irritably reminded her.

"I—I . . ." She looked everywhere but at him. When her eyes fell on the barn, she remembered the little hat. "I was looking for my hat. I think I left it in the barn."

Muttering under his breath, he strode quickly to the enclosure, threw open the doors, and disappeared inside.

She gulped and drew circles in the dirt with the frayed toe of her slipper.

Still muttering, he came out and handed her the straw bonnet. "Come on, and I'll walk you back to Sunny's."

She saw him start to reach for her and spun away. "No." Finding herself in the shadow of the saloon, she noticed the sun was about to dip behind a mountain-peak. The noise level had increased considerably with the number of men jamming the streets. Where had the day gone? She must have spent more time than she thought watching the people and looking over the town.

On the opposite corner, a man was thrown through a doorway and got up shouting vile threats. The color drained from her cheeks. Still, she couldn't accept Mr. Rawlins's offer. She wasn't sure how he would react when he learned she'd left the Turnbows' residence.

"I—I can find my own way back, thank you."

Looking from his outstretched hand to the fear—or was it desperation?—in her haunted eyes, he reluctantly backed away. There was a deceptive calm to his voice when he said, "Fine. You can reject my offer. But what will you do when you really need help?"

Craig Rawlins's parting words tormented Billie as she walked down the street, hugging the buildings as closely as possible to avoid being jostled and trampled by the hordes of men stampeding into town.

The two businesses of which she'd just inquired had both told her the same thing. They were just getting started. They didn't need help. The other places she'd passed were all saloons and gambling dens.

She hadn't checked across the street yet, but it was late and she was attracting too much attention. Sweat beaded her forehead. Her knees quaked as darkness settled over the teeming city. Black clouds that had billowed onto the western horizon before dusk obliterated the moon and stars.

Her spirits fell. She'd found no work, which logically meant she would have no place to stay and no food. As if sensing the dire situation, her stomach grumbled its displeasure.

She continued walking, having no idea where she was since few lights illuminated the street. Then all at once, she faced a boisterous group of miners weaving their way toward her. Uh-oh. Trouble.

Across the street, from beneath the portico of the

freight office, Craig Rawlins leaned against a post, arms crossed over his chest, watching the woman's progress with interest.

When he'd first seen her, he'd started to go after her, to ask what in the hell she thought she was doing, wandering the streets alone. But then he remembered her earlier admonition, her assurance that she would find her way by herself.

So, though it went against his better judgment, he'd decided to let her do just that, under his watchful eye.

And if he were truthful, he'd enjoyed these free moments of being able to study her without her suspiciously eyeing him back. The woman was a complete enigma. He had nothing by which to compare her. Her desperation, fear, stubborn independence, and serene beauty combined to make her mysteriously intriguing. His brows slashed together. He'd always been irresistibly attracted to mysterious situations.

As he watched her unconsciously graceful movements, he recognized a naiveté about her in the gingham gown that was completely contradicted by the sophistication of last night's gown. Which was she really? Sweet innocent or sultry seductress?

She was a beauty, that was for sure, but seemed unaware of her allure. She kept her head down, avoiding unnecessary contact with anyone who tried to catch her eye. The more he watched her from afar, the more tempted he was to forget his vow and go after her himself.

Suddenly, he stiffened. He saw the rowdy bunch of miners barreling in her direction. His entertainment was over. It was time to step in and save the lady from her damned foolishness.

As the miners weaved closer, Billie hesitated only a second. So far, they didn't appear to have noticed her and she hoped to keep it that way. She quickly ducked into the next open space and inched slowly along the side of a large tent until reaching the narrow lane. All she could see of the barns and shelters across the way were their shadowy shapes.

Stumbling forward, she shivered and wrapped her arms around herself as the wind blew stronger and colder. Craig Rawlins's barn. It was the only place she knew to go.

Off to her right, loud shouting erupted over the din of a hundred voices, clinking bottles, and out-of-tune pianos. Gunshots hurried her efforts to open the barn door. The hinge creaked. The horse snorted. She heaved a sigh of relief.

She'd barely closed the door behind her when angry shouts rent the air nearby.

"Damn Yankee. All I ever seen was yore blue coats. Come back an' fight."

Running feet trampled the earth within a few yards of where she slumped against the wall. Another dispute over the war? Would the dissension and turmoil ever end?

How long she stood pressing her aching back to the rough but sweet-smelling wood she didn't know. Eventually, her throbbing feet and trembling legs demanded that she make a decision as to what to do next.

Murmuring softly to the horse, whose outline she could barely make out in the darkness, she held her hands in front of her and felt her way along the top rail to the empty stall. Her fingers brushed something thick that moved at her touch. She gasped and jerked her arm. Her elbow banged into a board. Then she felt a row of boards as high as her shoulder. Ahhh, the something she'd felt was the blanket she'd used several nights ago, folded over the top rail. She'd reached her destination.

Wrapping herself inside the warm wool, she sank to her knees and scraped straw into a pile. After spending unnecessary moments patting and fluffing, she eased herself onto the soft heap and leaned back into the corner. Closing her weary eyes and gripping her necklace, she inhaled deeply and released the breath softly over a period of seconds.

She was exhausted and hungry, but felt safe from the prying eyes of all those men. Safe. Here, alone in the barn, with the rustlings and snorts of the horse, she felt more secure than inside Sunny Turnbow's huge mansion. It was a feeling she savored.

Pulling the blanket more tightly around her shoulders, she closed her eyes as the first plops of raindrops pelted the roof. Wind shook the building. The tempo of the rain increased. Curling into a tight ball, she snuggled down into the straw.

Craig Rawlins cursed and pulled his hat down tighter. He winced when his swollen knuckles protested the movement.

Damn it, where was the woman?

He'd rushed to her rescue, gotten into a fight, only to find out she'd disappeared. He'd searched everywhere. She was nowhere to be found. It almost made him wonder if he'd actually seen her or if his mind had been playing tricks on him and he'd only imagined watching her all evening.

Grumbling beneath his breath, he leaned into the wind and headed back to the freight office. One more shipment was due to arrive, then he'd go home, have a good stiff drink and try to forget he'd ever heard of Billie . . . whatever her name was.

Billie tossed and turned. Tears pricked the backs of her eyes. Before she could blink them away, they streaked her dusty cheeks. Her chest convulsed. A sob filled her throat, then choked past her chattering teeth. Her heartbreak raged along with the storm as she released a part of the terror that had haunted her days and nights since she'd apparently run from St. Louis.

What was it that tormented her so?

Images of her father flashed like bolts of lightning across her mind. Her stomach flip-flopped. She remembered her father. She struggled in the dark to claim more of him, but the harder she tried, the more elusive the fragment of memory became.

Suddenly, another face flickered and blurred her thoughts. She concentrated. Deep-set, odd-colored eyes fused with high cheekbones and a blunt nose. A square jaw and cleft chin blended with the other features to form the face of the owner of the Empty Barrel Saloon and the barn in which she hid.

A trace of warmth seeped into her body. He'd come to her rescue. He'd also tried to manage her and hold her, but in doing so, had averted her attention to someone and something besides herself and her problems. For that, she was grateful.

The day's ordeals took their toll. She was hungry and, quite literally, miserable. Her eyelids drooped. She yawned and squirmed to find a more comfortable position. Thoughts of whatever else she might be settling into only momentarily made her hesitate before sinking down on her fragrant bed. She closed her eyes and listened to the steady patter of raindrops.

She would rest a while, then get up and plan how to survive the next day. Living day to day had gotten her by this far. Somehow, she would continue to muddle through.

Sunlight shone through the only window in the barn, directly into Billie's eyes. She groaned, shifted, and covered her face with her forearm. "Go 'way," she mumbled, then turned to her other side. But the damage was done. She couldn't go back to sleep.

Sitting up, she stretched leisurely, then plucked bits of straw from her gown. She unpinned the bonnet from her head and maneuvered the brim until it had some semblance of shape again. Thank goodness she'd forgotten to remove it last night, or she'd never have gotten all of the stems out of her hair, which was so thick and unmanageable that she had to keep it braided to control it.

The horse whickered, and Billie's insides lurched. Someone would probably be coming soon to feed the animal and she had to straighten things and be gone before they did.

Scrambling to her feet, she shook out the folds of her skirt. The necklace flopped weightily against her collarbone. Heat suffused her cheeks. After her encounter with the saloonkeeper yesterday, she knew what the townspeople must think of her.

She sniffed and squared her shoulders. As soon as she earned enough to eat, she'd save her money for a high-collared dress.

Leaning against the stall, she dreamed about plain muslin. She'd always wanted a plain muslin dress like her nanny had worn. But her father wouldn't allow it. After all, his daughter had to uphold the image of the Glenn name. Glenn . . . Her last name was Glenn.

Billie straightened. She was really remembering. With that simple thought, a curtain of shadows fell firmly down on the past.

She grimaced and worried her lower lip. Though she was pleased with all of the memories, she worried that nothing recent flashed into her mind. Her chest deflated as she walked to the door. After opening it slowly and peeking outside, she saw that the town was busier today and didn't know how that could be possible. Wagons creaked. Several children shrieked and giggled. Men on horseback were everywhere. Businessmen who operated out of tents were repairing wind damage done during last night's storm.

Slipping from the barn, she'd just walked into the lane when the undertaker's wagon rolled by. The driver tipped his hat. At the sight of two bodies sprawled in the back, she tried to swallow, but her mouth was too dry.

She blinked. Water. Then food. Those were her first two priorities of the day.

She'd already checked the pail they'd used that first night she'd spent in the barn and it was empty. The horse had some left in his bucket, but . . .

Turning her back to the town, she spied a creek winding through the depression in the ground the freight driver, Buck, had called Alder Creek. She could get a drink there.

But the closer she got to the water, nearly every available space had been staked and men were busily panning or running water through sluice boxes. She was familiar with the better-known terms describing their apparatuses. But how? How had she known those terms?

She stepped daintily, protecting her feet. The minute she focused on where she was walking, rather than her thoughts, the answer came to her. Her father often dealt with miners and mine operators in the freight business.

Billie sighed and allowed a sad smile to form. She wouldn't get excited. It was easier to accept what comes, when it comes, she reminded herself.

After eyeing the miners closely, she chose to pass a youngish man who appeared cleaner than most and who had a round, friendly face. She nearly froze when he caught sight of her, but kept her feet moving and even managed to quirk her lips and nod when he offered her a smile.

But then the man moved toward her. She stopped and turned to flee.

"Please, Miss Billie, don't run away," he pleaded. "Remember me? Here, I want you to have this." He quickly clutched her wrist and turned her hand palm up. "You were at Sunny's party."

She tried to jerk free as granules of gold dust poured into her palm. When she realized what he'd done, she gasped, "Why? Why would you give me your gold?"

The man blushed, secured his pouch in his pocket,

then yanked a floppy-brimmed, stained hat from his head. " 'Cause last night you gave me a decent dance and today the prettiest smile I've seen in a coon's age."

"Smile?" she whispered. He'd given her money because she'd been polite and *almost* smiled? She curled her fingers over the gold dust and regarded him with wary speculation. He seemed to be in his right mind. He'd even stepped away and was just staring, albeit with a faraway glaze to his eyes.

"Thank you." He'd certainly given the gold to someone who needed it. She bobbed a quick curtsy and was about to retreat.

"Lady?"

She blinked at the awed manner in which he repeated the word and wondered what he saw that the bar owner and Sunny couldn't. "Y-yes?"

"You must be good luck. Where are you from?"

She gulped and blinked again. "Uhm . . . Missouri."

"I'm from Tennessee."

"That's . . . nice." She glanced cautiously about. What was he up to? Why was he keeping her there? "I've, uhm, never been there." She retreated a few steps.

His eyes took on a misty sheen. "My farm was in the most beautiful little valley you ever did see." As if embarrassed by his sudden sentimentality, he ducked his head. "Least it was 'fore the war."

She relaxed a little and nodded. Like this miner, many of the men around Alder Gulch wore articles of clothing from both sides of the conflict. Hot tempers concerning the War Between the States, as she'd learned last night from her safe haven inside the barn, had started several altercations.

"Miss Billie, you were headed toward the creek 'fore I interrupted. Was there somethin' you were wantin'?"

She swallowed and nearly choked. He'd surprised her so, she'd forgotten. "I—I was thirsty and—"

As if her words had lit matches under his feet, he turned and grabbed a bucket filled to the brim with fresh water. A ladle hung from the side. He filled it and handed it to her. "Don't worry. I washed it recent."

She took a long, deep drink, sighed gratefully, and drank again. Replacing the ladle, she glanced around uncomfortably. Then knowing nothing else to do, she wiped her mouth on the sleeve of her gown. The man beamed.

"Thank you, Mister . . ." She tilted her head, hoping he would supply his name.

"Lucky. Folks call me Lucky."

She clenched her hand more tightly around the gold dust. She could imagine how he got the nickname. "Lucky . . . Is there somewhere . . ." She felt her neck and face flush. She'd never had to ask this of anyone before. Never been so alone. "Someplace a . . . lady . . . can go for breakfast?"

He frowned and scolded. "Yep, but you don't want to go there all by your lonesome." He gallantly stepped closer and held out his arm. "If you don't have no one, that is." He looked behind her meaningfully.

"I . . . he . . . hasn't arrived yet." She recalled Craig Rawlins making the same gesture and how he hadn't accepted her refusal.

As if he hadn't noticed her hesitation, Lucky continued. "I'd be plumb proud to escort you, Miss Billie." He tilted his head in much the same manner as she had a moment ago.

She cleared her throat. "Thank you, sir."

Chapter Six

Lucky was being gentlemanly, she knew, and it took every ounce of willpower she possessed to appear relaxed and comfortable with him as they made their way to a dilapidated tent. The name "Raul's" was burned into a board nailed to a post in front. Adding to her discomfort, by the time they arrived, a small crowd of men trailed along behind, ogling her as if they'd never seen a woman before. Her grip on Lucky tightened, and she kept turning, keeping him between herself and the other men, until she was afraid he'd comment or question her.

Lucky did scowl at her and rasped, "Just look at all those growed men, actin' like a bunch of chuckleheads that don't know their . . . ah, I mean, actin' like they haven't seen a pretty woman before."

A man following close enough to have heard, piped up, "Reckon it's been quite a spell fer us 'chuckleheads,' Lucky. Didn't reckon no one'd mind if'n we jest *looked.*" He snatched his hat off and gave Billie a toothless grin.

A wave of heat flooded Billie's face. Being the center of attention would make anyone uneasy, but especially when the assembly was all male . . .

Lucky guided her to the door. "After you, Billie." He puffed out his chest and smiled smugly toward the gawking men.

She ducked beneath the flap Lucky held open and

clutched the gold against her breast for protection. Thick smoke from cigars, cigarettes, and the wood stove sucked the breath from her lungs as she straightened.

Her eyes burned and she blinked until they adjusted to the dim interior. Gradually, she became aware of the silence, a waiting kind of silence that caused the hairs on the nape of her neck to tingle. She squinted and looked around the small room. Her stomach muscles knotted. Every head at every table had turned in her direction.

And in the back of the room, because of his large frame, clean-shaven face, and immaculate suit that so stood out from the rest of the clientele, she spotted Craig Rawlins sitting all alone.

Lucky stepped up beside her and glanced importantly around the establishment. "Looks like the tables are full this mornin', Miss Billie. Reckon the wait won't be long—"

Craig raised his hand and motioned them toward the empty bench at his table.

Lucky grinned and took hold of her elbow.

Billie frowned. "N-no. Why don't we wait." She didn't like the look in those green eyes. They glinted with something—anticipation, anger, impatience? Whatever it was, she didn't want to face him yet.

If he'd found out she left Sunny's, he would try to send her back. All she wanted to do was eat, not cause a scene.

But before she could protest further, they were standing in front of the man, and she could swear his smile was nothing but wicked.

Craig flicked his hand in greeting. "Mornin', Miss . . . Billie," he drawled.

His soft voice crawled up her spine until she had to suppress a shiver.

Lucky hurriedly helped her take a seat on the bench, then scooted in beside her, beating three other miners who filled any empty space they could find.

Calling disinterestedly from the stove, a tall, bony

man with lank black hair and a handlebar mustache asked, "What's yer poison?"

Lucky turned adoring eyes on Billie, "You first, Miss Billie."

Grateful to prolong the time before she had to face Craig Rawlins, Billie gazed toward the man she assumed to be "Raul" and politely inquired, "What do you have?"

"Ham an' taters." He switched a long, fat cigar from one side of his mouth to the other.

She waited. When it appeared he had finished listing the choices on his menu and that everyone was waiting and watching to see what she would say, she gave her order over the rumble of her stomach. "I believe I shall have ham and potatoes. And lots of it, please."

Her eyes darted of their own volition to Craig Rawlins, then to her lap when he gave her a sardonic nod.

None of the other men ordered food. They just sat in their seats, staring. She started to wipe her palms on her skirt, but remembered the gold dust in her left hand. Her fingers were starting to cramp. If she wasn't very careful, some would slip through. She lifted her eyes and stared at the cleared tables. Where could she put it?

Craig watched the woman's furtive glances and the deepening furrow between her brows. He didn't know what was troubling her, but he had his own reasons for wishing the other men at the table would move on. He had a few questions he needed answered, not the least of which was where in the hell she'd disappeared to last night.

A sudden motion from Lucky's hand as he embroiled her in conversation drew Craig's attention to the young man. Although he remembered Lucky helped to get her out of the saloon that day and had danced with her at Sunny's, he hadn't realized the two were so friendly. His eyes narrowed. And what was she doing eating in a dirty establishment like Raul's instead of Sunny's dining room? Hadn't she gone back to the mansion last night?

Billie fidgeted beneath Craig Rawlins's blatant regard. She was so aware of the tall man that she jumped when a tin plate was plunked unceremoniously in front of her. Suddenly, everyone and everything faded from existence except the simple meal.

Her hand trembled as she picked up the crooked-pronged fork. Her stomach grumbled in anticipation as she raised a chunk of browned potato and slid it into her mouth. Her teeth sank into the flavorful softness, but she hardly took the time to chew before swallowing and gorging her mouth with more.

When she finished, she nervously noted the absolute silence of the place. Everyone watched her. Raul was on his way over. She flinched when he reached toward her, but he only grinned and set a steaming cup of very dark coffee beside her empty plate.

The aroma was strong and wonderful. She didn't hesitate to gulp down the first mouthful, though it scalded her tongue and throat. However, she did slow down and sip after that. Still holding the cup, she glanced around the table but couldn't see a napkin anywhere. She refused to wipe her mouth on her sleeve in front of all these men.

All at once, a fresh, crisp handkerchief was thrust beneath her nose. Her eyes trailed a dark broadcloth sleeve up to a wide set of shoulders, a sunburned nose, and knowing blue-green eyes, all effectively belonging to the too-dapper Craig Rawlins.

She reached out, took the handkerchief in her free hand, and daintily dabbed her chapped lips. A collective sigh echoed around the room, as if every man had just enjoyed the meal with her and also blotted her lips.

Their reaction deeply affected her. They seemed not to notice her imperfections, disregarded her impurities.

Blinking rapidly, she glanced at Lucky and thanked

him. Then her eyes sought the cook. "Mr. Raul, you are a gourmet chef. How much do I owe—"

Twenty male voices chimed together as each offered to buy her meal. Raul turned them all down, claiming someone with such good taste could enjoy breakfast as his treat.

Craig shifted on the bench. He was having a hard time erasing the memory of her lips caressing her fork, the languorous droop of her lashes when she bit into the food. She sat there so prim and proper now, looking properly contrite while men fought over who was going to buy her breakfast!

Just who was this Billie Whatever? Where had she come from? What was she doing in Alder Gulch? Was she a high-class con artist? Maybe Sunny was right. From the jewels she flaunted, she could even be some sort of fancy prostitute. Naw, no woman working the streets or in a bordello would shy away from a man the way she did. It wouldn't be good for business. Besides, she had manners and breeding one rarely found on a woman of the street.

He watched her modestly duck her head when Lucky asked her a question. Images of pearly teeth and a pouty mouth knotted his gut. An irrational anger suddenly consumed him. She'd put on one hell of a display for the men, whether she'd intended to or not, and he'd had enough.

By the time Billie noticed he was leaving and cheerfully realized she'd been spared having to explain why she was no longer living at Sunny Turnbow's, his back was turned and he couldn't see her holding out his handkerchief. Once he'd gone, however, she gratefully settled it in her lap and carefully emptied the gold dust from her hand into the clean folds.

The stiffly starched cloth reminded her of its owner. It was almost disconcerting to meet a man that immaculate.

When she rose to her feet, every man still inside the

eatery followed suit. Becoming accustomed to their
stares, she begged their pardon for a moment and
walked over to Raul. She held her breath as she approached, hoping the jar of her footsteps wouldn't
bounce loose the long, drooping ash from his cigar. It
dangled dangerously close to a large caldron of something that smelled and looked suspiciously like laundry
water, but which she'd heard him refer to as *stew*.

"Mr. Raul . . ." Her lips twitched when he glanced at
her with only mild impatience. "I—" Her eyes widened
as half of the ashes finally plopped into the stew when
he nodded. His large ladle stirred them into the brew as
if they were a natural ingredient.

"Are you in need of help? I could serve the . . . food.
Wash dishes. Anything."

He slid the smelly cigar way back into a corner of his
mouth, losing the remainder of the ashes down his shirt-
front. "Does it look like Raul need help?"

She gazed around at the dirty plates still on the tables
and stacked in a large tub beside the stove. More miners crowded inside, waiting to fill any empty seat.
"Well . . ."

"Raul work alone."

She'd been afraid of that. "If you change your
mind—"

He dished up a bowl of the stew and edged past her.
"Adíos."

Her steps were slow and dejected as she left Raul's.
She felt much better after having eaten, but was fairly
certain she'd find the same rejection from other businesses. Except the saloons.

"Where do you wanna go now, Miss Billie?"

She stiffened. How could she have forgotten Lucky so
quickly? "Mr. Lucky . . ." He frowned. She started over.
"Lucky . . . you've been very kind." She tilted her head
and included the rest of the men standing close by. "But
you have work to do. You can't spend your time escort-

ing me about town . . . no matter how much I would enjoy it," she added quickly and smiled—genuinely smiled.

A dozen sunburned, weathered faces turned even
darker.

Lucky scuffed his toe through the thin layer of mud
left over from the rain. "If you're sure. This ain't the
safest town, even in broad daylight."

How well she knew. "I'll be careful."

A man with dirt caked on his face and clothes spoke
shyly. "I hope you mean that, Miss Billie. You remind
me a lot of my sister and I'd hate for anything to happen to you."

Billie stared aghast at the unkempt fellow who spoke
precise, cultured English. At last she found her voice.
"I—I . . . thank you for your concern."

He grinned, tipped his hat, and wandered slowly toward the creek. Soon, the rest of the men followed.
Lucky was the last to go, but reluctantly conceded when
she waved him on.

A measure of warmth invaded her heart as she
watched them leave. She was beginning to understand
that these men were lonely, and starved for feminine
company. She felt less intimidated by their overwhelming numbers, but still vowed not to let down her guard.

She started down the street—alone. Her first stop was
the same mercantile she'd visited yesterday. The man
had seemed truly upset by his inability to help her and
she'd been touched. He was also the only person in
town she'd trust to weigh her precious gold. Of course,
there was Craig Rawlins . . .

She shook her head. No, she didn't want him to know
that she'd been reduced to accepting money from
moon-eyed miners. Besides belittling her in his eyes, he
would remind her how stupid she'd been to turn down
Sunny's hospitality, begrudgingly as it had been given,
and add another reason for him to think she had no
business in Alder Gulch.

What damaged her pride the most was her dawning realization that he might be right.

When the gold dust was weighed, she thought there was enough to buy a pair of shoes and several nonperishable food items. However, the merchant looked at her quizzically when she asked about ladies' footwear.

He led her to a shelf along the back wall. "This is it, lady. Take your pick."

"But those are . . . boots," she explained, as if maybe he hadn't heard her correctly when she'd requested shoes.

"Yep. That's what you got to choose from. *If* you want *shoes.*"

"Oh." She was learning that there was a lot about life she hadn't taught her young, wealthy charges in finishing school. She would have to make a few adjustments when she . . .

Her throat constricted. What was she thinking? She didn't even know if she could return to that life.

Another thought struck her. Had she let the school know she wouldn't be back after summer recess? Would they miss her? Somehow, she thought not.

"Hey, lady?"

She blinked and realized the merchant had been speaking to her. "Excuse me, what did you say?"

"If you want a pair, try 'em on till you find something that's a close fit. I may have some socks that'll fill up the rest of the space."

"Fine. Thank you." She looked down at her feet and couldn't help but also notice the fresh layers of dust coating her gown. A few new rends marred the once-beautiful material. "Wait. If I don't purchase the . . . shoes, would there be enough to buy a dress?"

"Lady . . ." He shook his head. "Don't know where you think you are, but I don't have any ready-made women's things. Got some material I could sell ya, though, if you want to make something up."

"Ahem, no, thank you. I'll just look through the boots." She had no needle, no scissors, no place to sew.

She finally selected the smallest of the seven pair of boots, which were still three sizes too big. But she had to have something, and her gingham skirt hid all but the toes from view. When she walked back to the counter, she asked the merchant if he'd found the socks he'd mentioned.

"Yep. Two pair. If you want them, I'll throw in the second pair for half price, since you seem like a nice lady an' all."

She swallowed and refrained from asking what he'd have done if she *hadn't* seemed like a lady.

"You hear me, lady?"

"Y-yes. Thank you." She snapped her eyes up to meet his. "It's just ... I'm not used to life in a gold camp." Uh-oh. When she saw that her comment brought a world of question to his eyes, she quickly snatched up her purchases.

Struggling through the door, she was about to drop the parcel of food when she backed into someone.

"Ouch. Damn you, you son of a—'scuse me, daughter of a—"

Billie's eyes rounded to the size of saucers when she spun around and saw a petite little girl of maybe sixteen, seventeen at most. She wore a dress that must have fit when she was thirteen or fourteen. Her face and arms were dirt-smudged, and her dark hair hung in limp, oily strands. And she seemed vaguely familiar.

"See what ya gone an' done? That man was fixin' to pay two bits, an' ya run 'im off."

"Two bits?" Billie blinked. She'd heard that before, too. "For what?"

The girl's hard brown eyes glittered with what Billie suspicioned was amusement.

"Are ya fer real?"

"Yes," Billie affirmed. "I would say so." She repositioned her packages and decided to take them back to the barn before continuing to search for work.

"Say, I 'member you." She swished her hips and stuck her face as close to Billie's as she could reach. "This's the second o' my gents ya scared off."

Billie frowned and shrugged, then felt a little miffed when the girl gave a big belly-laugh. The cheeky young thing had the nerve to also give her a thorough up-and-down perusal.

"I reckon yore fixin' to find out jest how much yore worth. But—" She shook her finger at Billie. "This is my last warnin'. This is my territory. Got that?"

Inhaling a quick breath, Billie was tempted to launch into the lecture she gave her girls at school about how young women respected their elders and spoke with deference, which this little hoyden definitely needed to know. However, even if she'd wanted to go to the trouble, the ragamuffin had turned her attention to another man and was trying to walk seductively toward him.

It looked more like she was favoring a sore hip.

The girl spoke briefly to the man, then glanced back over her shoulder. Seeing that Billie was still watching, she called out for everyone to hear, "Say . . . Lady. This here gent wants to know how much it'd cost him ta get under *yore* skirt?"

Billie's mouth gaped open. She snapped it shut. Two bits. Now she understood. The little hussy was taunting her.

Under her skirt. Billie's arms tightened around the parcels. Her body began to tremble. She quickly sucked in deep draughts of air. *No, I will not give in.* Everyone was watching. She had to act calm and in control. Like a lady.

With a voice that quavered only slightly, she lifted her chin and replied, "It will cost him much more than two bits, thank you." She regally turned and left the scene, hoping she could make it to the lane before her quaking knees buckled beneath her.

As she walked, though, she seemed to find a new strength. She'd actually found the nerve to stand up for herself, had not allowed herself to be intimidated. Heat surged through her body. Exultation rippled up her spine.

Yet she also felt a pang of remorse for the poor urchin. Imagine, being reduced to selling one's body for a quarter.

Trudging toward the barn, she glanced carefully around to make sure no one watched before slipping inside. A nagging thought had taken hold of her mind and wouldn't let go. Just how far would she be willing to go to survive?

Ice water raced through her veins. Perhaps the girl had been more insightful than she realized when she'd predicted Billie would soon discover how much she was worth.

Later that afternoon, upon returning to the barn for the second time, Billie worried that there might be no other option than to use her body to survive. She'd found absolutely no jobs available for a decent woman in Alder Gulch.

The only offers she'd had were from saloonkeepers. And it seemed that every other business in the town was a saloon or gambling house. There were certainly plenty of opportunities for employment in those places, *if* she wanted.

Yet, she'd also learned that the people of Alder Gulch liked the idea of having a lady around to look at and talk to—whatever little good that did.

Despair weighed heavily on her shoulders. Being a lady might win her nice comments, but it wasn't any help in earning a real wage.

A sob caught in her throat.

Sudden pounding from across the lane drug her from her self-imposed state of depression. She peeked through a space between the slats and saw Craig Rawlins replacing a board that must have blown off during the storm.

Pursing her lips, she scratched the horse's nose and studied the back of the Empty Barrel. Why was he keeping it closed? From the looks of the other businesses, they generated a lot of profit. One would think that with his evident sense of enterprise, he'd be after his share of the gold being spent in town.

She gave the animal one last pat and sank onto the piled straw. Hmmmm. She was certain he had the means to keep the saloon in operation. Maybe he just didn't have the time to run it himself. Maybe that was why he needed partners.

Well, his business acumen, or lack of it, was certainly none of her concern. She just needed to rest her feet before going out to look for work in one last place before dark. She slipped off a boot and rubbed her heel. Blisters. That was all she needed.

Stretching her neck, she looked outside. He was still there.

She sighed. Then perked up. With the saloon closed, she wouldn't feel so guilty about staying in the barn a few more days.

By the time Mr. Rawlins left the area and she was able to escape the barn, it was early evening. She slipped down the lane a ways, in the opposite direction from which he'd taken, before changing her path and heading for the main thoroughfare.

She'd no sooner turned the corner of the first business than a door swung open and bounced off her arm and hip. She staggered backward as three men stumbled outside, leaving her a clear view of the interior of the saloon.

It was nothing spectacular. The bar was a wide, thick board stacked on top of two upturned barrels. There was a rickety table or two, with chairs in even worse condition. She saw two women—very scantily clad. One was clearing empty bottles, the other was being swung

and bounced around like a rag doll while someone pounded the keys of an out-of-tune piano. No one paid a bit of attention to the awful music as more "couples," all men, laughed and kicked up their heels with no apparent care as to keeping time or rhythm.

Billie was sorry when the door slammed closed. The people inside had looked like they were having fun. But she sighed and hurried past the saloon toward the freight office. Hopefully, Mr. Rawlins had gone on about other business and only the manager would be present. She'd saved the freight office as one of her last possibilities just because she didn't want to lower herself to ask Craig Rawlins for work.

Stepping tentatively inside the small, spartan office of another all-wood building, she decided Craig Rawlins must be quite well-to-do compared to the rest of the businessmen in Alder Gulch.

It took a few seconds for her eyes to adjust to the dim interior. Then she saw *him.* Her stomach knotted. He was staring at her from behind a carved counter that took up almost the full width of the room.

"Ah, Miss . . . Billie. I've been looking for you."

Her eyes narrowed. She didn't appreciate the smug expression on his too-handsome face. And she knew better. He hadn't been looking for her. He'd been busy around his saloon for the past hour.

"I went up to the Turnbows' earlier, thinking I might catch you there."

She swallowed and backed up a step.

"Funny," he continued smoothly, though his eyes bored into her. "Sunny said she hadn't seen you since yesterday." He folded his hands on the countertop. "Imagine my embarrassment."

She darted her eyes toward the door.

Swifter than a bolt of lightning, his hand shot out and captured her wrist.

She repressed a shudder and took a deep breath before meeting his eyes. "I—I decided not to stay there."

His head snapped back. The truth reared in front of him like a brick wall. Of course. He should have realized it sooner. She'd hooked up with ole Lucky. Disappointment inexplicably coiled in his throat. She wasn't the lily-white flower he'd imagined. Quickly, he swallowed it down. What was the matter with him? He'd just met the woman. Who was he to judge her moral character?

He grimaced and released her hand. "I was just . . ." He was just *what*? Going to tell her he was worried about her? She'd think him terribly foolish. The only excuse he could think of as to why he would have been looking for her was, "I wanted to ask you a few more questions about the shooting."

Billie looked away and rubbed her wrist, worried about the tingling sensation that shot up her arm when he grabbed her. And she still felt the burning imprint of his fingers, though he hadn't held her so tightly as to bruise the skin.

She cleared her throat, knowing she had to ask him now or lose her nerve. "I have a question for you, too." She didn't want him to think she'd wandered into his office for no good reason. Under the cover of her lashes, she darted him a quick glance. But he was staring at his hand with a bemused expression on his face.

Craig shook off the strange feeling touching her soft flesh had invoked. He raised his gaze to her face, closely noting the dark smudges under her eyes, her drawn cheeks, and pale features. Something was bothering her, but he wouldn't dare to presume to question her about her personal problems. Lucky could do that. Damn him.

But maybe her question would enlighten him. He did the gentlemanly thing. "You first, Miss . . ." For the hundredth time, it seemed, he gave her the opportunity to fill in her surname.

The anticipation in his regard caused her to retreat another step. When she'd been turned down before, she'd been able to shrug it off and go on. But, somehow, his answer held the weight of the world and she was afraid.

"I—I—" She looked toward the door.

He swayed forward.

"I wonder . . . Would you like to . . ."

Craig drummed his fingertips on the counter.

"Could I . . ." She looked around the neat, spotlessly clean room. Her voice faded to a whisper. ". . . earn some money here?"

Chapter Seven

Billie inhaled quickly, not realizing she'd been holding her breath. A familiar tightness enveloped her eyelids. She concentrated, willing herself not to fall apart. Not again.

Craig stared in fascination as she closed her eyes and compressed her lips. Her full, sensual lips. What the hell? He cleared his throat.

"Earn money doing what?" He could hardly stand it, the way she waved those long, curly lashes at him.

Billie's eyes shot wide open. He was going to make her spell it out. Make her beg. "I need gainful employment," she said defensively. "I believe I could do almost anything."

"Yes, I bet you could." He thought of the way she looked on Lucky's arm—elegant, graceful—and rolled his eyes. Then his conscience berated him. He was being judgmental, and had no right.

"I'm sorry, Billie," he said in a more professional tone of voice. And he was, but he didn't think she belonged in this town and wouldn't help to make her stay permanent. "I hired a new man last week to keep the books. So far he's done a good job and there's really nothing else a . . . female can do around here."

"I see." And she did. From the looks of the office, he probably didn't even need some of the help he had.

"Oh, I believe this is yours." He reached under the

counter and lifted out two precisely folded articles of clothing and handed them to her. "Justin asked me to give these to you."

"My dress." She frowned. Evidently, Sunny hadn't appreciated her trade. But then she saw the other piece and brightened. "And my cloak." She shook it out and swirled it around her shoulders. "Thank you." Shivering slightly, she clutched it tightly about her, though the sun had finally come out and taken the chill from the afternoon.

She backed toward the door. "W-well . . . thank you for your time." At least he'd been honest. Hadn't pussy-footed around. Yet the disappointment cut clear to her soul.

"Wait." Craig shook his head as the door closed between them. Unaccountably, he'd just thought of the saloon. However, despite her dress, he had a hard time imagining her working there.

Outside, Billie put a hand on her chest to ease her thundering heart. How humiliating. She should have known he would be the same as the others, or even worse, she thought irrationally. Why had she asked him for work?

She sighed and glanced around the street with dull eyes. Once again it was getting dark and she was caught alone on the main road. She'd learned her lesson by this time. Hurrying back toward the barn, she was grateful that at least for tonight she would have food and had even thought to fill her bucket with fresh water. Also the horse's. She *almost* had all the comforts of home.

Home. She choked and tripped over a mound of earth. How she wished she could go a few hours without wondering about home or family.

Not paying close attention to where she was or where she stopped, she bent to run her hand into the top of her boot to catch a sock crumpling around her heel. When she straightened, she looked directly through a section of canvas that had come unbound at the corner of a tent.

The establishment she gazed into was nicer than the other ones she'd seen, at least as far as the furniture and the actual bar. The piano was in tune and the player knew how to coax out a melody. The song was so energetic and lively that she tapped her toes inside the too-large boots.

Several women were being kept busy dancing and, again, men were partnering each other. She was just about to move on when she saw a man grab the hand of a woman waiting tables and circled her onto the dance floor. He and the woman looked to be enjoying themselves so much that Billie had to stay and watch.

When the tune came to an abrupt end, the miner pulled on the woman's bodice and poured gold dust into her cleavage. The woman laughed, patted the man's bearded cheek, and went back to work.

Billie sagged against the corner support. Just as Lucky had given her gold for a dance and a smile, the miner paid generously for his fun. Her mind spun. The men of Alder Gulch were willing to pay for decent entertainment. And not only could Billie dance, she'd been taught by the finest master money could buy. Yes, she knew she had.

If she was to be forced to use her body to survive, why not do it using her *feet?*

"Come on in, 'stead of just standin' out there and watchin'."

She jumped when a face looked out at her through the unlaced canvas. "Oh, I—I couldn't. Really couldn't."

"Why not?"

The man was young and good-looking, in a cocky sort of way. Dare she ask—"Are you, perhaps, seeking help?"

The young man inclined his head. "I'm always on the

lookout for a pretty woman. If you're askin' if I could use *you* . . . You damn well betcha."

He reached through the canvas. "Come on."

She jerked back. "N-no. Not yet. All I want to do is . . . dance."

"*Just* dance?"

She nodded.

He scowled. "Sorry. If you dance downstairs, you gotta dance upstairs."

"B-but—"

"And any woman workin' for me's gotta lower her neckline and raise her hemline. Get my drift?"

Her eyelids slid half closed as she regarded the slimy character. "Oh, yes. I definitely *get* it." She shook her finger as close to his crooked nose as she could. "Mark my words, one of these days you're going to be very sorry you have such a high-handed attitude toward women."

He grinned and leered. "My attitude ain't all that's high, beautiful. Come on around and I'll show you how to make a lot of money and have a *real* good time."

"Oh-h-h!" she sputtered. What was wrong with the employers in this town? Did they think the only thing a woman was good for was to . . . to lie on her back?

Sweat suddenly broke out on her brow and neck and rolled between her breasts. Her body went numb. Of course that was what they believed. How could she be so naïve?

Seeing the agonized expression stealing across her face, the saloonkeeper held up his hands and backed away. "Look, lady, don't go and do somethin' . . . lady-like, and faint, or cry. Please don't *cry*. Didn't think you'd accept—"

She suddenly couldn't hear his words. Vague images of a struggle burned through her mind, then went up in smoke as quickly as a doused fire. Blinking rapidly, she looked into the man's shocked face. She gasped, spun on her heel, tripped, then finally ran toward the barn.

Billie had just reached the lane when she saw Craig Rawlins snooping around the back of the Empty Barrel. She slid to a stop and ducked behind a stack of crates. Holding her breath, she fidgeted and glanced wildly around, making sure she hadn't been seen.

Tears burned her eyes when he headed toward the barn. He'd find the water and food. She would have no place to go. Why, oh why, hadn't she hidden the things better?

"Hey, Rawlins? That you?" someone called from the next building. "Your wagon's comin' in. Looks like Buck's shot up."

Buck? Anguish tore at her chest. That nice old man who'd been so sweet to her during the trip? Craig ran toward the street and a sigh of relief tore from her throat—for Buck's sake and her own.

She peered up and down the lane before rising from behind the crates. Men were running toward the freight wagon, drawn by the threat of having their supply line cut. With everyone's attention directed toward the calamity, she felt it was safe to move. She rushed across the lane and fumbled the barn door open with trembling hands.

Collapsing on the piled straw, she closed her eyes and inhaled deeply. It was strange how such a small, almost uninhabitable space, combined with the horse's quiet presence, offered her a measure of security.

She'd left her home, traveled who-knew-how-far to get someplace in the middle of nowhere, was penniless, and had no hope for a job that didn't involve the use of her body—but she'd found this little haven in the midst of chaos.

An explosion shook the barn. The ground vibrated so violently that water sloshed over the rim of the bucket. Billie huddled on the straw, waiting for the world to end. When the horse just stood there calmly munching his hay, she decided it was safe to breathe again and stretched out her back.

She pulled out a strip of jerked meat and began to chew as she wondered what had happened. Logically, since the animal didn't react and this was a mining camp, it probably had something to do with the search for gold.

As the light in the barn faded, she delved into the package of food and withdrew a peppermint stick. Pleased and surprised to find the candy in the mercantile, she'd splurged on several pieces.

Sucking on the sweet in the growing darkness, she focused on Craig Rawlins and the Empty Barrel Saloon. It was a shame such a huge new building was going to waste. Surely he would do something with it. Not that it was any of her business.

Craig Rawlins helped Buck Benson into the freight office. "Sit in that chair, Buck," he commanded, "then shuck that shirt while I stoke the fire and set some water to boil."

After finishing those chores, Craig went back to his driver and felt around the wound in his upper arm. "You were lucky. Bullet just gouged the flesh."

Buck nodded. "Them rascals come at me right on the flat. Never expected 'em there. Got everythin' but the Glenn shipment. Had that cached in the box."

"Good." Craig frowned as he examined Buck closer. "How did blood get up here?" He wiped congealed flakes from the side of the driver's head.

Buck coughed. "I smeared it from my arm, then played dead." He shook his head. "Wasn't so sure they warn't gonna plug me agin just from pure cussedness."

"This is going to hurt," Craig warned, opening a drawer and pulling out a bottle. He poured rye whiskey over the wound, then handed the liquor to Buck, who drank down several swallows before handing it back.

"Did you see who they were, or recognize any

voices?" Craig was beginning to suspect that the outlaws
were getting inside information, or lived right in town.

Buck shook his head. "Naw. Didn't have a chance.
The weirdest thing happened, boss. I looked at the
blood on my arm an' fingers, an' heard this loud
buzzin'. My head spun. Must've passed out then an'
there."

Craig grinned at the grizzled old man. "Reckon you
must've."

"Well, damn it, I wanted to git them yahoos. We
gotta do somethin', or they'll ruin us."

Buck was right, Craig thought. No business had been
spared, but it seemed the freight line had been hit the
worst.

He'd been so certain that Alder Gulch would grow
and prosper that he'd risked everything to construct du-
rable buildings and employ dependable people. The
town had grown all right, but as evidenced by the rampant lawlessness, it wasn't a safe place.

Wrapping Buck's arm, Craig thought of the woman.
Billie. He cursed under his breath and tied off the bandage. A soft, seemingly intelligent, beautiful woman like
her was way out of her element in a town like this.

And he recalled when she'd first entered his office
that afternoon. She'd appeared so self-assured and determined, yet the minute she'd looked up and seen him,
her confidence had evaporated. Her reaction bothered
him. Why? What had he done to cause her to be afraid
of him? She was a grown woman. Had been stupid
enough to leave Sunny's house of her own volition.
What had she thought he would do about it?

And then, when he'd told her he didn't have a job for
her, she'd looked so lost—even desperate. Every other
day he turned someone down. Someone who'd sold everything they owned, or could borrow or steal, to race
to the gold fields to find their fortunes.

He felt that same sense of sympathy when the reality
was that only four or five of the thousands seeking that

dream actually found their fortune. Now they needed to earn just enough money to go back home and face their family and friends in disgrace. How many times had he denied them jobs but given them rides out of town on the freight line?

Craig sighed and patted his driver's shoulder. "You're all done here. Go home and get some rest."

"Thanks, boss. I'll be back in the morning' an' take that next shipment to Salt Lake."

"No. Wait another day. Don't want to take any chances of that wound getting infected on the trail."

"I don't know . . ."

"The load will still be here." He tried not to show it, but he was worried. Besides the shipments being stolen, several drivers had been killed the past month. By the time Buck left for Salt Lake, Craig would have a guard hired to ride with him. One way or another, the outlaws had to be foiled.

He frowned. This development also meant he wouldn't be sending the woman to Salt Lake. It was just too dangerous. No, he'd just have to keep an eye on her here, Lucky or no Lucky.

Rubbing his stubbled chin, he thought that it was too bad none of the jobs he had coming up were suitable for a woman. Hiring her would be one way to keep her out of trouble, after all.

Locking up the office, he headed toward the cabin he'd built on the side of a hill overlooking Alder Gulch. He stopped beneath trees, spared for shade in the summer and a windbreak during the winter, and again found himself thinking of Billie.

It had been a long time since a female had intruded into his business considerations. Well . . . at least she was a *gorgeous* female. Her skin was creamy and delicate, but no longer so pale. Since she'd been walking around town without the customary parasol, her cheeks had turned a soft, rosy color. Though her hair was strawberry blond and she was fairly light complected, she ap-

parently had the type of skin that tanned when exposed
to the sun. He grimaced. Unlike himself, who burned
and peeled and then burned again.

Her tall body moved now with a willowy grace.
When she'd left his office that afternoon, she'd felt pres-
sured and her steps had seemed ungainly. She'd lifted
her feet as if lead weights were attached to her shoes.
What haunted her so?

He shrugged and commanded himself to stop thinking about her. She was no different from any other
woman he'd known—just a little prettier. All right, a *lot*
prettier. But he had other things to think about. Like
who killed his cousin. How to put an end to the outlaws.
What to do with the Empty Barrel.

Yes, he had more to occupy his mind than a nicely
curved figure.

Twenty-four hours later, Billie hobbled to the creek in
the waning light. "Of all the stupid, idiotic things to
do," she muttered, while refilling the bucket she'd
tripped over in the barn.

It was the boots. They were so big and clumsy that
she forgot to make allowances for the extra space they
took up.

The too-big boots. They fit just like her life. Living
without answers to questions about a lost period of time
in her past was like trying to fill shoes three sizes too big.

She sighed and picked up the bucket. It was heavy
and she listed to the right as she struggled up the slope.
Thank goodness it was the time of evening when the
miners flocked to town, or she never would have ven-
tured out this far alone. It wasn't so much that she felt
threatened anymore—she felt smothered, swarmed by
helpful hands and grinning faces. But sooner or later,
that one man—the one who would want to do her
harm—would make his presence known, and then . . .
Then the terror would return.

She inhaled and released the breath quickly. This was not the time—though there was never a *good* time—to unravel the past. She needed to keep her mind in the present. She needed a plan.

Once again she was reduced to being penniless and hungry. For lunch, she'd eaten the last of the jerky and polished off the peppermint.

Paying more attention to hunger pangs than to where she was going, she stubbed her toe. Ouch! She banged angrily into the barn door, slamming it against the siding. It bounced back and hit her, spilling the water. Damn! She let loose a muffled shriek before catching herself. She needed control of these sorry boots—and control of her life. Self-consciously, she glanced quickly around to see if anyone had heard the commotion.

All was quiet. No one had noticed.

Craig was changing clothes, regretting his acceptance of another invitation to Sunny Turnbow's, when someone pounded on his door. He cursed beneath his breath as he dropped his watch and had to get down on his knees to search for it.

"Mr. Rawlins? Ya in there?"

"Yeah," he called. "Be with you in just a minute."

"Hurry, Mr. Rawlins."

Craig frowned. It sounded like that boy, Danny. What could he be up to at this hour? "That you, Danny?"

"Yeah."

Tucking the watch into his pocket, Craig strode across the planking in his bare feet. He threw open the door and gazed at the wide-eyed boy's harried face.

"Ya might wanna go see, Mr. Rawlins. Could be somethin' real important."

"Slow down, Danny," Craig tried to calm the excited boy. "What might be important?"

"One of the gents from the gamblin' hall next to yore saloon, he said there're noises comin' from yore barn.

The one behind the saloon. Anyways, he reckoned if'n I weren't real busy, ya might wanna know."

Craig rubbed his chin. He had been in the barn just that morning and planned to go by tonight and feed the paint. Hell, the fella probably just heard his horse. A rat could've knocked something over. A board might've come loose. There were any number of reasons . . .

His gut clenched. Or it could be a horse thief. Or even the murderer.

He'd spent a lot of time thinking during the past few days, and had come up with no good explanation for Big John or Bobby's deaths other than their connection with the saloon—or himself. What if he'd stepped on someone's toes getting his businesses started? What if someone thought they'd been cheated in the saloon and had a vendetta against the owners?

Whatever, or whomever, he'd decided to keep a close watch on his back.

He patted the boy's shoulder. "Thanks, Danny. You did the right thing."

Danny shuffled his feet. "Mr. Rawlins, 'member that time ya give me the job o' feedin' Spot an' all?"

"Sure I do. You did a real fine job."

The boy's Adam's apple bobbed as enthusiastically as his head. "Don't ya reckon, ya might put me on agin? Ain't no tellin' what all could happen without no one watchin' the place. Me an' my ma, we could stay there at night, an' ya wouldn't have to worry 'bout nuthin'."

Craig looked closely at the boy. Danny wanted more than just a job. There had been a plea to his voice when he mentioned his mother. Young as Danny was, Craig sensed the boy understood the need for her to have a safe place to go at night. A place off the streets.

"You know, Danny, I'd been thinking about hiring a reliable man to kind of keep an eye on the barn and . . ." He choked. "Spot." He bent and looked the boy in the eyes. "Think you could handle the job?"

Danny's eyes grew round as a full moon. His thin chest puffed out. "Yep. I mean, yes*sirr.*"

"Then the job's yours. When do you think you could start?"

Danny twisted the ragged hem of his shirttail around one grubby finger. "My ma, she's, uhhh . . ." He looked worriedly out the door. "Don't reckon it'd be tonight. That won't make no diff'rence, will it, Mr. Rawlins?" he asked anxiously.

Craig ruffled the boy's shaggy blond hair. "How's tomorrow? Think you could come to work then?"

"You betcha." Danny almost jumped up and down.

Taking some coins from the change he'd dumped into an empty ash tray, Craig held it out to Danny. "Here's a little advance for coming all the way up here to fetch me."

Danny gulped. He gripped the money tightly in his small fist, bobbed his head, and ran off down the hill.

Craig smiled fleetingly as he finished dressing, but sobered quickly when the buckle clicked on his gunbelt. He felt in his vest watch pocket to make sure the derringer was there. Crowning his head with his good black hat, he headed down the hill toward town.

If a man *was* in the barn, he was in for a big surprise.

Billie stood peeking out the window at the last red glow of sunset rimming the nearby mountains. Never one for just idling away time, she felt like a cooped-up pigeon with no hope for release. As much as she appreciated the safety of her hideaway, she wished she could be out there *doing* something.

The mountains were stark, rugged outlines amongst deep purple shadows encompassing the town. The dark image only served to blacken her mood. She rubbed her palms up and down her arms, trying to dispel the eerie feeling rustling down her spine. She sensed something was about to happen. Soon. She just hoped it was for the better.

About to return to the larger pile of straw she'd raked together to make a more comfortable bed, she could have sworn she caught a glimpse of a movement through the window. She stood stone-still and focused on the corner of the saloon.

There! There it was again. But the swiftly moving shadow was soon out of her range of vision. She couldn't tell if it went up the lane or . . . toward the barn.

She murmured to the horse, more to reassure herself, and backed into the empty stall. As she sank onto the straw, night faded the dimming light to almost black. She knew the blackness could rise up and overwhelm her. And she knew it would stay this dark until the moon came up.

She held her breath and listened, hearing nothing unusual. So far that evening, she hadn't heard any blasting or much noise-making from the street. She guessed the weekends were the wildest, when the farmers and ranchers from outlying areas came into town and joined with the miners in cutting loose.

Suddenly, she cocked her head. The door creaked. Her heart stopped. Her chest constricted. She couldn't catch her breath. The horse snorted, then whickered softly.

She scooted back into the stall, sacrificing caution to her terror and rustling the straw.

The deep shadows inside the barn loomed ominously. Billie froze, engulfed by a different blackness—the familiar blackness of an unknown past horror.

"No!" she whispered to the emptiness.

A cold determination edged out the dark. She couldn't just sit back and wait. With a shuddering breath she straightened. She knew she'd be at an even greater disadvantage, but crawled to her feet. Her skirt slithered across the straw, as loud as a gunshot in the silence. She sucked in her breath, glaring through the darkness until her eyes ached. It was too dark.

Her ears buzzed from the strain of listening. Nausea churned her stomach. Had someone actually entered the barn? She had to know.

From somewhere in front of her she heard a huff of breath. Straw scuffed. Her chest felt like it would burst. Slowly, with her back to the stall wall, she worked her way toward the corner where she'd seen rakes and pitchforks.

Why hadn't Craig built the barn so the door could be locked from the inside, then something like this wouldn't scare vagrants half to death.

Something bumped something. Water sloshed. A muttered curse sliced through the stifling air. Her heart jumped into her throat. Ice water trickled through her veins, but the blackness was only around her now, not inside her. Stronger, but weak at the same time, she had to squat down to keep her knees from quaking out from under her.

She sensed, but couldn't see, someone or something close—very close. The air was sucked from the room. Was the sudden heat she felt from a nearby body, or was she so frightened she was feeling, as well as hearing, things?

An indrawn breath hissed just to her left. Time, and her heartbeat, came to a standstill.

Gunshots exploded outside, scattering her wits. She jumped. Her elbow rammed into flesh and bone. She screamed. Running feet and shouting voices approached— but bypassed the barn.

Fingers grasped her shoulders. She shrieked and scrambled on her hands and knees. Her head thunked into a hard, flexible body. Someone grunted. She let out her breath, unable to hold it longer, and gasped for another. The fingers brushed her back, then caught in locks of her hair. She yelped with pain.

Craig cursed. Good Lord, a woman. He'd been about

to call out with the first screech, thinking he'd grabbed
Danny. But the boy didn't have long silky hair. Fingernails raked his neck and tore the top button from his
best shirt. He swore again.

His feet slipped in the loose straw. He lost his balance
and fell on top of the struggling, gasping woman. Petticoats tangled with his legs. Grasping her flailing arms,
he rolled until he lay atop her with her hands trapped
above her head.

"Wh-Who are you?" he wheezed.

Billie didn't hear his question. She was fighting another battle—the black terror from within.

Craig lowered his weight over the heaving, bucking
body until she stopped fighting from pure exhaustion.
When she finally quit struggling, her body was as stiff
and tense as a virgin on her wedding night. Feeling the
tendons in her wrist bunch, he frowned.

Her arms remained strained, but he thought a sigh of
capitulation brushed his cheek. "Who are you?"

She failed to respond, staring at him with eyes that
didn't recognize him.

"Billie?" He let go of her hands and pushed himself to
a sitting position. "Who in the devil *are* you?"

He cleared his throat and tried again. "What are you
doing here at this hour?"

Billie felt the chill of the night air as he moved away.
She tried to sort through his words as the door creaked
open. Moonlight illuminated a portion of the floor. The
horse snorted as a match flared. The smell of sulphur
wafted across the space. Flickering flares from a lantern
chased the frightening shadows back into their corners.
Then he stood before her, legs spread, hands splayed
across his narrow hips.

"You haven't answered a single question." He stared
down at the disheveled woman. With her hair all askew
and short wisps curling about her ears and cheeks, she
looked like a bedraggled, lost little girl.

From somewhere deep inside, where he hadn't allowed emotions to arise for a long, long time, he had a distinct urge to reach out and comfort her, to just hold her and make everything better. The notion stunned him.

Billie lay limp and exhausted, thankful he'd come like a shining knight into her darkness. "I—I've been staying here."

"What?"

The look in his eyes was frightening. She couldn't go on.

"What was wrong with Sunny's?" Suddenly, he stopped and stared at her. "You spent the night here last night?"

She nodded.

For some reason, the thought that she'd been here, all alone, wasn't nearly as disturbing as the thought of her spending the night with Lucky. But he didn't know quite what to say. He'd enlisted the Corbetts to make sure she stayed in the barn that first night. How could he denounce her for doing so now? At least she'd had the good sense to come here instead of . . .

"I couldn't stay at Sunny's."

Her voice was so low he had to bend forward to hear. "I'd rather stay here. May I, please?"

Chapter Eight

To refrain from acting on his impulse to reach out and comfort her—an impulse he was highly uncomfortable with and sure she would not welcome—Craig Rawlins fisted one hand in his pocket and scrubbed the back of his neck with the other.

"You know, Sunny wasn't offering you charity." Why else would he be going up there for dinner tonight? He'd promised to do a lot of things for Sunny in return for the favor, whether he liked it or not. "What were you thinking, coming here alone? You should've learned by now how dangerous this town can be—especially for a woman."

She managed to look him in the eyes long enough to nod. Then she shyly glanced away as she busied herself sitting up and brushing at the loose straw. His eyes were too disconcerting. Caused too many strange sensations to vibrate through her body. Her body. Which still felt the weight of him pressed upon her but not the after effects that usually followed her moments of unexplainable horror.

Confused by his own reactions, Craig glanced uneasily around. He saw the paper that had been wrapped around her food and the discarded slippers. "What's that?"

"I, uhm . . . bought some . . . shoes . . . and a few pieces of a jerky at the mercantile." She lifted her chin.

He spread his hands on his hips. "What'd you use for money?" He realized he was acting defensively, but he'd told Danny he'd look after her and didn't like the feeling that he'd let the boy down. Hell, a man couldn't keep tabs on her every minute.

"Th-that nice Mr. Lucky. He gave it to me." She stiffened her backbone straighter than a broom handle.

His eyes narrowed. "Now why would Lucky do that?" He knew Lucky. The miner was a smart man, squirreled away his money—when he had any. Unless . . . he'd bought something . . .

"For a dance and a smile." Shifting from one foot to the other, she looked him in the eyes, daring him to say any different.

Craig choked. A nice smile? What smile? He'd never seen it. Who did she think she was kidding? He'd seen the elephant too many times to be taken in by such an innocent-appearing woman. Suddenly, he lifted his shoulders in a nonchalant shrug, angry that he was angry. If that was the way she wanted to play the game, the outcome was none of his business.

But her living quarters were.

"Well, you can't stay here anymore." He grimaced and looked away from the desperation that filled her large green eyes again. He liked it better when they were a soft green-brown swimming with flecks that sparkled brighter than any gold he'd ever seen.

"Why?"

"I've already told you. It's not safe."

"It *is*. And warm."

"Sunny's house is much more comfortable. Why do you have—"

"Please? Just tonight?" she pleaded. "Tomorrow, I promise, I'll be gone."

He frowned. "Where do you think you'll go?"

"I—I . . . think I've found work," she lied uneasily. "I'll be able to get a place of my own."

He threw his hands up. The woman thought she was

dealing with a dunce. *Where* would she find a place of her own? There were no other *places*, unless she had enough money to build something. And he knew better than that. He looked at the empty wrappings on the ground.

He darted a glance to her face and inwardly sighed. Aw, there was that lost-little-girl expression again. What would one more night hurt? She had promised it would be the last.

"All right."

"What?" Billie wasn't certain she'd heard him correctly. "I can stay?"

"Just tonight. That's it. Understand?"

She nodded.

"Have you had something to eat?"

Unwilling to take the chance that he would change his mind for any reason, she nodded again. Her stomach couldn't grumble right now. It just couldn't.

"Well . . ." Craig didn't want to leave her alone. He figured she'd be safe enough as long as she stayed inside, but . . . His protective instincts seemed to be working overtime. "You'll leave tomorrow?"

She bobbed her head up and down. What would it take to get rid of the man? She'd given him her promise.

Stalling, he checked his watch. Late again.

Billie noticed. "You have an appointment?" Her eyes lowered. Why did she have this sudden empty feeling in the pit of her stomach that had nothing to do with the lack of food?

"Yeah. I've got to go. You'll be all right?"

"Yes. Of course." Why did he keep looking at her like that? Like he was concerned, or even worried? She was not his responsibility. Though it was his barn, he was being kind enough to let her stay, and she would certainly not hold him accountable if anything happened to her here. This was *her* decision.

She sighed with relief when he stiffened his shoulders

and slowly walked from the barn. After blowing out the lantern, she gave the horse a good scratching behind the ears, then went over and lowered herself on the blanket.

Closing her eyes, she tried to keep her mind blank. She didn't want to recall bad memories. Didn't want to think of all that had happened since her arrival in Alder Gulch. And she did *not* want to think about her reaction to Craig Rawlins. No matter her mind's negative thoughts, her body created a completely different interpretation.

But she didn't want to think about that.

Her eyes popped wide open. It was going to be a long, long night.

Craig walked down the hill from Sunny's house with his hands fisted in his pockets and his shoulders hunched against the cool breeze. He wished he hadn't worn his good suit. Wished he'd worn a heavier jacket.

Long strides carried him quickly down the lane behind the Empty Barrel. He stood there for a long time, staring at the darkened barn. Before he'd left Billie that evening, he'd already decided to come back. No matter how quiet things had been, some idiot could do something stupid at any time. So, here he was. Here he'd stay. Someone had to keep a watch on the barn. Billie . . . *Whoever* had herself a guardian, whether she thought she needed one or not.

The next morning, Billie smoothed the bodice of her gingham gown and looked over her shoulder at the two bank clerks. Both men glanced away, then looked again. She gulped and wondered for the hundredth time if she was doing the right thing.

All night she'd lain awake, thinking about what she'd do if she didn't find a job today. She'd also thought about the things she'd seen in Alder Gulch—the miners in the saloons, at Sunny's party. And she'd thought about the big Empty Barrel, which lived up to its name by being quite empty.

She'd had a brainstorm.

But now butterfly wings fluttered against her stomach as she stood in front of the sign announcing, PRESIDENT. She had nothing. No money. No collateral. All she could do was convince him she had intelligence and determination. And if she was successful here ... all she'd have to do was convince Craig Rawlins.

Her fist shook as she rapped lightly on the door. What if the banker turned her down? What if she was forced to leave town after all?

"Just a damn minute." Craig Rawlins rubbed his burning eyes and straightened from his slouched position in the chair. He brushed a stalk of straw off his sleeve. The prickly stuff seemed to be growing from his gray suit.

The rap sounded again. "I told you, just a minute." He'd warned his clerks not to bother him. All he'd planned to do was check an account, then go home to change. He hadn't intended to doze off in his chair.

The knock came louder, more insistent. "All right, come on in," he grumbled, "I thought I told you—"

Hoping her countenance displayed more bravado than she felt, Billie hesitated, then swung the door open and stepped inside. She stopped in her tracks. Bloodshot aqua eyes focused on her. A lock of reddish-brown hair tumbled from beneath a lopsided black hat. The crisp white shirt was wrinkled, the string tie loose and about to disappear inside the suit coat. Craig Rawlins was the bank president. She might have known.

Feeling more like fleeing through the door than staying, she closed it firmly behind her. She had business to discuss, and it looked like she'd be killing two birds with one stone. She nearly choked, but said as sweetly as possible, "Good morning, Mr. Rawlins."

Craig sighed and slumped back into his chair. Her.

Chaos should be her last name. Miss Billie Chaos. What the hell? Why not start the day out right? "Mornin'. What do you want?"

Billie twisted her fingers in the folds of her gown. "You . . . You're the banker . . . too?"

Craig rubbed his throbbing forehead. "You sound surprised."

Very slowly, she moved farther into the room. "No . . . Well, a little."

"Why?"

"You own so many things. I just never expected . . ." Yet, now that she thought about his *usual* well-groomed, stylish appearance, she guessed he did suit her concept of a banker.

"I've worked hard for everything I have," he grumbled.

Her eyes widened. "I'm sure. I didn't mean to sound condescending."

"And I didn't mean to snap." He sat up in the chair, then rose stiffly to his feet. Walking around the desk, he indicated a comfortable-looking chair in front of the desk. "I'm remiss with my manners. Please, have a seat. You're here on business?"

She felt the color drain from her face. The soles of her boots scuffed the floor as she slid timidly into the proffered chair. Fear clutched her throat. Suddenly unsure of herself, she realized that if they'd made a deal, she'd secretly hoped the banker would contact Mr. Rawlins.

Craig crossed his arms over his chest and leaned against the edge of the polished oak desk. His eyes drifted down to the floor. His heavy lids suddenly popped up. She wore thick-soled work boots that would probably be too large even for *him*. Boots. A gingham gown. Emeralds. What an outfit. One corner of his mouth twitched. Lord, but she became more intriguing and enchanting every minute.

With an invigorated sigh, he reminded himself she'd come for a reason and prompted, "So-o-o?"

She squeezed her eyes closed, then blinked them open again. She squirmed in the chair as his eyelids lowered to regard her intently. He appeared slumbrous, almost sensual. But she sensed it was a ruse to throw her off guard. He was waiting, watching for a chance to . . . She didn't want to know *what*.

"I, uhm . . . have a business proposition."

He arched his brows.

She frowned and primly continued. "It concerns the Empty Barrel."

He leaned forward and blinked. The last thing he'd been thinking about was the saloon. He couldn't even picture her in a saloon. The sun shone through a window, its rays reflecting off Billie's braided hair. The lustrous glow gave the impression of a halo shining above her head. He blinked again. Twice. The third time the sun had shifted far enough to dispel the image. But in his mind was entrenched the vision of an angel.

She took his movement as a favorable response. "I'd like to reopen the saloon."

The angel plummeted in a cloud of smoke. "Why am I not surprised?" There was something about her. Something innocent. Something bold. She defied definition. He'd thought she was different.

Billie sucked in her breath. She didn't dare spoil what chance she might have by being contrary, so gamely asked, "Are you interested?"

"No." He pushed away from the desk and walked toward the door.

"Wait!" Realizing he had every intention of showing her out, she scooted to the edge of her chair. "Just give me five minutes."

Swayed by her desperation, Craig hesitated.

"Surely you can spare that much time with your busy schedule." She gulped down a breath and rushed on. "It could mean a lot of money—for both of us."

He rubbed the back of his neck. If she only knew how much time he'd already spared for her. He shoved aside his inexplicable disappointment in the angel ... Of course, he had no intention of reopening the Empty Barrel, but it might be entertaining to listen to her "proposition." "Five minutes."

It appeared her high card had won his interest. She stood and began to pace. "While I've been looking for work—"

He held up his hand. "You haven't *found* a job?" He couldn't believe it. Any self-respecting saloonkeeper should've snapped her up in a second.

Stiffening her spine, she replied, "That's what I said. Now, I've noticed a lot of the other saloons—"

"I bet you have." He scowled at himself. Why couldn't he hold back the sarcasm? He couldn't seem to act like a professional around this woman.

She cleared her throat, but still stumbled over her words. "I—I have a few ideas to earn money."

He managed to keep from making any comment, but couldn't help the automatic arch of his brow. And she had aroused his interest. He'd been concerned about the loss of income the Empty Barrel provided. He hadn't realized just how much the establishment took in each night until the receipts had stopped.

"What do you have in mind?" If her ideas were that good, he could pass them on to the next proprietor.

Taking a deep breath, she repeated the words she'd practiced all morning. "Alder Gulch needs a classy place. Somewhere the men can spend their money and enjoy an evening of elegance and fine entertainment."

He ground his teeth. Ah, yes, fine entertainment. His eyes roamed down her lush figure. He felt a stirring in his loins and immediately tamped it down.

"There are too many places now for the miners to lose their dust. One more won't make that much difference."

"But it could. Give the men a choice," she suggested.

"They might enjoy cleaning and dressing up to consort with feminine company."

She could picture it clearly. A fine dance hall, where the miners had their choice of several clean, nicely attired women to squire around the floor. The men at Sunny's had conducted themselves as gentlemen. They loved to dance. And so she'd seen for herself they seemed willing to pay for the opportunity. But it would take a woman's approach to pull it off. It was the perfect solution to her dilemma.

Craig imagined the Empty Barrel all spruced up. The rooms upstairs occupied by several women and . . . Billie. He'd never permitted Big John or Bobby to hire prostitutes. Had always shied away from the profession. But the other saloons in town had always been more crowded. Had he been mistaken?

Thinking about Bobby and Big John reminded him of the bad luck associated with the saloon. He doubted a woman would be in danger, especially as starved as the men were for the companionship of a beautiful . . . lady.

He shook his head. It almost appeared as if he was considering her "proposition."

"Just how did you plan to open the saloon as this grand palace?"

She swallowed and almost choked. "I'd hoped to, uhm . . . borrow the money." She waved her hand in the air, indicating the office. "Why else would I be here?"

Why else indeed? he thought. "What do you have for collateral? If . . . I were to decide to loan you the money?" His eyes narrowed with disbelief. Had he really said that? He must be too tired to think straight.

"N-nothing." The muscles in Billie's face tightened. She felt queasy.

He laughed. "Nothing. And you expect me to lend you money."

"For a short time. I'll make it back soon. With interest."

Craig was impressed, though he tried not to be. The woman was determined, confident, and no doubt, very intelligent. She knew what she could do. The thought sickened him. But she also had an idea about how to make it really pay. That thought piqued his interest.

"Tell you what . . ." He rubbed his stubbled chin and frowned. "Instead of getting the bank involved, I'll fix up the place with my own capital." Why not? He'd be ahead in the long run. "And I'll take you on as a temporary partner."

She opened her mouth, but closed it when curiosity got the best of her. Her blood rushed through her veins, heating her cold body. He hadn't said no.

"If, after three months, you haven't earned back my investment, with interest, I buy you that one-way ticket to Salt Lake. No arguments."

Billie shifted in the chair. Three months wasn't very long. On the other hand, if the gold played out during that time, the town of Alder Gulch could cease to exist. She mentally shook off the negative feeling and thought about what had brought her to the bank in the first place. If her plan worked, she could make the money back in three *weeks*.

She cocked her head. "What happens if the grand palace is a success?"

"Well . . ." He didn't think he'd have to worry about that. "We'll discuss different terms, *if* that happens."

"When it happens, you mean."

"Whatever."

She continued to sit primly on the edge of the chair, her mind whirling with plans.

"There is one other thing." He stared into eyes alive with golden fire and sucked in his breath.

"Wh-what?" Uh-oh, she thought. She didn't like the smug look on his face.

"You have to be ready to open by Saturday night."

Her eyes widened. "Saturday? That's only . . . three days away."

He nodded.

"But . . . I haven't seen inside the saloon. I don't know what all will have to be done."

"I'll take care of any construction. And give you an allowance for hiring girls and adding a few fripperies." He peered at her intently. "It's all up to you. If you think you can't handle it, I've already checked on a wagon—"

"I can handle it," she stated with much more enthusiasm than she felt.

"If you think so . . ." He went behind the desk and hefted a stack of papers. "I have to finish this business. Come back around noon and we'll go over to the saloon and let you take a look."

Overwhelmed by the knowledge that she had a real chance to put her plans into motion, Billie only nodded and slowly rose. She felt hazy as she clomped across the floor. After she let herself out and closed the door, she momentarily collapsed back against it and gulped several deep breaths to gain control of her trembling body.

He hadn't made it easy, but he hadn't turned her down.

A genuine smile crinkled her stiff cheeks. It was within her grasp. Could regular meals and new clothes be far away?

Inside the office, Craig stared at the closed door. He hoped he hadn't made a mistake. *Another* mistake. The woman had already upset his happily ordered life. She popped into his thoughts at the most inopportune times.

She was a vagabond. Had no visible means of support. And he knew absolutely nothing about her.

Trouble. It was written on every angelic feature. What had he gotten himself into now?

A little after noon, Billie sat self-consciously in the only chair inside the bank's small lobby. After leaving

Craig Rawlins's office, she'd been busily making plans and thinking of things she'd need to begin redecorating the Grand Palace—she'd grown quite fond of that description—when she ran into her friend, Lucky.

He had walked back to the bank with her, complaining that his strike was playing out. In order to dig deeper down, he'd have to borrow money for heavy equipment. At that moment, he was in Mr. Rawlins's office and she was nervously hoping their meeting would never come to an end.

What would she say or do when she and her new partner inspected the saloon? She'd only been inside one once, and she'd just as soon forget that experience altogether. Would she be able to make intelligent suggestions and prove she could succeed?

As if thinking of the man caused him to materialize, the door to his office opened and he followed Lucky nearly to the spot where she was sitting.

Lucky looked despondent. Craig appeared apologetic, but resolved.

"Sorry, Lucky. Wish I could help, but you're the sixth or seventh man from that area of the creek who's been in to see me. The gold is about panned out. It's a bad investment, and I can't justify loaning you the capital to go on. Wouldn't be fair to the bank's investors or to you."

Billie stood up when Lucky dejectedly held out his hand and said, "I understand. Doesn't make it any easier, but I see your position."

Then he turned to Billie and smiled sadly. "Well it's your turn, Miss Billie. Hope you have better . . . luck." His grin turned into a grimace as he shouldered through the door.

Billie turned stunned eyes on Craig. The man didn't have a heart. Poor Lucky. Poor . . . She took a deep breath. Lucky had wished her "luck," but "luck" had nothing to do with her venture. She *would* make a success of her dance emporium.

Craig watched the changing emotions rioting across her expressive face. He especially liked the fierce gleam that literally blazed across the lobby and roasted him alive. Smothering a grin, he informed her, "I'm through now. Wait here while I get my coat." He waited until she nodded.

Billie seethed at Craig Rawlins's high-handed treatment. Why, if she weren't so desperate, she would never be reduced to standing, twiddling her thumbs, waiting on him.

"Let's go."

She jumped when he took her arm again. He certainly moved silently for such a tall man. When he began leading her down the street so quickly she had to skip to keep up, she complained, "Slow down, please."

He did ease his pace, but refused to release her.

A familiar claustrophobic feeling threatened, and Billie wondered what happened to the considerate man who rarely touched her.

Craig perversely wondered the same thing. "I thought we'd eat lunch before going to the saloon." When he looked down and saw her pursed lips and felt her continued efforts to escape his grasp, he added with a grin, "If that meets with your approval, of course."

Billie's stomach took that opportunity to voice its whole-hearted acceptance of his suggestion.

"I presume that settles it. Lunch, it is." He smugly lowered his grip and placed her trembling fingers on his forearm, where he promptly covered them with his again. A frown creased his brow, though, when he sensed her shaking was due to more than outrage. What had gotten into him? Why was he goading her, forcing her to accept his touch? Was it because he now knew the truth about her? That instead of an innocent, she was a fallen angel?

Beneath his lashes he noted the furtive glances she directed toward his hand. The gold sparks in her eyes seemed to drown amidst a sea of emerald green, the color blending perfectly with the stones in her necklace.

Was she angry with him? Why? Everything he'd done had been for her benefit. Surely she realized that.

To test how she would react, he removed his hand from hers. She immediately jerked away from him. He mentally shook his head. He'd give a day's profit to know what had caused that reaction.

"Why didn't you give Lucky the money he needed?"

It took a moment for Craig to shift his train of thought from his fallen angel . . . Miss Billie Chaos, back to business. "You heard what I told him."

"Yes-s-s." She walked through the door he held open for her.

"It's the truth."

She ducked under the flap Craig held open and entered Raul's. Relieved to find the place nearly empty, she scooted onto a bench at the first table. When Craig slid in next to her and his thigh brushed hers, her first instinct was to move away. But with one anxious glance through her lowered lashes, she again found every eye in the place trained on her and managed to stifle that reaction.

Sitting perfectly still, she began to find Craig Rawlins's looming presence comforting. His nearness created an aura of warmth and security she'd lacked for a long time. And not only was his touch bearable, she was beginning to find it reassuring.

Raul saw them and called, "What's yer poison today?"

Craig grinned at Billie and asked, "What do you have?"

"Venison chops and potatoes."

"We'll take two plates. And pile them high."

Billie ducked her head, flushing beneath his teasing smile. She remembered that he'd been present the first time she'd come into the restaurant and eaten like a starved pig.

Sensing her embarrassment and knowing he'd caused it, albeit not purposely, he told her, "There's nothing wrong with a good appetite. I think it's the altitude and fresh air."

It was Billie's turn to grin, although it was just a quirk of her lips.

Raul brought their meal and two steaming cups of coffee. She gulped and said, "Excuse me," when her elbow bumped Craig's with the first bite.

"I didn't know you were left-handed." Craig nonchalantly inched after her when she scooted away.

She nodded, chewing self-consciously. Why didn't he eat instead of watching her? What did he find so interesting?

Craig loved to watch her lips when she ate. The sensual way her jaw compressed their fullness and then circled . . . He cleared his throat and moved back to his original place on the bench. His body was reacting much too swiftly. Damnation. It was only a meal.

Billie released a grateful breath of air when they finished eating and Craig quickly suggested going on to the saloon. Hopefully, the change of atmosphere would take her mind off the tingles still radiating along her nerve endings where his body had brushed hers. These tingles were highly disturbing due to the fact she didn't find them terrifying. In fact, she'd almost . . . enjoyed . . . She swallowed and looked up when he rose from the bench.

While he paid for the food, she forced herself to think about her grand palace. She wondered what the interior looked like. How much work would need to be done before Saturday? Saturday. Only three days away.

"Are you ready?" Craig's voice boomed.

She gulped and nodded. As ready as she'd ever be.

Chapter Nine

Craig Rawlins pried off the board barricading the door of the Empty Barrel Saloon. He held it back and allowed room for Billie to enter. He was curious about her hesitant steps and the cautious way she leaned forward and peered inside, as if she'd never seen the interior of a saloon before. And he found himself somewhat nervous about what she'd think of the place.

He'd gone to a lot of trouble and expense to hire a good craftsman to build the bar and had constructed the entire building with an eye to the future. Now he had to admit concern over outlaw gangs and the potential failure of the mines. He'd originally assumed that the gold in Alder Gulch would last and had concentrated on the planning and plotting of the town, even going so far as to buying corner lots for most of his businesses.

Billie walked slowly into the darkened interior. The farther she went, the more her nose wrinkled at the stale smells of cigars and liquor. But she'd best get used to it. If—when—the dance emporium became a reality, she would smell those foul odors—and a lot more—every night.

Glancing over her shoulder, she asked, "Are there windows we can open? It's hard to see."

"Only one. But I guess if we're going to reopen, I could take the boards off now."

He didn't have to sound so grudging about it, she thought.

She stood in the semidarkness, peering toward a bulky shadow. Peaceful silence was shattered by the squeal of a nail and splintering wood. Light poured into the room. The shadow took shape and her eyes widened. While Craig took the boards outside, she walked toward the bar in awe.

The front of the bar had ash veneers intricately designed with alternating circles and diamonds. A brass footrail ran the full length and around both ends, with spittoons strategically located every few feet. Even after a few days of neglect, the heavily varnished mahogany countertop fairly gleamed.

The back bar ran the same length as the counter. The portion visible above the counter had shelves at each end, framed by fluted and turned columns. Between the shelves were three spotless mirrors.

Billie walked forward and peered at the lower part of the back bar. A row of drawers ran the full length. Beneath the drawers were closed cupboards and open shelves. Very impressive, she thought.

Facing forward, she leaned her elbows back on the counter and studied the rest of the room. Like the other buildings in town, this one was long and narrow. Her first impression, besides the elaborate bar, was of stark simplicity. Everything was serviceable, without frills or pretty tablecloths or decorations. That would have to change.

The walnut tables had solid iron bases, and the chairs' rounded seats and backs looked comfortable. The floor was so polished she could see her reflection.

But it was the fancy bar to which she turned her attention.

When Craig pushed through the rattan doors, he found her standing on the footrail, leaning over the countertop, staring at the assortment of bottles displayed openly on the shelves.

His chest expanded with pride. Most saloons in makeshift mining communities supplied only whiskey, brandy, and inferior beer. But thanks to his freight company, he'd been able to haul in fruit brandies, cordials, cognac, absinthe, gins, bottled beer, and a few wines.

"Well, what do you think?"

Billie tilted her head and glanced at him through shuttered lashes. She was thinking that her grand place was very well stocked, but couldn't help questioning, "Do men really drink all this stuff?"

"Stuff?" he gasped. He felt like the wind had just been knocked out of him. "I'll have you know that's the best 'stuff' money can buy." How could she call his treasures "stuff"?

"Miss . . . Billie, I get the impression that you've never actually worked in a place like the one you plan to open." He unwittingly searched for and found his leather wallet.

"You afraid of trying something new?" she asked evenly, displaying a confidence she was far from feeling.

He cleared his throat. "I didn't mean the liquor. What do you think of the saloon?"

Once again she turned on the rail and set her elbows on the countertop as she seriously regarded his question.

Craig's eyes widened as her breasts pushed against the constriction of her bodice, presenting a lovely lily-white threat to the scooped neckline of the simple gingham dress.

"It's very nice."

He choked. "Nice?" His gaze shot back to her face. Just "nice"?

She nodded. "But there's a lot of work to be done."

"What kind of work?" If she ruined his saloon . . .

Eyeing him warily, she rubbed her chin, smearing it with a streak of dust. "Improvements."

The cute smudge made her look innocent and playful—a far cry from the courageous female who stood before him and dared to suggest he change the saloon.

Damn! "I'll have you know, lady, this is the finest saloon in Alder Gulch just the way it is."

Oops. She'd made a faux pas. "Of course it is. But we want to make it the finest and fanciest in the territory, don't we?"

Flustered, and somewhat placated, he stammered, "Yeah, but—"

"This is truly a magnificent bar." She snuck a peek at his flushed face as she ran a hand over the shiny counter. At least *she* thought it was. She had nothing by which to compare it.

"You think so?" He puffed out his chest and eyed his bar with pride.

"Yes." She nodded enthusiastically. Then remembering something else, she asked, "Where does the orchestra play?"

"Pardon?"

"The orchestra."

"I . . . we . . . have a piano. That'll do fine."

"Oh, no, it won't do at all." How could men be expected to pay good money to dance without an orchestra? "And we'll need curtains and tablecloths and flowers."

Craig frowned. "I said I'd fix the place up, but . . ." She was talking about making the saloon into . . . into a home. He'd be the laughingstock of every man in town. And where did she expect to find an orchestra? This was a mining town. They'd be doing good to be as lucky as Sunny and put together a three-piece band.

"You'll get your expenses back. I promise."

He leaned against the counter and crossed his arms over his chest. "You promise?"

Her temples started to throb. She nodded.

A strange light crept into his eyes. "So, are you ready to see the upstairs?"

She glanced up, carefully masking her reactions.

What those rooms had once been used for didn't matter. The important thing was whether or not they would be adequate for her plans.

There were two sets of stairs. One in the front and one in the rear, both on the left side of the building. They walked up the front stairway and Billie took note of the narrow hall down the center of two rows of rooms.

When Craig opened the first door to her right, she hesitated. Rooms above a saloon were a mystery to a finishing-school teacher. But Alder Gulch wasn't St. Louis. It wasn't a fancy girls' school they needed here. This was an opportunity she'd never have back home, and her feet moved forward with a curiosity all their own.

She stopped in the middle of the doorway, and craned her neck. Her eyes narrowed with disappointment.

"What do you think?"

Why did he keep asking her that in a tone of voice that gave her the impression he'd be hurt if she didn't give her approval? "It's empty."

She peered over her shoulder and was sure she'd caught him staring at her derriere. But when his eyes met hers, their expression was almost angry.

"I meant the size. And notice that each room has a window. The corner rooms have two." He debated saying anything else, but finally blurted out, "I'll expect the rooms, and the women, to be kept clean." There. He wanted to get things straight right from the start.

"Don't worry." She sensed a double entendre in his words, but it escaped her. She was elated that he intended for her and the girls she hired to live in the building. That solved one of her major problems. Upstairs accommodations would keep wages down, reducing expenses and increasing profits.

"Will I have a say in decorating the rooms?" she asked hopefully.

"I suppose." Her earnest gaze pinned him to the floor before she wandered on to the next room and opened the door. "You'd know more about what the girls need than I." He'd frequented a few classy brothels in his time, but he'd been young and hadn't paid much attention to a prostitute's needs.

As for his own personal tastes, he'd never touched a whore in an intimate sense. Sunny Turnbow offered herself every now and then, but she'd been a prostitute when Big John married her. Though Big John was gone, Craig couldn't bring himself to overstep the bounds of friendship, or principle. Sunny was a friend, nothing more. No matter what *she* might think.

He walked up behind Billie, still figuring what he could do about Sunny, when Billie suddenly turned and slammed into him. His toe caught on her large boot. Losing his balance, he grabbed her, but she, too, was tottering. Together, they tumbled to the floor.

Finding herself on her back, with a man's weight on top of her, allowed a familiar panic to suffocate her.

"Sorry, Angel." His fingers brushed the side of her cheek and the column of her neck. "Hope I didn't hurt you."

The gentleness of his touch, the warm comfort of his solid frame, immediately soothed her. The darkness that had been descending evaporated.

As he rolled away, Billie's flesh rippled with the tender caress of his movements. The sensation was . . . nice.

"Well, now, isn't this sweet."

Startled, Billie and Craig, in unison, turned their heads. Sunny Turnbow and her son stood at the top of the stairs, watching. Craig continued rolling off Billie and rose gracefully to his feet. Hoping Billie wasn't too embarrassed and that she had pulled herself together, he held out a helping hand.

Billie blinked and grasped his hand. Distress at having been caught in such a compromising position brought heat to her cheeks. She let him pull her to her feet and attempted to smooth her gown, but her hands shook too badly. When she finally glanced up, expecting to find the Turnbows' condemnation, all she saw was Craig's broad back.

He was shielding her, providing her a few extra seconds before having to face the new arrivals. The fact that he'd thought about *her* feelings touched her.

". . . tripped and fell."

Hearing the last of his explanation, Billie sniffed and stepped out from behind him. Unconsciously proving the truth to his words, she brushed at the dust clinging to the back of her skirt.

"You poor thing. Are you hurt?" Sunny hurried forward to give Billie a very thorough once-over, placing herself between the two.

Billie nodded. *Poor thing. Poor dear.* The lack of sincerity in Sunny's tone made her straighten. She was tired of being the *poor* victim.

Seeing that Billie was all right, but noting the apprehension in her eyes, Craig joked, "What about me? You didn't ask if *I* was hurt." He winked at Justin, who scuffed his toe on a warped plank.

"You big handsome thing," Sunny purred. "You're too strong and powerful to let a little fall slow you down."

"What you all doin' up here, anyway," Justin interrupted. "Thought you'd closed the place."

Craig ushered them all down the stairs. "I was showing Billie around. She had a notion that she could reopen and make us both rich." He slanted Sunny and Justin a conspiratorial grin.

Heat vibrated up Billie's spine as three pairs of eyes skewered her. She knew she'd better get used to people's curiosity if she planned on bringing a new form of entertainment to town. With a smile, she nodded, confirming Craig's comment.

"Sunny, I'm glad to see you. I did't get a chance to

thank you personally for your kind hospitality. It was appreciated."

Sunny looked surprised and a little relieved. "Appreciated? I thought Craig was going to make ... You mean you aren't coming back?"

"I'll be living here now."

"What?" Craig looked at her like she was crazy. "There's no bed, no furniture. It'll be several days before you can stay here."

"I'll make do. Maybe I can get a few blankets at the mercantile." Now that she had made up her mind, she wasn't going to be dissuaded. She'd certainly slept in worse places during her journey.

Craig started to ask just how she planned to purchase blankets, but refrained in front of Sunny and Justin. After all, as a partner, she should be allowed to buy things when she needed them.

"I'll open an account there for you on my way back to the office."

Billie was surprised, but didn't question her good fortune. After all, her purchases would all be for the saloon's benefit.

"Sunny, Justin, come on. I'll walk you home." Craig glanced back to Billie. "We can talk about the rest of the changes later."

Justin hesitated and shyly asked Billie, "Did you get your cloak and gown? I sent them down with Mr. Rawlins."

"Yes. That was very thoughtful. Thank you."

She followed them to the door and watched as they walked up the street. They hadn't gone very far before Sunny grabbed Craig's arm. Billie blinked and dejectedly turned back inside.

Sunny squeezed Craig's forearm, slowing his pace. "Craig Rawlins, what's gotten into you? You can't mean to have taken that woman on as a partner," she scolded. "Why, you don't know anything about her."

Justin moved up to walk alongside the pair. "She seems pretty nice." He watched Craig intently.

Craig shrugged and walked faster, dragging Sunny a step or two until she fell into the pace. "I'm not worried about her. We made a deal and I think she'll hold up her end. If she doesn't, she's gone."

Sunny smiled and batted her long lashes.

Justin shoved his hands in his pockets and trailed silently along, though his eyes seldom left his mother and her companion.

Billie wandered through the saloon, imagining what it would look like after she'd finished the renovations. A pang of trepidation shot through her as doubts battered her mind. What if they couldn't find musicians? What if no women wanted to work here? What if no one came to the opening? What if she didn't finish everything by Saturday night?

Which reminded her, Craig had said he'd open an account at the mercantile.

She felt another jolt of insecurity. Had she made a rash decision by blurting out that she planned to stay here? This was a huge building and she'd be all alone.

Passing the window, she noticed it was already late afternoon. If she planned to get those blankets, she'd better go now.

Fifteen minutes later, she walked into the mercantile. She'd forgotten to fetch her cloak from the barn and suddenly felt silly in her gown, necklace, and boots. Chewing her bottom lip, she wondered if Craig would mind if she brought the items she'd need to make another dress. She could use the scissors and thread when it was time to stitch up the curtains . . .

A bolt of calico lay on the counter. She ran her hand over the soft cotton as if it were expensive velvet.

"Yes, ma'am. What can I do for you now?"

All at once it struck her that if Craig Rawlins had

opened an account for *her*, it would appear as if . . . that they . . .

"You want some of that calico?"

"Uhm . . . has a Mr. Rawlins been in this afternoon?" she croaked.

"Yes, ma'am. Said I should be expectin' a pretty young lady. I reckon that's you."

She felt heat crawl up her neck. "D-did he open an . . . a-account?" The situation was awkward, almost embarrassing. What must the proprietor be thinking?

The merchant opened his records as if he couldn't recall. "Yep. Right here. He left a deposit and said you had free rein till it was spent." He grinned.

"I see." Craig had certainly kept his word.

"Now what do you need?"

So many things . . . "A blanket. Make that two blankets. And eight yards of that calico. Scissors. Thread. Needles . . ."

As she followed the man around the mercantile, she thought back to what he'd said earlier. A pretty young lady. Craig Rawlins had said she was pretty?

Thirty minutes later, Billie left the mercantile loaded with parcels. Her arms were so full that she couldn't see her feet and prayed she didn't trip or step in something really horrendous.

She'd walked a full block with no major catastrophes, then something bumped her legs. Something groped her knee. She gasped and dropped everything to grab at whatever was attacking her.

"Please, lady, I didn't mean no harm. The puppy . . . Miss Billie!"

Her fingers dug into thin, bony shoulders. She bent to find herself face-to-face with the grinning Danny.

"Danny! Danny Corbett, what've you gone an' . . . Oh, it's Billie." Anna smiled, then turned her attention back to her son. "I swear, I cain't take my eyes off ya fer a second."

For the first time in a long time, Billie felt the sides of her mouth curve. Friends. It was good to see her friends.

Anna stared at the packages strewn in the street and horses' hooves coming within inches of trampling them. She shook her finger at her son. "You get busy an' pick up Billie's things."

"No," Billie admonished. "I can get them." She bent and started snatching up the parcels, but Danny was quick to help and and handled the items with care.

"Want me to help ya carry 'em?"

Billie was looking up the street, watching Craig and Sunny as they strolled into the freight office, together. Evidently he hadn't been in a hurry to walk Sunny home after all. Just in a rush to get out of *her* clumsy presence.

"Hey, ya want me to help, or not?"

"Danny! Watch yore mouth. You're talkin' to a lady, not yore poor ole ma." Anna shook her head and told Billie, "I'm sorry. But it seems I'm always sayin' that lately."

"But Ma, Billie don't—" Suddenly, the boy's eyes widened. His features brightened. "Fer a penny, or . . . a nickel, I'll carry 'em all fer you."

Billie sadly said, "You forget, I don't have money."

He looked at all the parcels and screwed up his face to argue.

Anna scowled.

Billie quickly explained. "Remember Mr. Rawlins?"

"Yeah. He's rich."

"He and I are partners now. But until I can start earning my own money, he's the one paying for these things."

He seemed to contemplate that for a few seconds, then very seriously, asked, "Reckon he could use my ma? He's done hired me."

Anna inhaled sharply. "Danny Corbett! Shame on

you. Miss Billie don't need to hear ya talkin' fer yore
ma. An' when did you see that Mr. Rawlins, young
man?"

Billie's chest constricted. She looked at Anna. Why
hadn't she thought of her sooner? Although it hardly
mattered, she asked, "What all can you do?"

Anna waved aside her anger at her son and suddenly
found the dust in the street extremely interesting.
"Cain't say, 'xactly."

Danny piped up. "Sometimes men give ya money fer
walkin' with 'em behind a barn." He grinned up at Billie.

Billie blinked. She didn't know who turned redder,
Anna or herself. "Can you dance?"

Anna glanced fearfully at her son.

"I mean, really *dance.*"

"Well . . . I used ta step out right fine, back a few
years."

Billie gathered the rest of the packages. "Then I'm
sure you still can. You have a job." She looked from
Danny to Anna and added a little less aggressively, "If
you want it."

Anna chewed on a jagged nail. "Jest dancin'?"

Billie nodded.

Anna smiled.

Danny tightened his grip on the parcels he'd collected
and looked hopefully between the two women. "Ya
gonna walk with my ma an' give 'er money, too?"

"Uhm . . . not exactly. But you and your ma . . .
mother . . . are going to walk with *me* over to that building." She looked askance at Anna. "You haven't found
another place to stay, have you?" Billie found herself
feeling guilty for being so caught up with her own problems that she hadn't given them much thought since
they'd left her in the barn that day.

"N-no."

Danny clomped alongside Billie. "We been campin'
down by the creek. Shore's been cold 'fore mornin'." He

shuffled his packages into one arm and grabbed Billie's hand. "Ain't talked to 'im yet today, but Mr. Rawlins hired me to look after Spot. Reckoned my ma'd be warmer in the barn." He puffed out his scrawny chest and looked so grown up that Billie's heart melted.

"I'm sure she would. How old *are* you, Danny?"

"I'm nine, I think." He glanced up at his mother, who nodded affirmation.

They entered the saloon and Billie placed her purchases on the countertop before collecting Danny's. "Our rooms will be upstairs, but there's no furniture yet. I'd planned to sleep down here on the floor tonight . . ." She opened the paper-wrapped bundles until she found the two blankets. Why hadn't she gone ahead and asked for more?

Seeing Billie's frown, Anna said, "That's plenty. Danny and I always share the covers."

The little boy rubbed his grubby hands over the scratchy wool. "It's gonna be warm, Ma."

Billie saw Anna looking questioningly around the saloon. "It's been closed several days, and we have to reopen by Saturday night or we don't open at all. It'll be a lot of work in just three days. If you'd rather not stay, I'll certainly understand."

"I'm a good worker." Anna didn't even blink. "An' yore the first who's offered me a decent job. But . . ." She gazed around the large room and up to the ceiling and the second floor. "We gonna do it *all* ourselves?"

"I hope not. I'm going to try to find at least two more girls as quickly as possible. Hopefully, we can all work together. And Mr. Rawlins may help." She doubted he'd do it personally, but miracles could happen.

Billie watched the restless little boy walk around the tables trailing his fingers through the dust, then suggested, "Why don't you take Danny upstairs and pick out a room. Maybe you can come up with a few ideas on how you want it decorated. It may take a while, but—"

"Think we kin have a real bed, Ma? Huh?" He pulled on his mother's hand and led her to the stairs.

Danny's excited chatter trailed off as they ascended. Billie sorted through her purchases. The first thing she needed was a proper day dress, one more versatile than the casual gingham and more sensible than the green gown, but with a higher neckline than either dress.

The swinging doors creaked. Billie turned. "Sorry, we're not open . . . Oh, hello."

"Hi." Craig stepped into the room, astounded by his body's instant reaction to the mere sight of the woman. He remembered the tumble they'd taken earlier and each blessed point where her curves and valleys had met and yielded to his. And, damn it, he'd liked it.

He'd tried to put her out of his mind all afternoon. Had even squired Sunny around town while she did a few errands, thinking it would help. It hadn't.

"I see you've been to Ike's."

Her fingers were long and smooth as they fondled the calico. He wondered how they'd feel caressing his skin with that same easy stroke.

Billie frowned. "Ike's?"

"The owner of the mercantile."

"Oh, yes. Th-thank you for opening the account." She stifled the addition of, "like you promised." Partners should trust each other. Shouldn't they?

"You're welcome. What did you get?" He used the question as an excuse to get closer.

She showed him the material she'd gotten for curtains and the sewing items. But she hesitated when she touched the calico.

He saw how lovingly she ran her hand over the fabric and shuddered. "What's that for?"

"Uh . . . I thought I'd make . . ."

He frowned.

"A new dress." The words came out in a rush. If she spoke fast enough maybe he wouldn't question her.

"Good."

She gulped. "I'll pay you back for personal expenses."

"Don't worry. I should've thought to tell you . . . I mean, you need something to work in . . ." He hunched his shoulders. Like the dreaded disease, he couldn't keep his foot out of his mouth. "And you will be working. For the saloon." The thought made him sick.

He just couldn't picture her upstairs—with a man.

Nodding, she turned away, trying to forget the nice feel of his hard, lithe body next to hers that afternoon. She was still stunned that the memory didn't bring on another fit of apoplexy.

Craig cleared his throat. "I thought you might be hungry and would like to go to supper. Maybe tomorrow I can get someone to check the stove in the back. We've never served food here, but you'll need a place to take your meals."

"Well, I—"

"Hot damn. Ma, c'mon. Mr. Rawlins is gonna get Billie an' us somethin' to eat."

Chapter Ten

Craig Rawlins stared in surprise at the grimy little boy and the mousy woman. But he inclined his head and greeted them warmly, "Hello, Danny, Mrs. Corbett. What are you folks doing here?"

Billie clutched Danny and pulled him close to her.

Craig scowled. She acted as if he was going to hurt the boy.

"Anna's accepted a job with us."

"I see." His gaze roamed from Anna to Danny to the defensive Billie and back to Anna. Though she wasn't exactly a woman he would've chosen, he wouldn't cause Billie embarrassment this early in their association. He'd let the men show her her mistake. Later, when Danny wasn't around, he'd have a little chat with Billie. Anna would have to take precautions against producing more "Dannys" while in his employ.

Danny gawked at Mr. Rawlins's stern features and screwed up his face. "Why's he lookin' so mad, Ma? I thought he liked us. This mean we won't get no supper agin? Betcha he fergot ya was gonna give me a job, too."

Anna's already pale face turned even whiter. "I don't think he . . . Mr. Rawlins, meant—"

"Of course you're going to eat. And yes, you're hired. But first, young fella, you have to wash up. There's a bucket of water and a towel behind the bar. Make use of it."

"Yes, sir." Craig's commanding tone sent Danny into action.

"Mr. Rawlins, you really needn't——" Anna began, her voice threatening to crack.

"I know I needn't, Mrs. Corbett, but an invitation," he narrowed his eyes at Billie, warning her not to say different, "is an invitation. This will be a good chance to get acquainted and plan our activities for the next few days, don't you think?"

"Well, yes."

In two shakes Danny was back with a full display of freckles dotting his cheeks and nose.

"That's better." Craig had a hard time keeping a straight face in front of the boy's engaging grin.

Billie looked upon Craig Rawlins with kinder eyes. The man had just taken the charity out of his forced invitation. She was proud of him for leaving Anna Corbett her dignity in front of her hungry child.

Several minuets later, Billie found entering Raul's easier with Anna and Danny along. The men inside the eatery, and those trailing behind, had more to gawk at than just herself. Now that Anna and Danny seemed to have latched on to someone, the miners were more at ease and teased and joked with the boy.

In the crowded eatery, she found herself walking close to Craig, allowing his size and confidence to lend her courage.

During the meal, Craig kept the conversation moving in the direction of the saloon, telling the trio that he'd arranged for men to build minimal furniture for the upstairs, plus a dais for a band, provided Billie scared one up.

As they'd already discussed, Billie would be in charge of hiring more girls and decorating.

Craig refrained from adding, "As if the men who frequented a bar would care."

Billie listened, but her thoughts centered on her own reactions. She'd had a few rough moments when the shadows grew longer and the voices of the male customers grew louder, the brief time between the sun setting and Raul lighting several lanterns. But sitting with Anna and Craig, she felt quite comfortable.

Craig was directly across the table and she'd had several opportunities to study him whenever Danny captured his attention. His patience with the boy raised her estimation of him even more. She also enjoyed watching the changing expressions on his handsome face, which was highlighted by slashing brown brows and lashes so thick, they seemed to allow his lids to open only halfway.

Even devouring a platter of Raul's potatoes and ham, Mr. Craig Rawlins was seductive. His eyes sparkled blue tonight, matching the color of the sky on a clear Montana day. They were a vibrant contrast to his brown hair with its streaks of burnished copper.

She leaned her elbow on the table and supported her chin in her palm. Everything she knew about the man was a contrast—from his stern business demeanor to the way he grinned and answered Danny's constant stream of questions. From the strength in his hands as he hammered nails to the tenderness of his fingers when he touched her.

Craig felt her regard. Every time her eyes toured his face, the hair on the back of his neck prickled as if a bolt of lightning had streaked across the room.

"Ahem . . . it's late. Is everyone finished?" He placed his palms on the table, ready to push himself to his feet.

"I wanted a chunk o' that pie." Danny pointed to a tin on the cook's workbench.

Anna ducked her head, kicked her son under the table, and hissed, "Dann-n-ny."

Appearing not to have heard, Craig got up, walked

over to Raul, paid for the meal and turned around with the whole pie in his hand. As he started for the door, he eyed the gawking trio still sitting by the table. "Anyone coming, or do I have to eat the whole pie by myself?"

Danny, Anna, and Billie scrambled from their seats and quickly followed him. Danny jumped up and down as he tried to catch up, like a puppy trailing the smell of cooking bacon. "You really gonna eat that pie all by yourself, Mr. Rawlins?"

"I might."

"Ya'll get sick."

Craig stopped and looked down. "How do you know?"

That almost shut Danny up, but he looked over his shoulder to see if his mother was within hearing. When he discovered that she and Billie were still a ways behind, he whispered loudly, "I ate one once, when I was a tad. Ate so much my gut pooched out like a cat 'bout to drop kittens."

"Guess you'd know then," Craig choked. He hefted the pie. "Maybe I better have help after all."

Danny nodded.

Billie and Anna caught up at that point.

"Think we should share with the womenfolk?" Craig winked at the boy.

Danny looked at the women as if seriously considering the question. But then he grinned and bobbed his head.

Craig led them all into the saloon and took them to a small room near the back door that contained a stove and several cabinets filled with odds and ends of kitchen utensils and a stack of tin plates.

"I thought we'd make this room into a real kitchen. Move in a table and chairs for those of you who'll be living here." He put the pie tin on top of the cabinet.

All at once, what he'd just said hit him like a kick to the stomach. He was talking as if this crazy venture would turn into something permanent.

He sighed. There was a side of him that actually wished it would. The sentimental, gullible side. But just because he'd enjoyed the company at supper didn't mean Billie would be able to pull off this fantasy of a plan, even with his help. To be completely honest, he wasn't sure he wanted her to. He was beginning to *like* the woman, and that unsettled him.

An insistent tug on his coat sleeve diverted his attention.

"When ya gonna cut that pie?"

"How about right now?"

"Yeah!"

Billie set out four plates and scrounged up forks and a knife. She offered the knife to Craig, but he backed away. Typical, she thought.

The knife almost bounced off the top crust. Finally, she managed to slice through it and slid the first piece onto a plate.

"What kind is it, Billie? Is it good? I ain't had pie fer years. Since I were a tiny baby."

"Why, young man, I made a pie . . ." Anna stopped and looked sheepish. "Reckon it has been a spell."

Billie handed Danny that first plate. "Looks like it's peach."

"Mmmm. I like peaches. Don't I, Ma?"

"You like just about everything, son."

Once they all had a slice, they went back into the saloon and sat at a table. Craig admonished Danny not to get anything sticky on the tabletop.

Billie took a bite of pie, chewing and chewing the rubbery crust. At least the peaches were tasty. All in all, they decided the pie was a treat and better than no pie.

A few minutes later, Craig pushed his chair back. "Hate to leave good company, but there's a lot to do tomorrow. Better turn in." He glanced around the large room. "Where you folks goin' to sleep?"

Danny squirmed out of his chair and ran to a folded

blanket. "Ma an' me git to sleep inside agin tonight. Even got a cover. Ain't we lucky?"

Tears burned the backs of Billie's eyes. She knew just how Danny felt.

Craig gazed at the misbegotten trio and mentally shook his head. Then he ruffled Danny's hair, walked to the door, and said gruffly, "Yes, I guess you are."

Early the next morning, Billie blinked open one eye. She stretched, then curled up inside the blanket. This place was good for her. She'd had the most wonderful dream ... Of home ... the huge brick house in St. Louis. Her loving father. She remembered her mother had passed away years ago, and a pang in her heart reminded her of how much she still missed Arianna Glenn.

Billie sighed. She'd even dreamed of her best friend, Selena Jenkins. Selena had the biggest crush on her stepbrother, Samuel. An involuntary shiver shook her. The morning air must be chillier than she thought. But she had her memories now to keep her warm. A tiny frown wrinkled her brow. All of her memories except the ones that explained why she'd left St. Louis and why she knew by intuition alone that she shouldn't go back.

All at once, she cocked her head.

Crash!

There it was again. She sat up and arched her aching back.

A door slammed.

Wiping her eyes, she crawled to her feet and peered toward the back door. She glanced quickly at Anna and Danny. They still slept, cuddled together on their blanket. She debated waking them, then decided they needed all the rest they could get. From bits and pieces of Danny's conversation, she'd gathered they hadn't slept well out in the wilds.

Wrapping her own blanket around her shoulders, she

tread softly toward the small back room. Through the open door she heard muffled grunts and curses, then saw a tall, heavy man lever open the door and stumble inside with a large box. He muttered in surprise when he saw her.

"Sorry if I disturbed ya, ma'am."

"Wh-what are you doing?" She stepped back, pulling the blanket more tightly around her.

"Why, I'm deliverin' these supplies for Mr. Rawlins. He wanted you should have 'em bright an' early." He stared at her for a moment. "Didn't he tell you I was comin'?"

"Uhm, well . . ." If he had, she didn't remember. "Thank you, anyway." She took a deep breath to calm her jittery nerves.

"S'right." He set the box on the floor and went out to fetch another. Billie held open the door for him, and after he'd put it beside the other, he said, "That's it for now. Reckon I'll be back again later." He scratched behind his ear. "Want I should knock first?"

"Please. There should be someone here most all of the time."

He nodded and clomped out.

Billie looked inside the boxes. They were filled with sugar, salt, baking powder, cans of milk, and other canned goods. Everything a person would need to stock a kitchen, if a person knew what was needed and how to cook. She grimaced. She was more adept with a pot than a needle, but not to any great extent.

A gasp behind her alerted Billie that Anna and Danny were awake. She turned to find Anna staring wide-eyed at the supplies.

Anna walked into the room and ran her hand over a sack of flour standing on end in the corner. "My goodness . . . Heaven musta done opened up."

Billie wasn't sure about comparing Craig with heavenly entities, but told Anna, "Mr. Rawlins sent it over. Do you think we have everything we need?"

Anna gave the boxes a closer inspection. "For a while." Opening the cabinets, she found a chipped bowl and pulled it out. Then she opened the flour, took some, and searched through the boxes again. Glancing at Billie, she asked, "Can you start a fire?"

Billie nodded. At last, something she was good at. Her father had taught her even before she'd learned the technique at finishing school and then had gone on to teach it to others. Her throat clogged, but she quickly shook off the sensation and went outside to where she'd seen some split wood stacked. Before long, she had a cheerful fire crackling in the potbellied stove.

Anna brought over a pan with a thin-looking mixture that Billie was afraid to even ask about. Sensing Billie's hesitation, Anna smiled and set the pan on the stove's lid. "It'll taste better'n it looks."

"Ma? Ma, where are—Oh." A sleepy-eyed Danny padded barefoot into the room. "Ma, I gotta . . . You know."

Anna rolled her eyes. "You know where it is."

"But I don't wanna go alone."

Billie held out her hand. "I'll go with you." At last, the little man was showing signs of being just a young boy.

He just nodded and slid his small hand into hers. She closed her eyes, relishing his childish trust.

After they'd gone out and then returned to the kitchen, Billie walked over to the stove. Sure enough, the mixture was thickening and smelled pretty good.

"Where did you learn to cook?"

Anna shrugged and stirred the gruel. "Been cookin' ever since I could reach the top o' the stove. My ma was always busy with the rest o' the younguns and ready ta pop another. Us kids jest grew up somehow knowing what ta do."

"How . . . why did you come to Alder Gulch? There aren't many women who . . . well . . ."

"Aren't prostitutes?"

Billie nodded. She didn't think of Anna in those terms, no matter what Danny alluded to.

Anna's chin quivered at the same moment Billie's eyes rounded. "Oh, no, I didn't mean to be so nosy. Please—"

"It's all right. I ain't really ever told no one. No one ever thought enough to . . . Anyway, my man heard there be good farm land in the West an' had been itchin' to come take a look see. An' then when the war done busted out, he didn't have no heart to fight. So we hid out an' started makin' our way West. Only we run outta money faster'n he figured, an' we stopped here'n there fer 'im to work at whatever needed doin' wherever he could find it."

She stirred faster. "Sometimes . . . he couldn't find no work. We was starvin'. I didn't have no choice. I had ta feed my Danny." Her voice cracked. "My man got to where he'd help pick out someone who looked rich an' . . ."

Billie wanted her to stop. Her fingers clenched in the folds of the blanket she'd forgotten she was still wearing. But Anna had a faraway look in her eyes and a desperation to her voice that told Billie she needed to talk.

"An' then one day, a man didn't want ta pay. Said I wasn't worth what Saul charged 'im. They fought. My Saul was shot in the chest. He killed the other man. We had to run."

Anna gulped and continued to stir, unmindful that the gruel was done. "He never recovered from the wound. When he heard 'bout a gold strike not far from where we was camped, he figured it'd be easy money. Gold nuggets layin' around fer 'im to just pick up and stash away."

Silence dragged on so long that Billie finally found a towel and removed the pan from the stove. She was too curious not to ask what happened to her man. "I mean, you husband?" she added.

Anna's voice was lifeless. "The trip was too rough.

We was within sight o' town when Saul jest laid down
an' died."

"Oh, Anna. I'm so sorry."

Billie tried to reach out to the woman, but Anna
stepped away. "I ain't. He made me do things no good
man woulda asked his wife ta do." A tear rolled down
her cheek. Then another.

Billie stood by and let her cry. She didn't think this
was the time to explain that she wasn't sorry for the husband. She was sorry for the pain Anna and Danny had
suffered. So terribly sorry.

Danny scampered into the room, his face scrubbed
and shiny. "Somethin' sure smells good." He looked between the two somber women. "What's wrong, Ma?"

Anna wiped her sleeve across her face and eyes.
"Nuthin', son." She gave Billie a watery smile. "Things
may jest be startin' ta get right."

Billie experienced a pang of conscience. People were
depending on her. What if she couldn't make a success
of her dance emporium? What if, after the three
months, she failed? What would Anna and Danny do
then?

Her own problems melted in fate's fire. Others had
been more badly burned than she.

Anna spooned the gruel into three plates. She'd also
boiled coffee for herself and Billie, while Danny drank
watered canned milk with a little added sugar. Billie
found the meal more than satisfactory.

They ate and talked over the things that needed to be
done. First they would clean downstairs, and move tables and chairs to make room for a dance floor. Then
they'd start upstairs.

"What kin I do, Billie? I wanna help."

Billie pursed her lips and studied the boy. Both he
and his mother looked like they needed a month of
good food and rest with no hard labor of any kind. Yet
the enthusiasm Anna expressed for what, in her eyes,
was a respectable job, meant she wouldn't stand for not

pitching in and doing her share of the work. And Billie wouldn't dare deflate Danny by denying him some task.

She looked toward the bar and the glasses sitting atop the shiny counter. A thin layer of dust had accumulated since the saloon had closed.

"Danny, would you mind cleaning those glasses, and maybe wiping off the counter? It will impress our customers if everything is polished and bright."

The boy grinned. "Yes'm. I can do that." He puffed out his chest, clearly believing he'd been assigned the most important chore.

Billie handed him a towel, but admonished, "You finish eating first. And if you get tired, promise me you'll stop and rest." She squared her gaze on Anna. "That goes for you, too."

Both Corbetts agreed.

They worked all morning. Billie enjoyed the physical labor and the camaraderie that slowly evolved between herself, Anna, and Danny. During a break, she found sarsaparilla and divided some amongst them.

Anna looked down at her faded, stained dress. "Don't know, Billie, reckon anyone'll wanna dance with me lookin' like this?"

Billie gasped. She'd completely forgotten. "You won't be wearing that. I plan on everyone having something dressy and classy." She tapped her finger on her chin. "I'll get some material and we'll make something really fancy."

Her eyes widened. "I bought some calico yesterday to make a dress so I could change out of this gingham." She looked at the damp splotches and streaks of dirt coating her skirt and sighed. Thank goodness she had the green gown to wear the first evening the dance hall opened—if she needed it. Hopefully, she'd have a new one.

"You two rest a while longer. I'd better go to the mercantile and see about more material." She glanced hesitantly toward Anna. "Are you good with a needle?"

Anna shook her head. "Not very. My two older sisters had that chore. I cooked."

So much for *fancy*, Billie thought. "Well, maybe between the two of us, we can work something up."

As she left the saloon, Billie wished she could make it a requisite that the next woman she hired to dance be an expert at sewing. But, the way it looked, she'd do good to find two more women, period, before Saturday.

Billie strode unhappily from the mercantile. The owner had said he expected more material to arrive with an order tomorrow, but that would certainly make it difficult to get the dresses done in time. And what if the shipment were late, or didn't even arrive?

"Miss Billie?"

She angled her neck to see over the other purchases she'd made. "Mr. Lucky. How nice to see you."

"You, too. I've wondered where you were. Haven't seen you the past few days."

"I've been rather busy."

The lines in his face deepened. "That's nice."

Billie suddenly remembered his financial problems. "And you? Have you done anything about your mine?"

He shook his head.

"I'm sorry. What will you do?"

"I don't know." His shoulders lifted slightly, then fell. "Guess I'll go back home. But there's nothing left for me there anymore. My family's gone. My girl married last month. Decided she'd waited long enough, I suppose."

Not knowing what she could say that would help, Billie just nodded.

"Could probably get my old job back, but it'll be like going home just to admit that I failed."

"What did you do . . . back home?"

Lucky's eyes brightened. "I was a mixologist. And a damn . . . darned good one."

Her brows furrowed. "A mixologist?"

"I mix drinks. All kinds of drinks. Even invented a few of the more popular ones myself," he declared proudly.

"Oh, a bartender."

"No. A mixologist is a specialist. And very prominent in a community. That's why I'm ashamed to go back. I bragged I would make my fortune. Everyone believed me."

Billie understood his disappointment. People had expected better things of her, too.

All at once she had an idea. She'd have to talk to Craig first, but . . . "You aren't leaving town right away, are you?"

"No. I still have *some* money left. Thought I might as well enjoy spending a little of it."

"Good."

Lucky blinked. "Good?"

"Yes. I would hate to lose my very first friend in Alder Gulch."

He ducked his head. "That's a right nice thing to say, Miss Billie. It's been my pleasure."

"Do you still live on your claim?"

He nodded. "Why?"

"Just wondered," she told him vaguely, lost in thought.

Lucky seemed to notice her bundles for the first time. He plucked several from her arms. "Let me help you with those."

"Sure you don't mind?"

"Can't say as I have anything better to do right now."

"All right, then." She handed him two of the biggest packages, keeping the lighter ones for herself.

When she reached the Empty Barrel and started to go inside, Lucky frowned. "Miss Billie. This is a . . . saloon."

"Yes, I know."

"You can't go in there."

"Yes, I can. I'm a partner now," she stated matter-of-factly.

His jaw sagged. "You an' Mr. Rawlins. . . ."

She didn't like his tone. "Are just partners. We're re-opening Saturday night."

"But you're a lady. Ladies don't—

"You're right, Mr. Lucky. I *am* a lady," she huffed. "And I will conduct myself as such—even in a saloon." She turned and stalked inside. Men and their antiquated attitudes. Why did they all think they had the right to make assumptions on her character because of the way she was dressed or because she lived in a saloon?

She stopped abruptly. Was that the reason she'd run from St. Louis? Because she was afraid of what the good people there would think of whatever had happened? And hadn't she looked down her own nose at the *women* who worked in saloons? In St. Louis, as well as Alder Gulch?

Why, she was no better than the men. With a grimace, she decided to remember this lesson. If it made her more open and accepting of others, then living in a saloon might be good for her, regardless of why she'd come here.

Turning to Lucky, she said with a kinder ring to her voice, "I appreciate your help. Please, just lay those things on the counter."

She saw him looking raptly at the back bar and the display of liquor. Though her experience with such things was close to nonexistent, she was sure Craig Rawlins stocked only the best, and that it was being fully appreciated by Mr. Lucky. Her idea grew in magnitude. She could hardly wait to talk it over with her partner.

In fact, she was willing to wager he'd be in his office that very minute.

"Mr. Lucky, if you'll excuse me, I have another errand to run."

Lucky touched the brim of his hat, but his eyes were now directed toward the rear of the room. Billie followed his gaze and saw Anna dusting off a table. He stared so intently at the woman that Billie's chest tightened with fear. But when his eyes swung back to her, she saw no threat, only question.

She cleared her throat. "Anna, I have to leave again. This gentleman, Mr. Lucky, was kind enough to help me. Would you mind getting him something to drink?"

Anna wiped her hands on a rag and walked forward. Lucky unconsciously backed up.

"N-no, really . . . It was nothin'. I don't need—"

"Nonsense. It's no trouble. Is it, Anna?" She glanced back as she made her way to the door and saw the two red-faced people awkwardly trying to converse.

Grooves momentarily deepened in her cheeks as her lips quirked in a semblance of a smile.

Craig Rawlins *was* in the bank's office. She knocked on the closed door. His voice rang loud, clear, and confident when he bade her enter. Though she had something important to discuss, she felt her usual trepidation as she pushed open the door and walked into the room.

She peered through lowered lashes into his bright blue eyes and felt something in her chest soften. Displeased with her body's reaction, she forcibly stiffened her spine and strode determinedly to the chair in front of his desk and settled daintily into it.

Craig Rawlins arched a brown brow and invited, "Won't you have a seat?" It suddenly occurred to him, as he watched her sitting so prim and proper, that she didn't seem like a *Billie*. Who was she really? Where was she from? Would he ever get the answers to his questions?

All at once he blinked. A shimmering glow rose above her head. Just as before, a ray of sunshine reflected from the crown of her hair. Why'd she have to come at the same time and sit in that same chair? Now he'd never get the image of that angelic sight out of his mind.

"What do you want now?" he snapped, more harshly than he'd intended.

Billie scooted deeper into the chair, as if a few more inches between them would make a difference. Perhaps this wasn't a good time . . .

"I—I need to talk to you."

"So? I'm a busy man."

"It's about the saloon."

He stared at the stack of papers that hadn't gone down at all that morning, mainly because he'd been daydreaming about Billie and wondering if she and the Corbetts were getting along all right.

"First . . ." She folded her hands in her lap and looked him directly in the eyes. "Thank you for the food. That was very . . . thoughtful."

"Ahem . . ." He gazed out the window. "Danny looks starved. I wanted there to be plenty to eat." *For yourself as well,* he added silently. She appeared to have had every bit as hard a time of it as the Corbetts. If he only knew more about her . . . what she was hiding.

"Have you hired a bartender yet?"

"What?" The question caught his mind wandering. She repeated slowly, "Have you hired a—"

"Bartender. I heard." He steepled his fingers. Bobby had run the saloon and done the bartending. A replacement? He answered honestly. "No."

"Good." She almost clapped her hands.

"Why?"

She leaned forward, unwittingly allowing Craig a glimpse of bare, rounded flesh and a deep cleavage. Damn Sunny and her penchant for low necklines. Billie couldn't make a new dress fast enough to suit him.

"I know just the right person."

"Who?" His eyes narrowed.

"Mr. Lucky," she sighed with satisfaction, knowing that he'd be pleased, too. Having to turn down Mr. Lucky's request for a loan had probably been upsetting for Craig. Now he had an opportunity to make amends.

"No."

"What?" she gasped.

"I said, no."

"You can't mean it."

"But I do."

She stood so quickly her chair tottered. "As a partner in this venture, I must insist we hire him."

Craig also flew to his feet, placed his palms on the desktop, and leaned over so his face was only inches from hers. "As the partner with the *money* in this venture, my *no* is final."

She lifted her chin. "We'll just see about that."

With every ounce of what she recalled of the Glenn family pride in her step, she spun, stalked to the door, and slammed it satisfyingly behind her. As her blood boiled through her veins, she felt more alive than she had in months. Come Saturday night, Mr. Lucky *would* have a job.

Yet she was curious. Why? Why had Craig Rawlins thrown the gauntlet? Shaking her head, she decided it didn't matter. She'd picked it up.

She'd barely taken two steps out of the bank when a quick movement to her right startled her. A sharp slap ricocheted into the street. A woman screamed.

Chapter Eleven

"Touch me again an' your balls'll be pig swill."

Billie turned wide eyes on a pretty, red-haired woman standing in front of a huge, bald-headed man whose entire head and face was red as a beet. Though the day was cool, sweat ran down the side of his face.

"Let go, Pearl. I swear—"

"Go on an' swear, but don't you never raise a hand to me again."

Billie saw the woman's right hand stretched between the big man's legs. She gasped. No wonder the fellow stood so still and had such a desperate glaze in his eyes.

"Don't need to worry none 'bout that, Pearl. You ain't workin' here no more. Yore fired." The man suddenly sucked in his breath and spread his legs wider apart. But he blustered on. "An' won't no one else take ya on, neither. I'll pass the word to every barkeep in town that 'sides havin' the clap, you're a goldurned thief."

"That's a lie, Lem, an' you know it."

The big man carefully lifted his shoulders in a shrug. Men standing nearby groaned. Women were too scarce for them to like the thought of any woman being banned from any brothel in town.

Billie watched a guarded look of fear steal over Pearl's flushed face before it was quickly wiped away with a determined act of bravado. She gave the giant's privates a jerk, then quickly stepped out of his reach.

The bartender growled and raised his ham-sized fist. Billie reacted instinctively, shoving two men aside to throw herself in front of the woman.

She flinched when her eyes met Lem's. She knew immediately that she had made a mistake. His little black eyes were glazed. He wasn't going to hesitate to hit a woman. Any woman. His hand was already descending. Hunching her shoulders, shutting her eyes, Billie waited for the blow.

She heard the smack of flesh on flesh, but felt nothing. She had not been the recipient of the blow. Another body was leaning over her, protecting her. Hard muscles pressed against her hip and side.

The body suddenly moved and she straightened. She was trapped between the woman and . . . Craig Rawlins. The big barkeeper's fist was inside Craig's palm. Craig stood steadily between herself and the threat of harm.

"Get out of here. Now!" he ordered.

She grabbed the other woman's wrist and pushed her way through the mob that had gathered.

"All right. Let me go. You're breaking my friggin' wrist," the woman demanded.

"I—I'm sorry." Flushing, Billie released the protesting woman.

Pearl rubbed her wrist as she glanced back at the milling men. "Thanks for helpin' out. Lem can get kinda mean when the mood strikes 'im."

The smacking thud of a fist sinking into flesh caused Billie to wince. The crowd suddenly roared. She stood on tiptoe but couldn't see what was happening. Were Craig and that huge man fighting? Craig—Mr. Rawlins—wouldn't stand a chance.

He had come to her rescue. He just couldn't be injured for such a gallant act.

Sharp nails dug into Billie's arm. "Can you see Lem? He isn't comin' for me, is he?"

At that moment, Billie saw through the woman's tough veneer to the frightened, insecure girl. Sympathy constricted her chest. "I can't see anything except a lot of hats."

The fingers gradually eased their grip. "Then I'll be on my way. Thanks again."

Billie put her hand over the other woman's before she could slip away. "Where will you go? Do you have a place to stay?"

Pearl looked down the street. "Dunno. But if I hurry, I might get a job before Lem—"

"I'll give you a job."

The crowd moved, apparently following the punches. Both women were jostled. Billie pulled Pearl to the wooden sidewalk.

"What did you say?" Pearl asked.

Billie took a deep breath. "I can give you a job. And a place to stay."

"You got a house, or what?" Pearl cocked her head. "Don't think I've seen you around here before." She narrowed her eyes. "And I know I ain't heard of any *woman* runnin' a place here.'

"Well . . ." Billie gulped, trying not to show her nervousness as she glanced quickly over her shoulder toward the ongoing commotion. "It's not a house, exactly. I'm the new partner over at the Empty Barrel."

Pearl scrutinized the woman with newfound appreciation. Now she understood the classy, albeit a bit frayed, gown and expensive jewels. "You got yourself a new girl. Call me Pearl. What's your name?"

"Billie."

Pearl stuck out her hand. "Pleasure."

Billie anxiously glanced toward the front of Lem's saloon. Where was Craig? At that moment, some of the crowd shifted. She caught a glimpse of a white apron and then the man's huge body on the ground.

"Whoooee, would you look at that. Ain't seen no one that could lay Lem out like that. That fella of yours must be purdee somethin'!"

"But—"

"Maybe we best get outta here. Don't wanta be any-where near when Lem comes to."

Billie couldn't leave until she knew Craig was all right. He had put himself in danger on her behalf.

"How're you ladies?"

Billie's spine tingled. She spun to find every hand-some, confident inch of Craig Rawlins standing beside them.

"What do you mean, sneaking—" She snapped her jaws closed, just relieved he was in one handsome piece, then turned her head. She didn't want to acknowledge her deep concern.

Pearl glanced questioningly at Billie, then beamed at their good-looking rescuer. "We're doin' just dandy. How 'bout you?"

"Fine." Craig smiled at Billie, then shook his head at the loudmouth who'd started the whole altercation. He unconsciously rubbed his bruised knuckles as he studied the powder-caked face and curvy figure pushed out and plumped up by a too-tight corset.

Irresistibly, his eyes wandered back to Billie. She was beautiful and ladylike and even brave—as she had just proved—but she was also Miss Chaos. What had she hoped to accomplish by getting into a street brawl with Lem over the likes of Pearl?

On the other hand, his well-bred new partner was about to become a madam. He shook his head again. This fallen angel was a bundle of contradictions.

Pearl leaned over and squeezed his upper arm. "Ooooh. Just feel those muscles. Poor ole Lem didn't have a chance."

"You may have inflicted more damage than I did."

All three of them turned to watch several of Lem's customers drag the unconscious man off the street.

Billie's breath caught in her throat. It could have been Craig in that condition. The thought chilled her. She closed her eyes. In a few short days she'd come to rely on his strength and character.

When she finally looked up again, Craig was walking away. She twined her fingers together. She hadn't even thanked him for stepping between her and the huge Lem.

"Just look at those long, muscular legs and tight backside. You ever seen such a handsome man as that Rawlins?"

"No, Pearl, I haven't."

Pearl laughed and winked. Billie flushed as if she stood next to a blazing fire.

"Come on," she indignantly ordered Pearl. "We have a lot to do." As they moved down the street, she asked, "Can you sew?"

Pearl tilted her head. "Sew?"

"Oh, never mind."

By that afternoon, Billie had introduced Pearl to Anna and Danny. New shelves had been built in the kitchen and all of the food was stored neatly away. Workmen were upstairs constructing beds and stuffing ticks with feathers bought from a local farmer.

She was overseeing the building of the stage for the orchestra and a gate across the stairs. At some point she had to go to the mercantile for cotton to make sheets and more blankets.

All in all, she thought, things were going quickly and smoothly. Another girl or two were needed. And the musicians. And she still hadn't come up with a plan to convince Craig to hire Mr. Lucky.

Craig chose that moment to shove through the swinging doors. With sun behind him, his face was shadowed and he seemed to loom eight feet above the floor and completely blocked the doorway. She gasped for breath as all of the air seemed to be sucked from the room.

Craig stood just inside the door until his eyes adjusted. Spotting Billie, he strode purposely toward her. The peculiar expression on her face caused him to gradually slow his pace. He surreptitiously lowered his eyes. He hated to admit it, but her strange gaze unsettled him.

When her huge, gold-flecked eyes locked with his, he momentarily forgot his purpose for coming. Until he heard feminine laughter in the kitchen. Then his face hardened with resolve.

"Billie—" He stopped directly in front of her.

Billie stiffened and hated herself for backing up. The last time she'd heard her name spoken with such authority, her father had been scolding her for some misdeed. And as she'd always done, she bristled in preparation for battle.

"Billie . . . I've just heard that you hired that . . . that . . . woman."

"You mean Pearl?" Her chin jutted at a stubborn angle.

"Yes. Pearl." He blinked, feeling like a child standing up for himself for the first time in front of a dreaded teacher. He didn't appreciate the inept feelings she brought forth in him. He quickly shrugged them away.

"What's wrong with Pearl?" She spread her hands on her hips.

"I won't have her here," he stated with unequivocal authority.

"Why not?"

"Why, I . . . Because Lem . . ." Come to think of it, he had no better reason than that Lem Bowden had said not to. And, damn it, why did she make it so difficult to say what he was thinking? "She's a troublemaker." That was a fact. He had the sore knuckles to prove it.

"Has she ever caused *you* trouble?" Billie stepped

closer. So close she could smell leather and cigar and a faint hint of spice. Nice. She blinked the realization away.

Craig scowled. "No." In fact, Pearl had had a lot of admirers in the crowd gathered that morning. She was pretty and saucy. Men liked *that*, though they didn't like *everything* about her. Especially her strong fingers and quick hand. "She'll ruin us."

"How?"

Exasperated, he took a deep breath. "Lem says she has the clap."

Billie gulped, staring wide-eyed at him and feeling the heat of embarrassment warm her cheeks and neck. "I don't care to believe that man. So unless you know for a fact that what he says is true . . . or plan to ask the lady yourself . . ."

Craig bristled. "Absolutely not. I would never . . . No."

"Then, shouldn't she have a chance?"

He almost chuckled at the way she stood like a banty hen, challenging, but with a glint of fear in her eyes.

"A week. But if she causes any problems, she's gone. Understood?"

Billie nodded.

"Good." He lowered his chin, wondering why every encounter with his new "partner" turned into a confrontation.

"Who's going to tend the bar?" Though Craig seemed through with their conversation, Billie was just getting started.

A muscle rippled the length of his jaw. "I'll find someone."

"Why—"

"We've been through this. I need someone who knows what he's doing."

"But—"

"No more arguing. I'll find the bartender, and that's that." Speaking of arguing, he couldn't explain why he'd taken such an aversion to hiring Lucky. He liked the man. He just didn't want him hanging around . . . the saloon.

Billie sputtered, looking for words suitable enough to describe the oaf.

"There you are, darlin'. What are you doin' here? I thought you didn't like saloons." Sunny Turnbow sidled up next to Craig and rubbed her body against his side.

"I don't." He moved toward the bar, breaking contact as gently as possible in front of Billie and the interested carpenters.

Sunny smiled at the stormy-faced Billie. "Hello," she purred.

"Good afternoon," Billie countered with forced graciousness. She didn't know why the other woman always seemed so perturbed at her, but it was wearing on her good manners.

"You seem to be keeping Craig awfully busy lately."

Billie's eyes widened. "Me? He's the one who insists we open in two nights. There's a lot of work to be done."

"But he's letting his other businesses suffer. I thought you were supposed to be in charge. Can't you handle things?"

"I—I . . ." Guilt consumed Billie. She couldn't believe Craig hadn't been keeping a close watch over his business ventures. And why was the woman harping at *her?* She didn't control Craig Rawlins's actions, and had no desire to.

Her eyes drifted to the man and ran up and down his back of their own volition. Pearl's brash description of his backside earlier in the day burned her cheeks.

Sunny smugly rubbed her palms together. "Once this is over, he'll be concentrating on what's *important.*" With a toss of her dark curls, she sashayed over to Craig.

Billie understood quite well what, or *who,* was most important in Sunny's mind. Guilt seeped into Billie's conscience even as her blood boiled when the conniving woman latched onto Craig again. No matter what she thought of Sunny now, the woman had taken Billie into her home at a time when the hospitality had been needed and appreciated.

"Ma'am?"

Billie's fists unconsciously clenched when Sunny stood on tiptoe and kissed Craig's cheek.

"S'cuse me, ma'am, but do ya wanna look at this, or not?" the workman shouted.

Billie started, blinked, then gratefully turned her attention to the stage. She didn't understand what had come over her. Well, perhaps she did, a little. She'd let Sunny Turnbow use Craig Rawlins to get to her. He was just a man, a business partner, who had been very nice to her. That was all. And she was appreciative. That was all.

"This high enough?"

"Uhm . . . what did you say?"

The man huffed and pointed out that the carpenters had erected the ten-by-ten square platform about a foot off the floor. Her eyes widened. Thoughts of anything but the stage fled her mind. She just hoped it wasn't too late as she pleaded, "Would it be possible to raise it?"

He shrugged. "How high?"

"At least twice that much." She wanted the dancers to be able to see the orchestra members and for the music to be clear.

Several workers groaned, but their boss nodded and went out through the back door. When he returned, he had more two-by-four supports.

Billie headed toward the bar as Sunny and Craig made their way over boards and through sawdust to the door, with Sunny obviously working her wiles to keep Craig's full attention.

". . . hoped you wouldn't have to spend so much time here." Billie overheard the end of Sunny's conversation as the pair sailed through the swinging doors. Thwapping sounds drowned out his reply. Leaning her elbows on the countertop, she watched them meander up the street with unwittingly wistful eyes.

"Hey, you gonna pine after that man all day or help us cut sheets and make up beds?"

Billie jerked upright and gazed into Pearl's grinning face. "I'm not pining. There's no man in the world I'd waste such time over."

"Sure. Sure. Whatever you say." Pearl didn't believe a word Billie said.

For the next few hours, everyone busied themselves upstairs. Anna had just mentioned the calico dress and asked about a pattern when Billie's face went white.

"Oh, no."

Pearl and Anna looked up. Danny furtively tried to untangle a wad of thread.

"What's wrong?" Anna asked.

"Dresses!" Billie gasped.

"Yep, that's what we were talking about. At least this time you paid attention." Pearl patted a red curl in place.

"No." Billie ignored Pearl's brassy sass. She was beginning to learn that Pearl hid a multitude of insecurity behind a smart mouth. "Dresses. We need something fancy for Saturday night." She still had hopes of wearing something besides the green gown. For some reason, she could hardly bring herself to look at it any more.

Pearl and Anna glanced at each other, their smiles dying on their lips.

"Oh, dear. What will we do?" Anna nervously poked her needle into the white muslin she was hemming to make into a sheet for Danny's small bed.

"And how will we ever get them finished in time?" Billie shook her head. They hadn't even started on her calico dress, and the owner of the mercantile hadn't unpacked the crate which he thought contained his fancier materials.

Pearl cleared her throat. Two pairs of eyes looked

askance at her. "In case you ladies haven't noticed, I've done two sheets and you're still on your first."

Billie arched her brow and looked behind Pearl. Sure enough, two sheets were stacked haphazardly on a stuffed mattress. The hems were crooked, but the sheets were finished.

"Are you trying to tell us you can sew dresses?" Billie asked hopefully. It was almost too good to be true.

Pearl grinned impishly. "I am."

Anna smiled.

Billie was skeptical. "I've never met a professional seamstress who could sew three dresses in that short a time."

"There's the nights, too," Pearl reminded her. "When was he gonna find that material?"

Billie rushed to the hallway, calling over her shoulder, "Keep your fingers crossed the mercantile's still open."

Ike was standing in the shop doorway when Billie hurried past.

"Now hold on a minute, young woman," he protested.

"Please, sir. This is very important. I need that material." She glanced to a table and saw with relief that he had unpacked a few bolts of beautiful materials.

"But it's time—"

"Some of that blue silk" would look attractive on Anna. "And that dusky rose velveteen" was perfect for Pearl.

"I'm sorry, but—"

"And that aqua satin" would do nicely for herself.

"Look, lady, I—"

"Of course, we'll need thread and lace and—"

The proprietor stepped in front of her and waved a hand in front of her face. "I've been trying to tell you . . . I can't give you any of those things."

"Can't?" Billie blinked.

He shook his head. "Believe me, it's not that I don't

want to make the sale. But a man has to look out for his business. I wish—"

"Why? Why won't you let me have the material?" She stood braced with her hands spread on her hips. His explanation had better be good.

"You've used the credit in your account. Mr. Rawlins hasn't authorized more purchases."

Her spine sagged to the consistency of just-washed flannel. No more credit? Although she realized Craig had not given her carte blanche with his funds, surely the merchant would allow her just a *little* leeway.

"I—I'm sure if Craig, Mr. Rawlins, knew why I need the material, he'd tell you to let me have it. I really need everything *now*. Please . . ."

"I've been in business less than two months and already had five customers skip out on their bills. I won't give no more credit to strangers."

"But . . ." She could understand his reasoning. The dresses were just too important. Unconsciously, she lifted her hand to the necklace and fingered the largest emerald.

"Now, if you had some kind of collateral." He grinned innocently.

Collateral? Her fingers tightened on the stone. She had only one item of value. The necklace.

Her hand trembled. The tendons in her neck corded. Her heart pounded. No. She couldn't part with the gems her stepbrother had claimed would keep her safe—the one thing that had given her the courage to go on.

But she had a chance now to start her life anew. If she had to part with the necklace to accomplish that . . . Wouldn't it be worth the sacrifice? And Anna and Danny and Pearl had cast their lots with her. They were depending on her to do the right thing.

Craig swung around the doorjamb and came to an abrupt stop. He'd hurried from the saloon after Anna and Pearl had told him where to find Billie. He knew his original line of credit had to be about spent.

The cost of renovating the Empty Barrel had gone far beyond what he'd planned and he and Billie needed to have a long talk.

His suspicions were confirmed when he saw Ike's out-thrust chin and determined glare.

However, he wasn't prepared for the look of utter defeat on Billie's profile. Her entire body shook. She clutched at that damned necklace as if it were a lifeline. Her eyes swam with tears. What the hell?

It took Billie some time, her fingers were trembling so, but at last she laid the necklace on the table. "Will this do for collateral?"

The merchant's eyes took on a greedy glitter. He actually rubbed his hands together before reaching for the jewelry. "Well, it might cover most of your purchases. However, the lace—"

Seeing the sacrifice she was about to make, Craig knew that whatever she wanted to purchase had to be important. He sauntered on inside the store.

"That necklace is worth more than everything in this building and you know it, Ike."

The merchant and Billie jumped simultaneously as Craig strolled over to them.

"I'm surprised at you, Ike. Truly surprised." Craig clicked his tongue. Then, making a gesture that even he couldn't believe, Craig picked up the necklace and handed it back to the stunned woman.

As soon as she took it, he wished he'd taken the thing and thrown it into the street.

"But—"

"But—"

Both Billie and Ike spoke at the same time, glanced at each other, and started again.

"The funds you left—"

"There wasn't any credit—"

Craig held up his hand. "I know. I know." To the

proprietor he said, "Go ahead and give the lady what she needs." Then he pulled Billie aside and warned, "Fixing up the Empty Barrel has gotten completely out of hand. We're reopening a saloon, not the Taj Mahal. Any more purchases will be made with profits. Understand?"

Still trembling, Billie tried to refasten the necklace. She managed a weak, "Y-yes," and continued her efforts. Secretly, though, she was pleased. Craig was finally coming around, talking as if he believed her plans would succeed. And once the dance emporium began to show those profits, she would repay Craig and not have to feel beholden to him for financing her—their—business.

Craig couldn't take his eyes off the delicate curve of Billie's neck and her nearly bare, sloping shoulders. Her skin looked as soft and silken as the satin material Ike was measuring. And somehow or other, she always managed to smell as fresh as a mountain meadow.

Without thinking, he brushed aside her fumbling fingers and took the necklace.

When his hands touched hers, Billie jerked. He might as well have pricked her with needles, so sharp was the jolt to her senses. Why? What was it about this man that attracted and distracted her so?

"There you are. Material. Lace. Thread."

Craig finished hooking the necklace and quickly stepped away, as if he'd been caught trying to steal the damned thing. Her scent lingered with him. What was it about her that made him feel like a terrified teenager and a randy stud at the same time?

Billie gulped and nodded at the merchant. She wrapped her arms around her upper body to ward off the chill threatening to ripple down her spine from Craig's swift departure.

While Craig paid the merchant, Billie began gathering the items without allowing the proprietor to take the extra time to wrap them. The sooner she got them back

to the Empty Barrel the sooner Pearl could get started.
And the sooner she could sort out the confusing feelings
Craig Rawlins aroused.

"Hey, wait." Craig saw that she was heading for the
door loaded down like a pack mule. He rushed to reach
the opening ahead of her, trying to take a few of the
things. Suddenly, from the corner of his eye, he saw a
small cannonball on two feet barreling toward them.

Realizing the material was unwrapped and that all
the needles and thread were loose, he threw himself in
front of Billie.

Chapter Twelve

"Damn ya, ya blasted monster."

"Ouch!"

"Ummphhh." Billie stubbed her toe on Craig's heel and barreled full force into his hard back, fighting to retain her grip on her purchases.

"Let go o' me, ya two-eyed swamp rat."

Craig cursed and tightened his hold on the petite person with the big, bad mouth.

Billie peered under Craig's arm. Her eyes widened. It was that young girl. The one in the too-tight dress who'd tried to embarrass—had succeeded in embarrassing—her so.

The girls saw her, grinned impishly, and quipped, "I see ya got ya one what pays more'n two bits, huh?"

Heat suffused Billie's face as she looked from the girl, to the purchases in her arms, to Craig's scowling features, and back to the obnoxious ragamuffin.

"What's the brat talking about?" Craig asked, aware of a subtle undercurrent between the two.

"It's, uhmm . . . a private joke," Billie stated, raising her chin in an indication she didn't care to discuss the matter further.

But the smudge-faced girl didn't take the hint. She shrugged loose from Craig's grasp. Instead of backing away, though, she stepped closer and ran a hand up his hip and ribs, eyeing him with blatant invitation. All the while, her challenging gaze flickered to Billie.

Craig decided he was not a bone to be fought over, but searched Billie's eyes closely. Disappointment deflated his chest when all he saw was disgust. What had he expected? Jealousy?

He quickly disentangled himself from between the two glaring women and stepped away. With a warning glance toward the young street girl, he told Billie, "Since it appears you have things under control . . ."

Billie frowned at the amusement dancing in his eyes and the wicked grin slowly curving his appealing, roguish lips.

"I'm late for an appointment and have to hurry," he lied.

Billie's eyes flashed. She had a feeling she knew just where his appointment would take him. With a toss of her head, she gave him permission to leave, as if he needed it, then turned her back on him and headed toward her grand palace. But with each step, she became more irritated. He couldn't help her carry all of her parcels because he had a rendezvous. The thought tainted everything. Suddenly, she felt she was walking to a saloon rather than her home and her hope for a brighter future.

Craig watched her go. Watched the seductive sway of her hips and the straight, fragile column of her neck and spine. The woman had class and dignity, that was for sure. He shook his head, wondering how he'd let her become such a time-consuming interest.

Turning, he walked in the opposite direction, regretting a bit the fact that he'd resisted another invitation from Sunny. Going home alone to his empty cabin was less and less appealing every minute.

Billie walked several yards before she realized the young girl was trailing after her. She stopped and waited till the urchin drew even. "Where do you live?"

The girl stuck out her lower lip. "Nowhere's in partic'lar. Why? What's it to ya?"

Billie shrugged as easily as she could while maintaining her grasp on the heavy material. She happened to glance over and caught the youngster wistfully eyeing the pretty colors. But when she lifted a grubby hand, Billie swung the fabric out of reach.

"It doesn't matter to me at all." She arched her brows and wrinkled her nose. "I just wondered why your mother never gives you a bath."

"I'm full growed. No one gives me a bath," the girl hissed.

"Perhaps," Billie conceded. "But I still think your mother—"

"Look, lady. I ain't got no mother. Don't need no mother. Don't need no one but a man what's got four bits in 'is pockets."

The girl started to stomp away but Billie quickly balanced her goods in one arm and clamped the other hand over the ragamuffin's bony shoulder. "Four bits? You've raised your price."

"What's it to ya?" Her pointed chin raised defiantly.

Billie sighed. "I—I think you're worth more than two bits, too." There were so many questions she wanted to ask, so many things she wanted to say. But she knew too much sympathy would scare the girl away.

Skeptical brown eyes darted a look at Billie's face.

She nodded, reinforcing her words. Then, her arms getting tired, Billie readjusted her load and started walking.

The girl fell into step beside her again. "What ya gonna do with all them things?"

Billie noticed she'd spotted the lace. "Make dresses."

Some of the hardness left the girl's face. "Dresses? Are they all fer you? Did the big gent buy 'em fer ya?"

"Well . . ." Billie hesitated. "Yes, the man bought the material, but there'll be three of us wearing the dresses."

"Wheweee. He's got *three* wimmen?"

Billie chuckled once at the implication, then chuckled again at her own amusement. "You misunderstand. The other ladies work for me and I work *with* Mr. Rawlins. I'm opening a dance emporium."

The little face became animated. "Empo-ri-um. Is that like a cat house? I seen lots o' cat houses. None o' the wimmen had dresses as purty as those'll be, though."

Billie hid a grin and shook her head. "No, it is not a 'cat' house. The girls will be able to live upstairs, but there will be no prostitution in my establishment."

"Then what ya gonna do?"

"Dance."

"Just dance?" the girl asked, astonished.

"Just dance."

"Wheweee. How kin ya make money dancin'?"

"What's your name?" Billie had forgotten, if she'd even heard it before.

The girl's eyes shuttered. Her steps slowed.

Billie matched her pace to the youngster's. "*My* name is Billie."

"Billie?" She snorted.

"Yes." Billie stopped in front of the Empty Barrel.

There was a long silence. The girl stared back and forth between the saloon and Billie as if she were considering something of grave importance.

Billie finally moved toward the door.

"My moniker's Molly."

The words came out so softly Billie almost dropped her bundle in an effort to hear. But hear she did. "Molly. What a pretty name."

Molly scuffed shoes whose stitching had worn through the thin leather and exposed toes on both feet. "T'ain't purty. It's common as crow bait."

Billie opened her mouth to argue, but Molly interrupted. "Ya need another girl? Er . . . dancer?"

"Well . . ." Billie pursed her lips, then voiced her

main concerns. "My 'girls' have to be clean. They can't backtalk the customers, or lose their tempers and curse."

Faced with a choice, Molly quickly made a decision. "I kin do that. I—I mean, watch my language an' all."

"What about a bath?"

Molly reluctantly nodded.

"I just don't know ... Won't someone be worried about you? Don't you have a father, or a guardian?"

Molly's face contorted, but smoothed when she remembered her promise. "I done told ya. Ain't got no one."

If she was telling the truth, Billie felt there was no other choice. She couldn't—wouldn't—leave the girl on the street. No telling what might happen to her. No telling what had already happened to put the doubt and distrust in those sharp brown eyes.

"I suppose we could give you a try. But I'm warning you, Molly, I'm going to run a strict business. I intend to make a success of the emporium and can't have my girls driving away the customers."

"I won't," Molly sullenly retorted, but then looked at the things in Billie's arms and brightened. "Kin I have a dress outta one o' them?"

Billie frowned. She'd only bought enough for three gowns. "We'll have to see how much material there is left. But I have some calico we can use until enough money is earned to buy something fancier." She winced at the mix of disappointment and strength filling the girl's eyes. Billie had a feeling Molly had had a lot of disappointments in her life, but the girl was clearly a survivor.

"Come on inside," she invited, "and meet the rest of the girls." They walked into the darkened interior. Once Billie had deposited the materials on the counter, she lit a lantern and turned to study Molly more intently. "How old are you?" she bluntly inquired.

Again, Molly's features shuttered. "Nineteen."

Billie arched a brow.

"Seventeen?"

"Try again."

"Oh, gol durn it. Fifteen." Her lower lip jutted out.

"That's better." Billie took hold of Molly's shoulders and slowly turned her around. She was such a tiny thing. It wouldn't take much to make up something nice for her. Something fitting to her age. Rubbing her chin, Billie decided to discuss the matter with Pearl.

At that very moment, Pearl and Anna and Danny came into the room from the kitchen.

When she caught sight of Billie, Pearl announced, "Sure got dark in a hurry. Looks like we might get another storm tonight. Were you able to get those things we needed from the mercantile?" Upon seeing Molly, Pearl scowled. "Why'd you drag her in here?"

Anna took hold of Danny's shoulders and kept him close to her side.

Molly just eyed everyone with a belligerent expression.

Sensing that in a town with so few women, Anna and Pearl and Molly had probably met, and knowing firsthand how rude Molly could act, Billie took a deep breath. "I'm going to give Molly a try. She's promised to behave herself with the customers, and that goes for those of us working here, too. Doesn't it, Molly?"

Molly shuffled her feet.

"Doesn't it, Molly?"

"Yeah." She mumbled something under her breath. Billie frowned. "I didn't hear you."

Molly threw up her hands and dramatically confessed, "I said, 'Yeah. Gol durn it, yeah.' But that's the last time I'll say it. Just had ta git it out o' my system."

After making sure they all knew each other's names and that peace was reigning while everyone began to look through the new materials, Billie excused herself and went upstairs. Luckily the workmen were still there. She asked them to construct another bed when they had

he time and was pleased to learn they had to come
back the next morning anyway. They could do it then.

On the way back downstairs, Billie thought she'd give
Molly the room with the bed that was already assembled and she'd sleep downstairs on her pallet.

Pearl looked up, saw her entering the main room,
and called her over.

Clicking her tongue, Pearl asked, "Just how much of
this are you planning to use? The men don't like it if
you cover up *everything*."

"They'll have to *learn* to like it, then. We're going to
wear beautiful gowns with full skirts that will billow and
twirl when we're spun around." Billie was thinking of
some of the balls she'd attended before the war. They'd
been elegant and sumptuous and were what the ladies
seemed to miss the most. The men, too.

Anna smiled.

Molly appeared awed.

Pearl fisted her hands on her hips. "This isn't going to
be like any saloon I ever worked in. What makes you
think men will want to come in here and spend their
money?"

"Because . . . this will be a dance emporium. The
men will be required to clean themselves up and come
here for drinks and the opportunity to dance with a
beautiful woman in a grandiose atmosphere. And drinks
and dancing is *all* they will pay for. My 'grand palace'
will not become a brothel. Understood?"

Anna's cheeks flushed. "But, Billie, I'm ain't no
beeuutiful woman."

Danny frowned and twisted until he could look up at
his mother. "Ya are too, bea . . . bee . . . purty. Yore the
purtiest ma in the whole wide world."

Billie nodded. "You can't argue with that."

Anna swallowed painfully and hugged her son.
"Don't reckon I kin. Don't reckon I want to."

Molly looked at the other women and shrugged as if

she could care less what the rules were. All she had to worry about was controlling her temper.

Pearl's face remained reddened with displeasure. "But what if I meet a man I want to . . . entertain?"

Billie stood her ground. "Then you can go to his room or camp. Outside of this building, you can do as you wish. But inside—"

"That what Mr. Rawlins wants, too?" Pearl asked with a sly gleam in her eyes.

Billie shifted her weight from one foot to the other. Truthfully, she had no idea what Craig Rawlins wanted. "Mr. Rawlins is my partner. Our agreement is that I will run the Empty Barrel and make a profit. How I do it is of no concern to him," she bluffed.

Pearl smirked. "We'll soon see about that, won't we?"

Then, as if the argument had never occurred, she grabbed the things from atop the bar and headed for one of the large gaming tables. "Come on, girls. Let's get started on these gowns. This might take longer than I expected."

She slanted one last smirk at Billie, who stood rooted to the floor, wondering what she'd gotten herself into. What if she couldn't get everything organized? Time was running out. As far as she knew, there was no bartender and no orchestra. Where would she find anyone who knew how to play an instrument?

Billie gulped. Sunny. Sunny'd had musicians at Justin's birthday party. But no, she couldn't go to Sunny.

Tomorrow morning, first thing, she'd discuss it with Craig and make sure he gave her his undivided attention. She'd also find Lucky and have a little chat with him.

She would be ready to open Saturday night if it killed her, and everyone else.

Later that night, after a brief argument with Molly over who would sleep on the pallet, Billie pulled a blanket up to her chin and stared at the ceiling, which she and Danny had dusted down after supper. Her back ached, every muscle in her body was tender, and she felt . . . exhilarated. For the first time in her life, she was in control of her fate, using her own knowledge and labor to direct her life.

She snuggled deeper into the blanket as the chill night air began to cool the building. The rain they'd had earlier had been soft and steady, much different from the storm earlier in the week. Creaks of new wood and groans from the settling building actually lulled her eyes closed.

She didn't know how much time had passed, but a different noise sounded from behind the bar. Her eyes shot open. She turned her head and stared toward the counter, back bar, and mirrors. Her muscles tensed as she held her breath and waited and watched. But she heard nothing else. It was probably just a mouse, she rationalized. She'd seen one in the kitchen just that evening.

Her lungs threatened to explode. She gradually released the pent-up air, but remained alert, just in case. Minutes dragged by and her vision began to blur. She blinked. Blinked again. Yawned. Her lids fluttered shut.

Suddenly, she stiffened, sensing someone was near. Her flesh felt as if a horde of ants crawled over every bare inch. Something slid across the floor. Someone grunted. Someone? Immediately, she scrambled to her feet. Grabbing the first bottle she encountered on the bar for a weapon, she hunched down and crept slowly toward the sound. Her bare feet padded soundlessly as she crunched the edges of the blanket she'd remembered to throw across her shoulders in a one-handed death grip.

The "someone" was in the kitchen. Inch by inch she slunk toward a steady stream of muffled noises. Stopping near the doorway, she peeked around the corner, saw a shadowed form, and charged into the candlelit room, bottle upraised, before she could lose her nerve. As dear as food had become during the past few weeks, she darned sure wasn't going to let anyone steal it.

"Get out right now, I'm warning—"

"Stop. Don't break that bottle." Craig Rawlins's face drained of color when he saw what she was wielding. Rushing forward, he tried to wrest it from her fingers.

Billie hadn't recognized Craig, casually dressed in dark trousers, cream shirt, and brown leather vest. When the man whom she'd identified as an intruder spun toward her, she'd already started her arm in a downward arc. His hand hit hers, numbing her fingers, and the bottle crashed to the floor.

"Damn."

Billie jumped sideways to avoid being splattered with dark-red liquid.

"Why in the hell did you do that?" Craig demanded, glaring at her with his hands splayed on his narrow hips.

"I—I thought you were a . . . thief." She shuddered as a wave of relief rippled up her spine. Then she scowled at him. "What do you think you're doing, sneaking around in my kitchen?"

"*Your* kitchen?" he asked, astonished.

She nodded.

"I'll have you know, lady, this is *my* saloon. *I* paid for everything in this . . ." He waved his hand around the incomplete room. ". . . kitchen."

Taking a step back, she conceded, "All right, *our* kitchen. I'm going to repay every penny you've spent."

"So you say. We have yet to see any proof."

"That's beside the point." She lifted her chin. "You nearly frightened me to death. You should have told me it was you when you went to the bar."

"To the bar?"

"I heard you. Behind the bar. But I thought you were a mouse." A really big mouse, from the way it set her nerves on end.

He frowned. "Then that's what it must have been. I came in the back and this is as far as I've gone."

She gulped. "Oh." Sure, it was just a mouse. What else could it have been? She was tired. Sleeping inside such a large, empty space was unsettling. She'd jumped at nothing.

"So, what are you going to do about the mouse?"

"Nothing." Observing her crossed arms and unblinking expression, he added, "Tonight. I'll set a trap tomorrow." And he'd give the doors and windows a thorough inspection. He had a gut instinct that no four-legged mouse could've made the kind of noise that had startled her so badly.

"Good."

"Anything else you need me to take care of?" he asked, eyeing glimpses of lacy chemise and frilled drawers wherever her blanket slipped.

She yawned. "Have you arranged for an orchestra yet?"

"No."

She waited. When it appeared he had nothing more to say, she ground her teeth. "No? Just, no?"

"I'm working on more important things." He clenched his jaw, thinking of the hours he'd spent trying to mine out any little nugget of information to help him discover a murderer. So far, he'd dredged up nothing. "I'll find a band when there's time."

Her lower jaw dropped almost to her chest. Her eyes widened in horror. More important things? What could be more crucial to a dance emporium than musicians? "You *have* to find men and instruments. We already have a stage and . . . everything." She inhaled, refusing to beg.

Craig cocked a brow at the hint of desperation in her voice. "I promise to have one within at least a week." There, that should satisfy her.

"No." She literally stomped her foot, then winced. "It's imperative we have music opening night."

Exasperated, he spread his arms. "What do you expect of me? You're getting a kitchen. As you've stated, the stage is erected. There are beds in most of the rooms and more furniture coming tomorrow—"

"You act as though you did it all personally, but you *hired* people to do the work. Why can't you just as easily hire an orchestra . . . And a bartender?"

"I've done that already."

"Who?" Billie's brows furrowed, nearly slanting them together.

"Me." What on earth had caused him to go and blurt out such nonsense? He stood still as a statue, but his mind worked faster than a Chinese labor camp.

Sure, he knew how to mix drinks. Had done all the ordering for Bobby. And yes, he suddenly couldn't seem to stay away from the place. For a man who'd sworn to never set foot in another brothel, he'd certainly undergone a swift change of heart.

Just like this evening. He'd gone home and found himself sitting around the cabin with nothing to do. In reality, there was a lot to do—business, picking up the place—but he kept finding himself at the window facing town, wondering what was happening down at the Empty Barrel.

And he was bound and determined to be there opening night to witness Billie's comeuppance. His chest constricted. All right, so he wouldn't enjoy it, but she had to learn that there was more to operating a saloon than she could ever hope to be prepared for. Working the upstairs didn't give a woman the knowledge to the whole business.

Billie stood in silence. Craig was going to tend the bar? The same man who used to force himself to even enter the place? At least that was what Sunny had inferred. As far as Billie was concerned, she couldn't seem to find a minute when he wasn't underfoot.

She swallowed and questioned reasonably, "Have you tended bar before?"

His eyelids lowered a fraction. "I've never done it as a 'job,' if that's what you're wondering."

"That's what I was wondering," she admitted, futilely trying to mask her dejection. What kind of opening night were they going to have?

He looked affronted. "I can make the best Knicker-bocker within two hundred miles."

She looked skeptical. He took her hand and led her into the saloon, stopping to light a lantern at the end of the polished bar before moving behind it. She didn't even think about jerking away. His company, and his touch, were too enjoyable.

Bottles clinked. Liquid splashed. The next thing she knew, she was holding a glass containing a small amount of . . . she had no idea what. The only liquor she was familiar with was her father's decanters of aged brandy and bourbon.

"Go on. Try it."

She glanced at him through her lashes. Saw the look of expectancy on his suddenly boyish features. "But . . . I don't drink. I won't know if it's good or not."

"If you can take a sip without making a face, it's good." He grinned. "Go on. Test my prowess."

She shuddered at the double entendre. To keep from showing her unease, or causing him to question her reaction, she raised the glass to her lips and took a tiny sip. Her eyes shot wide open. Though the liquor itself was cool, it traced a hot trail over her tongue, down her throat, and to her belly. She unconsciously shivered, then licked her lips. She gasped and said, "It tastes like raspberries."

He nodded and watched her intently. "Do you like it?"

"I don't know," she answered honestly. "I've never tasted anything like it." The drink wasn't exactly sweet, or sour. Her insides tingled with a strange, yet not unpleasant, sensation.

In order to give him a fair chance, she took another

taste. Warmth stole through her entire body. This time she didn't shiver. "I guess it's good."

His lips turned downward. "I'm not so sure that's a compliment."

"Is this what everyone drinks in a saloon?" She had one more sip. The taste kept improving.

His brows furrowed at her naive question even as he chuckled. "No. Most men have different preferences. They can choose between fancy drinks like that one or whiskey, bourbon, brandy, and beer. We also keep a cheaper homemade brew in barrels in the cellar." He cocked his head. "You don't drink, but have worked in saloons?"

She gulped. "I, uhmm . . . just didn't realize there was such a variety. And I was never required to get . . . Well . . . you know."

"Drunk?"

Suddenly, she stiffened. A memory overwhelmed her, coming to life with the smell of hot, fetid breath. A dark shadow seemed to loom behind her.

"Angel? Are you all right? The drink isn't making you sick, is it?"

She blinked and the frightening images vanished. She quickly straightened, set her drink down, and found several wrinkles to smooth from a corner of her pallet. Where had the memory come from? What did it mean? What she'd conjured up so far hadn't been more scandalous than events from the average person's past. But this was different. It seemed to give credence to those awful feelings of worthlessness that plagued her.

"Hey, watcha all doin'? I *told* Ma I thought I heard voices." Danny, outfitted in nothing more than an oversized shirt, hopped down the rest of the stairs and skipped over to Craig. "Did ya bring another one o' them pies?"

"Danny!" Anna reprimanded, following closely on her son's heels and clutching her blanket around her.

"Don't pester Mr. Rawlins. Now that ya know who's here, we should go on back to bed."

"Aw, Ma . . ."

Billie smiled at Danny, glad for the interruption.

A few seconds later, Pearl and Molly stumbled down the stairs. Pearl wore a flimsy robe over a long flannel gown and Molly, like Anna, was shrouded in a blanket.

Pearl looked at Billie, then frowned toward Molly who was moving around the others and inching toward the gaming tables. "Can't keep the kid away from the material, and there's just barely enough for our three dresses."

"Jest wanted to see if'n he'd come to take back that fancy material."

Understanding Molly's obsession with the unfinished dresses, Billie told Anna, "We'll let Molly use the calico."

Anna nodded. "It'll be perfect fer a girl her age."

Molly made a face. "I'm not a dad blamed baby." All at once she recalled her promise to Billie and sucked in her breath. "Cain't I have jest a scrap or two o' that fancy stuff?"

"Well . . ." Billie slanted a glance toward Craig, who was watching with unmasked interest.

"Please?" Molly begged, dragging Billie's attention away from Craig Rawlins.

"I don't see what it would hurt if she kept the remnants." Billie looked askance at Pearl, who frowned, but finally shrugged her acceptance.

"Danny, what're ya drinkin'?" Anna glared at Mr. Rawlins.

The boy smacked his lips, then wiped his mouth on his sleeve. "Don't know, but it shore is good."

Craig picked up a towel and dried his hands. "It's just sarsaparilla, Mrs. Corbett. Want some?"

Anna declined, but Molly wasted no time accepting. Pearl sniffed the glass Billie had. "What's that?"

Billie announced, "A Knickerbocker," as if she were well acquainted with the drink.

Craig surreptitiously arched his brow, which she disdainfully ignored.

Pearl took a sip and smacked her lips just as Danny had done. "Best I've tasted in a month of Sundays."

Beaming at Billie, Craig said, "Then there's no more arguments over who's tending bar."

Billie was disappointed for Lucky's sake. The poor man needed the work so he could go home. But . . . this meant she would see more of Craig. Her stomach suddenly felt fluttery.

Danny puckered his forehead. "But I was talkin' with this kid what said ya didn't like saloons. He said we wouldn't have a job very long. That right, Mr. Rawlins?"

Chapter Thirteen

Craig cleared his throat as five pairs of questioning eyes turned upon him. He dropped the towel and squared his shoulders. "What 'kid' are you talkin' about, boy?"

"He's older an' taller'n me. An'—"

"Who said it, isn't important," Billie interrupted. She stared directly at Craig. "Is it true?"

"I guess it's no secret that I've never had anythin' to do with the saloon before. But—"

"Do we have a business agreement, or not?"

"Yes, damn it, we do."

"Then we have jobs for three months, guaranteed." She didn't ask. She stated.

His teeth ground together as he hissed, "Yes."

Danny ran around the counter and threw his arms around Craig's legs. "I knowed he was fibbin'. Ya shoot fair an' square, don't ya, Mr. Rawlins?"

A fist of guilt squeezed Craig's gut. It was hard to imagine that he'd only agreed to this fiasco because he figured it would fail. Now, looking around at the frightened, yet hopeful, faces of the outcasts Billie had dragged in, how could he desire anything but success for her?

However, one unanswered question still bothered him. "Danny?" He mussed the boy's already flyaway hair. "Have you seen the boy who told you I'd close the saloon before?"

Danny nodded while gulping another glass of sarsaparilla. Then, licking his lips and short of breath, he gasped, "Don't know 'is name, though."

Craig glanced at the women. "Any of you happen to see who it was?"

No one had seen any youngsters hanging about.

Finally, Craig shrugged it off. No harm had been done. "You'd all better go get a good night's sleep. There's a busy day ahead."

Pearl yawned and headed toward the stairs. Molly trailed along behind, fingering a fragment of lace she'd filched. Anna rounded up Danny, then looked doubtfully around the huge room. "Think we kin really do it? Open Saturday night?"

"Of course we can," Billie assured her, though the task looked daunting.

After they were once more alone, she darted a glance to Craig's somber face. She hated to keep arguing with the man, but . . . "If you can't find an orchestra by tomorrow evening, may I at least try to find a piano player?" She nodded toward the cherry-wood piece sitting forgotten in the corner behind the bar.

He tilted his head and regarded her so intently that she shifted uneasily from one foot to the other. Her fingernails ached from their deep grip on the blanket.

"Tell you what . . . If music is so important to you, I'll leave it up to you to find whatever you want."

Her eyes rounded. Up to her? She'd have to do something so vital, all by herself?

Reading the sudden insecurity in her eyes, he spread his arms. "I don't have the time. My other businesses have been neglected and there are things I need to catch up on if I tend bar Saturday night."

Billie opened her mouth. Craig narrowed his eyes. "Don't say it. My mixin' drinks will save us money. That's to our advantage, isn't it?"

Unable to come up with a reasonable argument, she sighed and nodded.

"All right. Now ... I suggest you get some rest."

"What about you?"

He finished cleaning up behind the bar. "I'm on my way home right now. Sorry I disturbed everyone."

She blinked, feeling strangely abandoned. She was beginning to really like this hard-headed man.

"Good night, Angel."

She flushed. "Good night, Mr. Raw— Craig."

Waiting until he'd left and secured the door behind him, she made her way back to her pallet and sat quietly for several long moments. Angel. It wasn't the first time he'd called her that, but it was the first time she'd allowed herself to think about it.

Did he really believe she was an angel? Why? It seemed all she'd been was an annoyance to him.

At last she sighed, laid back, and closed her eyes. Somewhere, from deep inside, she battled a disturbing feeling that he was wrong. Terribly wrong. She was no angel at all.

Saturday morning found the saloon a bustling center of activity. Workers were sawing and hammering from the kitchen to the upstairs bedrooms, including the room Billie had chosen to use for her office.

Crates of liquor arrived from Salt Lake. Bottles were unloaded behind the bar and any surplus was stashed in the cellar.

Pearl stitched on their dresses and Mollie had taken her scraps and hidden herself away in her room.

Anna was cleaning off tables and washing glasses. Danny swept up after the carpenters, but left some sawdust on the dance floor.

Outside, it was cloudy, with a chill in the air. Billie donned her cloak and set out to find her orchestra.

Halfway down the block, she saw Lucky crossing the street toward her.

"Mornin', Miss Billie."

"Good morning, Mr. Lucky. What brings you into town?"

"Aw, nothin' much. Just wastin' time."

"Are you going to come to the opening of my grand palace tonight?"

"Grand palace?"

She flushed. "I prefer to think of my dance emporium as a grand palace. It sounds more elegant than the Empty Barrel Saloon."

He grinned. "You're right. But to tell you the truth, I'd forgotten all about tonight being the grand opening." Seeing the disappointment in her eyes, he relented. "Sure. I'll be there. Promise you'll save a dance for me?"

It suddenly dawned on her that *she* would also have to dance with the customers. Just like at Sunny's party, only for hours at a time, night after night. She took a deep breath and gave him a weak smile. "Of course. Maybe even . . ." she gulped, "two."

He took off his battered hat and slapped it against his thigh, billowing a cloud of dust around his legs. "Then I'll be there with bells on."

Looking toward the freight office, she hesitated, then suggested, "If you don't have anything else to do, why don't you come early."

He looked puzzled, but shrugged. "Sure. Why not?"

As he was about to walk on, she called, "Do you know of anyone who can play a piano, or any other instrument?"

"Hhmmm." He scratched his head, then replaced his hat. "Two of the fellas that played at Mrs. Turnbow's party have moved on to another strike. But there's Dawkins. He played the fiddle. Crespin's got a banjo. He's good. And Hanshaw used to play piano at the

Gold Nugget but got his heart broken by one of the gals and now just mopes around his claim."

Billie could hardly contain her excitement. "Will you see those men today?"

"Reckon I will. Except Hanshaw."

She clapped her hands. "Would you ask them to meet me at the saloon around two o'clock?" Her eyebrows drew together. "I'll even guarantee you free drinks tonight if you can find Mr. Hanshaw and ask him to come, too."

"Free drinks, you say?"

She nodded. She was taking a lot for granted, thinking that Craig would allow her the right to make such a decision. But she could bear his anger as long as her dance emporium opened with at least a three-piece orchestra. Although most she'd seen in St. Louis were at least four pieces, she doubted the men in Alder Gulch would mind. And perhaps she could find another person in a day or two.

The emporium was destined to fail for sure if she couldn't offer decent music.

Lucky glanced down the street. "Hanshaw'll be there if I have to carry him over my shoulder."

"Oh, thank you," she sighed. "I don't know what I'd do without you."

"As long as I'm able to remain in Alder Gulch, Miss Billie, you'll never have to worry about finding out." His eyes filled with worshipful adoration.

Already thinking about hurrying to finish her errands so she could return to the saloon and get ready to meet with the musicians, Billie just nodded and waved without paying much attention to Lucky's vehement declaration.

Billie was surprised to see Craig Rawlins behind the bar when she entered the Empty Barrel about an hour later, talking with a pinch-faced Sunny Turnbow.

"But Craig darlin', you promised you'd come by to-night."

"Yeah," Craig sighed irritably. "But I forgot this was opening night for the saloon."

"Justin will be so disappointed." She patted her perfect coiffure and bent slightly, accidentally on purpose allowing Craig a glimpse of her generous bosom. "You said that your partner, that woman, Billie, had made you a bargain to run the saloon. Why do you have to be here?"

Bartender, or not, Billie hesitated on her way through the room to hear his answer. She'd wondered the same thing. What had happened to his declaration that *she* would be solely responsible for the success of the business once it opened?

Craig frowned. He didn't have a reasonable explanation. It was an . . . obsession. That was the only word he could think of to describe his need to spend more time at the Empty Barrel.

"I just want to make sure everything runs smoothly the first night. After all, it's a big investment."

Billie shook her head. Money. The man thrived on success. Was it what drove him? Was profit all he cared about?

At that moment, Pearl stopped in the middle of the stairs and called to Billie, "There you are. If you want a new gown tonight, you best come up here and let me take some measurements."

Billie was on the first step when she heard a disgusted huff and the click of Sunny's heels as the woman marched across the floor and out the swinging doors. Stifling the surge of pleasure flooding her chest, Billie reminded herself that what Craig Rawlins did, or whom he saw, should be of no consequence to her. Yet her heart felt light as she ascended the stairway.

Her flight of fancy took a decided downward spiral, however, when she entered the chaos inside the empty room Pearl had commandeered to spread out the material and do her needlework.

Anna was nearly in tears as she donned the beautiful blue silk dress. She ran her hands lovingly over the soft material, but hiccuped at the sloppy way it hung on her slender body.

Pearl put a pin in the hem and leaned back. "There ya go, Anna. I'll finish the rest of the hem after I fix up Billie."

Anna's eyes locked imploringly with Billie's.

"Uhm ... before you start on my dress, why don't you go ahead and take up Anna's." Billie, admittedly, wasn't an expert on dressmaking, but she definitely recognized there was still a lot to be done to assure Anna's dress was a perfect fit.

Pearl spit out a pin. "Naw. That's the way I figured it ought to fit. You know, loose ... so she can move when she dances."

Anna threw up her hands in despair.

"But, Pearl ..." Billie tried to explain again, "we want to look elegant and neat. Classy."

"Provocative?" Pearl grinned.

"Alluring is more what I had in mind. Show off our figures, yet leave something to the men's imaginations." She purposely omitted the fact that she wouldn't mind having her own dress fit like Anna's—to hide her body behind as many layers of material as possible.

While Pearl cocked her head and pretended to scrutinize the dejected Anna, Billie thought about what they would do once the doors were open. She'd considered what would be a fair price to charge for each dance. It couldn't be an outrageous sum, yet enough to not appear cheap. One dollar. That was affordable to the type of clientele she wished to attract.

Anna turned from looking out the window to ask Pearl, "What does your dress look like?"

Pearl just fluffed her bright red hair.

Anna's voice rose. "Does yours fit like this?" She waved her hand down her body and made a face.

"Well, not exactly. But it's easier to make things for myself than for someone else."

Molly wandered into the room and took in the situation with wide eyes. She lowered her lashes and shook her head at the sight of Anna's baggy garment.

Trying to think of a solution to Anna's dilemma, Billie asked, "How's your dress coming, Molly?"

The younger girl stepped over scraps of cloth. "It's done."

"Can I see it?" Anna anxiously wanted to compare her gown with another.

Molly bit her lower lip and darted a glance to Billie. "Do I have to?"

"No, you don't *have* to. But I'd like to see it, too," Billie encouraged. Then she turned to Pearl. "But if we don't get started on mine soon, it won't be ready." She sucked in her breath. There was always the green gown, if worst came to worst.

All of a sudden, Molly offered, "I kin help."

Pearl sniffed. "Sure. I can just imagine what something *you* stitched together looks like. No wonder you don't want anyone to see it."

Her back stiff, Molly spun and stalked from the room.

Billie shook her head and walked over to the folded aqua satin fabric and wished she had the expertise to turn it into something wonderful. She definitely didn't want *her* dress to look like Anna's.

Anna took off her dress and handed it to Pearl before putting on her old one and walking over to stand beside Billie. "Don't know . . . The grand openin' could be a grand disaster."

"Anna!" Billie reprimanded. "Please don't talk like that."

"Why? 'Fraid it might come to pass?"

Billie gulped and nodded.

A slight rustling came from the doorway. Just enough

of a whispery sound to attract the women's attention. Anna gasped. Pearl cursed. Billie stared, then moved toward the brown-haired vision.

"Molly."

The girl shyly backed up. "Whatcha think?"

"Oh . . ." Anna and Billie both sighed.

"Aw, that's nothin' special. Why, I made—" Pearl realized no one was listening. They were circling Molly, oohing and aahing. Huffing disdainfully, Pearl nonchalantly joined them.

Molly's dress was made mostly from the beige calico patterned with tiny multicolored flowers. The scooped neck of the tailored bodice was scalloped with the blue silk. Ruffles of dusky rose velveteen adorned the sleeves. A sash of aqua satin tucked in her waist. The long, full skirt was divided with alternating panels of all four materials. It was very simple, yet extremely elegant. And perfect for a young lady.

"Molly . . ." Billie was stunned. "Where did you learn to sew like that?"

Molly flushed crimson and clasped and unclasped her hands. "My ma had her hands full with ten of us kids. Pa purty much took care o' the boys, teachin' 'em how to plow an' handle the stock an' such. But ma had six o' us girls. She divided the chores amongst us. Sally an' Raebeth, the two oldest, helped with the cookin'. I was the third girl an' then Sue Ann. We sorta took to the mendin' an' sewin'. The youngest two were barely old enough to start sweepin' when I were sold to my first husband."

"*What?* Sold? Husband?" Billie's stunned disbelief turned to shock. "How old were you, for heaven's sake?"

Molly lifted her chin. "Twelve."

"Why, I've never heard—"

"Happens all the time." Pearl had a faraway look in her eyes, but blinked and added, "Some are just lucky ta escape and do something different with their lives." As she talked, she rubbed her hands up and down her arms as if recounting unpleasant memories.

Anna cleared her throat and patted Molly's shoulder. "Would ya mind . . . helpin' to fit my gown?" She darted a worried glance to Pearl. "That is, if Pearl don't mind."

Pearl waved her hand and finally grinned. "Naw. I never claimed to be an expert. Just volunteered to get them done. Fact is . . ." She rubbed a finger down her own folded gown. "Might get you to take a gander at mine."

Billie heaved a pleased sigh. She'd been afraid Pearl might take offense, but Molly was by far the better seamstress. And from the animated light in the girl's eyes as she chatted with Anna and pointed out tips to Pearl, she enjoyed sewing.

A family was evolving here. Anna had taken over the cooking, Molly the sewing. And Pearl was organizing everyone and everything. As for herself, Billie had them all fooled. They thought she was in charge and alternately treated her like a madam and a mother superior. Only *she* knew she was unfit for either position.

"Miss Billie, there be some fellers downstairs askin' fer ya," Danny shouted as he burst into the room.

She brushed her hands together. It must be the musicians Lucky said he'd find. She turned to Molly and Pearl. "If you don't mind waiting, I'll be back soon to start my gown."

Nobody minded. Billie hurried on down to interview her orchestra. Descending the last step, she was surprised to see Lucky among the gathered men. Then she recalled that he'd said he would get the piano player here if he had to carry him.

Of their own volition, her eyes darted around the rest of the room. She was vaguely disappointed Craig wasn't there.

Lucky grinned broadly as she approached. "Miss Billie, here they are. Just like I promised."

Billie stopped just before she reached the motley group and inclined her head. "Gentlemen, thank you for coming on such short notice."

The men shuffled their feet and grumbled, but quieted and jerked off their hats after a glare from Lucky.

Lucky pointed to a too tall, too thin, bowlegged man with a full, bushy beard. "This is Jack Dawkins. You may remember him playing the fiddle at Sunny's."

As if to emphasize the fact, Jack Dawkins produced the instrument, which he'd been holding behind his back. It was well used, and so oiled and shiny that Billie knew he took special pride in it.

"And this is Eduardo Crespin."

Billie nodded to a short, thin fellow with slicked-back, coal-black hair, a mustache and goatee. He produced a banjo. And from the look of the worn area beneath the strings, he played it often.

Lucky tugged on the arm of a pudgy, bald-headed man who was incongruously blessed with a face full of gray-streaked brown hair that he kept neatly trimmed. "This is Ben Hanshaw. He plays a mean piano."

Ben nodded shyly.

"Gentlemen, the reason I asked to meet with you is that I'm interested in putting together an orchestra." Billie wasted no time in getting to the point since the men seemed uneasy in her presence.

The men glanced at each other, as if taking due measure of the talent and ability of each—and taking due measure of Billie.

She finally seemed to have their attention. "The problem is, you have to start tonight."

"Aw, well—"

"I don't think—"

"Couldn't do it—"

"Gentlemen . . ." She waited until they all met her eyes. "If we draw a big crowd and encourage the townsmen to dance, the pay could be very good."

"How good?" Jack blustered.

"As I said, it will depend on how well you play."

The men eyed each other warily.

Lucky pointed to the piano in the corner. "Let's move the piano over by the stage and see if you boys can tune your instruments."

Billie let out a long breath she hadn't realized she'd been holding. Thank goodness Lucky was there to help. She still felt intimidated, giving orders to men.

Stiffening her spine, she splayed her hands on her hips as they hefted the piano past her and set it down on the stage.

Billie noticed Ben Hanshaw eyeing the piano longingly, yet hesitantly. She wondered if he'd played at all since he'd been so unfortunate with love. Her insides constricted. Love. Was there such a thing?

She mentally shook herself and strolled over to where the men stood uncertainly.

"Mr. Hanshaw?"

He barely met her eyes. "Yeah."

"Mr. Lucky—" Her comment was interrupted by the snickering of the musicians. All eyes were focused on Lucky, whose neck turned beet red. She ignored them and continued. "Mr. Lucky said you played a mean piano. Would you mind playing something? I haven't had a chance to enjoy good music since . . ." She choked. Since she couldn't remember exactly when.

The men turned suddenly sympathetic countenances upon her, as if they, too, empathized. Billie was grateful. It seemed to bring them together on a level that didn't pit male against female. They all shared a common emotion.

Lucky hurriedly fetched a stool and Ben sat down. His fingers hovered over the keys only a few seconds before he began to play the song, "Twenty Years Ago."

She was so enraptured, Billie didn't notice Jack Dawkins tuning his fiddle. When he pulled his bow across the strings and took up the melody along with

Ben, she had to back up and sit down. Soon, Eduardo strummed in time.

When they stopped, she sat mesmerized, then clapped. "That was beautiful."

She gazed into their grinning faces. "May I assume you will all agree to play in our orchestra?"

Their gazes interlocked with each other, at Lucky and then at Billie. All three nodded.

Ben Hanshaw cleared his throat and asked, "Would you want another member?"

She nodded as if she didn't dare to hope.

"There's this fella, Joe Smith."

She frowned at the vague expressions flitting over the four faces. "What about Joe Smith?"

"Well, he's a fair hand on the cornet. Might be we could talk him into joinin' us."

She was a little hesitant, but finally shrugged. "Please ask him."

"What hora we come?"

Eduardo's English was broken, but Billie understood perfectly. "Mr. Rawlins suggested we open the doors at eight o'clock. Perhaps you gentlemen could be here at seven-thirty."

They preened with her continued use of the term "gentlemen," straightening their shoulders and expanding their chests.

Jack was the one who, after some hemming and hawing, finally asked, "What should we wear?"

Her eyes narrowed. She hadn't thought about that. "Uhmm . . ." Not knowing just what they might have in the way of spare or fancy clothing, or how much money they had at present, she tried to think of something they might all have in common.

"Do you all have a white or light-colored shirt?"

They nodded.

"What about a tie?"

Only Jack nodded.

Lucky joined the discussion. "I have one someone can borrow."

Ben grinned. "Let Eduardo have it. I can get one from my partner. And I think Joe has a string tie."

"Wonderful," Billie exclaimed. "Soon, we'll have the funds to make matching vests, or whatever you all decide you'd like to wear." At their looks of relief, she inwardly grimaced. What had they thought? That she would dress them up like matching dolls?

Fifteen minutes later, Billie stood in front of the bar listening to the orchestra practice when Craig Rawlins elbowed through the doors with a huge bowl in his arms.

Unable to stem her curiosity, she wandered as nonchalantly as possible toward the end of the counter where he'd placed the bowl. As she approached and saw that it was filled with crackers, an idea began to form.

Craig spotted Lucky and snapped, "What's he doin' here?"

She inclined her head and followed his hard gaze. "Mr. Lucky's been a great help," she said enthusiastically. "I don't know what I'd do without him."

A muscle in Craig's jaw jerked as he swung around the end of the bar and muttered. "The man's a real saint."

Unaware that he was being sarcastic, she nodded. "Yes. Isn't he?" Then, when she noticed Craig was leaving again, she called, "Wait."

Surprised, he turned and regarded her intently.

"Where are you going?"

"To bring a barrel of pickles to go with the crackers."

She wrinkled her nose at the thought of pickles and crackers as the only snacks for her classy emporium. But . . . since she hadn't considered offering anything at all, she supposed they would have to do.

"Would you mind putting a punch bowl out with the crackers and pickles?"

His chin dropped, but he recovered quickly. "Punch bowl?"

She nodded.

"In a saloon?"

She nodded again. In her grand palace.

"What the hell?" He threw up his hands. "Why not? This is like no saloon I've ever seen. You even managed to find an orchestra—of sorts."

Damn it all. How had she done it? He wouldn't have known where to round up one piano player and he was the best-informed man in Alder Gulch.

Chapter Fourteen

Seven o'clock. The ladies descended the stairs.

Anna had finished feeding and tucking in a very tired little boy. She caught up with the others as they looked in dismay at the tables spread across the dance floor.

Pearl, the only one who didn't seem the least bit nervous about the coming evening, locked her gaze on Billie. "Mr. Rawlins doesn't have a clue that you're turning his saloon into a dance hall, does he?"

Billie inhaled deeply, released a long, worried sigh, and began moving chairs against the wall. Everyone hesitantly pitched in until the seats were neatly arranged on either side of the room, all the while watching Billie with questioning eyes.

"Does he?" Pearl persisted.

Billie swallowed. The women anxiously awaited her answer. "Well . . ."

Pearl slapped her palm on a tabletop. "I knew it. I knew this was too good to be true." She shook her head. "Pack up, ladies. Two minutes after Mr. Rawlins comes through that door, we'll be leavin'."

"No!" Billie's voice rang with much more authority than she felt at that moment. "All that was mentioned in our agreement was that I had three months to turn the grand . . . Empty Barrel into a money-making proposition."

Pearl grinned. "Hope he made your 'proposition' worthwhile." She winked at Molly and Anna.

Billie sputtered. "I've already told you where I stand on *that* matter." Splaying her shaking hands on her hips, she cleared her throat and looked each woman in the eye. "If there are any complaints, state them now."

Like a cat worrying a mouse, Pearl couldn't let the subject drop. She took an indignant breath, nearly spilling her generous bosom from her low-cut, high-hemmed, tight-as-skin dress. "What about Mr. Rawlins? What if *he* wants us to entertain upstairs?"

"Did Mr. Rawlins hire you? And you'll follow *my* rules." Billie exhaled her breath in a huff. "Understood? This is the last time I want to hear about the subject."

Anna and Molly nodded.

Pearl glared for a long moment, but finally acquiesced. "Whatever you say. But if I decide to take a man someplace else, I keep the money. All of it."

"That's strictly your business," Billie agreed.

"Damn right." Pearl grinned saucily. "It's my *business.*"

Further discussion of the matter was brought to an end when Jack Dawkins and Eduardo Crespin banged through the front doors. Behind the men, Billie delightedly glimpsed several spectators craning their necks to peer inside. She glanced to the window. Blurred faces stared back at her. Someone even used his bandana to wipe away the grime in order to see better. She made a mental note to be sure to clean the outside of that window tomorrow.

She turned to face the door just as Lucky and another man squeezed through the gathering crowd. Lucky shrugged out of his jacket. "Joe, this is . . ." He got his first good look at Billie. His eyes widened. Then he glanced at the rest of the women. His jaw dropped. "My Gawd . . ."

Suddenly, Billie realized the other orchestra members were standing in the middle of the floor, also gawking at

her and her girls. She fidgeted for a second, then gave
them a shy smile.

"Miss Billie . . . you all look like . . . jewels."

She reached up, felt her necklace, and quickly lowered her hand. "Now, Mr. Lucky . . ." Yet, she had to
admit they all looked nice. She was even pleased with
her own appearance. Aqua was a good color on her,
and accented the rich sheen of her emeralds.

To get the group into action again, though, she introduced the ladies to the orchestra, then stepped back as
they all began talking about songs everyone knew.

Her gaze fell one by one on her dancers. Pride
swelled her chest. Even Pearl, in her typical risqué saloon garb, displayed her hourglass figure and rosy-
cheeked beauty to perfection. Molly's sweet gown set off
her youthful complexion and took the sting from her
worldly ways. And Anna. The blue silk, with a gathered
ruffle on the high collar and on the cuffs of her three-
quarter-length sleeves, emphasized her femininity, as did
the long, full skirts. Excitement and pride lent color to
her otherwise pale, plain features. Molly and Pearl had
pinned Anna's thick mass of brown hair in a curly array
atop her head, leaving several artfully teasing strands
loose. If they were all jewels, Billie thought, Anna was
the gemstone of the collection.

Billie started to wipe her damp palms down her skirt,
but fisted her fingers instead. Her gown was pristeen,
with its high neckline and long sleeves. Lace scalloped
the neck, which was cut only far enough to display the
emeralds, and ran from her waist to the hem to divide
the skirt into panels.

She sighed, thinking that even in St. Louis she
wouldn't have been able to find a more elegant gown.
Molly's workmanship was almost professional.

At last, Billie stood back and cast a last critical look
around the room. It wasn't yet the palace she imagined.
There was still so much to be done that it boggled her
mind, but . . . it would do for the first night.

The floor had been sanded and swept. Clean horse blankets covered the tables. The orchestra—she sighed and gazed heavenward as they attempted to tune their instruments—was in place. The bar, counter, and back bar had been polished until one could see one's reflection as clearly as in the three mirrors dividing the back panel.

Craig had the liquor bottles set within easy reach. He'd even chopped ice from the huge block he said had been dragged down from the mountains this spring. A scale was set to weigh gold dust for those men who didn't have currency.

Only five minutes until eight. All that was missing was the bartender. What was keeping Craig Rawlins?

Craig couldn't believe his bad luck. For the hundredth time, he checked his watch. What was keeping that damned payroll? Stuffing his hands into the pockets of his black evening pants, he paced back and forth in front of the bank.

One of the larger mines between Alder Gulch and Bannock had sent word they were sending a payroll and a month's earnings in gold to be locked in Craig's bank until Monday morning. Nothing would do but that Craig receive the delivery and assure the gold was locked inside the safe himself.

He snapped open the lid of his watch one more time. Five minutes until time to open the saloon. The gold was fifty-five minutes late. A worried frown creased his brow. What if the outlaws knew of the shipment? What if . . . he was late for Billie's big grand opening?

He rubbed his stomach, wondering if one of the knots he was feeling might be apprehension over even opening the Empty Barrel again. After all, he'd lost every partner he'd had there. He took a deep breath. Surely Billie was different. She had no connections in Alder

Gulch. No enemies. No score to settle. Surely no one would be hurt this time.

Sighing, he glanced down the empty street. Where was the damned wagon? If Billie thought he'd been a complete jerk about hiring Lucky, what would she think when he was late for her debut? He had no control over the payroll shipment, but he might have exercised better judgment where Lucky was concerned. He had been a mite hard-headed. Yep, he'd purposely gone out of his way to keep from hiring the miner. And now, he might have to go and—

"Here comes the wagon, boss."

Craig smashed his watch closed and quickly replaced it. Hell. There wasn't even time to let Billie know he would be just a little late.

At five minutes after eight, Billie opened the doors to, in her mind, the Grand Palace Dance Emporium.

Lucky slanted her a cocky grin from behind the bar. The orchestra struck up a lively tune. Pearl, Molly, and Anna smiled tremulously as a horde of men tried to push through the narrow opening at one time.

Billie took a deep breath and blocked the doorway. "Please, gentlemen. Read the sign. Only those of you who have taken baths and are wearing clean clothes may enter."

Loud grumbling vibrated through the crowd.

Billie held up her hand. "Anyone who follows the rules will be readily welcomed. We look forward to entertaining each and every one of you with dancing and the best in fine liquor."

Those men who were literate and had taken the time to read the sign and had cleaned themselves up, shoved to the forefront. Once they gained entrance, they stood spellbound by the changes that had been made in the place.

One man whispered to his friend, "Murdock . . . there ain't no gamblin' tables."

Another looked curiously around and questioned, "What's goin' on?"

"Gentlemen?" The din continued to rise. "Gentlemen!" Billie shouted. Only those closest few paid her any mind.

From the back of the room, a man said, "You hear what she called you, George? A gentleman. Haw! Haw!"

"What's a *gentleman?*"

"Where she think she is? New York damned City?"

"Aw right, ya blasted double-eared varmints. Listen to the lady." Molly's loud voice succeeded in quieting the throng.

Billie jerked her astounded gaze from Molly, then hesitantly stepped up on the bar's foot rail. "Gentlemen . . ." Her voice cracked as at last, every eye focused on her. Her throat constricted even more tightly, but she managed to croak, "Welcome to Alder Gulch's first dance emporium."

An excited buzz hummed through the crowd.

"Please come in and take a seat or stand at the bar. Mr. Rawlins has gone to considerable effort to afford you the finest drinking selections. The orchestra has a wonderful variety of music planned for your listening and dancing pleasure. The girls and—" she choked, "*I,* are available to dance with those of you willing to part with just one dollar." Her eyes closed. It was the longest speech she could remember making since her arrival in Alder Gulch. Her throat was dry. So dry. She reluctantly blinked her eyes open, afraid of what she might see.

The hum began to fade.

More grumbles echoed around the room. Some men turned and walked out. Others began filtering to the tables. Still more shoved through the door, trying to find out what was happening.

Lucky poured punch and dispensed drinks so quickly

she could hardly see his hands as they moved from one bottle to another.

But no one was dancing. The men sat at the tables, or along the walls, or stood at the bar, staring from the perspiring orchestra to the nervous women. Even Pearl had lost her usual saucy demeanor.

Billie's stomach sank to her toes. Sweat coated her palms.

"Uh-oh," Pearl whispered loudly enough for Billie to hear and pointed toward the door.

Billie glanced in that direction. Her heart froze. Standing in the center of the opening, his tall frame and broad chest effectively blocking the others from either leaving or entering, was Craig Rawlins. A thundercloud appeared about to rage from his eyes.

Uh-oh was right, thought Billie. He was going to stalk over and tell her what a fool she'd been, what an idiotic idea she'd had. What had ever made her think she could do something this important on her own?

He started toward her, moving large men, heavy men, tall men, *any* man in his way, aside as if they were mere weeds in his path. Her heart thawed and began to climb up her throat.

He stopped in front of her. She swallowed and backed up a step. He held out his hand. She stared at it, unable to fathom what he intended.

"Would you do me the honor?" He bowed slightly at the waist. His head canted at an angle so that his eyes never left hers.

She saw the storm still brewing in his gaze, but had no choice. This was, after all, a dance emporium. What impression would she give prospective customers if she refused her first offer?

"Y-you must f-first pay your dollar to the," she gulped, "bartender."

His eyes sparked fire. His nostrils flared.

She flinched, but stood her ground.

"Ahem. Yes, ma'am." Craig swallowed down the urge

to strangle the little liar. He was so angry he could have chewed the damned silver dollar and spit out pennies.

He mentally chided himself for letting her get to him again. When he'd first walked in the door, he'd been tempted to shut the place down. Then he'd seen Billie. Seen that familiar look of fear and despair. What could he do but play along with her? But just this one night.

After the saloon cleared tonight, when he had her all to himself, she'd get the dressing down . . . Poor image. He couldn't think of her dressing—or undressing—right now. What was it he'd been promising himself? Oh, yes. He would give her a real piece . . . damn . . . of his mind.

He strode over to the bar, glowered at Lucky, paid his dollar and received a wood chip in return. Stalking back to Billie, he handed the chip, and with a slight click of his boot heels, said, "Now . . . Would you care to dance?"

She dropped the token into a special pocket on her gown, then tentatively placed her fingertips on his muscled forearm, allowing him to lead her to the center of the dance floor.

Jack Dawkins ran his bow across the strings of his fiddle and announced loudly, "All hands round." Billie's surprised gaze darted to the fiddler, who shrugged and smiled as the orchestra began to play "Lily Dale."

Craig turned her to face him. Her flesh quivered before he even touched her. She sucked in her breath as his arms came around her. She closed her eyes, willing herself not to panic. After all, she'd danced with him once before. Her eyes blinked open. He held her firmly, but at a distance. It was going to be all right. He guided her deftly to the rhythm of the music. His steps were sure and graceful, his hands warm and supportive. She felt weightless and almost giddy. It was going to be fine.

Craig felt the subtle changes in her body as the tension began to ease. As pleased as he was that she was beginning to feel comfortable around him, he had to ask, "Billie?"

She swayed close to his body. "Uhmm?"

"What made you think you could turn my saloon into a dance hall?" He spat the last two words with distaste.

Billie blinked. She was enjoying the dance. "Wh-what?"

"What idiotic notion caused you to ruin my saloon?"

Her mind snapped to attention. Idiotic? She caught her boot on his toe. "It's a wonderful plan. We'll both make a fortune," she hissed. "Just you wait and see."

"Set your partners." Jack called the end of the dance. "Parade to the bar."

Billie glanced again toward the fiddle player, impressed by his knowledgeable handling of the situation. Why hadn't he mentioned his experience earlier, and eased some of her trepidation?

Then she looked around the room at the staring sea of faces, the empty dance floor, and doubted the confident declaration she'd made to Craig.

"All hands round." The orchestra started "Sweet Betsy From Pike."

Several men stood up and casually strolled toward the bar. When they saw others heading in the same direction, they rushed the remaining few feet to pay their dollar.

The next thing Billie knew, a grinning miner came to a stop in front of her, nodded to Craig, handed over a chip, and wiped his hands on his pantleg. Shyly, he held out his arms. Over his shoulder, she saw a young man leading a pursed-mouth Molly to the floor. Then Pearl was robustly swung into a round of boot-stomping circles.

Billie inhaled and took the gigantic step into the man's waiting arms. She had not time to think of being afraid as she, too, swung around and around until she had to close her eyes to keep from becoming dizzy.

For the next hour, Billie was whirled from one pair of

arms to another. Every girl danced every dance. Craig and Lucky were both busy behind the bar. And joining the male–female pairs, number upon number of men danced with men for the pure pleasure of it. Some vocal fellows had pulled a table near the stage and were singing accompaniment to the music.

The orchestra took a ten-minute break to rest their burning fingers and to quench their thirst. Room was made for the women to sit at the tables and ease their aching feet. Lucky hurried over with a precious pitcher of iced water and glasses. They all downed at least one glassful, but Pearl grimaced, set her glass on the table, and shouted, "Who's gonna buy a thirsty gal a real drink?"

A fight nearly broke out when over ten men held out their pokes. Craig quickly diffused the prickly situation by pouring free punch for the "losers." He frowned toward Pearl, then shot a warning glance at Billie.

She deciphered his message perfectly. Tomorrow, there would be a few new rules added to the list.

Much too soon for Billie's tender toes, the orchestra returned and played the first strains of a slow waltz. A huge man, wearing a too-small suit, came to stand in front of her and held out a token. He grinned, exposing crooked, stained teeth.

She suppressed a shudder and held out her hand. If the man paid his dollar, he was due a dance. He snatched her arm and dragged her to the floor where he embraced her in a gigantic bear hug. Holding her so tightly she could hardly catch her breath, he moved his lower body suggestively against her.

Unlike the men she'd danced with earlier, this one frightened her. Suffocating fear surged into her throat. She tried to pull her hand free from his ham-sized fist.

"What'sa matter, honey? After this here dance, let's you an' me go upstairs."

His rubbery lips slobbered over her cheek. She struggled harder. He huffed his foul breath in her face. She gagged and twisted her head. Her eyes locked with Craig's and she quickly averted her gaze. It wouldn't do at all for him to think the proprietress of a dance emporium could be frightened almost immobile by the first man who became aggressive.

She gulped several deep breaths. It didn't help. Nausea choked her. Again he rubbed against her and she tried to free herself.

Suddenly, the man stopped moving. But his hand tightened around her waist, trapping her to his massive body.

"Whadda ya want?" the giant growled.

Billie realized he wasn't talking to her. She looked around to find Craig standing beside them.

Craig Rawlins smiled genially at the big man. "There's a free drink at the bar. Someone said *it*, and two more, were for you."

The big man's eyes narrowed suspiciously. "Free?"

Craig thumbed the man's gaze toward Lucky, who held up a schooner of beer.

"For me?"

"That's what he said."

Gradually, the grip on Billie was eased. He couldn't keep from staring at the tall, foaming glass. Finally, he headed toward the bar, pulling Billie with him.

Craig stepped into his path. "Sorry. Got to keep my girls busy."

The fellow frowned, smacked his drooling lips, and shoved Billie toward Craig. "Hang on to her for me, pal. This won't take long."

Billie turned and headed for the kitchen, thinking to find a few minutes alone. She was cut off after two steps. Looking up, her eyes were captured by Craig's intense gaze.

"Now you see what a stupid idea this was."

"*Is*," she corrected. Drawing up her chin, she conceded, "There are always a few troublemakers in any business. We just have to stay a step ahead of them."

"Like you did with the giant?"

She swallowed. "I'm new at this. Next time——"

His eyebrows shot up at her confession of being "new at this," but he was too worried about the danger she could have been in if he hadn't come to her defense.

"How many next times are you willing to risk before you run up against something you can't think your way out of?" He stared at her defiant features, the slight quiver in her lower lip. A shiver spiraled down his spine, as he suddenly realized she'd somehow squirreled her way into his mind—into his life. The thought of losing her was painful.

All at once, he drew her into the kitchen shadows. He lowered his head and took her lips in a kiss whose spontaneity surprised him.

A kiss was the last thing Billie expected after his scolding. Caught off guard, she was pleasantly surrounded by the warmth of his hard, smooth mouth and the security of his embrace. His masculine scent, sensual mastery, and extreme tenderness slipped through her protective barricade and teased her senses.

Unconsciously, her hands slipped beneath his jacket, and she splayed her fingers across the taut muscles on his back. Soothing strains of music wafted into the darkened kitchen. Her eyelids fluttered shut. Her knees weakened and she swayed forward.

Craig felt the delicate softness of her feminine form and wrapped his arms more tightly around her. She fit against him perfectly. He groaned with pleasure as his lips sought the throbbing pulse at the base of her throat.

His hot breath tickled. She shivered and felt the constriction of his embrace. A tightness began to build in her chest. Her eyes blinked open. Apprehension and anticipation battled for dominance. Her breath came in sharp gasps as she lifted her head and pushed away from him.

Craig was also breathing heavily. Driving his fingers through the hair that had fallen across his forehead, he said, "Sorry. That shouldn't have happened." What in the devil had gotten into him? All he needed was a cape and fangs, the way he'd swooped down upon the woman. He'd never done anything like that before. Usually he considered all the consequences before engaging in any type of relationship with a woman. And then along came Miss Chaos. He slowly turned and, rubbing the back of his neck, walked away. This strange turn of events was something he needed to think about.

Billie ran the fingers of one hand across her damp lips. Lordy, she tingled all over. Her insides felt like they'd been set on fire. She couldn't take her eyes off the man, even when he shrugged helplessly and headed back to the bar.

Well after midnight, Billie sighed with exhaustion as she sank onto her new bed and feather mattress for the first time. The soles of her feet burned. Her ankles were swollen. She didn't think she'd ever worked so hard.

But it was a good tired. By the time Jack Dawkins had called out, "Last dance, gentlemen. Only this one before the girls go home," every chair had been taken and men stood two and three deep around the bar. A satisfied grin curved her lips. Craig had asked Lucky to stay on as bartender. It had been all the two of them could do to keep up with the orders.

Craig Rawlins had even promised not to be late the next evening. The thought made her chuckle sleepily. Shortly after opening the doors to the Grand Palace Dance Emporium, she'd have sworn there wouldn't be a next night.

She stretched and wriggled her toes. A pleasant warmth invaded her insides at the thought of her partner. He wasn't nearly the bear he wanted everyone to think he was.

With the shock he'd received upon entering his establishment, he could have stood by and let the evening deteriorate to the point where all he needed to say was, "I told you so." But he'd had the decency to take charge and ask her to dance. And he'd come to her rescue when the giant wouldn't let her go. Come to think of it, she'd never seen the beast again. What had happened to him?

Now the emporium was being given another chance. *She* had a second chance. The girls and Danny's mother had a decent place to live and work. Lucky had a job.

Craig Rawlins was a good man. She'd learned first-hand how much he cared for the people in his community. In his own way, he'd taken Danny and Anna Corbett under his wing even before she'd offered them the opportunity to work for her.

Quite a few of the businessmen she'd approached and asked for work last week had come into the emporium tonight. They appeared to respect Craig and had taken him aside for a serious conversation. She'd heard only a few snippets as she'd been danced by the group, but by the end of the evening she'd surmised another gold shipment had been stolen. Two men had been killed. She was certain she'd heard mention of a Vigilance Committee. She shuddered. What did they want from Craig?

She yawned and pulled the blanket up to her chin. Craig. Reaching up, her hand grazed the necklace before she traced the outline of her lips with her fingers. The kiss. The kiss had been . . . spectacular. She'd never thought that the mere touching of lips could set off such fireworks in her body. She'd certainly never experienced the explosive sensation with any other man.

Why Craig Rawlins? What exactly was it that set him apart from anyone she'd ever known? She liked him. Genuinely liked him. Even considered him a friend. Who else would sacrifice time from a busy schedule to look after someone he hardly knew?

A friend. What a nice thought.

* * *

"Hot damn. Flapjacks." Danny scooted forward in his chair. "An' ain't that real butter?"

Anna rolled her eyes at her son's continued use of profanity.

Billie sat next to the boy. "One of the men who came by last night traded the butter for a dance." At Danny's look of utter delight, she asked, "Was it a good trade?"

"Mumph. Damn right!"

"Danny," Anna scolded. "Don't talk with yore mouth full. An' quit that swearin'."

Molly shuffled sleepily into the kitchen. All of her energy seemed concentrated on the effort it took to pull up a chair and sit down. She rubbed her bleary eyes, sniffed, and suddenly sat up straight. "Do I smell flapjacks?"

"Yep. Ma's makin' 'em. An' there's real butter."

Billie smothered a grin when Molly's young features became almost as animated as Danny's.

They were almost finished with breakfast by the time Pearl ambled into the room, but all she wanted was a cup of coffee. Billie gave her a chance to finish before broaching the subject of rules.

She inhaled, exhaled, and inhaled again. "While we're gathered together this morning, I want to thank you all for helping to make our opening night a success." She twined her fingers in her lap. "There were a few minor incidents, but everything seemed to go smoothly . . . except for one thing Mr. Rawlins asked me to mention."

Pearl grimaced. "I have a feeling I know what it is. I didn't know my askin' for someone to buy me a drink was going to start a brawl. This place is different from those other places I been in, and I just didn't think. It won't happen again."

The breath Billie had been holding released in one gush of air. "Thanks, Pearl. I imagine it will take a while for *all* of us to adjust."

Flushing scarlet, Anna asked, "Did we take in as much as ya'd hoped?"

"I don't know. Mr. Rawlins took the night's receipts to the bank. Maybe he'll tell us later how well we did."

Pearl frowned. "You're a partner in this operation, aren't you?"

"Y-yes."

"And we work for you. Wouldn't it be smart for you to be there whenever he counts *our* money?"

"Uhmm . . ." Billie didn't have an immediate answer. She'd never thought about it. Never considered that Craig Rawlins wouldn't be honest with her.

As if sensing her indecision, Pearl narrowed her eyes and prodded, "He's a man, isn't he? And you can't trust one of the sons . . . suckers any further than you could a hungry weasel in a hen house."

Chapter Fifteen

True to his word, when the emporium opened the next evening, Craig was already there, helping Lucky with the punch bowl and replenishing the crackers and pickles. Anna had baked fresh bread, so they sliced the loaves and set out tins of sardines. Though Billie wrinkled her nose, Craig assured her the men would like the repast.

Once the doors opened, it was almost a repeat of the night before. Until the bar became busy, Lucky took over the job of standing in the doorway, making sure all that entered appeared to have made an attempt at bathing. Damp, slicked-back hair, and freshly scrubbed faces were the common sight as men began to wander inside, purchase drinks, and find a place to sit. Conversation was more subdued and the trouble encountered by the last freight wagon was on everyone's mind.

While shaking a champagne cocktail, Craig noticed several of the other saloon owners coming in to check out the competition. From the smiles on their faces, he assumed they were pleased he was offering something different instead of competing with them directly, as the Empty Barrel had always done before.

Watching Craig from the corner of her eye, Billie admired the handsome figure he cut as he proficiently went about the business of mixing exotic drinks. When his head turned in her direction, she quickly shifted her gaze to the girls standing near the stage. They all wore the same dresses as the previous night, but she hoped the receipts after two nights would be rewarding enough to purchase more material. They needed a good selection of gowns.

Once he'd spotted her through the crowd, Craig surreptitiously kept his eyes on Billie, noticing things he'd been too preoccupied to heed the night before. Though modestly cut, her aqua gown accentuated every hill and valley of her slender, but curvaceous, figure. The gathered skirt swayed with each graceful movement of her hips. Both the gown and the emerald necklace drew attention to burnished highlights in her hair that were warmer and richer in color than his best aged brandy. Yet, when she stood beneath a lantern, as she was doing now, the strawberry-blond in her hair sparkled, lending her that aggravating angelic appeal.

Shaking his head, he forced his attention from the enticing woman to the rapidly filling room. He scowled at the men sitting quietly in their chairs or leaning against the walls. What was wrong with them? They never acted so shy and retiring in the other saloons.

He slipped a dollar into the cash box, hesitated, added another, and pocketed two dance chips. Then, motioning for Lucky to take over the bar, he wiped his hands on a towel and walked to where Billie stood fidgeting and twisting her fingers together. As before, he bowed slightly and held out his hand, displaying one of the wooden chips. His pulse leaped when she didn't hesitate to accept.

She gave him a diffident smile. His chest constricted. He hadn't seen her smile more than once or twice since they'd met. He'd like to see the upward tilt to her lips more often. When she smiled, even so uncertainly, her entire face smiled. Her eyes twinkled. Her teeth gleamed. Her cheeks blushed prettily and rosily. She literally stole his breath.

The orchestra finished the tune they were playing and

began a slow ballad. Craig stifled a groan when he pulled her into his arms. An ever-increasing sense of *rightness* settled over him. Her tall form nestled against him perfectly. She was soft and feminine and . . .

He stiffened. What was he thinking? She operated a saloon. Though she termed it a dance emporium, it was still just a glorified saloon. And the rooms upstairs . . . reminded him of a dozen different places he'd grown up in—though so far they were used only for sleeping.

He glanced down at the top of Billie's head, at her shining tresses, her delicate feminity. She hid a mysterious past, and though it gave her a certain allure, she was still just a woman who worked in a saloon. The type of woman he'd always vowed to avoid.

His eyes shuttered as he swung her in step with the music. His grip tightened on her hand. She flinched and he quickly loosened the pressure.

Damn it, he hadn't thought about his mother in ages. Now, suddenly, it was as if the years melted away and he was seven or eight again. His mother had been a prostitute. She hadn't known who his father was, she'd hauled him around with her until one day, she just gave him away.

His heart thudded against his breast. How could a mother give away her child? Sure, there'd been other children, food, clothes that fit. But the man, the head of the family . . . the monster in coveralls . . . He mentally shook the disturbing thought from his mind.

Eventually he'd clawed his way from the degradation of being labeled a whore's bastard to a position of wealth and respect. Now his fortune ensured that no one would dare risk knocking him down again. He'd earned the title of successful entrepreneur. And he'd done it on his own merit.

"Mr. Rawlins?"

He stubbed his toe on her boot.

"Craig?"

"Sorry. Didn't mean to step on you." He started to twirl her again.

"Craig! The music has stopped."

He blinked. He heard the buzz of deep voices and a few soft chuckles. "So it has." Heat burned his cheeks as he led her from the dance floor.

"Is there something wrong?"

He cleared his throat. "Yes. You need better shoes."

She lifted her chin. "At least the boots protect my feet from clumsy dancers."

He frowned and started to remind her that his treading on her foot was an accident. But when he looked into her eyes, he saw nothing but a teasing twinkle. She was joking with him. The dash of humor snapped him from his reverie faster than a bucket of ice water.

"Your feet have to hurt, wearing those clumsy things all day, and at night, too."

She glanced away so he wouldn't see her hurt. What choice did she have until extra money was available? She sniffed. "There's something I need more than fancy shoes."

He quirked a brow.

"Did we make enough profit last night to buy more material?"

"Material? What do you need that for?"

"The girls and I need more gowns."

He gazed from the soft mass of red-gold hair piled atop her head, down the length of the elegant gown to the tips of brown leather boots peeking from beneath the full skirt. He couldn't help a slight twitch of his lips. "There's nothin' wrong with the dress you're wearin'. Why do you need another?"

She stepped away and fisted her hands on her hips. "Do you wear the same clothes every night?"

"Sometimes," he choked.

"Well," she gasped. "That's all a man knows. I should think you, of all people, would want us looking attractive and appealing to the customers. They won't want to pay to see us looking the same night after night."

For some reason, he liked the notion of all the other men finding her unattractive. However, she'd made a valid point. Bored customers meant bad business.

He shrugged. "I guess we did pretty good last night. I suppose you could buy some material." She grinned, and his heart flipped upside down.

When the orchestra struck up another song, and the men began asking the other ladies to dance, Craig discovered he wasn't ready to give her up just yet. "Dance with me one more time?"

Unsure as to whether it was proper, Billie nevertheless found it difficult to refuse when he pressed the second chip into her hand. She liked dancing with him. Enjoyed the strength and warmth of his tall body. He pressed her closer than before. She felt no momentary panic and reveled in the haven of security she'd found in the arms of this man. The arms of her partner. The arms of Craig Rawlins. The man who'd looked after her and been kind to her. A man she respected.

His right hand engulfed hers. Their fingers threaded together. Tiny shock waves heated her palm. His left hand settled firmly at her waist. Her skin rippled. She felt a sizzling imprint from each of his fingers, even through several layers of clothing. She might as well be wearing nothing at all, so vivid was his touch.

His leg moved sensuously between hers when he spun her out of the way of a miner who thought he and Molly were dancing to a merry hoedown rather than a waltz. She stiffened, but then sighed and gave in to the pleasure of the movement and the music.

Across the room, men turned their heads and made room for someone to come through the doorway.

Sunny Turnbow, smothered by the crowd, called over her shoulder, "Hurry up, Justin. There's an empty space ahead." She pushed her way inside. Taking in the milling men and the busy dance floor, her steps slowed and finally stopped at the edge of a row of tables. Her dark eyes rounded as she stared openmouthed at the changes that had been made.

Toe-tapping music drew her attention once again to the dance floor and raised stage. An orchestra. No one had mentioned there would be an orchestra. Brightly colored gowns attracted her gaze. Besides the stomping male couples, there were four beautiful women from whom the men could choose.

Lips pursed, she was about to return to the bar when one couple made a spectacular spin and she saw Craig swinging that . . . Billie person.

"Craig darlin', over here," she called. But Craig either didn't hear or paid her no mind. His eyes were half closed and he seemed lost to everything and everyone except the music and the woman he squired.

White-hot rage seared her. Her eyes sparked fire. Suddenly she spun and headed toward the door. Justin had finally managed to clear the mass of humanity when she grabbed his arm, turned him around, and shoved him in front of her.

Outside, she fumed, "Why that no-good two-timer. I've wasted some of the best months of my life on that ungrateful man."

Justin frowned. "What happened?"

"Craig an' that . . . that scarecrow. That's what happened. He led me on. That's what he did. He ruined everything. Ruined my life."

"But, Mother . . ." Justin hurried behind her, his longer legs hardly able to keep up with her furious pace. "You don't need him." He huffed and puffed and gasped, "You've got me."

"Yes, yes. That's nice." Sunny secured some strands of hair that had fallen loose during her vigorous walk. "I'm not giving up. Mr. Craig Rawlins will be mine."

* * *

Several hours later, Craig watched Lucky mix drinks. "You know, you're good at this."

Lucky grinned. "It's my profession. At least when I'm not standing knee-deep in freezing water or shoveling buckets of mud and rock."

"Your profession?"

"Mixologist." Lucky grinned. "Miss Billie acted real pleased when I told her. Didn't know she was gonna end up bein' my boss." He cocked his head to the side and eyed Craig. "Half boss."

Craig hunched his shoulders. So that was why she was so insistent that he hire Lucky. She'd heard him turn down Lucky's loan. Knew Lucky needed work and that the saloon needed a bartender. Why hadn't she just come out and told him instead of letting him think . . . believe . . . Or had he jumped to conclusions and not given her a chance to explain?

A commotion from the dance floor snapped his gaze in that direction. The orchestra was between songs and two men were arguing over which one would dance next with Billie. One had pulled a knife and everyone gave the pair a wide berth, except for Billie, whose forearm was caught in the other man's harsh grip.

The taller man, whose right cheek was scarred, pointed the tip of his blade toward the other fellow. "I wanna dance with 'er."

"Ah got here first," the long-haired, mustachioed man holding Billie drawled.

"Don't give a damn. She's dancin' with me."

"Ah got her. Ah'm keepin' her." He yanked Billie closer.

Billie gasped, "Gentlemen, please . . . I can't dance with you both at the same time. You've got to take your turn."

The one holding her said belligerently, "Fine. Ah'm first."

The knife tip wavered toward Billie. She watched it,

a little nervous, but, amazingly discovered she wasn't all that scared. "This isn't the way to cut in."

The scar-faced miner suddenly demanded, "Come over here, little lady. You an' me'll heat up them floorboards."

"Please—"

"Put the knife away, mister," Craig said softly as he eased up close to Billie.

"An' what if I don't?" The tall man waved the blade recklessly close to Billie.

"Then you won't be welcome here again." Craig glanced toward the mustachioed man. "That goes for you, too, if you don't let the lady go." He kept a tight rein on his temper, afraid if he followed his instinct to fight, she'd get hurt.

The taller fellow laughed. "Hear that, Simpson? We won't be welcome. Now ain't that a fine howdy do?"

The man named Simpson snorted. "Reckon we ain't so *gentlemanly* aftah all, eh, missy?" He jerked Billie's arm.

"Please . . . You're hurting me."

Craig took another step closer. "Look, we don't want trouble. Come on up to the bar and I'll buy you both a drink. *After* you put the knife down and release the woman."

For a minute it appeared they were considering his offer. But then Simpson pulled Billie into his arms. "Nah, Ah'd rather dance with the *lady.*"

Liquor on his breath. Hurtful hands. Black images assaulted Billie's mind. She sucked in her breath, but couldn't get any air. Violent shudders rocked her body.

"Hey? What the devil's the matter with her?" Simpson stepped back.

Everyone's attention turned to Billie. Craig took the moment of opportunity to yank Billie from the man's grasp and swing her clear of danger. She stumbled, but Anna grabbed her arm and pulled her to safety.

Pain sliced through Craig's upper arm. He winced,

realizing his heroism had won him a knife wound. He focused on Scarface as the man brought the blade up to take another swipe. Craig kicked his wrist. The knife rattled across the floor and under the stage.

With Craig's back partially turned, Simpson locked his hands together and swung his arms like a club. The crowd shouted warnings. Craig sensed the blow coming and ducked. Simpson's knuckles hit his partner square on the end of the nose. Bellowing with pain and rage, the taller man fell to his knees and covered his bleeding nose.

A feral grin curved Craig's lips. His right fist buried into Simpson's gut. His left clipped the man's chin. Simpson fell next to Scarface.

Breathing heavily, Craig rubbed his bruised knuckles and grated, "Are you leavin' peaceably, or do you want some more?"

"We're goin'. We're goin'," the scar-faced man hissed, barely understandable, with one hand still holding his nose. With his free hand, he helped Simpson to his feet. A path opened for them as they staggered to the door.

Gentle hands touched Craig's arm. Taken by surprise, he jerked and spun, only to find Billie rolling up his sleeve. "What're you doin'?"

"You're bleeding. Come to the kitchen where I can see better." She started toward the kitchen, thinking he would follow. When she missed the warmth from his body, she stopped and looked over her shoulder. He just stood there, staring. "Well, are you coming, or not?"

Undecided, Craig glanced fretfully around to see that Lucky had brought a towel and was wiping up the blood. But nobody else moved. Craig sighed. With a payroll missing and two men dead, maybe a fight had been inevitable. The town was just itching to let off steam. Catching Hanshaw's eye, he nodded to indicate that the orchestra should begin playing. Within minutes, dancing resumed.

He flinched when fingers curled around his hand. His eyes locked with Billie's.

"Come with me. Please?" She tugged insistently.

Unable to resist the husky plea, he trailed after her like a puppy on a leash. He was amazed that she was so adamant about caring for him. His heart thrummed double-time. Why? Why was she concerned about him?

Billie made him sit. He hung his jacket neatly on the back of his chair while she filled a basin with water and set it on the stove to heat. When she turned back to him, he'd already finished rolling up his sleeve.

"It's just a scratch."

Her eyes narrowed on the long, ugly gash. She quickly went over and dipped the end of a towel into the warm water, then cleaned the wound. He winced as a trickle of water dripped into the cut. She flinched at his pain, but continued her ministrations.

"Why are you doin' this?" he demanded.

She frowned. "Why wouldn't I?"

"I—I . . . don't know."

"As many times as you've helped me since I arrived in Alder Gulch, shouldn't I return the favor?"

The tightness in his chest eased. A favor. *That* he understood. No one had ever done anything for him out of the goodness of their heart. There was always a deal, or a business proposition, or money involved.

"Ouch!"

"Sorry. I've got to get this clean so it won't get infected. No telling what that man had used his knife for."

Her fingers brushed his bare flesh. He headed off a shiver of delight. She was tender, but sure in her actions. "Have you done this much before?"

She blinked, then shook her head.

"Then how do you know what you're doin'? I hope you're not using me for some sort of practice." He was only half joking.

"I just meant that I'm not that familiar with knife cuts. But I've doctored other wounds." She specifically remembered many occasions when she'd helped the servants with burns or scrapes. And her stepbrother had needed her help a time or two after he'd gotten into fights. A shudder rippled down her spine. It seemed he'd always been fighting over something.

"Are you cold?" Craig reached for his jacket.

"No. No, I'm fine."

"What were you thinkin' about?"

"I . . . Blood. I just don't like the sight or taste of blood." She stiffened. Taste? Where had that thought come from? When would she have ever tasted something so horrible? Another chill raked her spine.

This time Craig didn't ask, but draped the coat over her shoulders. The backs of his fingers brushed the flesh above her bodice. A red-hot current sped from his hand to his lower belly. He shifted uneasily in the chair.

The accidental contact jerked Billie from vague images of the past back into the present. Grateful to take her mind off the disturbing subject, she fetched the hot water and thoroughly cleaned the wound. Then, taking a clean cloth from a drawer, she tore it into two strips. One she folded into a pad. The other she used to bind the pad to the wound.

"There. That should stop the bleeding. In a while, we'll clean it again and use an antiseptic."

He tilted his head toward the main room. "Got a whole case behind the bar."

"You mean whiskey?"

He nodded.

"Surely we can find something better."

"Like what?"

"Well . . ."

"Whiskey'll do just fine."

Anna tiptoed into the kitchen. "How is he?"

Craig flushed. *"He's* goin' to live."

Anna's cheeks filled with color. "Good. We were all worried." She turned to leave.

"Wait. I appreciate your concern. Is everything all right out there?"

Anna shuffled her feet, but nodded.

"We'll be back in shortly."

She nodded again and fled.

Craig frowned. "Don't know why that woman acts so timid around me. I don't bite." He winked at Billie. "Too hard." In fact, he bit back the urge to remind her again what a risky idea this emporium thing was. She might get the miners to dress like dandies, but acting like them was something else. But he refrained from telling her so. She'd been so sweet . . . And he liked the way she fussed over him.

The look in Craig's eyes caused liquid heat to flow through Billie's veins. She felt it sizzle all the way from her fingers, through her insides, and down to her toes. Her nerve endings were so sensitized that she felt the teasing huff of his breath.

When Billie also turned tail and ran, Craig scowled. These ladies could do tremendous damage to a man's self-confidence. Chuckling, he got up and went back to the bar. Though his injured arm had stiffened, once he started working, he was able to pour and mix with just a slight ache.

No matter how hard he tried to concentrate on what he was doing, his eyes kept drifting to the dance floor. His gaze followed Billie as she twirled with one man after another. Her lips would move. A man would smile or laugh. Yet he never saw *her* smile.

And even from the bar, he could see her body tense ever so slightly each time a man put his arms around her to guide her through a dance. Her reaction was always the same. Something had happened to cause her apprehension. But what?

At least she didn't seem to be as frightened of *him* now. She didn't flinch and pull away anymore. Maybe he'd begun to win her trust.

A slow grin curved his lips. What she needed was

constant presence, sincere companionship, consistent touching. It would be his pleasure, as a red-blooded male, to do his part in easing her fear and gentling her. After all, she was as precious and unique as the high-strung horses on his ranch. She needed an easy, guiding hand.

A few minutes before closing, Lucky handed Craig a dollar, took a dance chip, and walked nonchalantly over to Anna. Craig arched a brow. The woman ducked her head and shyly nodded. Craig stifled a grin. His bartender's smile could have lit the town for a two-mile radius.

Several men approached the bar and requested beers. "Sorry, fellas," Craig told them. "We're closing up soon."

One of the men shrugged and slapped the top of the counter. "Ya got a good business, Rawlins. I sure never s'pected to say this, but it's kinda nice to wash the mud off an' come to a *genteel* place."

Another man standing nearby agreed. "Yeah. Reminds me some of home. Makes me not quite so lonely."

As the crowd began to file out, Craig thought about what they'd said. Their perceptions matched exactly the atmosphere Billie had hoped to create. And if he was any judge of his new partner, she probably had a few more projects being planned to make the saloon even better. Maybe . . . just maybe . . . there was something to this idea of hers. Business was certainly booming. And it wouldn't hurt to hire more women.

Fifteen minutes later, Craig closed the door behind Lucky and the boys in the orchestra. When he turned back, he chuckled. All four ladies were sprawled in quite *un*ladylike positions, with their feet propped up, exposing a few daintily turned ankles—several of which were swollen from too much dancing.

Pearl fanned her face with the hem of her skirt. "How we doin', boss?"

He noticed that she consistently looked at him rather than Billie. Perhaps it would be a good idea to start going over the books and receipts with Billie. That way she would know everything about the business and be able to answer the girl's questions.

But not tonight. She looked exhausted. The fight. His injury. Dancing every dance. Even a hearty soul would be drained. Since arriving in Alder Gulch, Billie's recovery had been remarkable, but Craig couldn't so quickly forget her condition when he'd first seen her.

He walked over and placed his hand briefly on Billie's shoulder. "Tomorrow we'll take the receipts into your office and find out exactly how well we've done. All right?"

Billie gulped. "Uhmmm, sure."

He felt a tautening of her muscles and noticed a warmth seep into her eyes that hadn't been there before he touched her. He smiled and removed his hand. Gentling her was best done slowly, always leaving her wanting more.

His arm began to throb and he rubbed it. "Sleep tight, ladies. See you in the mornin'."

"Oh no you don't. You're not leaving yet."

Everyone looked at Billie, who was standing and crooking her finger at Craig.

"I told you, we need to doctor that wound before you leave."

Chapter Sixteen

Craig held out his hands and backed up a step. "Thanks anyway, but it's fine. If it needs to be cleaned, I can do it at home."

"But you won't." Billie shook her head. She rose stiffly from the chair and hobbled toward the kitchen. "Come on. And bring some of that . . . antiseptic."

"Yes, ma'am." Craig gave a mock salute, said good night to the trio of girls filing up the stairs, and tucked two bottles under his good arm. Hooding his eyes, he glanced at the row of clean glasses and snatched up two as he went by.

Billie had water heating and was tearing another clean towel into strips by the time he arrived and set the bottles and glasses on the table. She cocked a wary brow. "What's all that for?"

After removing his jacket, he sat in the same chair he'd occupied earlier. Then he lifted the cheap whiskey. "This is for the cut." Then he pointed to the other, very expensive, bottle of aged brandy. "That's for a toast."

"Toast? What, exactly, do you want to toast?" she asked as she began removing the old bandage.

"Ouch!"

"Oh, did that hurt?" she asked innocently. She hadn't meant to pull the pad off so quickly, but the cloth had stuck to the wound and would have hurt much more had she removed it more slowly. Besides, he deserved to suffer a little. The man had spent the entire evening making her infinitely aware of his presence.

The hot water stung and Craig clamped his teeth together. The woman wouldn't drag another word of complaint past his lips. She'd invented her own special form of torture and looked much too pleased.

"Now this might sting a tiny bit."

When she poured the whiskey over the wound, he nearly forgot his intent to keep quiet. The only sound he made, though, was his breath hissing between his teeth.

"Well, it wasn't as bad as I thought it might be," she chirped. But seeing the sweat beading his forehead and his hooded expression, Billie cleared her throat, wishing she could snatch back her silly comment. Instead, she took pity and wrapped the injury as gently as possible. She had to admit that seeing him in real pain caused her stomach to roil. Any aggravation she'd felt had evaporated as quickly as dew in the desert.

Contrition ached in her chest. He wouldn't have been hurt in the first place if it wasn't for her. Once again he'd stepped in and plucked her from a prickly situation.

"You never said what you intended to toast."

Craig started. He'd been staring at her profile while she studiously secured the bandage. She had all of the classic features—high forehead, straight nose, rounded cheekbones and hollow cheeks, and a delicate jaw. In the lanternlight, her skin looked as soft and healthy and delectable as a plump, ripe apricot.

A devastating urge to touch her, to feel if her flesh was as velvety as it looked, surged through his fingers. With extreme gentleness, he slid the backs of his knuckles down her cheek. His gut knotted. She felt much, much softer than she looked.

Billie jumped when he touched her. It might have been a moth, the brush had been so brief. She inhaled and held her breath. No one had ever caressed her like that before, so soft and sweet. She gave him a shy smile.

He watched her eyes warm like simmering honey. That reaction was for him alone, and he knew it. But rather than explore further in that direction, he preferred to find out why she tensed around other men.

"Who's hurt you, Angel? Who's caused you to shy away from a man?"

She gasped. "Why, I—I . . . don't know." Tears blurred her vision, but they were a result of the husky timbre of his voice, the deep growl that indicated his concern.

Yes, she was frightened of men, but couldn't tell him why.

Craig caught one of her hands and held it. "It's all right. You don't have to tell me anything if you don't want to."

How reassuring his touch was, how kind. She sniffled and cleared her throat. "What about that toast?"

Reluctantly releasing her cold hand, Craig poured them each a small glass of brandy. His lips twitched when Billie surprised him by eagerly accepting hers. He tapped the rim of her glass with his. "Here's to the success of the Empty Barrel." He took a healthy sip and felt the warmth ease down his throat.

"To the Grand Palace," she whispered, and took a tiny swallow. Her nose wrinkled. The back of her throat burned.

Craig frowned. "Did you say somethin'?"

She coughed and ducked her head. "I think of the emporium as a grand palace. At least, maybe it will be soon."

He chuckled. "I've got to admit it, you've spruced the old dog up. It's grander than any place in town."

She smiled and took another sip of brandy. "Thank you."

He smiled back.

* * *

During the next few days, the girls kept busy cutting material for new gowns. Molly did most of the stitching, with Pearl helping when something elaborate was needed. Downstairs, Billie and Anna hung curtains and fashioned brightly colored ribbons into bows to decorate each end of the five beams.

In the afternoons Billie enjoyed walking by the creek and picking wildflowers. Craig let her use the fancy glasses he seldom needed for vases. Every night there were colorful fresh bouquets of yarrow, columbine, and Indian paintbrush.

Inside the Grand Palace things were going smoothly. Outside, Billie often listened to concerns about supplies and passengers bound for Alder Gulch. One evening she overheard a group of men talking about the war. She'd been so caught up in the town's troubles and her dance emporium that she'd almost forgotten there was a civil war tearing the nation apart.

Not daring to ask who was winning in a room full of supporters of both sides, she nevertheless asked a man she'd danced with on several occasions if he knew what was happening in the East.

"Just got a paper off the freight wagon, Miss Billie. It's near a month old, so don't have no current news."

"I got a letter from my little brother," said a boy who didn't look more than eighteen. "Gen'ral Lee won the battle of Chancellorsville."

Rebel yells echoed around the room. Complete silence engulfed the Union sympathizers who, so far, had no major victories to cheer.

"But Eddy says the southern boys are hurtin'. Most of our troops ain't got shoes, or nuthin'."

The man with the paper added, "It says here, there's a rumor President Lincoln's gonna call up a hundred thousand volunteers 'cause he's scared General Robert E. Lee's gonna camp on his front lawn."

From the next table, an inebriated miner pounded his

glass on the wood and hollered to the piano player, "Play 'John Brown's Body,' Professor."

" 'Dixie.' I wanna hear "Dixie.' "

" 'Battle Hymn of the Republic.' "

" 'Bonnie Blue Flag.' "

"Gentlemen, please." Billie raised her voice. "This is not the place to fight the war." She held her breath until some of the more vocal customers settled down. Then she turned to the orchestra. "Let's make everyone happy. Do you know, 'When Johnny Comes Marching Home'?"

The grumbling she'd become familiar with ricocheted around the room until the music started. No one danced. The men stopped drinking. More than a few tears trickled down weathered cheeks to be harshly scrubbed away.

Anna walked up to Billie. "Why'd ya say that song, 'When Johnny Comes Marchin' Home,' would calm all the gents?"

Billie slid into a chair at an empty table. "I don't recall who wrote it, but the song started originally in the North. Then before long, the South adopted it. Both sides can identify with the lyrics."

Anna nodded. "I reckon."

Craig turned the bar over to Lucky and joined them. He stopped beside Billie, lightly placed his hand on her back, and leaned down until his chest brushed her shoulder. "Just wanted to tell you, you did a good job back there. A fight could've started very easily."

Billie swallowed. Her nerve endings tingled whenever he touched her. Her palms and the soles of her feet itched. She wanted to move, to put a stop to her uncontrollable reactions. But with Craig so close, her brain couldn't focus on any one command. So she sat still and listened while Anna wondered aloud if she shouldn't go over and carry the drinks to the tables since no one appeared to be in a dancing mood.

Craig was the first to answer. "Sure. Maybe the other

girls will help. They look like they could use something to do. And the fellas might cut loose a little change so the whole evening won't be a bust."

Billie glanced toward a table where Pearl and Molly sat glaring at each other. Pearl was Union. Molly was Confederate. Each had the support of grinning admirers sitting nearby.

After Anna spoke to Pearl and Molly, all three walked to the bar. Watching her girls, Billie suddenly realized Craig still stood closer to her than a Persian carpet to a parquet floor. The tension building between them jolted her to her feet and she moved away.

Craig followed, pressing his hand firmly against her back. "Come outside with me for a while."

"But I should—"

"Please."

"Why?"

"Because I want to talk to you—alone."

Her lips narrowed. "There is something I need to tell you."

He inclined his head, stepped through the door ahead of her, then gently replaced his palm on her back.

She shifted her shoulders and walked faster. He stubbornly kept pace, moving with her as surely as if he had a bridle on her, she thought. At the corner of the building, she finally stopped and turned to face him. "What did you want to say?"

He grinned. "Ladies first."

"But you're the one who—"

"I insist. You first." In truth, he had no need to speak with her, only a need to be with her.

Sighing, Billie spilled what was on her mind. "What are we going to do about the fighting? The first two nights there were altercations. Now they're choosing up sides over the war. This isn't the business I envisioned."

Craig wasn't nearly as concerned. In fact, he felt pretty good because there'd only been one real fight— and no more murders. "Don't get discouraged. This isn't a fancy city where controversy is kept on the editorial page of the paper. It'll take the men some time to get used to the Empty Barrel bein' a Grand Palace. Their drawing-room manners are a bit rusty. But they're comin' around. Tonight we didn't have to turn away one person who hadn't spruced up."

Suddenly, Craig blinked. Surely that hadn't been *him* encouraging her? Not him, the one person who'd hoped her emporium would fail.

Billie arched her brows. "Still, I wonder—"

"Stop wonderin' then. Everythin's fine."

Something buzzed past his ear and thunked into the siding just as he heard the report of a gun. He cursed and dove at Billie, knocking her to the ground. Scrambling to her side, he covered her body with his own. He should have known better than to become too confident too soon. Footsteps could be heard crunching gravel between two buildings across the street. Craig scanned the shadows, saw nothing, and reassured her. "It's all right. They're gone."

Billie looked up to find Craig's shadowy face so close to hers that she could almost taste the faint texture of bourbon on his breath. His chest flattened her breasts. His thighs seductively encased one of her legs, pressing tantalizingly close to her feminity. Her belly coiled. A moan strangled in her throat as, with their own volition, her hips rose.

Craig groaned out loud at her primal reaction. His lips lowered within a fraction of an inch above hers. "Angel, I—"

The swinging doors slammed again. Men rushed from the saloon. Lucky was the first to reach Craig and Billie. "You folks all right? Did you see who did it? Miss Billie, you hurt?"

Craig's weight continued to hold her to the ground. Her voice was a throaty rasp. "No. I think I'm fine."

Still unable to see Craig's features because of the shadows, she nevertheless felt his gaze. Felt it delving clear to her soul. "Y-you can get up now," she hissed, although it was the last thing she really wanted him to do.

"Do I have to?" he teased, his voice a husky rumble that only she could hear. Then in a louder voice, he said, "Yep. I think we're both in good shape."

She shivered, then narrowed her eyes at his mocking leer. "Y-yes."

Several miners helped Craig to his feet. Even more offered Billie their assistance.

"Don't like our Miss Billie bein' used fer target practice," said one of the men. A murmur of agreement rippled through the crowd.

"The bullet went right through a crack and hit the brandy. Broke a whole bottle of your best stuff. Who'd a done such a thing, Mr. Rawlins?"

Craig crooked an eyebrow at the speaker. "Don't know. Thank God there weren't more casualties, right?"

The man looked down and shuffled his feet. Craig grinned and put a hand on his shoulder. "I appreciate your concern," he said, eyeing the crowd to see who might be missing. He noted Scarface and his buddy were not in the group gathered.

"I couldn't see who it was." Lucky asked, "Did anyone else see anythin'?"

Several *no*'s followed as Billie was ushered back inside. Anna and Pearl and Molly rushed to help her to a chair where they brushed dirt from her hair and skirt. The musicians returned to the stage and resumed playing, though no one moved toward the dance floor or the huddled women.

"Who on earth coulda done such a thing?" Anna demanded, clucking over Billie like a mother hen.

Molly snorted. "Prob'ly jest some jackass full o' tarantula juice."

"I'm just glad you weren't hurt," Pearl admonished.

Billie snapped her head around. Of all the girls, Pearl was the last one she would expect to make such a sincere declaration of concern.

"Thank you. All of you. But I don't think it was me the gunman was after." Her gaze fell worriedly on Craig, who stood with a group of men, massaging the healing knife wound and talking more adamantly than ever about forming a Vigilance Committee.

While Craig listened to Ike and several other saloon and business owners, he darted a glance toward Billie and caught the tail end of her conversation. He tensed. She thought *he'd* been the target. And given the life expectancy of Alder Gulch saloon owners, it was possible.

The business of running a saloon was naturally risky. Drunks and men with chips on their shoulders didn't always sleep off their anger. A well-nursed grudge could make a man do crazy things.

And the memory of his cousin Bobby and Big John Turnbow still haunted Craig. All of his quiet inquiries had turned up nothing more than the fact that both men were connected to Craig's saloon when they died.

Well, he damned sure wasn't going to hole up and let some sneaky bastard ruin his business—or endanger Billie's life. But he wouldn't get careless, either. When . . . if . . . the murderer tried again, Craig would be ready. He actually looked forward to catching up with the sonofabitch.

Suddenly, the doors swung open and Sunny Turnbow rushed into the saloon. She ran straight for Craig and threw her arms around him. "Darlin', Justin told me what happened and I ran all the way down the hill," she gushed. "Are you all right?" She stood back and began running her hands over his body.

The men standing with him smirked and Craig flushed. He took hold of Sunny's shoulders and pushed her to arm's length. "I'm fine. Really. Whoever took that shot didn't aim very well. Hell, like Molly said, it was probably some drunk having a little fun. He just got carried away." He managed to curve his lips into a semblance of a smile, wishing he could believe that story himself.

The musicians finally put down their instruments and joined the assembled group. "Since no one's danced a lick all night, or paid much attention to the music, reckon we'll hang it up, if there ain't no objections," Hanshaw said.

"Good idea," Craig agreed. "We'll close up early, and start all over again tomorrow night."

He allowed the crowd to disperse naturally, smiling congenially at those who stopped to buy one last drink. What he really wanted to do, though, was send them all home and lock Billie safely inside. There was no telling when the bastard who'd shot at them might try again. But playing the part of friendly bartender, he nodded at his customers' proffered wisdom on the war, missing payrolls, and the shootings in Alder Gulch.

Sunny continued to fuss over Craig.

Craig continued to keep an eye on Billie.

Billie looked around and sighed. She'd learned one thing tonight. It had only taken a single sour event to turn her Grand Palace back into a saloon. And that wasn't acceptable. Something had to change.

The next morning, Danny hopped downstairs after everyone else had taken their seats. It always amazed Billie how late the child slept in the morning despite the fact that he was turning in earlier now than when he and Anna lived on the streets. Clearly, having his own bed, his own room, a place to call home, felt comfortable to Danny. Billie smiled at the boy. This was one of the things she'd hoped to accomplish.

Anna set plates of biscuits and bacon on the table, followed by a steaming bowl of gravy.

Danny was unimpressed. "Ain't any more o' them dancin' fellas traded fer no more 'good' stuff?"

Billie fought to keep a straight face. "Sorry, they haven't. What kind of 'good stuff' would you like?"

The boy wrinkled his freckled nose and licked his lips. "That butter was durned sure good." He kicked his feet, since his legs were too short to reach the floor, and gazed up at the ceiling. "An', uh . . . a big ole glass o' fresh milk. That'd taste real good."

Molly nodded her agreement.

"An' a big ole roastin' ear. An' a juicy, ripe tamater. Ya know . . . *Good* stuff."

Billie's mouth watered. She dug into the biscuits and gravy with renewed vigor. As she ate, she thought about the prospect of advertising that they would trade dances for food. It might lure the farmers who came to town into the emporium. Yet, would that be a sound business practice? Soon, everyone might want to barter something.

But . . . what if they opened up the emporium for a kind of farmer's market? Maybe on Saturdays, when most everyone from the outlying farms and ranches came into town anyway. That way, everyone—businessmen, miners, townspeople—would have access to fresh vegetables and meat. Dysentery and mountain fever were much too prevalent in the mining camp. Healthful food would help everyone.

Craig sauntered into the room and came up behind her chair. He casually placed his hands on the tops of her shoulders. "Mornin', ladies. Danny. Sure smells good in here."

"D'ya like bis'cits n' gravy, Mr. Rawlins?" Danny asked excitedly.

"I shore do."

Anna lowered her eyes, but invited, "There's plenty, if ya want some."

"I'd love some, Mrs. Corbett. Thanks."

Danny pointed to an empty chair, which placed Craig between Billie and the boy. Craig grinned, surreptitiously moving the chair closer to Billie, and slid into his seat.

His breath fanned her cheek when he inquired, "Sure you weren't hurt last night? I didn't mean to fall on you so hard."

Pearl snickered. Molly chuckled. Anna blushed. Danny gulped a mouthful of food and half rose from his chair with his fists clenched. "Yeah, Mr. Rawlins, ya better have a durned good reason fer fallin' on Miss Billie." His eyes took her in as if checking for injuries.

"Whoa, Danny." Craig laughed.

Billie shot the boy a reassuring smile. "I wasn't hurt. He . . . he was just protecting me." She met Craig's mischievous gaze and frowned. "I don't think I ever gave you what you deserved for that moment of . . . sacrifice."

"No," he said huskily, as his calf brushed hers. "You didn't."

"Then . . ." She squirmed in her seat, trying to swing her foot back, but hoping not to draw anyone's attention. As she smiled at him, she kicked his shin. "Thank you."

"Ow-w-oh-h . . . No need to thank me like that again." His left hand just grazed her elbow as he reached under the table to massage his leg. But he grinned. She hadn't really hurt him and she was teasing back. Flirting. It stunned and delighted him.

She gulped, trying to ignore the warm sensations crawling up her arm. Her eyes darted around the table. Could they tell how little control she had when *he* was around? The observant Danny couldn't, she decided as she watched him contentedly chomping a slice of bacon.

"Craig," she began, suddenly remembering the bartered butter. "What would you think about opening the emporium on Saturdays to provide a place where the farmers and ranchers could bring their goods to sell or trade?" She nervously pleated a fold in her skirt.

"It's a great idea." Craig sighed as he swallowed a

heavenly mouthful of flaky biscuit and just-right gravy. He nodded toward Anna. "Bet you could sell some of your bread, too."

Anna's eyes widened with undisguised pleasure.

Billie let out the breath she'd been holding. A great idea. He thought she'd had a great idea. She smiled.

Just before time to open the doors that evening, Billie heard a knock on the door. Instantly, the unidentified gunman from last night came to mind. She glanced around with the hope that someone else would answer it, but Craig and Lucky were in the cellar checking on the beer supply and the women were upstairs settling Danny in and getting dressed.

She cautiously cracked open the door. Her heart sank. Sunny Turnbow stood there, dressed fancier than an organ grinder's monkey. Billie forced a pleasant tone to her voice. "Yes? Is there something I can do for you?"

Sunny shoved her way inside, pushing Billie back with the door. "I thought I'd do somethin' for you, honey. Like offer my services this evenin'."

Billie scowled. "Services? What kind of services?"

"Dancin', of course, silly. I noticed you're short of women. I'd be glad to help out."

"We can't pay you much—"

"Oh, honey, I'll do this for free."

"What?"

Sunny patted a lock of black hair into the coil at the nape of her neck. "I've been awfully bored lately, what with Craig workin' so hard an' all."

Billie cocked an eyebrow.

"So, here I am."

"But—"

Craig and Lucky came up the narrow stairway be-hind the bar. When Craig glanced up and saw Sunny, gaudily dressed in a revealing kelly-green gown with a matching plume in her hair, he muttered an oath.

Behind Sunny, he glimpsed Billie, wearing a soft pink gown whose décolletage barely exposed her collarbones and just capped her shoulders. A modest vee gave just a hint of the firm roundness of her breasts. He felt a swift tightening in his loins and hurriedly set down the small keg he'd brought up from the cellar.

"There you are, darlin'. I was just explainin' to little Billie that I'm goin' to help out for a while."

"H-here?" His eyes narrowed. "Why?"

Billie took a deep breath and stepped forward. "You've been neglectin' her, darlin'. Sunny's bored."

Craig shot a quick glance to Billie. Though he detected the amusement in her voice, he saw no sign of it in her stoic features. Seeing no gentlemanly way out of the situation for the present, he shrugged and told Sunny, "Whatever. If you want your toes tromped by a bunch of rowdy miners, that's fine with me." He nodded toward his partner. "You'll be workin' for Billie, so mind what she says."

Sunny seethed.

Billie beamed. She didn't know what she'd been expecting, but it wasn't for Craig to welcome the woman to join them in quite that manner.

Before she could say anything to Sunny, Jack Dawkins, Ben Hanshaw, and the rest of the orchestra came through the doors. Then Anna, Pearl and Molly floated downstairs wearing the beautiful creations they'd worked all week to make. They hesitated upon seeing Sunny, but eyed her gown curiously and seemed to silently reach a conclusion that was announced by Pearl. "It's okay. She's one of us."

Anna eyed Sunny closely. "Ain't I seen ya afore?"

Everyone in the room turned to hear the answer.

Sunny raised her chin. "Perhaps. I'm Big John Turnbow's widow. You might recall, he made the first

big strike in Alder Gulch," she drawled in her fake
southern-belle accent.

Winking at Billie, Pearl grinned. "Yeah. I remember.
He married a gal that worked in Lem's cribs." She stuck
out her hand. "Nice to meet you."

Sunny's jaw dropped open, then snapped shut. She
ignored Pearl's hand. "I'll have you know—"

"Time to open the doors, ladies," Lucky announced
loudly. "Everyone ready?"

With a lot of noise and movement, the musicians
tuned their instruments and warmed up. Ten minutes
later the room was filled. Jack Dawkins called out, "All
hands round." As the orchestra started the first dance
tune, Billie waited in silent anticipation for Craig to
claim her. She'd come to enjoy their ritual of beginning
the evening with the first dance.

She watched him walk around the end of the bar. He
looked so dashing in his boiled white shirt with garters
holding up the sleeves and a fawn-colored leather vest.
His tan trousers hugged his lean hips and muscled
thighs like a second skin and she felt a familiar warmth
of appreciation curl in her lower belly. A slow smile
tilted her lips. He had to be the most handsome man
she'd ever seen.

Suddenly, a green serpent slithered into his path. Billie sucked in her breath. Sunny Turnbow snatched
Craig's hand and led him directly to the dance floor.

Chapter Seventeen

Billie Glenn stood, in the middle of the dance floor, as still as one of the bare, lifeless stumps along Alder Creek. She tried to tell herself it didn't matter . . . But it did. She'd come to look forward to Craig's fetching her for the first dance. And she felt betrayed that he'd allowed Sunny to keep him from coming to her.

Pulling her pride around her as a protective cloak, she held her head high, and with a sad heart headed toward the bar. A hand reached out. She gasped and jerked back. Her eyes met those of a man she didn't recall ever seeing in the emporium.

" 'Scuse me, ma'am. You look very familiar. Have we met before?"

She controlled the urge to frown and started to respond with a laugh, "Why, no—" But the seriousness in his eyes stopped her cold. She studied his face, but couldn't remember him. "I don't think so."

"I'm sorry. I could've sworn I saw you in St. Lo—"

"Miss Billie," Lucky called. "Come quick."

"Excuse me. I have to go." She left the stranger as quickly as possible, a disturbed feeling setting her feet in motion. Could she have known the man? Was he a part of the world she'd misplaced?

Lucky directed her mind away from the past when he pointed to a man sitting just outside the doors. "That fella passed out. Heard him tell someone he hadn't eaten in three days. Think we oughta ... I mean, it's not my right, but—"

"Yes, it is. The man needs help. I'll fix him something to eat right away." Thankful for something to keep her busy, she threaded her way through the crowd of men singing "Yellow Rose of Texas" along with the orchestra. This errand would help her put things in perspective. Craig was her friend. After all, just a few weeks ago, he'd helped her out when she'd been in nearly the same situation as the poor stranger outside.

Watching every move Billie made, Craig Rawlins's fingers unconsciously tightened around Sunny's hand.

"Land sakes, darlin'. You don't have to hold on so tight. I'm not goin' anywhere." She nestled her head onto his shoulder.

He silently cursed. No matter how hard he tried to keep her at a distance, she took advantage of his every lapse of concentration to snuggle against him.

Damn. What was Billie thinking? Was she hurt? Did she miss dancing the first dance with him?

Then he scolded himself for feeling guilty. It was probably best this had happened. He was getting entirely too comfortable with his partner. What had he been thinking when he'd vowed to "gentle her."

Getting involved with a woman like Billie would be the height of stupidity. She stirred too many unfamiliar and unwanted emotions—emotions he'd buried too long ago to want to dredge out again.

Still, he'd never had a partner who felt so good in his arms.

He jumped when Sunny suddenly reached between them and caressed his manhood. He grabbed her hand and held it firmly. Although he didn't want Sunny, she was the type of woman who didn't expect or ask for a commitment.

His gut spasmed at the sight of Billie dodging human

obstacles on her way to the kitchen. She darted one
glance at him and looked quickly away, but not before
he'd seen her pain. He hated himself for treating her
callously. And that knowledge left him feeling strangely
uncomfortable, too.

Sunny blew in his ear.

He twisted his head. "Damn it, Sunny. Stop that.
What do you think you're doin', behavin' like an alley
cat in heat in front of all these people?"

She touched him intimately again. He instinctively
hardened. She purred, "You like it."

He shoved her hand away. "No, I don't." Yet he had
to admit it had been a long time ... And it had felt
nice. But he couldn't encourage her.

The music stopped. He immediately led Sunny off
the dance floor. With a smile, he handed her off to the
first man he saw with a dance chip. "Here you go, pard.
Keep a tight rein on 'er."

Craig turned his back to Sunny's sputtered oaths. The
man he'd given her to was cajoling, "Now, come on,
honey. Let's see ya kick them pretty heels."

The orchestra played a rousing polka. Craig heard
Sunny shriek. He chuckled. *Served the vixen right.*

He'd taken only a few steps when he saw Billie coming from the kitchen, balancing a cloth-covered plate.
Hadn't they put plenty of food on the counter? Trailing
behind, he was surprised when she passed the bar and
headed out the door.

What in the hell was going on? he thought. Rushing
after her, he stopped short when he found her kneeling
beside an extremely emaciated, extremely filthy man.
She held out the plate filled with sliced beef and biscuits.

The man's hand trembled so violently that Billie had
to hold the food to his mouth. After he'd eaten several
bites, she told him to wait and let his stomach digest the
food before eating more. She then wiped the man's
mouth with the towel she'd draped over the food.

Craig watched, amazed. His chest contracted. He had

to drag in the next breath. He was like most folks—
doing kindnesses here and there that called for little real
sacrifice. This was something different. This was his . . .
Angel. And right now, that starving man was the center
of her universe.

He backed into the saloon, unsure how he felt about
that. He longed, just once in his life, to be the center of
someone's world. No. He longed to be the center of *her*
world.

He shook that notion out of his head and strode to
the bar. "Pour me a glass of milk, Lucky."

Lucky glanced beneath the counter. "Not much left,
Mr. Rawlins. If anyone wants—"

"Just give me the damned milk. They can drink
somethin' else."

"Yes, sir." Lucky frowned as he poured most of the
liquid into a glass and handed it to Craig. The frown
turned into a brief grin, however, when he saw his boss
walk back outside and hand the milk to Billie. Yep,
Lucky thought, even though he fought it, Craig Rawlins
was a good man.

Billie almost dropped the plate when Craig knelt beside her and shoved a cool glass into her hand. His long,
strong fingers brushed hers, sending a jolt of fire up her
arm. She'd known immediately who it was. It didn't surprise her that he'd thought of the milk. He was a compassionate man. She turned her head and smiled.

Craig rocked back on his heels. He'd rarely seen a
more beautiful, more genuine expression of appreciation.

"Thank you." She turned back and held the glass to
the man's lips. When he sputtered, she said, "Slowly.
Drink slowly. That's the way. Now, would you like a bite
more to eat?"

The man nodded and was able to hold a piece of biscuit on his own. "Th-thank ya, missy. An' you." His
voice was thready and weak as he glanced briefly at
Craig.

Craig looked into the fellow's hollow, haunted eyes and suppressed a shiver. "What's your name, pardner?"

"Fr-Frederick."

"Where you from, Frederick?"

"Den-Denver."

"You want to go home?"

Frederick nodded once.

Billie handed him a small slice of beef.

"Tell you what," Craig patted his shoulder, "when you feel strong enough, go over to the bunkhouse behind the freight office. Tell a man named Buck that Craig Rawlins said you were to work your way to Denver on the next wagon."

When Frederick smiled, Billie was shocked. The face she'd thought old and haggard changed to that of a young man. After Craig went back inside, she slid the food into the cloth and set it in Frederick's lap. "I've got to go back to work. Stay here as long as you wish, then follow Mr. Rawlins's instructions."

"Yes, ma'am."

She started when bony fingers wrapped around her wrist. But he only gently squeezed before his hand dropped limply to his lap.

Inside the emporium, Billie was met by the sight of a furious Sunny confronting Craig.

"I was lookin' all over for you, darlin'. What kind of man are you to go off an' leave me just to feed that trash?" She looked scornfully at Billie. "If Miss Priss there wants to get her thrills—"

Billie froze, wide-eyed. She suddenly recognized Sunny Turnbow for what she was. A manipulator. And she was good. Almost as good as . . . Billie flinched. One blink dissipated a hazy image taking shape in her mind.

Craig opened his mouth to respond, but Sunny thrust out her chin and pushed past him, heading for the target of her venom.

In the wake of the disturbing wave of memory, unanticipated fury consumed Billie. The woman had picked the wrong moment to attack. "Get out, Sunny. Now."

Sunny's eyes narrowed. "I will not." She smirked. "I work here now. Don't I, darlin'?" Batting her long black lashes, she looked at Craig.

Craig didn't answer. He was too busy watching Billie. What would she do next?

"Your job is terminated, especially since the only man you came to dance with was Mr. Rawlins."

Craig hooded his eyes. Billie hadn't disappointed him.

"Yeah!" the man who'd danced the polka with Sunny hollered.

"You tell the bitch, Miss Billie," another lanky miner agreed.

Billie silenced the supportive onlookers with a sharp glance.

Sunny's jaw opened, then closed. "Why, I'll have you—"

"Another thing . . ." Billie interrupted. "That man outside is not *trash*. He's a decent human being down on his luck. Who among us cannot see himself in the same predicament but for the turn of a card or failure of a strike?'"

"You said it, Miss Billie!" came from more than one bystander.

Another added, "I happen ta know the boy's daddy's a judge in Virginia."

Again Billie shushed those gathering to listen.

Sunny turned pleading eyes on Craig. "Darlin'?"

Billie fisted her hands on her hips. "You're barking up the wrong tree, *honey.*" She repeated the word with the same syrupy sweet tone Sunny had used on her earlier. "As my partner told you earlier, I'm responsible for hiring the women who work here. *And* the firing." She glanced quickly toward Craig.

He held up his hands and backed away.

Sunny frowned.

Billie let out a tiny sigh of relief that Craig hadn't contradicted her.

"Darlin'," Sunny cooed, "are you goin' to let her get away with this?"

He shrugged. "You heard the lady. She's in charge."

Sunny sputtered, then splayed her hands on her hips and stepped threateningly toward Billie. "You'll be sorry, slut. Just you wait and see. You picked the wrong—"

Suddenly Pearl and Molly stepped between the two women. Billie tried to force her way past them, but Pearl pointed to Sunny and then the door. "Git. I was mistaken. You aren't one of us. We don't need your kind here."

In unison, the two women took a menacing step forward. Billie shadowed them, insisting that she could fight her own battles. Sunny retreated, shouting, "All of you. You'll all be damned sorry for this.'

"Sure. Sure," Molly hollered. "Only thing I regret is we didn't toss ya out sooner." She rubbed her hands together as if just itching to lay them on Sunny.

Screaming shrilly, Sunny turned and fled through the doors. The curses flowing from her lips made even the raunchiest of the miners blush, but were drowned by the crowd's laughter.

Billie turned her frustrated ire on Craig. "I won't have her here again. If you bring—"

"She won't be back."

"If—if you bring her—"

"She's gone. For good."

"I— Really?"

Craig nodded.

A man standing close to Billie chuckled and slapped her on the back. "Any time ya wanna get in a good cat fight, my money's on you, Miss Billie."

Heat suffused Billie's face. She suddenly realized just what she'd done. Covering her cheeks with shaking hands, she glanced shamefully at Craig. "You really don't mind that I threw her out?"

"She deserved it." He'd been about to do the same thing. The uppity Mrs. Turnbow's inhumanity toward the starving man struck a nerve, especially after witnessing Billie's unselfish concern. And bitching about his partner had been Sunny's last straw.

"Well, I . . . Thank you for taking my side."

He put his arm around her shoulders and pulled her close to his side. As she began to stiffen and stammer, he commented, "Why wouldn't I? We're partners, aren't we?" Squeezing her gently, he looked down and smiled. "Aren't we?"

"Y-yes. Yes, we are." She blinked and gradually relaxed. Dare she allow herself to enjoy a moment of closeness? He felt so strong, so steady, so reliable. So warm. So good. Her chest constricted. She needed his hug. No. She needed more. She needed him.

On top of the hill, in her big house, Sunny sat alone in the parlor. She didn't move or make a sound when the front door opened and Justin slipped quietly inside.

He stopped in the hallway and lit a lantern, turned the light low, and walked toward the stairs.

"Where've you been?" Sunny demanded.

Justin yelped, backed up and shined the light into the small room. "Mother? What are you doing in the dark?"

"As if you care. I came home, needin' someone to talk to, and my son wasn't even here."

"What happened, Mother?" Justin knelt in front of her and laid his head in her lap.

Sunny threaded her fingers through his fine hair. "Damn that woman. She made a fool of me."

"What woman?"

"That bitch Billie." She stroked his head over and over.

"She wouldn't do—"

"Don't you dare defend that woman. I'm tellin' you, she did. In front of Craig an' half the town." Her lips compressed into a thin, ugly line. "She's goin' to pay for humiliatin' me, Justin. She'll pay dearly."

The next morning, Billie limped downstairs to the kitchen. Her left foot had been trod upon so often the night before that her boot had done little to protect her big toe. It was so sore that she'd hardly been able to slip into the clodhoppers again.

Anna looked up when Billie entered and grimaced. "You, too?"

"What happened to you?" Billie asked when she saw that Anna's right ankle was wrapped.

"While ya was busy outside, they played a darned polka. A German fella grabbed me an' we got to spinnin' so fast we went plumb to the floor." She stuck out her foot to emphasize who'd taken the brunt of the fall.

Billie started the coffee and watched Anna prepare the batter for flapjacks. "Must be Danny's turn to choose what we have for breakfast."

Anna grinned and pointed to a cupboard. "Found some molasses in the supplies this mornin'."

Billie found the crock, carried it to the table, and sank into a chair. As the pressure on her toe eased, she sighed loudly.

"What's this? Did I hear my partner bemoaning success?" Craig said, as he entered the room.

She perked up quickly. "Success? I thought when we checked the books, we'd just broken even."

"That was for last night, and the night before when we closed early. For the full two weeks, we've made a profit."

"Th-that's wonderful." She could hardly believe it. Was she actually going to be able to make this a success? Of course, there were still two and a half months to go,

but surely the first two weeks were the hardest, attracting customers, building a reliable reputation, working
out the kinks.

"Yes, it is. And as a reward, I thought I'd take my
partner for a Fourth of July ride."

"A ride?" Suddenly, her eyes widened. "The Fourth
of July? Already?"

Craig grinned and nodded.

Anna looked surprised, too. "Cain't imagine ya
wouldn't wanna hang around fer the horse racin', an'
all."

Craig shrugged. He hadn't taken his eyes off Billie,
who was dressed in a simple calico gown with little
green flowers that matched the emerald necklace. Her
hair was pinned in a soft coil at the nape of her neck,
except for a few wild strands that had escaped and
curled around her ears and hung in ringlets down her
back. He wondered if she always looked this beautiful so
early in the morning. But he couldn't imagine her otherwise.

"Well, partner? What do you say?"

Billie's heart beat ecstatically. A ride. With Craig.
What a wonderful way to spend a special day. But now
that the emporium was on the way to being a profitable
concern, she had responsibilities. "I'd better not. I have
things to do—"

"Like what? What's so important it can't wait until tomorrow?"

"Well . . ." She wanted to make muslin tablecloths to
replace the horse blankets, needed to pick fresh flowers.
But then again, how much business would they do on
the Fourth of July? A rising note of excitement tinged
her voice. "When?"

"I have a buggy waiting outside now."

Anna clicked her tongue. "No one's goin' anywhere
till ya eat a good meal."

She didn't have to twist Craig's arm. He scooted up

a chair and slid in close to Billie. His knee brushed hers, then nestled there.

Billie darted a glance at him from beneath her lashes. She looked back and forth between him and her plate, hoping he would notice and move his leg. Not that she wanted him to move it, but a peculiar warmth quivered along her thigh and upward. In desperation, she scooted her chair over.

With a semblance of control, she attacked the thick molasses poured over hot-from-the-griddle flapjacks. She had a forkful halfway to her mouth when she realized Craig's leg was once again invading her territory, resting completely against her. It was a warm leg. She could feel his body heat through both their clothing. She watched the molasses drip slowly from her fork as a delightful sensation flowed over her.

Craig hid a smug grin. Billie's eyes were as languid and sweet as the thick syrup. So, she was as jolted by his touch as thoroughly as he was jolted by hers? Good.

"Glad ya admire 'em, but the cakes are better if'n ya eat 'em," Anna teased.

Billie tried to focus on her food.

Embarrassed at being caught, Craig twiddled his thumbs until Anna literally shooed him from the room.

"Go on an' take 'er outta here," she scolded the impatient Craig. "We'll get along without 'er jest fine."

"But—"

"Go on an' git."

Craig rose and held out his hand. "I promise to have you back in plenty of time to get ready for tonight."

She waited until he'd escorted her outside and handed her into the buggy to ask, "Where are we going?"

"Thought we'd go for a ride in the country. You haven't been out of town since you got here, have you?"

She shook her head. Not only that, she couldn't recall much of what she'd seen, if anything, coming into town.

The team jerked the buggy into motion as Craig

tapped them with the reins. Billie held herself stiff to
keep from bumping into Craig. Watching his hands,
lean and long-fingered, she marveled at how easily he
made the horses obey. She knew the feel of those hands
on her neck and shoulders, on her waist as they danced.
The buggy hit the first of a series of deep holes. She
jounced all over the seat. Her only handholds were either the flimsy support for the canvas top, or Craig. She
chose Craig.

Clutching his arm, she felt the need to draw closer
yet, at the same time, pull away. Her left leg bounced
over his right one. She looked down at their intertwined
limbs, unable to move. The bonnet Molly had made to
match her dress flopped into her face and pulled free of
its pins. Then, as the horses pulled the buggy up a steep
incline, every other pin loosened. Her hair tumbled in a
flaming red and gold mass of disarray down her back.
Billie groaned.

Craig could hardly take his eyes from the thick russet-
and-honey mane. Shorter locks impishly teased her
cheeks. If he didn't have to keep such a tight rein on the
team, he'd like nothing better than to bury his hands in
her wild, windblown curls.

"Your hair is gorgeous."

"Th-thank . . . you. But you don't have to be nice."
She pushed several heavy tresses out of her eyes and
managed a syllable with each bounce.

Craig glanced down to where her leg was wrapped
over his. He shifted to his advantage and gave her a
heated, slow smile. "I'm not being nice."'

She ignored him and forced her gaze back toward the
town. She was instantly amazed by how dirty and unkempt the tents and false fronts and the mounds of piled
dirt and garbage looked from a distance. Adding to the
stark scene were the dying stumps of the alders that had
originally given the camp its name. A discoloration in
the creek from mine tailings was obvious from this van-

tage point. She frowned. Over and over again dull booms vibrated the air as well as the earth.

"Not a pretty sight, is it?"

Jerking around, she saw him looking back, too. "I never realized . . . Living down in it, you don't notice."

When they reached the top of the hill, Craig pulled the horses up and let them take a breather. He climbed down and adjusted one of the reins.

With his attention diverted, Billie snuck a long look at a very different Craig Rawlins. Away from his business environment, he could pass for a rancher in his knee-high boots and buckskin leggings all fringed along the seams. And buckled around his waist was a belt and holster and knife sheath. If it were possible, out here he seemed more dangerous . . . more male.

He still wore the crisp white shirt, but it was open at the neck and he wore no tie or bandana. Only the shaggy ends of his copper-hued hair were visible beneath a black felt hat. Definitely dashing and dangerous, she thought.

He turned, caught her staring, and grinned.

She quickly averted her gaze.

When he swung back into the buggy, she could've sworn he sat much closer. Before, she hadn't felt his shoulder brushing hers, or his thigh pressing so tightly against her hip.

"Ahem . . . Will you tell me now where we're going?" She attempted to slide to the right, but was brought up short by the rail at the end of the seat.

His lips twitched as he clucked the team into motion. "I want to go to the ranch and check my mares and foals."

"Ranch? Foals? I thought you owned the freight office, saloon, and bank."

"I do. But I also have an interest in the stables. I bought some brood mares and I intend to raise the horses to stock it. To do that, I needed a ranch."

She shook her head. "Your family must be very wealthy."

"Why would you assume that?" he said sharply. At her innocent expression of hurt, he closed his eyes. "I didn't mean to snap." Then, looking her in the eyes, he said, "I have no family."

Her fingernails dug into the seat as the buggy bounced down the rocky hill. "I'm sorry."

"I'm not."

"But everyone needs . . ." Ah, she remembered that he'd once said his cousin Bobby was his only relative. Touching his arm, she repeated, "I really am sorry."

"I get along fine on my own."

She'd said nothing. The man hadn't appeared out of thin air. He'd had a family once. Yet all he seemed to have now were emotional scars.

He inhaled sharply. "How about you? Where's your family?" He tentatively held his breath, wondering if she would answer.

She'd dreaded this moment. "I have a father and stepbrother in St. Louis." Goose bumps dotted her arms.

He tilted his head and frowned. "Have you told them where you are?"

"Uhmmm, no."

"Why not? They're bound to be worried."

"I—I kind of just remembered them . . . recently."

He stopped the buggy and swiveled his hips until he looked directly at her. "Is that what was wrong when you first arrived? You had amnesia?"

She intently twisted her fingers into the folds of her skirt. "I wouldn't call it amnesia, exactly. Everything was . . . is . . . foggy. But . . ." She glanced into his eyes and read his concerned interest. Could she trust him enough to tell the truth? Would he, perhaps, be able to help?

He brushed a finger down her cheek. She leaned into his hand and he inwardly smiled. He was afraid to push, but wanted to know everything there was to know about her.

"There are still some things I can't remember."

"Like what?" Ever so gently, he massaged the back of her neck.

"Like why I left St. Louis, and when. It's as if . . ." She choked, "weeks, or months—maybe *years* of my life never existed. I don't know what to do." A tear wandered down her cheek.

"I could send a message to your family on the next wagon."

"No!" She couldn't explain why. Just knew she didn't want anyone to find out where she was. At least not yet. Suddenly, she trembled.

Craig noticed and took her in his arms. It seemed the most natural thing in the world to mold her body to his and kiss her. Long. Hard. Deep.

Chapter Eighteen

As Craig's mouth met hers, Billie clutched at him like a drowning woman grabbing for the sturdiest tree trunk. She held on tightly, drinking from his lips, replenishing her soul.

Craig embraced her as if she were a porcelain treasure, a fragile doll needing to be handled with care, but needing to be *handled*. So, as any gentleman would, he let her have her way with him. A silent chuckle rumbled through his chest. He felt wonderful—almost happy—for the first time in years. He released a part of himself into *her* care now just as easily as he'd released a part of his past to her a moment ago.

His arms tightened convulsively around Billie. Not only did he have an intelligent partner, he had a friend. A warm, soft, very appealing friend. He lifted his head, gave her a squeeze, and laughed out of sheer delight. He couldn't restrain himself. Who'd have thought that Craig Rawlins, bastard son of a whore, despiser of women in general, would wind up with a woman—a dance-hall Terpsichore—as his dearest friend? Life was truly a riddle.

When Craig first pulled his lips from hers and laughed, Billie was befuddled. But his arms never left her. In fact, his embrace tightened into a hug and his laughter bubbled with joy. What had sparked his spirit of camaraderie and gaiety? Her lips curved into a smile as she leaned back in his arms. "What's so funny?"

He squeezed her again. "Life. There's nothing you can do about the past. Who knows what lurks in the future. So, why not enjoy today?"

"Sounds good to me." Another small grin tugged at her lips as she struggled to a sitting position and primly smoothed her clothing.

The sudden feeling of emptiness without her in his arms disquieted Craig, yet, at the same time, he discovered that the laughter had left an unfamiliar lightness in his chest. It was a sensation he treasured. Clicking to the team, he guided the horses into a grassy valley and with a flick of the reins, commanded them to trot.

"Thank you." Billie's voice was barely a whisper.

"For what?"

She closed her eyes, inhaled, and blinked them open again before saying, "For not making me feel like a fool a while ago."

"Angel, the *last* thing I'd ever think was that you were a fool." He threaded his fingers more firmly in the lines as the team rounded a stand of green willows. His eyes softened when he heard Billie's hushed gasp.

"Oh, my goodness. Is that yours?" She gazed hungrily upon a very simple but picturesque scene. Nestled toward the end of the valley, shaded by willows and huge cottonwoods, sat a small, cozy, white one-story home. Several steps led up to a wide veranda covering the entire length of the front of the house.

She sighed. A porch. A real porch. Strange as it seemed from a person who'd lived in a stately brick three-story home, she'd always dreamed of rocking in the shade of a porch, sipping from a big glass of lemonade.

"Well? What do you think?"

She smiled. He sounded as boyishly excited as Danny. He must be very proud of his ranch. "It's beautiful. Truly beautiful." On the left side of the lush green val-

ley, situated a short distance behind the house, was a
huge brown-and-white barn and pole corrals.

As the buggy approached, the horses Craig had mentioned nickered and trotted to the rails, ears pricked forward, nostrils flared. Peering timidly from the mare's
sides were smaller replicas with huge, curious brown
eyes and fragile, spindly legs.

"You're so lucky to have all of this."

His eyes widened. "All this? Believe me, it's not that
much." He studied her. Remembered the necklace she
always wore, though often now it was hidden beneath
her necklines. Remembered the elegance and style of
the green gown she'd worn into town. Even her cloak
had been expensive. She looked, talked, and acted like
a wealthy woman. And she considered his run-down little ranch "all this"?

Billie saw her dreams in this one small package. She'd
always loved horses, had spent all of her free time in her
father's stables. She'd watched the stablehands and
grooms until she knew everything they did about the
care and feeding of the animals, cleaning stalls, oiling
tack, even training.

But then her father discovered what she'd been doing.
Three days later, she'd been sent off to finishing school.

Craig pulled up near the barn door. A large black
man came out, wiping his hands on a smithy's apron.
"Mr. Rawlins, suh. Didn't know you was comin' today."

"Neither did I, Ezekiel." He handed Billie from the
buggy. "This is my . . . friend, Miss Billie . . . Billie, meet
my foreman, Ezekiel Jones."

Raised by a father who believed all men were created
equal and stood up for his convictions even in racially
volatile Missouri, Billie had no hesitation about holding
out her hand. "How nice to make your acquaintance."

Ezekiel's eyes rounded. He backed up, looked down
at his ash-smudged hands, and cast a questioning glance
at Craig.

Craig nodded, indicating the man should take her hand.

The foreman's fingers trembled as he pumped her arm so hard she thought she heard her teeth rattle.

Craig looked upon Billie with ever-growing appreciation as he led her into the barn. "How many foals do we have, Ezekiel?"

"Gots two new ones since yo was last here, suh. One gent, an' one little gal."

Craig stopped at the first stall on the right of the aisle and peered over the top rail. Billie followed and peeked between the first and second poles. "Oh, look how little. Isn't it precious?" The red-and-white foal was lying stretched out on the straw. A sorrel mare stood guard close by.

"That's the gal."

"Is Spot . . . I mean, your horse in town, the daddy?" Billie asked.

Craig grimaced. 'Spot.' But then he laughed. "I've caught myself callin' him that. His name is Medicine Blanket."

"Spot's easier." She chuckled.

"And the horse answers to it. Every time Danny calls, he nickers." Craig moved on to the next stall. A brown mare with a star on its forehead nuzzled a colt with a star on its forehead.

"This one doesn't have as much white." Billie was surprised after seeing the first foal.

"Sometimes it happens that way. The mare's color can be the more dominant one."

"Yo gonna stay up at yore home tonight, suh?"

"I'd like to, but the Empty Barrel's open again." He cast a surreptitious glance at Billie, wishing nothing more than to be able to carry her up to the house and make mad, sweet love to her all afternoon and night. He'd been a witness to her hidden passion and wanted more—much more.

Ezekiel ducked his head. "Would ya mind, suh, if I run out an' check on the mare in the east pasture?"

"The one about to foal?" When Ezekiel nodded, Craig continued. "That's fine. We'll be here until you get back."

"Yo sure?" The foreman cocked his head. "It'll take a while to ketch 'er."

"Take your time."

As Ezekiel walked away carrying a rope halter, Craig took Billie on down the row of stalls, showing her several more mares expected to foal within the next week. In the last stall, she saw a tall, dark-brown mare with long, slender legs and a delicately muscled body. The horse extended a graceful neck and nuzzled Billie through the rails.

"Look at those big brown eyes," Billie cooed, fondly rubbing the mare behind the ears.

"You like her?" Craig arched his brow. Billie was praising his best mare. The one he'd chosen to breed for his own personal stock. His eyes took on a decided gleam as he looked at the special woman.

Billie darted a quick glance at Craig. "She's the most beautiful horse I've ever——" The last of her sentence ended abruptly when her eyes connected with his. They were filled with such hunger and longing that her body instinctively responded with an aching desire to be held in his arms again, to feel his burning need as his lips devoured hers.

Craig watched her closely, his hands clenching and unclenching at his sides. Lord, but he wanted her. So badly, he ached. But he remembered how fragile she'd been in the beginning and thought about how far she'd come. She was beginning to trust him, and he'd be damned if he'd do anything to give her reason for regret.

But the yearning glow in her eyes, the dilation of her pupils, told him all he needed to know. She wanted him, too.

His voice was a deep, resonant growl when he warned her, "I'm goin' to kiss you, Angel. If you have any objection, you best tell me now."

The fact that he'd told her of his intent swelled her chest with an almost uncontrollable eagerness. He'd been so gentle and patient with her since they'd first been drawn together ... He seemed to have sensed her special needs and had gone out of his way to assure her safety and security.

Her voice was thick as she gulped and placed her hands on his shoulders. "Kiss me. Please."

He spread his fingers on either side of her slender waist. *Please.* The huskily spoken word was the only thing that kept him from crushing her to him. His lips feathered hers as he gently pulled her closer. "I please, Angel. I definitely please."

He sipped and licked and tugged her lower lip until she twisted her head, trying to meet his mouth, pressing her body fully against him as she unconsciously begged him to take her lips completely.

Without breaking the kiss, Craig edged her backward until she leaned against the barn wall. Her fingernails bit into his shoulders as he coaxed her mouth open. He dipped in and out, tasting, teasing, tempting until she groaned and their tongues mated.

His hand worked up her rib cage and rested just beneath the enticing swell of her breast. Caressing the soft mound, he felt her shudder as her nipple pebbled between his fingers. He ground his lower body against her.

Billie's hips arched. Need seared through her veins. She wasn't sure where she left off and he began, so tightly did she cling.

Suddenly, Craig jerked. His teeth grazed her lower lip as he raised his head. Colorful oaths polluted the air as he quickly smoothed his shaking hands down her bodice, then brushed his fingers over her flushed cheeks. His thumbs tilted her chin and his lips touched hers fleetingly before he regretfully whispered, "Stay here."

276   *Judith Steel*

Billie blinked in confusion. She felt cold and empty where only seconds before she'd been consumed with heat. And then she heard his voice. And Ezekiel's. Her face ignited. Ezekiel. Craig must have heard the foreman returning.

The clip-clop of a horse's hooves alerted her that they were entering the barn. With a sigh of thanksgiving for Craig's thoughtfulness, she busied herself in the back of the barn while the men discussed the mare.

She wasn't certain how much time had passed, but Billie was disappointed when Craig finally said that it was time to leave. She held a lapful of kittens and hated to put them down.

Craig had watched her paying special attention to a cuddly calico kitten. When she stood and shook hay from her skirt, he scooped up the mewing baby. "You know, when this one's a few weeks older, we could use a cat at the emporium."

"Do you think so?" She reached out and stroked the fuzzy ears, casting sidelong glances at his flushed features.

"Yep." He loved the delight glowing from her eyes. He wished he could make her happy forever.

Suddenly, he stiffened and quickly handed the kitten to her. What was happening to him today? Why were the words "we" and "forever" coming so easily to his mind? He stuffed his hands in his pockets and hunched his shoulders. "We . . . It's time to go."

She held the kitten to her breast, hiding her confusion. What had happened? He'd been so friendly, then turned cold and distant. Had she done something to upset him?

Craig swallowed hard as he watched the kitten nuzzling the fabric between the rounded mounds of her exquisite breasts. He envied the tiny creature. Already he ached to hold her again. What had she done to him?

Giving the kitten a last pat, Billie put it back with its mother.

The trip back to town was silent. Both people were lost in thought, both wondering what kind of magic spell they were under, both hoping for miracles.

When Billie and the girls came downstairs that evening, they saw Craig talking with two big, blond-haired giants wearing plaid flannel shirts, denim trousers, and lace-up boots. They didn't appear to be buying dance chips. Each held a double-barreled shotgun and watched intently as Craig pointed to one chair in the corner behind the bar and another near the back stairs.

"Those will be your stations, but feel free to wander, one at a time, through the tables now and then," Craig was saying as Billie walked over.

He saw her and motioned her closer. "This is Miss Billie, my partner. Billie, these are the Swenson brothers. They'll be keepin' an eye on the place for a while."

She inclined her head toward the men, then followed Craig when he went to the bar. "Do you really think it's necessary to hire armed guards?"

"We've handled things so far, but with the near miss the other night, the war escalating, and tonight bein' the Fourth of July, even supposed *genteel* establishments need to be prepared for trouble." He quirked a brow at her.

"Well, I guess . . ." Although she knew he was right, she didn't like the idea that her dance emporium might not be regarded as a safe place for her customers, or employees. She glanced around to find the girls. So far, there'd been only a few minor scuffles. But who knew how long their luck would hold?

She canted her gaze back to the two burly brothers. Perhaps Craig was right. At least help was here if the need arose.

Hours later, after the doors had been closed and Craig, Lucky, the orchestra, and the guards had gone

home, the women sat around a table fanning themselves.

"Wow. I ain't never danced so much afore. An' look
here at my new slippers. Some jackass stomped all over
'em." Molly scowled at the smudges streaking her new
white shoes.

Billie looked at her own feet, propped comfortably on
another chair. She stared at similar marks on her new
yellow slippers. "Thank goodness Mr. Robins has decided to open a shop. He'll be able to make us new
ones."

She'd been so thrilled when Jack Dawkins, after
watching her clomp around in her boots, had told her
about a miner who used to be a cobbler. It had been
good for Leonard Robins, too. His strike had played out
and his situation was similar to Lucky's. When Billie
provided the hide and material, he'd been more than
happy to make all of the girls shoes. Once the townspeople heard about it, they crowded around Leonard with
shoes that needed repair and even ordered new ones.
Craig, bless his heart, had found Robins a cheap loca-
tion to start the new business.

Pearl drew Billie's attention by counting the tickets in
her lap. "Forty of the suckers. Yep, this is the best night
yet." She smoothed down the skirt of her new red silk
dress. " 'Fore long, I'll have a silk dress in every color of
the rainbow."

Anna didn't have as many tickets as Pearl, but smiled
anyway. "This is more money than I made in two
weeks, sometimes a month, turnin' tricks."

A tingle skittered down Billie's spine. She shivered. "I
just hope our luck continues. We still have two more
months on the agreement I made with Mr. Rawlins."

Pearl wagged her eyebrows. "You and him been
spendin' lots of time together. Maybe your contract with
him ain't as important as your relationship with him."

"He's shore one handsome gent. Why, if he'd even
look my way, I'd pay *him* four bits ta—"

"Molly!" Anna scolded. "Shame. We work fer the man."

All at once, Billie realized she was being teased. She grinned. "I'm sure he wouldn't take less than a dollar. A man who owns half the town wouldn't come so cheap."

The other three girls looked at Billie with open mouths. Pearl was the first to chuckle. All four giggled. Soon, they were doubled over with laughter. It had been so long since Billie had laughed with women friends that she had to wrap her arms around her tender ribs.

"Oh-h-h," Billie moaned. "I don't know about the rest of you, but I'm exhausted."

"Yeah, me, too." Pearl stretched and rose slowly to her feet.

They all went upstairs together. Billie's room was the first on the left and she waited until everyone had gone inside and closed their doors before entering hers. She shook her head, thinking that she was acting like a mother waiting until her brood was tucked in before she could retire. But that was all right. Pearl, Molly, Anna, and Danny were like family. It was her duty to worry about them.

She'd just let down her hair and was brushing through a tangle when she stopped and cocked her head. Had that been a noise from downstairs? It sounded like someone whispering . . . her name. She listened, heard nothing else, but felt strangely uneasy.

She heard it again and froze. A chill ran up her spine. Craig had secured and double-checked the doors before leaving. Who could have gotten inside?

Craig. Craig had the keys. But why had he come back? Perhaps she should go see. Her heart gave an unexpected leap. Yes, she should definitely go down and find out what Craig needed. Giving her hair a final brush, she left it hanging loose and hurried to the stairs.

She hesitated on the top step. It was dark. Very dark. She hadn't brought a lantern and there didn't seem to be a light on the lower floor.

Taking a deep breath, she started down. She heard another noise. It definitely came from the kitchen. Uh oh. She wondered if he was searching for a lantern. A wave of guilt assailed her. She remembered bringing the one from the kitchen into the dance hall because the one behind the bar had run out of oil.

Her right foot slid under something thin and straight that bit into her toes. Forward momentum and the sudden catch unbalanced her. She reached out, but it was too late to grab the banister.

"Help!" She pitched down the stairs, tumbling head over heels, then bumping sideways. At last she slammed to a sudden stop on the hard floorboards.

Her head spun. She felt numb, except for her right foot, which throbbed as if it might be broken.

"Who's down there?" Pearl called from the top of the stairway.

"I—it's me," Billie gasped.

"Billie?"

Someone held up a lantern. Light spilled down the stairs. "It is," Anna cried. "It's Billie. I think she's fallen."

"Don't move!" Pearl yelled. "We're comin'."

"Be—be careful. Something on . . . stairs."

Molly moved in front of the rest with the lantern. "Foller me."

Anna grabbed Danny as he tried to dash around them. "Ya stay with me, young man."

"Aw, shucks. I wanna see Miss Billie."

"An' ya will. Just hold yer horses fer a minute."

Molly stopped and held the light close to the steps. "Look here. A cord. An' it's tied across this here stair."

All eyes stared at the strange trap that could only have been deliberately set. The women exchanged knowing glances.

"Kin I have it, Ma?"

"Leave it be right where it is fer now." Anna held his

hand as they walked carefully over the cord. "First we gotta see ta Billie."

Molly set the lantern down beside Billie. "Ya all right? Anythin' broken?"

Pearl clicked her tongue. " 'Course she's not all right, ninny. She just fell down a bunch of stairs." She bent over and looked into Billie's eyes. "Tell us where you hurt."

Billie winced when Danny's little hand touched her shoulder. The numbness was wearing off. Where did she hurt? "All . . . over."

"Think ya kin git up?" Anna asked.

"I—I don't know."

Between the four of them—Anna, Danny, Pearl, and Molly—they managed to help her stand. She swayed, caught hold of Anna, then balanced herself. "I think it's mostly just bruises. But my ankle . . . I can hardly put any weight on it."

"Someone oughta fetch Mr. Rawlins." Pearl grimaced at the swelling already visible on Billie's foot.

Billie glanced toward the dark kitchen. "I thought I heard him earlier. That's why I came back down."

Danny raced off to see. "Nope," he hollered over his shoulder. "Ain't no one here."

"Anyone know where he lives?"

"I do," Danny announced proudly.

Anna shook her head. "Why'm I not surprised." She looked around at Pearl and Molly in their night dresses. "Since Danny and I are still dressed, we'll fetch 'im."

"There's no need," Billie protested. "He won't be able to do anything."

"Well . . ." Anna was undecided.

"Mebbe she's right," Molly agreed with Billie. "We kin get 'er back upstairs. Tomorrow we kin hunt up a doc."

"Ain't none. Mr. Rawlins said so," Danny informed them all.

"Ain't none that hung out a shingle. But I danced

with a gent what said he'd been a doc back in the East, or somethin'."

After more arguing, they all decided to wait till morning.

But there were some things that couldn't wait for morning. "Anna, why don't you put Danny back to bed?" Billie suggested, locking eyes with Pearl, who nodded brusquely.

"Darn it, I miss all the good stuff," the boy complained. "I oughta be the one figurin' out what hap'ned an' guardin' ya wimmen folk." He thumped his bony chest. "I'm the man around here."

Anna smiled indulgently at her son's bravado but placed her hands on his shoulders and urged him to their room.

"That was a good idea," Pearl said. "I've been itchin' to ask you about what you thought you heard down here?"

Billie leaned against the stairs. "A whisper. I distinctly heard someone whisper my name."

"An' ya thought it be Mr. Rawlins?" Molly squatted in front of Billie.

"Yes. He's the only other one with a key."

Pearl rubbed her chin. "I can't see Mr. Rawlins stringing that cord."

"Naw . . . But . . . reckon the varmint's still around?" Molly asked, glancing nervously over her shoulder.

"Pearl, there's another lantern behind the bar. With it and this one, we can check this place out."

"*We* nothin'. I'll get the lantern, but Molly and me will do the checking. A lame horse ain't no good in a search party."

Billie listened while the two women searched behind the bar, into the cellar, and through the kitchen. Anna soon rejoined her and, to everyone's relief, nothing unusual was found.

"Might be best if we bunk together tonight. Jest in case," Molly suggested, shuffling her feet. Suddenly, she looked up and stuck out her chin. "Not that I'm afeerd, or nuthin'."

" 'Course not," Anna said. "There be two beds in our room. We kin push 'em together."

Billie glanced at the others. Molly, clearly nervous, would be happier not sleeping alone. And they all might be safer. "All right, ladies. Let's do it."

It was a struggle going up the stairs, but with pushing and prodding, Billie made it to Anna's room. Danny seemed glad it had turned into a party, and he gathered everyone's pillows and blankets. The girls insisted Billie forgo a nightgown and robe and that she sleep in her dress.

Once Billie convinced them she was comfortable, they turned down the lanterns and took spots on the corners of the beds and snuggled down for the night. Pearl was nearest Billie and touched her arm to get her attention. The little redhead twisted the edge of her cover in her fingers. "You've got some pretty nasty bruises," she whispered. "Reckon you're gonna be awful sore tomorrow."

"I'm afraid you're right," Billie whispered back, trying to lift her shoulder.

"Ahem . . . What I'm gettin' at is, whatever you need done, far as workin', and all . . . just let me know."

Billie was speechless. Pearl, the brassy loudmouth, had offered her support and services in a shy whisper! "Th-thank you. That means a lot to me." She sighed. "From the way it looks, I may have to take you up on your offer."

"I wasn't sure you'd want to, after all the spats we've had. But if you need me to, I'll do a good job."

"I know you will."

Billie groaned and sagged back on her pillow. Wincing, she shifted until she found a spot she could rest on that didn't hurt.

She closed her eyes, but found it impossible to sleep. All she could think about was the strange whisper and the cord. That cord hadn't been on the stairs when they'd gone to bed. It was no accident. But which of them was the target? Her? Surely not. Still, it was her name that had been whispered.

She shivered and pulled the blanket higher. Why? And more important—*who* could have done such a thing?

By the next morning, Billie ached from the tip of her nose to the bottom of her toes. She blinked and gingerly threw back the blanket.

Anna poked her head around the door. "Good, yore awake. We was gittin' worried. Ya ready fer vittles?"

"Thanks, Anna, but I'm not very hungry. Besides, there's no way I can get out of this bed."

Another head poked around the jamb. "Why, Miss Billie, did I just hear you might need *help?*" Craig stepped into the room, his hands splayed casually on his hips. The grin half formed on his lips turned into a worried scowl when he got a closer look at her. "My God, Danny said you'd fallen, but—"

"I'm fine," she hastily assured him, although her efforts to sit up and smooth her rumpled dress went for naught.

He strode to the edge of the bed. "You don't *look* fine." He stroked his finger along the delicate line of her jaw and inhaled sharply at the sight of bruises on her arms and the parts of her legs exposed to his view.

And then he saw her swollen, discolored ankle. "Aw, look at that. What in the hell happened, Angel?"

Pearl and Molly entered the room at that moment and relieved Billie from tedious explanations. All the while, she studied Craig's face. For what, she wasn't sure.

At the mention of a cord, Craig cursed.

"But ya know . . ." Molly said, rubbing her forehead.

"They was some men fixin' some loose boards yesterday. Mebbe one o' them left it."

Billie wished that could be true, but she'd already thought about that possibility last night—and rejected it.

Craig shook his head. "Naw. One of you would've found it on the way upstairs last night." His brows slashed together. Which meant only one thing. Someone had deliberately tied that cord to hurt . . .

"Billie?" he questioned. "Think very carefully. What made you go down those stairs last night?"

She shot the others a glance that said she'd be the one to tell him. "I heard a noise."

"What kind of noise?"

She gulped. This was not going to be easy. "A whisper, I think."

"What was whispered that would make you go downstairs in the dark?" He was getting a little exasperated with her reluctance to tell him anything without his having to drag it from her.

"I thought someone called my name." His eyes were so intense, she couldn't hold his gaze. She stared at her twined fingers.

"Did you recognize the voice?"

She lifted her head slightly. "Not really." She hadn't thought about it before, but how could a person *recognize* a whisper? She did look him in the eyes, however, when she said, "I thought it was you."

"Me?" He was genuinely startled. "Why me?"

Relief flooded over her. She was certain it hadn't been Craig. Still, she couldn't admit the truth. That she'd hoped it was him. That she'd been so excited that she'd left her hair down just for him.

"I—I remembered the night I'd found you in the kitchen. I thought you might have come back for a snack, or maybe forgotten something."

Craig's eyes narrowed. Someone had purposely set a trap for her. But who? And why?

Anna timidly asked, "Could we talk downstairs? Breakfast is gonna be ruined."

Everyone readily agreed, except for Billie. "You all go ahead. I'll . . . get something later."

Realizing there was no possible way Billie could get around on her own, Craig stepped over to the bed and gently lifted her into his arms. She groaned. His own body ached. "Sorry, Angel. I'll do my best not to hurt you."

"I—I know." She wrapped her arms around his neck and rested her head on his broad shoulder.

Craig's heart thudded so hard his ears rang. And then something hit him. She'd said she thought the person downstairs had been him. He fought to keep his arms from tightening around her and aggravating her bruises. Lord, but she felt good in his arms. Perfect. His perfect Angel with the passionate kisses.

"Huh unh, nobody's allowed in the Grand Palace unless they're cleaned up, honey," Pearl partially teased, looking at Billie's dirt-encrusted scabs.

"She's right," Craig agreed, but frowned as he carried her to her room. Leaving Pearl and Molly to help Billie with her private matters, he waited in the hall, slumped against the wall. Although he didn't like to think about it, he recognized the irony of yet another attack on one of his partners while he was far from the Empty Barrel. Whatever was going on, he vowed to get to the bottom of it before someone else, especially Billie, was injured—or worse.

Molly called. He sighed and stepped into the room. Billie was sitting on the side of her bed, wrapped in a blanket.

"Since she's gonna need a bath anyway, we didn't dress her. Just be real careful of that blanket, hear?" Pearl grinned and winked.

Molly giggled.

Billie clutched the edges of the blanket so tightly her knuckles turned white.

Craig felt his face flush with heat as he collected his precious bundle. All the way down the stairs, the only thing he could think about was that beneath the blanket, Billie was naked. Naked. More than just his face heated.

Billie was every bit as aware of her state of undress as Craig. Tendrils of sensation wriggled through her nerve endings. She squirmed slightly, but the movement threatened her hold on the blanket, which seemed to cling to the fabric of his shirt and slither down her body with every movement.

He breathed in her heady scent and decided he liked her like this—hair hanging loose down her back, naked, resting in his arms.

She decided that maybe this wasn't so bad, nestled in a handsome man's strong arms, being carried wherever she wished to go. Sighing contentedly, she returned her head to rest on his shoulder.

As they entered the kitchen, Billie raised her head and looked at Craig.

His eyes smiled at her. His lips smiled. It seemed his whole face smiled.

She frowned. "What are you up to?"

Her question was answered after breakfast.

Chapter Nineteen

Much to Billie's dismay, Craig dragged in the large tub used for bathing and put it in a partially concealed corner. He instructed Pearl to heat water, Danny to re-fill the lanterns, and Anna to serve breakfast. Billie sat helpless with her ankle raised, watching and listening as the others discussed what they could do to make her more comfortable until Molly returned with a doctor.

So far, some of their ideas for "making her comfort-able" caused her to squirm with the desire to stagger to her feet and hobble away as quickly as possible.

The only reason that she remained rooted to the chair was the thought of a nice warm soak. Her muscles were screaming for relief.

Danny sat with her until he became bored and left to feed Spot and clean the stall.

A wagon pulled up at the back door and Anna took the driver down to the cellar to show him where to put the boxes and crates.

Carpenters came to the front door and Pearl led them upstairs to Billie's office where they were going to build more shelves.

Craig took the last bucket of steaming water and poured it into the tub. "There you go, Angel. It's all ready." When he looked up, his brows knit with puzzle-ment. "Where is everyone?" If the hot water was going to do Billie any good, she had to get into the tub. Now.

Billie looked from Craig to the inviting water, then back to Craig. Except for them, the room was empty. When he started toward her, she held up her hand and shook her head. "Oh, no. Don't you dare."

He grinned. "Don't dare what?"

"Uhmm, whatever you're thinking of doing."

"All I was going to do was help you to the tub. But if you don't want to—"

"I want to." She glanced around at the back door where Danny or the driver could come through at any time, and to the other doorway where the carpenters could barge in to ask a hundred questions. Usually when one of them took a bath, there were enough ladies around to hold up towels.

"Come on. I'll carry you over and help you get out of . . . Well, carry you over and move a chair so you can un—" He swallowed down erotic visions of Billie slipping out of the blanket. He mentally watched the wool slide sensuously off her creamy shoulders. The hem would glide over her rounded breasts and catch on her taut nipples. Pebble-hard nipples, just waiting for him to claim them . . . forever, for better or worse.

Billie raised her eyes. They locked with his. What she saw thrilled and excited and terrified her. His desire nearly leapt out and engulfed her. Surprisingly, she felt no need to flee. There, lurking in the aqua depths, was something . . . a bare-your-soul, tell-your-secrets kind of feeling that she couldn't face. At least not now, not yet—if ever.

She awkwardly cleared her throat. "All right, you can help me. But one of the girls should be back soon." Because of her own agitation, she didn't feel the tension in his arms, or notice the stiffness in his gait as he picked her up and carried her the few feet to the tub. But she did feel the burning brand of his touch and the way her body seemed to melt into his.

Pearl bustled into the room. "There you are. That water ready? Want me to . . ." She looked at the owner, holding her boss, and stammered, "Want me to stay? Or leave?"

"Stay," Craig growled.

"Stay," Billie pleaded.

Pearl chuckled and muttered, "This is gonna be interestin'."

"What?" Billie asked.

"I said, your water's gettin' cold."

Craig reluctantly set Billie on the chair. He turned to Pearl and ordered, "Let me know if Molly comes back with that doctor." He walked toward the door, but couldn't stop himself from taking one more look at Billie.

She had her back turned and Pearl was unwrapping the blanket. Billie's smooth, silken skin was marred by huge discolorations. His breath hissed between his teeth as he slammed the door behind him. Whoever had done that would be sorry. So very sorry.

"I don't see anything that needs attention except your ankle," Dr. Timothy Andrews told Billie. "The bruises and soreness will heal with time, as will the ankle. You just have to use common sense and stay off your feet." He shook his finger at her. "No dancing for at least a week."

"A week!" she moaned. "But—"

"No buts."

She sighed.

"We'll see that she—"

"We'll hog-tie 'er—"

Pearl and Molly both spoke at once, then looked at each other and grinned. When they turned their combined gazes on Billie, she knew she was outmaneuvered—for now.

The women took their leave while the doctor used strips of cotton material to wrap Billie's ankle. Then he handed her a roughly hewn pine cane Craig had ordered the carpenters to fashion immediately. "That should give you some support so you can at least get up and down the stairs."

"Thank you." She tilted her head and studied the middle-aged man's receding hairline as he bent over her foot. "Dr. Andrews?"

He glanced up. "Yes?"

"Why aren't you practicing medicine here in Alder Gulch?"

"Ahem. Here?"

She nodded.

His eyes clouded, became almost vacant. His hands trembled as he tied off her bandage. "I left my practice, my belongings, and my soul April 7, 1862, at Cornith, Tennessee." Standing up, he turned his back and whispered, "I'm afraid I also left my nerve."

"Bull!" Billie gasped. Had that come from her?

He met her eyes. "What do you mean by that?"

"What are you doing here?"

He spread his hands. "Working my claim."

"No, no. Here in this kitchen."

"The girl said someone had been hurt and that I had to come with her."

"But you didn't *have* to, did you?"

"I . . . guess not."

"So, why did you?"

"I—"

"Am I the only one you've helped in Alder Gulch?"

He hesitated, but answered, "No."

"Who else?"

"Some miners were injured in a cave-in. I did what I could. And a fellow shot himself in the leg."

"And I bet you could go on and on."

He shrugged. "I do what I can."

"Mr. Rawlins's freight company can bring you medical supplies. People here need you."

"I—"

Molly came in and looked at Billie's foot. "Got ya fixed up, huh?"

Billie nodded, but kept her eyes on the doctor.

He backed up and stammered, "Make her keep that foot up."

As he turned to leave, Billie said softly, "Dr. Andrews?"

He ducked his head. "I'll think about it." He spun and hurried out.

"What's he in such a all-fired hurry about?" Molly watched him rush through the swinging doors.

"He didn't say."

"Well, me an' Pearl's gonna help ya up ta bed."

"Please. I don't—"

"Pearl . . . Hurry up."

"I'm here. She gonna give us trouble?" She spread her legs and scowled.

Billie held up her hands. "I give up. Do with me what you will. Just cut me a piece of Anna's pie first."

Billie couldn't stand staying in her room that night. She might not be able to dance, but there had to be *something* she could do.

Craig just happened to see her standing at the top of the stairs, all dressed up, her hair combed and gathered in an ornamental net. She leaned heavily on the ugly cane and seemed to be trying to figure out which foot to put down first. He rushed up and swept her into his arms. A habit he was becoming rather fond of. "Damn it, Angel. You're supposed to stay off that ankle."

When he would've taken her right back to bed, she braced the tip of her cane against the doorjamb. "No. Please don't take me in there. It's lonely, and I want to help."

He gazed deeply into pleading, gold-flecked eyes and realized he couldn't refuse her. He carefully descended the stairs and walked toward the bar. It was strange, but he'd felt the emptiness when he'd come to the saloon during the course of the day. The Grand Palace was just the Empty Barrel without her around—tilting her head that certain way, or, on very rare occasions, favoring him with her heart-melting smile.

She'd only been in that room a few hours and he already missed her.

He'd been up to see her several times, and then he'd had to force himself to leave her to take care of all the mine shipments and payrolls coming to the bank in preparation for first-of-the-month payments.

Which reminded him. "I've hired more guards. You ladies shouldn't be in here alone at night." He could kick himself for not having done something earlier, before Billie got hurt.

Billie gasped. She placed a hand on his taut cheek and turned his head until he looked her in the eyes. "No. I'll not have strange men prowling my home at all hours." Her eyes softened. "Please."

He frowned, but could see her point. Her home. It pleased him that she thought of the Empty Barrel, her Grand Palace, and perhaps even Alder Gulch, as home. But he would not be swayed from his purpose.

"I'll post them outside, then." His eyes narrowed when she opened her mouth. "No arguments!"

She gulped and shook her head. The last thing she'd intended to do was complain about someone guarding the building from outside. Now, maybe she and the girls could feel safe sleeping in their own rooms tonight.

Feeling quite pleased with himself that Billie and the other ladies would have more protection, Craig halted in front of the bar, but continued to hold Billie. Lucky and Anna stopped polishing and stacking beer schooners, tumblers, and hot punch cups. They glanced from Craig to Billie, then looked at each other quizzically. Craig noticed, but still held on to Billie, relishing the fact that she nestled her head on his shoulder.

"What do you reckon we can put this lady to doin'?" he asked the two gawking employees.

"I don't know," Lucky said, gazing around the room to see if anything came to mind.

Suddenly Craig had a thought. "I know . . ." He settled her on the counter, then quickly pulled up a table and two chairs. Giving her a gentle squeeze and tender peck on the cheek, he lifted her from the bar and sat her in one of the chairs. Very carefully, he raised her injured foot into the extra seat.

Billie watched him, dazed by his absentminded kiss. His every movement fluid and sensual, he made his way around the room, speaking to Molly and the musicians. She'd become so engrossed in her study of the man that she was taken by surprise when he suddenly stopped beside her, cocked his head, and stared in return.

"What do you think?"

"I-I don't know." She felt the heat of a blush. He'd been talking to her and she hadn't paid a bit of attention—to his words.

Exasperated, he straightened. "You'd be taking a load off Lucky, and I know you'd do an excellent job."

He reached for the dance chips and scale. Without acknowledging that she'd been caught watching his lean, muscular body, she pretended that he'd talked her into giving out the chips.

"Well . . . all right, I'll give it a try."

Craig smiled and patted her shoulder.

She covered his hand with one of her own.

Their eyes locked. There was nothing, no one, but the two of them. Her fingers felt numb and tingly all at once. She squeezed, needing to touch him, feel him.

Craig's breath caught. His stomach played leap frog with his heart. Sweet, special Billie. He couldn't make himself break the contact.

"Mr. Rawlins?"

He started.

Billie jerked her hand away and folded both hands demurely in her lap.

Pearl grinned and tapped her foot. Oh, yes, this "friendship" was getting better every minute. "You going to open the doors?"

Craig plucked his watch from his vest pocket. The lid snapped open, revealing that he was already five minutes late. "Why, yes. I was just making certain Ang— Miss Billie was comfortable."

"Uh huh," Pearl grunted. "Looks like she's real *comfortable,* all right."

Heat crawled up Billie's neck and flushed her cheeks. She didn't know what to expect when she glanced into Pearl's eyes at the same time Craig's voice now drifted back to her from outside.

Pearl just winked.

Billie's chest expanded as she drew in a deep breath and grinned.

The next hour passed swiftly. The men crowded around her table, more enthusiastic about buying from a finely dressed lady than they'd been about buying chips from the bartender. Some told her how disappointed they were she wouldn't be able to dance. Some cracked jokes. Some just smiled shyly and held out money or gold dust. She enjoyed it all.

The emporium filled. Music floated on the air. Glasses emptied and were filled again. Couples danced. Ticket sales were finally slowing when a young man staggered through the door. Blood trickled down the side of his head. Heads turned and conversation ground to a halt. Billie gasped, frantically trying to pull her foot off the chair so she could stand with the aid of her cane. The guard stopped her.

"Craig!"

"Mr. Rawlins," the injured man rasped. "Mr. Rawlins."

The dancers stopped in midsway and turned to see what the excitement was about. The music screeched and plinked to a stop. Like clouds slowly drifting across the moon, a shadow of foreboding moved through the room. Molly's loud voice carried across the building as she cried, "It's the bank clerk."

Craig's face paled. The glass he'd been filling thudded onto the work shelf. Running swiftly around the bar, he and several other men helped the young man to a chair.

"Bring a glass of water," Craig called, and took out his handkerchief. He held it firmly against the oozing scalp wound. "What happened, Lawrence?"

Lucky placed the water in Craig's hand. He knelt and put it to his clerk's mouth. Lawrence gulped, and water spilled down his chin. "Enough," he sputtered.

He looked guiltily into Craig's worried features. "They got it, Mr. Rawlins. They got it all."

Craig carefully set the glass on the table, afraid he'd shatter it in his hands. "The safe?"

Lawrence nodded. "I tried to stop 'em. But there were too many of 'em."

"How long ago?"

The young man ducked his head, winced, and said, "I don't know. They hit me. But I come runnin' the minute I woke up."

Timothy Andrews stepped out of the crowd. "If you like, I'll take a look at that wound." He slanted a glance toward Billie, then quickly looked away when she nodded.

Craig rose to give the doctor room. Two merchants came to stand in front of him.

"There's no other choice, Craig."

"Something has to be done."

Craig's face hardened. "Gather what men you can. I'll go to the stables and have saddled horses ready for those who need them."

Ten or more men moved to the door as Craig nodded to the orchestra. Instantly, music filled the room. The customers milled around the bar, but nobody danced.

Craig walked over to Lucky, who'd gone to stand close to Billie.

"I've got to go. Think you two can handle the place?"

"Craig—"

" 'Course we can." Lucky put his hand on the back of Billie's chair.

The Swenson brothers also assured Craig they'd be watching for trouble.

He finally glanced down at Billie. "I'll be back as soon as I can."

Stricken with terror, she gulped and nodded. The thought of his riding into danger stole her ability to speak.

Before he realized he was going to do it, he leaned over and captured her mouth in a long, tantalizing kiss. He felt her lips soften and respond. She swayed toward him. He stifled a groan and reluctantly lifted his head. For her ears only, he said, "Will you welcome me back with another just like that one?"

Through the noise of whistles and cat calls, she forced her tingling lips into a semblance of a smile. *If* he came back, she'd almost be willing to do anything he wanted. He *would* come back. He *had* to.

Billie was looking out her upstairs window about noon the next day when she saw the first bedraggled riders from the posse pass the emporium. Their horses' coats were caked with dried lather and their hooves scuffed dust with every step. The men's faces were drawn and haggard, their shoulders slumped.

Craig rode near the middle of the group, leading two riderless horses with gunnysacks tied to the saddle horns. In contrast to the others, his back was ramrod straight and deep lines grooved his cheeks on either side of his mouth. His eyes, when he glanced toward the emporium, looked . . . haunted.

She frowned at his strange impression. The distance was distorting. He was probably just exhausted.

All at once she shivered and brushed her fingertips over her lips. He was back. She'd promised him a kiss when he returned. Would he remember?

The afternoon dragged by one minute at a time. Cooped up with nothing to do, Billie counted every second.

"Miss Billie . . ." Lucky finally complained when she asked him the time *again,* "why don't you take my watch." He finished wiping down the counter, erasing one last smudge with the elbow of his sleeve.

"No, no." She leaned forward and fluffed the towels under her ankle. "I guess I'm just nervous about opening tonight. Do you think Mr. Rawlins will be here?"

Lucky put down his towel and went over to sit across from her. "Everything went smoothly last night. Don't you think we can do it again?"

"Oh, no." She'd hurt Lucky's feelings. "That wasn't what I meant at all. You did a wonderful job. We all did."

His shoulders relaxed on a deep sigh of relief.

Anna, who'd been replacing wilted flowers with fresh ones, listened to the conversation. Sympathy shone from her eyes as she walked over and patted Billie's shoulder. "I reckon our Billie's uneasy 'bout seein' her *partner* agin, too."

Lucky's raised brows wrinkled his forehead. "So that's the way the wind blows." He winked at Anna. "And here I thought *I* was Miss Billie's best fella."

Loosening up a little with the teasing banter, Billie looked between the two and quipped, "I can't admit to that. Anna would have my hide."

Glancing surreptitiously toward her friend, she caught Anna's flaming cheeks. Then, looking at Lucky, she found his features ruddier than usual. She'd been kidding them, but perhaps her comment was more on target than she suspected. She smiled, hoping it was true.

"Guess what?" Pearl gushed as she pushed through the swinging doors. Before anyone could take a guess, she rushed on. "They got most of the money back. Can you believe it? Our men actually caught up with the outlaws. That oughta slow the bastards down some."

"Was anyone hurt?" Billie asked anxiously. Although he hadn't appeared to be injured, she worried about Craig. Where was he? Why hadn't he come to the emporium yet?

"Ole Lem, from the Gold Nugget, got a broke finger, but that's all I heard," she called excitedly over her shoulder as she headed for the stairway.

Relief flooded over Billie. When she glanced up and found Lucky and Anna nodding knowingly at her, she fidgeted with the towels propping up her ankle. "Well, a lot of men we know went out with the posse. I just wanted to—"

Anna grinned. "Sure. We understand. We're glad *nobody* was hurt, too."

Craig downed another glass of the rotgut served at Colonel Pugh's gambling house. The odors of flaming coal oil, stogies, and accumulated sweat assailed him. His nose wrinkled every time he took a breath. Any other time he would have bypassed the place, but it was the closest to the stables and was as far as he'd gotten before deciding he needed something to burn the events of the night from his mind. It hadn't worked.

He poured another drink. Tossing it down in one gulp, he gritted his teeth as the whiskey burned clear to his toes. His head lolled forward. He reached twice for the bottle before he caught it. He filled the glass and held it up. *To Bobby,* he silently toasted, again swallowing the amber liquid all at once. It had been too long since he'd thought of Bobby. Too long since he'd found any clues to lead to his cousin's murderer.

And poor Big John. The man probably was still

aroused in his grave by the fiery, sensual woman he'd
left behind. *To Big John.*

"Ya want a card, or not, Rawlins?"

He blinked, gazed blearily at the hand he held, and
shrugged. "I'll play these." His fingers toyed with the
stack of chips that had steadily grown in front of him.

The man to his right took two cards. Curly Jim, the
dealer, stayed pat, and the fourth player, Colonel Pugh
himself, asked for one.

Craig drained another glass. His lips curled. The
more he drank, the more it burned.

The bet was five dollars. He met it and bumped another five. The colonel folded. Curly Jim raised another
five, cleaning his poke. The man to Craig's right folded.

Eyes narrowed, Craig met the bet and, for pure or-
neriness, raised another ten dollars. With a slight curve
to his lips, he watched Curly Jim squirm. Craig didn't
much care for the mountain man with the scarred
pate—stark evidence that some Indian hadn't liked him,
either.

Craig waited. Curly Jim fished in his pockets, came
up empty, then slapped a big, elk-horn-handled knife on
the table.

"Got a knife." Craig signaled for another bottle of
rotgut.

"Ya gotta take it. It's all I have," Curly whined.

"Then the pot's mine." Craig lifted his hand to rake
in the money and chips.

"Wait." Curly wiped beads of sweat from his pink
forehead. "Com'ere, gal."

Craig kept his features blank as a young Bannock
woman stepped silently from the shadows. Olive-
skinned, with thick black hair, the girl's beauty was evident, even beneath a swollen eye and bruised cheek.

Curly Jim grabbed the girl's arm and dragged her
closer. She winced. "Don't worry, gal. I ain't gonna
loose ya."

The Indian showed no emotion as Curly Jim smiled

at Craig. "This be my wife, Black Eyes." He chuckled. "Ain't never been able to pernounce 'er Injun name." Then he speared Craig with a sharp glare. "She be worth more'n ten dollars. Ya take 'er on the bet?"

Looking at the Indian girl, Craig thought of Billie and the Empty Barrel and all of the misfits she'd assembled. Billie would take to the girl like a peafowl to grain. His eyes hooded. She might even be real appreciative of his good deed. *If* he won, of course.

"Yeah, I'll take her."

Curly snorted and grinned an ugly grin. "Figured ya would."

"You're wastin' my time, Curly. Show your cards."

Sneering, Curly turned over two pair, queens high.

One by one, Craig displayed a spade straight.

Curly shot to his feet, shoving his chair over backward. "Ya cheated, damn ya. Ya cheated. Ain't no one kin be that lucky."

"You dealt the cards," Craig pointed out calmly, though his right hand lowered to rest near his gun.

Colonel Pugh laid a pistol on the table, his finger curled around the trigger. "Ain't gonna be no fightin' in my establishment. The hand was won fair an' square."

Curly growled, shoved the Indian toward the table, and staggered to the bar.

Craig pocketed his winnings, then looked at the girl, whose eyes had never left the floor. Her demeanor brought back memories of an emotionally injured lady with fancy jewels.

"You speak English, girl?" He hiccuped and grinned.

She shuffled her feet, but finally nodded.

"Good. Let's get outta here." When he reached the canvas flap, he cast a wary glance through the dim lanternlight toward the bar where the surly Curly Jim was giving the bartender grief.

The girl didn't hesitate to follow, but no matter how hard he tried to get her to walk beside him, she refused.

At last, just outside the door to the Empty Barrel, he asked, "What's yore name?"

Eyes downcast, she replied, "Black Eyes."

He shook his head. "Your real name."

She muttered something in her native language.

Craig nodded and translated, "Falling Water." Taking hold of her shoulders, he forced her to look squarely at him. "I promise no one's going to hurt you here." He swayed and caught himself. "You may even li-like it. Will you shstand right here . . ." His finger waved around in a huge circle as he tried to pinpoint a certain spot. "until I c-call for you?"

She nodded once and lowered her eyes.

When he turned to open the door, it was already open. He frowned. Music and smoke and laughter filtered out. Suddenly, he blinked and looked around. It was dark. Real dark. No wonder the lanterns had been lit at the colonel's.

Taking a deep breath, he shoved through the doors and strode unsteadily inside. The place was crowded and men were lined up in front of both the bar and Billie's table. So far, she hadn't seen him. He hiccuped. Good.

Motioning to Erik Swenson, he pointed out the door. "There's an In-Indian gal right outshide." He leaned close to Erik as if whispering a close-kept secret. "Keep an eye on her for me, will you?"

The big man took a whiff of his boss's breath, arched a brow, and nodded.

"An' when I take off my hat . . . an' wave it in the air," he gave a demonstration and stumbled, "es-escort 'er over to Billie."

"Yes, sir." The guard shook his head, bemused by Craig Rawlins's very unusual state of intoxication.

Craig scratched his chin, felt the raspy stubble, and remembered he hadn't cleaned up since entering town. For a second, he hesitated, then thought of Falling Water. He had to stay.

There were only two men left in the ticket line, so he fell in behind them. In front of Billie at last, he shoved his hat back on his head and just stood there when she held out one hand and reached for a chip with the other.

Wondering what the hold-up was, Billie impatiently fumbled with the stack of dance chips and said, "One dollar, please."

When all she received was more silence, she glanced up quickly. At the sight of Craig, her mouth dropped open, then snapped shut. "Craig." He looked so handsome, still dressed in his buckskins, shirt and vest and tall boots. And dangerous, wearing his gun and knife. And devastating, with his shirt half open, heavy-lidded eyes, and stubbled beard.

He leaned close. She sniffed and wrinkled her nose. She smelled smoke and damp flesh and alcohol. Lots of alcohol. He grinned boyishly and grasped the table. Inebriated? Craig Rawlins?

"I have somethin' for you, Angel."

His breath teased her ear. She shivered with anticipation. Her eyes drifted shut. She licked her lips. *The kiss.* Drunk or not, he'd remembered.

Chapter Twenty

Craig looked over at Erik and waved his hat. When he glanced back to Billie, her eyes were closed and her breath was coming in short, wispy gusts. She was so beautiful, and he wanted nothing more than to lean down and kiss her with every ounce of his being . . . But Erik arrived at that moment with Falling Water. Drawing her to his side, Craig proudly announced to Billie, "Here she is."

Here *she* is. His words rattled through Billie. She?

Billie's eyes popped open. Craig stood before her, grinning, his arm around the shoulder of a beautiful Indian girl. The backs of Billie's eyes began to burn. She fought the disappointment welling in her chest. Very calmly, very properly, she asked, "Who is this?"

"This's Fallin' Water. I know you've been tryin' to find more girls to dance. Ishn't she perfect?"

"Perfect." Billie would've had to have been blind not to notice the girl's black eye and bruised cheek. She felt an instinctive twinge of sympathy break through her suspicion. "H-how did you meet her?"

"Ah, in one of the gamblin' hells." He blinked, wondering why he suddenly felt guilty.

Billie pursed her lips. "Is that where you were all afternoon?"

He thrust out his chin. "Yep. And if I hadn't been there, I never woulda won her."

"Won her?"

Falling Water at last found her voice. "Curly Jim bad man. Bad husband." She turned huge, luminous eyes on Craig. "Now have good man. This man be good husband to Falling Water."

Billie's eyes rounded.

Craig froze.

With her heart plummeting to the pit of her stomach, it was hard for Billie to clear her throat and croak, "Congratulations." She felt so hurt. So betrayed.

Craig gaped at the Indian woman. "No, no. Big, big misunderstandin'. I'm *not* your husband. I'm not married and never will be."

Billie blinked back hopeless moisture in her eyes.

Falling Water crossed her arms over her chest and stared stonily at Craig.

"The only reason I agreed to Curly Jim's wager was to help her," Craig explained to Billie, whose features seemed carved in marble. He looked around to find raised eyebrows and curious stares. Finally, he turned to Falling Water, gesturing with his hands. "I just wanted to bring you here, where you could earn a little money and be free. Free to do as you pleased."

Falling Water's face showed no emotion. "This is true?"

Craig nodded.

"I free? I free from being wife of Curly Jim. I choose to be wife of Rawlins." The Bannock girl looked around at the other ladies laughing and dancing. "And I work here."

"Well, partner," Billie said in a tone so sweet she hoped it turned his blood to sugary sludge. "Does this mean you've taken over the hiring and firing of employees?"

Craig swayed and took a step backward. He held up his hands. "No."

"So you're just taking over the girls?"

This time he shook his head. "No." The last thing he

wanted was more female trouble. "If she works here, she works for you ... Miss Billie."

Billie turned her gaze on the stoic native and gave her a disarming smile. Thrusting her hand forward, she told the girl, "Welcome, Falling Water. Glad to meet you."

Falling Water looked suspiciously at Billie's hand before running her palms down her dirty leather tunic. Awkwardly, she placed her hand in Billie's. "Want dress like you."

"Well ... The dresses we wear are a kind of uniform. Something everyone wears when they work in an emporium." She held her breath, watching the girl closely. "Unfortunately, Falling Water, we cannot have women who have husbands. Our women dance with many men. One husband would be a problem."

Falling Water looked stricken. She glanced from Craig to the couples on the dance floor. At last, she nodded. "I stay." She looked shyly through her lashes at Craig. "I free, so no husband."

"No husband," he agreed emphatically.

Falling Water grunted. "Good."

Craig wondered if he should feel hurt.

Billie called Pearl to take Falling Water in hand and, ignoring Craig, turned sad eyes to the man behind him in line. "One dollar, please."

Over the next few days, Billie's ankle steadily improved to the point that she could get around without the cane. Falling Water and Molly had become fast friends and the Indian girl caught on quickly to the waltz, polka, and shottische.

Sunday morning, Billie sat in the kitchen, extremely pleased with the success of the Saturday market. Several farmers had offered eggs, which sold up to a dollar apiece. Milk went for twenty-five cents a quart. And there were heads of lettuce, peas, and beans. Ranchers contributed sides of beef, deer, and antelope.

She grinned as she thought of the ingenious Danny. Paper was too scarce to waste wrapping meat, so he'd sharpened sticks and sold them to folks needing to carry the meat home. Falling Water had shown a couple of little girls where to find lamb's-quarter and they sold the greens for a dollar and fifty cents a bucket.

Everyone seemed pleased with the way the market was working. More and more people came each week. Farmers and ranchers made a profit on items that might otherwise spoil. The miners and townspeople were assured of fresh food. Even Ike was happy, for he bought up surplus to sell during the week from his mercantile.

"Miss Billie . . . Miss Billie. Guess what?" Danny skipped into the kitchen.

"I don't know. What?"

"I'm gonna be a porter."

Billie cocked her head, then looked behind him into the main room. "Has Molly been teasing you again?"

Danny giggled. "Naw. Mr. Rawlins done give me a new job. A real important job. He says I'm a porter."

"My goodness. That certainly sounds impressive." Billie wondered what Craig was up to, meddling in employee management again.

"Yep." The boy beamed and puffed out his chest.

"Just what does an important porter do?"

He wrinkled his nose and several freckles winked at Billie. "It's so much stuff I don't know if'n I kin 'member it all. But Mr. Rawlins, he's gonna show me ever'thin'." He held up one finger. "Gotta sweep, but cain't raise a speck o' dust. Wow! I ain't never seen no one do that."

He held up two fingers. "Gotta clean winders without no steaks."

"Streaks," Billie corrected. "That would be in the early morning or late afternoon."

Danny bobbed his head and held up three fingers. There was a long pause. All at once he used the same hand to snatch a cookie from the plate in the center of the table. With his mouth full, he garbled, "An' there's bunches more stuff. Polishin' an' oilin' an' all."

Billie frowned. "That's a big responsibility for a little boy."

He gulped down the cookie. "I ain't little no more. An' Mr. Rawlins says I'm a good worker."

"You like Mr. Rawlins a lot, don't you?"

A wide grin displayed his recent loss of a front tooth. "He's the bestest."

Molly walked into the kitchen, holding a paper. She sat down next to Billie and just stared at the print.

"Molly? What's wrong?"

"Yeah, ya look like ya jest puked, or somethin'."

Molly stuck her tongue out at Danny, then darted several covert glances at Billie, as if trying to decide whether to admit to something, or not.

"This here paper come in with the freight an' caused a hell of a . . . ah, ruckuss. Men're bawlin'. I seen it with my own eyeballs. An' fightin'. Bawlin' an' fightin'." With one last considering look, she shoved the paper at Billie. "Reckon ya could read me what it says?"

Danny climbed up on another chair. "Yeah, read to me, too."

Before she took up the paper, Billie asked Molly gently, "You can't read?"

Molly flushed and shook her head.

Danny hollered, "Me, too."

"Well, we might have to rectify that situation," Billie declared.

"Huh?" Two voices echoed each other.

"Would you like to learn?"

Molly shyly nodded.

Danny bounced in the chair. "Me, too."

"I could teach you."

Molly and Danny grinned at each other.

Still thinking about teaching, Billie pulled the paper over and absently glanced at the headline. Her breath caught. Nausea churned her stomach. "Oh-h-h . . ."

"What, Miss Billie? What's it say?" Molly eagerly leaned forward.

Billie thought back to the evening several weeks ago when a young man had talked about receiving a letter from his brother saying how badly in need of shoes and supplies the southern army was. A tear trickled unnoticed down her cheek.

Molly's fingers squeezed her arm. "Please, Miss Billie."

"It seems there was a huge battle . . . at a place called Gettysburg . . . in Pennsylvania."

Pointing to the large, bold-faced type, Molly asked, "What's that say?"

Billie swallowed. Her heart was breaking so, she didn't know if she could repeat the words. "M-more than fifty thousand men killed, wounded, and missing . . . Ten leading generals d-dead . . . Both armies crippled . . . The coun-countryside littered with bodies of soldiers and horses . . . Crops trampled and fences shattered. Relatives flocking to seek sons and brothers. Every building a hospital."

She stopped, covering her face with her hands. "Dear Lord, how can we do this to each other?"

"Fif-fifty thousand?" Molly whispered.

"How many is that, Miss Billie?" Danny's eyes rounded. He'd never seen her cry before.

The back door opened. Lucky dragged himself through, closed the door, and leaned back against it. From the main room, Anna bustled into the kitchen. She stopped abruptly at the sight of the silent, ashen-faced occupants around the table and of Lucky's stiff, still form.

"What's happened?"

Lucky stumbled into the room. Without a second thought, he wrapped Anna in a bone-crushing hug. Sensing his need, she responded in kind, whispering a repeat of her question. "What happened?"

Billie brushed the back of her hand across her eyes. "There's been a terrible battle, Anna. Terrible . . ."

Anna gasped, unconsciously squeezing Lucky tighter.

Danny scurried over and threw his arms around his mother's legs. "How many's fifty thousand, Ma?"

"Fifty thousand what?" She lifted one of her arms from around Lucky and ruffled her son's blond hair.

Lucky kissed Anna's cheek and stepped back, mouthing a silent *thank you*. Noting the paper drooping from Billie's trembling fingers, he bent and took hold of Danny's shoulders. "It's more people than live in Alder Gulch. It's more people than live in the whole Montana Territory. It's more than should . . . should . . ."

Danny straightened and very solemnly patted Lucky's back. "That's all right. Reckon it's more'n I kin count, anyways."

Lucky nodded and smiled through brimming eyes.

Billie gently inquired, "Did you lose someone, Lucky?"

"I don't know." He ran his fingers through his hair. "I have two brothers who, last account I had, were in the cavalry under General Buford. Buford's troops were there. All I can do is hope. And pray." He sadly sank onto a chair.

From outside came the sound of gunfire and angry shouts. Someone yelled, "The Union won, by God. We won."

Billie shook her head and looked at the paper. "Doesn't seem like either side won."

The back door swung open again and Craig stomped inside. Scowling, he walked over to the assembled group. "I'm tempted to close down tonight and let some of these idiots cool off."

"No," Billie disagreed. "There're a lot of men who will need a familiar place to come and seek a few smiles and arms to comfort them, even if it's for just one dance." She stood and tested her ankle. "I'll be dancing tonight, too."

"I think it's a mistake," he reiterated. "And your foot

isn't ready to take that kind of pressure. What about your bruises? Those men will be touching—"

Billie held up her hands. "I'll be careful. We all will. I'll talk to the girls before we open, along with the Swensons."

"At the first sign of trouble, I make the call. If I say close, we'll close."

"Fine." She might be compassionate, but she was no fool.

The evening was surprisingly quiet. There was little laughter, and many of the men just sat and stared into their drinks. The girls were all kept busy dancing, but few man-to-man couples bothered to expend the effort.

Two men traveling by horseback had been attacked and robbed by outlaws and Craig was called out to ride with the Vigilance Committee. Billie could tell something bothered him when he left, but she didn't question him about it. They'd had little reason or opportunity to talk since Falling Water had come to the emporium.

During the orchestra's last break, about half an hour before closing, Falling Water came over to Billie, who kept watching the door as if she expected someone to walk through at any moment. Someone special.

"That Craig Rawlins. He your man?"

Billie sucked in her breath. "No. Of course not. Why do you ask?"

"You look him. He look you. Later, him look you. You look him. Both no see." The girl shook her head and walked away.

"But—" Billie put out her hand, but it was too late to call her back. The orchestra had started to play.

Falling Water was mistaken. There was nothing between herself and Craig. At least on his part. He'd forgotten the promised kiss, had barely touched her since the Vigilance Committee had formed.

They were friends. That was good. That was enough.

So, *why*, she asked herself, did she suddenly feel like she was going to cry?

The next morning at breakfast, everyone was there, even Craig. Billie would catch herself watching him, and find him watching her. Then she'd jerk her eyes away. Once, she met Falling Water's amused gaze and felt the heat of embarrassment.

Before the dishes were cleared, she announced, "I'm going to start a school."

Her declaration was met by total silence, but she quickly captured Molly and Danny's attention. "And you two will be my first students."

Surprisingly, Molly nodded.

Danny crossed his arms over his chest and stuck out his chin. "I ain't goin' to no school."

"But you said yesterday you wanted to learn to read with Molly."

He shook his head.

"Thought you wanted that job as porter." Craig also crossed his arms over his chest and glared at the boy.

Danny scowled and nodded.

"A man has to be educated to have that job."

"But ya said I—"

"That was before I learned you couldn't read."

Danny's eyes brimmed with tears.

"But I'll hold the job open for you, should you prove to me you can read, and understand what you read."

Danny straightened in his chair. His look was belligerent, but he informed Billie, "Reckon I'll be there."

"You know . . ." Pearl arched a perfectly plucked brow. "I promised a gent that I'd teach him to speak French. Might be others that'd like to learn."

"Where ya gonna do all this?" practical Anna asked.

"That's a good question. If it was just going to be Molly and Danny, we could do it here."

"I know a gal 'bout my age . . ." Danny's freckles

turned bright red. "Her ma works down at the Gold Nugget. Bet she'd wanna come."

Craig scratched his chin. She wasn't just teaching a reading class. She planned much more than that. So she was a teacher. It figured. Anybody but an experienced teacher would think opening a school an overwhelming proposition. It was one more piece to the puzzle of her past, a piece she wasn't aware she'd revealed.

"There's a vacant building next to the freight office. A merchant went broke and left it for me to sell. So far, nobody's been interested."

"How much does he want for it?" Billie had saved most of her money, and had accumulated a tidy sum.

"I could probably make you a good deal." Craig grinned. "Maybe even rent it to you till you're sure—"

"I'm sure." She was becoming more and more excited about the venture. "We can contact the women in town who have children." She glanced at Pearl. "And mention it here at night." To Craig, she said, "Perhaps you can send an order for books and supplies with your next wagon." She knew just the place to get them in St. Louis.

He shrugged. "Sure."

She smiled. "Wonderful."

He felt as if he'd been kicked in the gut when her smile fell full force upon him. Damn but he wanted that woman, more than he'd ever wanted any woman. And from the way she looked at him every now and then, she seemed to return his feelings.

But things had changed. He'd done something he wasn't proud of, and when she found out, and she was bound to find out, she'd want no part of him. And why should he blame her? He could hardly stand himself.

Yet a little later that morning, when he received word from Ezekiel that another foal had been born, he went straight to Billie.

"Are you busy this afternoon?"

Billie's pulse leapt at the sight of him. As he came

closer, it felt like her blood boiled through her veins. That afternoon? She had so much to do it would take two days to catch up. "Uhmmm . . . no."

He smiled. "Then how would you like to take a ride out to the ranch? Spot's sired a new foal."

When he laughed, she melted inside.

When she laughed, jolts of desire ricocheted throughout his body.

"I'll go get the buggy."

"And I'll get a wrap."

"You won't need one. It's a gorgeous day."

"Then I'll fix a lunch basket."

He flicked the brim of his hat and strolled jauntily out the door.

She quickly packed bread, cheese, and sliced roast venison. A bottle of wine from the bar completed her basket just as Craig pulled up out front. She could hardly stop grinning as she walked out to meet him— felt like a schoolgirl with her first crush.

But what she felt for this man was more than a crush. Much more. Somehow, he'd worn through her defenses. She'd grown to like and trust him to such an extent that— She gulped, afraid to further explore her feelings.

Craig took the basket and set it behind the seat. He fought to keep from trembling as he helped her into the buggy. They both stared straight ahead, surreptitiously darting glances at each other as they rode out of town.

But both were extremely aware of their joined hips and shoulders. They sat stiffly, but maintained the contact.

Billie twisted her hands in her lap. She couldn't stand the strained silence. "Business has been good."

He nodded.

"Uhmmm, Falling Water seems to like working at the emporium."

He cleared his throat. "About that night . . ."

Her chest tightened. "Yes?"

"I—I . . . never intended to be so late. Or to show up . . ."

"Inebriated?" she added helpfully, her lips quirking slightly.

"Drunk's more like it." He cast her an embarrassed grin. "I just got to thinkin' and didn't realize . . ." He shrugged.

Billie straightened her spine and gazed fully at his chiseled profile. "Thinking? About what?" Even now he appeared to carry the weight of the world on his shoulders. It must have been something very profound.

He'd been afraid she'd pick up on his slip of the tongue. Sighing, he decided he might as well tell her the truth. Something he probably should've done a long time ago.

"You remember the day you arrived in Alder Gulch?"

She nodded. There were still some foggy areas to her life, but she recalled that day clearly. "I don't think I'll ever forget it. The sight of your . . . cousin . . ."

"Me, too. Anyway, I made a vow to Bobby and Big John Turnbow that I'd find their killers."

She gasped. "It's my fault, isn't it? I've kept you too busy at the emporium."

"No," he chuckled. "That's not it at all. I've had time to do some checking around. But there's nothing left to go on. No one saw or heard a thing. And I guess after . . ." He hesitated. He wouldn't tell her the real reason he'd stopped off at Colonel Pugh's; he couldn't stand to think of it himself.

"Guess I just drank more than I should have." He turned his head and looked her in the eye. "I'm sorry."

"So am I. I didn't exactly help the situation when you came in with Falling Water." She wrapped her arm around his and scooted closer. Her heart felt like it could float from her body, so elated was she that he'd shared his feelings.

He grinned and pressed his arm, and hers, against his

side. "It was kinda nice, though, having two women fight over me."

"Why . . ." Her eyes widened. "I never . . ."

"You were damned sure jealous. Your face turned as green as that grass when you looked up and saw me with another woman."

She sniffed. He was right. But she didn't have to admit it.

Laughing at her indignant expression, Craig was surprised when they turned the bend and saw the ranch ahead. The time had flown by so quickly he'd never had the chance to tell her he'd bought that building next to his office and that she could use it free of charge. Hell, he'd donate the damned place to the betterment of the community. Anything that would keep Billie interested and busy enough to want to stay in Alder Gulch.

Ezekiel met them as they pulled up in front of the barn. "You shore gots a purty li'l filly, suh."

"How's she doing?"

"Healthy as a hoss." The black man chuckled at his own humor. "How do, Miss Billie?"

"Hello, Ezekiel. Just fine, thank you." She smiled and received one in return from both men.

"Let's go see the little gal." Craig swept her into his arms and carried her over the uneven ground.

Billie giggled and wrapped her arms around his neck.

At the back of the barn, Craig reluctantly released her legs, but maintained his hold on her upper body so that she was still in the circle of his arms, her breasts molding firmly to his chest, as she found her footing. She gazed up into his eyes. He looked down and caught his breath. His head lowered.

A horse nickered.

Craig briefly rested his forehead to hers, then turned her to look inside the last stall. It was the dark-brown mare Billie had become so fond of on their first trip to the ranch. The mare whickered softly. Craig stepped into the stall. "Afternoon, Beauty. Where's your little one?"

A rustling in the straw drew their attention to a sorrel filly with a white blaze, four white stockings, and white splotches on its neck and sides and rump that looked as though the good fairy had stood back and thrown snowballs that melted and stuck to its hide in a truly artful design of color. The filly stood on awkward, wobbly legs in the corner. A ray of sunshine squeezed through a crack in the rafters, illuminating the snowy white and deep-red coat.

Billie came in behind Craig. "She's precious."

He had just turned to look at Billie and believed the description to be quite appropriate. "Yes. She certainly is."

"May I touch her?"

The mare snorted and moved stiffly to place herself between her baby and the humans.

Craig patted Beauty's neck. "All right. We'll give you two a chance to get acquainted first." He put his arm across Billie's shoulders and walked out with her. "You can love on her all you like the next time."

Next time. She hugged the words to her heart. Would there really be a next time? She truly hoped so.

While Craig closed the gate, she looked back at the nursing filly. "What're you going to name it?"

Craig didn't hesitate. "Angel." From the first moment he'd seen the foal in the beam of light and then Billie's wondrous expression, he'd known.

She snapped her head around, but Craig was busy talking to Ezekiel. When he turned back, he asked if she'd like to walk up and see the house.

"I'd love to." She'd been fascinated with the house their first trip. She could hardly wait to see the inside.

Clouds had boiled up since they'd arrived. A gusty wind twirled her skirt. Lightning flashed. They were a hundred yards from the house when thunder rumbled directly overhead. Huge plops of rain soaked into the dust. Craig grabbed Billie's hand. "We better make a run for it."

She limped along as best she could. When the wind blew harder and the rain fell faster, he scooped her into his arms. She squealed and clamped her arms around him. His long, muscular legs covered the rest of the distance in no time flat.

Once beneath the porch overhang, he laughed, feeling like a kid again, until he looked into her glowing amber eyes. Then he felt like a man, holding a very desirable woman.

With her still in his arms, he opened the door, carried her inside, and closed it behind them.

Billie felt the beating of his pulse where her fingers pressed into his neck. The steady rhythm increased. Her own heartbeat responded in kind. A ripple of excitement vibrated up her spine.

"You're cold." As he had in the barn, he released her legs, but let her twist until the soft mounds of her breasts flattened provocatively against the hard planes of his chest. But when he felt her body quiver, he completely released her and went over to kneel in front of a stone fireplace.

"I'll have a fire started in just a second."

Billie followed him over, crossing her arms and rubbing her hands up and down in an attempt to ward off the arousing sensations his body had ignited. Start a fire? He'd already done that.

While he was busy, she used the time to look around the living room. The two chairs and sofa were made from knotty pine and cowhide. Brightly colored rag rugs added to the varnished pine floor. Stretched animal hides and a painting of "Spot" decorated the walls. It was exactly the way she'd pictured a man's dwelling.

"Do you like it?"

His voice carried an expectant note. She cocked her head and pretended to make a close examination. Then she grinned. "I love it."

"So do I. I come here whenever possible, which hasn't been often lately."

To keep from completely melting beneath the searing glow in his eyes, she asked, "How many horses do you have?"

He rocked back on his heels and wiped his palms down his thighs. "Besides my personal stock, which you've seen, I furnish the saddle horses for the stable and the teams for the freight business. Plus replacements for any animals sick or injured."

"That's . . . quite a few."

He inclined his head, then pulled her down beside him on a bearskin rug. "Are you warming up?"

She was. But the warmth came from the closeness of his big body hovering at her side rather than the fire, which was blazing brightly. Every once in a while a raindrop survived the heat going up the chimney and sizzled on the logs.

His finger touched the side of her neck. She shivered and unconsciously tilted her head. The gesture allowed her to look anywhere but at him. She wasn't sure she wanted him to know that she liked the way he touched her, that she wanted him to do it again, or that she might combust if she looked into those wickedly colorful eyes.

He chuckled. His breath teased the nape of her neck. She started and straightened her back. Too late, she realized the movement brought her almost nose-to-nose with the irresistible man.

He traced the outline of her lips. "I've been waiting."

"Waiting?" She frowned, but he smoothed the wrinkles from her brow.

"You were going to welcome me back one night, but I didn't make it."

Her breath caught. She trembled all over. Lightning crackled. Thunder boomed. Her heart stopped.

"Thought I better collect what's due me."

Her lips parted. He hadn't forgotten. *The kiss.*

Chapter Twenty-one

Craig's firm, warm lips met Billie's gently, sweetly. An aching sensation spiraled through her body as he leaned back against a chair leg, coaxed her onto his lap, and cradled her protectively in his arms. An unfamiliar pressure began to coil in her belly.

She spread her fingers over the taut muscles of his back. Treasuring the feel of power and strength beneath her touch, she became emboldened and explored the contours of his smooth flesh.

Her hands flittered over his skin as lightly as butterfly wings. He quivered and shifted his legs beneath her bottom.

Hard evidence of his desire nudged Billie's backside. Desire that she inspired. It was a thrilling confirmation.

The kiss was everything—and more—that she expected it to be.

Craig was astonished by her ready acceptance and then full participation in the delicate joining of their mouths. He eased his tongue over the softness of her lips and, with gentle insistence, the smooth ridges of her teeth.

Billie sighed. Leaning against him, her body felt like butter melting over hot bread. Her jaws relaxed. His tongue dipped into her mouth—hot, wild, and wet. Blood raced through her veins. Her breasts grew heavy.

A strange moistness at the juncture of her thighs drew her knees tightly together.

Craig groaned as she snuggled against him. Her innocent squirming aroused his male need to a pulsing urgency. She was the most naïvely sensual woman he'd ever known. Though her hands and lips seemed inexperienced, she had the body and instincts of a courtesan.

He lifted his head. His breath rasped across his lips—lips that throbbed the demand that he taste her again.

Billie whimpered when his mouth left hers. He'd teased her with mind-boggling pleasure and now left her bereft, yearning for . . . for an unknown, elusive something she instinctively sensed only he could provide.

She raised her eyes. His gaze seared through her, igniting primal urges she'd never known she possessed. She wanted—no, needed—to experience every temptation he offered. He'd been so many things to her—savior, protector, friend, companion, partner. Through his tender care and patience she'd learned to live again, to feel and to . . . love.

Lightning popped. Thunder vibrated the house. She placed her palms on his cheeks and gazed adoringly into eyes that were a softer brown than she'd ever seen before. "I—I've never been kissed like that."

He reverently touched his lips. "Neither have I."

Her heartbeat matched the fury of the storm. Reaching for another kiss, she melded her breasts to his chest, her hip to his thigh.

Craig swallowed, enfolded her in his arms, and scooted down until they stretched full-length on the rug in front of the fire. He growled with ravenous hunger when she rolled into him, filling the depressions in his body with her soft, rounded flesh.

He hoped to God she knew what she was doing, because he wasn't sure how long he could control his body's raging needs. "A-angel . . . Are you sure?"

She couldn't find the breath or the will to speak. Instead, she slipped her hands beneath the hem of his

shirt, which must have pulled loose from his trousers
when he shifted them to the rug. Once again her fingers
massaged his taut, quivering muscles as she gently tested
their resilience with the smooth edges of her nails.

Inhaling several deep breaths, Craig stroked his fingers down the elegant column of her neck, over the
smooth roundness of her shoulder, and then cupped her
breast. She arched into his palm. The hard bud of her
nipple sent shock waves rippling directly to his loins.

"My God but I want you, woman." His voice shook
with the power of his declaration. His entire body trembled from the force of his desire.

Tracing his lower lip with her finger, Billie startled
herself as well as Craig when she stated firmly, "And I
want you."

Discarded clothing soon littered the brown fur rug.
Billie purposely tossed a petticoat over the blank eyes
and gaping jaw of the bear's shaggy head. For just a second, as she stared into the immobile features, her breath
caught. A wispy fog distorted her vision. Another pair of
eyes—evil eyes—gleamed through the haze.

Craig placed his finger beneath her chin and turned
her face to his. "Shy, Angel?"

She blinked and took a breath. Flames from the fire
sensuously warmed her chilled skin and reflected from
the liquid depths of soft, aqua-colored eyes—eyes that
were anything but evil. An erotic and intense heat van-
quished the haunting image. Slowly, she inclined her
head.

Sensing her hesitation, he whispered, "You are so
very beautiful . . . I'd never do anything to hurt you.
You know that, don't you?"

She nodded. He'd more than proven his caring and
tender ways—not by spouting sweet words, but by his
everyday actions. Her uncertainty was caused by her
own wild, unladylike response to his touch.

"Craig?" She wriggled her hips as his fingers played
up the inside of one thigh and down the other.

"Uh-huh?" He kissed her nose, her cheeks, and her chin. When her legs parted under his continued caressing, he swiftly filled the space with his lower body. She cradled him perfectly.

"Kiss me. Please?"

"Yes, ma'am." His lips and tongue adored every naked inch of her. When her fingers brushed his manhood, he sucked in his breath and groaned, "Yes-s-s. Touch me. Again."

Then his mouth replaced his hand on her breast. The suckling sensation from his lips pulsed through the core of her being.

Sliding his hands beneath her firm buttocks, he lifted her hips and slid the tip of his manhood against her femininity. Indescribable pleasure rocked through his body when he discovered she was hot and wet and ready for him.

As aroused as she was, when his hard yet silken flesh sought entrance to her body, Billie experienced another moment of doubt. Everything she'd done until now had been from pure instinct. What if she couldn't please him?

Sensing her retreat, Craig claimed her mouth with a searing kiss and undulated his hips in short, sensual strokes until her body naturally responded.

He pushed deeper and came up against a restrictive barrier. His breath hissed through his teeth. He paused, withdrawing slightly.

Billie clutched his shoulders when he stilled above her. Her eyes sought his, pleading for surcease from the aching pressure spiraling within her.

His gaze probed the wild, yearning, hazel depths. He gasped, "I didn't know . . ."

Her hips moved of their own accord. "Please," she begged, her voice a dry whisper. She dug her heels into the fur, lifting herself higher and higher, seeking, wanting . . .

Her honeyed moistness urgently surrounded him,

sucking him down ... down ... until her maidenhead yielded him entrance. He eased in and out slowly until her inner muscles gradually relaxed and she accepted him fully.

Billie felt the slight, tearing sensation, but the discomfort was soon replaced by tiny, rippling shock waves as he thrust deeper and deeper, filling her over and over with pleasurable sensations so intense that they were almost painful.

The pressure intensified. She wrapped her legs around his hips, demanding he release her from the shuddering sensations wracking her body. Her body convulsed. She gasped. Sparks exploded behind her eyelids. It felt as if her spirit separated from her body and soared. And when she floated to earth, she landed in the safe haven of his arms.

Craig held back as long as he was able. With one final, shuddering thrust, he joined her in flight. Ragged breaths lifted and deflated his chest. Collapsing beside her, he pulled her into the crook of his arm and kissed her damp forehead.

Breathless, and unable to express her tumultuous feelings, Billie curled against him and swirled her fingers through the wiry curls matting his chest.

Craig captured her hand and raised her fingers to his lips. "Are you all right, Angel? Did I hurt you?"

Languidly, she traced his lower lip. "I-I'm fine. Wonderful," she admitted in a hushed, awed voice.

"Good." He nuzzled his nose into her hair and glanced out the window. The storm had almost abated. Squeezing her tightly, he patted her bottom and reluctantly sat up. "As much as I'd like to cuddle in front of the fire the rest of the afternoon, I'm afraid we'll have to hurry to get back to town before dark."

Billie warily studied his eyes. She saw nothing to indicate that he was trying to worm his way out of an indelicate situation and sighed with relief.

Sensing her trepidation, he leaned down and tenderly

kissed her passion-swollen lips. "Thank you for the most beautiful moment of my life."

Her throat clogged. The backs of her eyes burned. If she'd had any doubts about giving herself to this man, he'd just set her fears to rest. A euphoric feeling settled over her as she stretched and watched him dress with uninhibited fascination.

He caught her watching and gave her a wolfish leer.

She laughed delightedly. The man was a rogue.

But when he then came over and helped her into her own clothing, she revised her description. He was sweet. She cupped his cheek in her palm. "You're wonderful. Oh." She hadn't meant to say that out loud.

Flushing, he teased, "I've hoodwinked you good, haven't I?" Then he tweaked her nose. "What I am, though, is hungry. Where's that lunch you promised?"

Bemused by the thought that she'd embarrassed him with her compliment, she blinked and said, "I guess it's still in the wagon."

He tossed another log on the fire. "The rain's about to quit. Stay right where you are and I'll get the basket."

Sighing, she rose to her feet as he rushed out the door. Through the window, she watched him lithely run an obstacle course around puddles of mud, the muscles in his long legs clenching and stretching . . . He was magnificent.

Touching her kiss-swollen lips, she closed her eyes and thought of another word that had come to her in a startling revelation. *Love.* She loved him. The man who'd announced adamantly to Falling Water and the world that he wasn't married and never would be.

The ride back to Alder Gulch was once again a silent one. Craig was lost in thought over the gradual weakening of his vow to remain uninvolved. The woman was storming his defenses and he didn't from one minute to the next know what to think or how to act. All he did

know was that he thought of her. Almost every second
of every day, every minute of every night. And now that
they'd made love, he wanted her even more. He wanted
to feel her silken skin, taste her sweetness, hear her
husky voice moan his name. He wanted all of her, for all
time. Damn!

Billie quietly watched Craig's profile, noting the tense-
ness in his jaw, the muscle that jerked in his cheek.
What was he thinking? Had he been as affected by their
coming together as she? Or was he already pondering
his next business venture?

As Craig pulled the team to a stop in front of the emporium, she looked up at the sign announcing the
Empty Barrel Saloon. She closed her eyes and imagined
it someday reading: The Grand Palace, Emporium of
Dance. A sigh slipped through her lips. Dreams. Only
dreams. And for some reason, she didn't want to think
about the future.

Craig stepped out of the buggy and went around to
hand Billie out. But when he reached up, she wasn't
looking. Her gaze was directed down the street.

The buggy rocked when Craig got out. Billie grabbed
the delicate brass and had just regained her balance
when she noticed a passing rider. His back was to her,
but there was something terribly familiar . . .

She frowned. The western garb seemed strangely out
of place on his narrow shoulders and slim frame.
Shaggy, chocolate-brown hair stuck out from beneath
his hat. A tremor quaked through her body. A dark
cloud blocked her vision. Her ears rang with memories
of shouts and curses and screams and—

"Billie! Snap out of it." Craig, unnerved by the blank
stare creeping into her eyes, shook her shoulders. Her
entire body trembled. The sight chilled Craig. She'd
come so far, what had happened to suddenly make her
revert to behavior she'd given up weeks ago? Whatever
it was, he wouldn't allow it to consume her again.

The sound of Craig's commanding voice penetrated

the fog clouding Billie's mind. She squeezed the rail until it bit into her palm. An overwhelming urge to sink back into oblivion hovered in the recesses of her mind, tempting her to make the easy choice.

"Billie! Look at me!"

She swallowed. No. She would not give in. She would not take that route of escape again. Looking determinedly into Craig's worried features, she drew the strength she needed.

Slowly, she released her grip on the buggy. She held out her hand. "Help me?"

Craig drew her into his arms, grateful her retreat had only been momentary. Still carrying her, he entered the Empty Barrel and, ignoring the curious stares of Lucky and the girls, took the stairs two at a time. Once inside her room, he kicked the door closed and set her gently on her bed. Taking her face between his palms, he forced her to look at him.

"What happened out there?"

She smiled brightly and forced a chuckle. "I—I'm not sure." But she reached up to touch her necklace and realized her shaking hands might have given her away.

They had. Craig steadied her fingers with a light touch. "Come on, Angel. Talk to me. I haven't asked you anything about who you are or where you came from because I could tell it would be distressing. But something is wrong. What can I do to help you?"

She took a deep breath and shook her head. "I wish I knew. I really do. There are so many things I don't know . . ."

"What *do* you know?"

"I've remembered my name. Wil—Billie Glenn. My home was in St. Louis. I have a father and stepbrother." She wrapped her arms over her chest, suddenly afraid.

"Is that all you've remembered?"

"No. I remember everything. Everything up to a certain time. Then there's a gap until I bought passage to 'anywhere' from Denver."

He waited patiently for her to continue.

"It's that time in between . . . When I try to remember . . . dark shadows creep out at me." She shrugged. "Silly, huh?"

Craig reached out again, tugged her hand from the necklace and held it. "One thing I've noticed . . . Whenever you feel uneasy, you reach for the necklace. Does it have something to do with your running away?"

She shivered. The stones suddenly seemed to burn the flesh beneath them. "I—I'm not sure. All I know is, I always feel *safe* when I touch them. I can hear someone whispering, *They will keep you safe,* over and over."

Craig sat beside her on the bed. He put his arm reassuringly around her shoulders.

She turned to him and held on for dear life.

Some of the puzzle had fallen into place for Craig. He finally knew her last name—a name that was oddly familiar. And he knew where she was from. He was also certain that his original assumption that she'd suffered some sort of emotional shock was correct.

He squeezed her shoulders. "I wish I knew how to help you, Angel."

"You already have. In many ways." She sniffed and slowly released her tight hold on him. "I was afraid if I told anyone, people would think I was crazy."

"You're definitely not crazy. But something must've happened outside today to bring on this reaction all over again."

She nodded. "It was the strangest thing . . ." Too strange to share. If she admitted she'd panicked at the sight of a stranger's back, Craig might refuse to leave her alone. She wouldn't allow her fears to alter her life—or his.

He watched her lower lip tremble and grasped her hands. "Look at me. That's better. I'm going to help you. Somehow. You're not alone now. Do you hear me?"

* * *

Things were almost back to normal that evening in the emporium. Billie planned to dance. Lucky was once again in charge of the chips. Craig would tend the bar. The only hitch was that Joe Smith, the cornet player, hadn't come to work.

Billie approached the other orchestra members. "Have any of you seen him today?"

No one had.

"Could he be hurt? Should we send someone to look for him?"

Eduardo shook his head. "There is rumor. Maybe José bought new claim with money he earn here."

"But would that keep him from sending word? Surely he couldn't work twenty-four hours a day." She frowned. "What?" The men were looking at her and shaking their heads.

"Miss Billie . . ." Jack Dawkins tried to explain. "When you think you're about to hit a strike, you don't notice if it's daylight or dark, or if it's Tuesday or Sunday. You just keep diggin'."

"I see," she sighed. "Will we need to find someone to replace him?"

"Don't reckon." Ben pointed to a man with a beard growing halfway down his chest. "Ole Whiskers has a guitar. We'll see if he'd like to sit in sometime."

Jack called out, "All hands round," and the music started.

As Craig made his way toward her, her heart skipped a beat. Her palms grew sweaty. Her eyes drank in his incredible good looks. And her heart swelled with the knowledge that he cared for her.

Craig swung her into his arms and moved in a graceful 1–2–3, 1–2–3, stepping in rhythm to the waltz. "Where's Joe?"

She leaned close so he could hear and told him what Eduardo had said.

Craig inhaled sharply. His eyelids drooped as he smelled her feminine scent. "Hope he strikes it rich."

A sudden succession of blasts shook dust from the ceiling. She arched her brows. "I hope they all do before the town comes down around our heads."

For the next three days, clouds came up every afternoon. Rain soaked the streets, making walking in the thick mud hazardous. On her way to the freight office, Billie slipped in a puddle and bumped someone who shrieked, then cursed like a miner.

"Well, if it isn't Miss Billie. I shoulda known. Still walkin' around with your head in the clouds?"

"Hello, Sunny." Billie found a dry spot under an overhang.

"Where's Craig? Thought you two were joined at the hip," she sneered.

"You thought wrong," Billie countered, although she couldn't help but wish it were true. "How've you been, Sunny? We haven't seen much of you lately." Thank heavens. She'd liked the woman at one time, but their last few encounters had been too unpleasant.

Sunny jutted out her chin, ignoring Billie's question altogether, and slyly cast her eyes toward the freight office. "Are you goin' to see Craig?"

Gritting her teeth, Billie admitted, "Yes."

"Good. I'll join you."

Billie lagged behind as Sunny barged full speed into the office. Ever since the afternoon at the ranch, she'd felt like she was walking on eggshells, never quite sure of what to say or do around Craig. It was nothing he'd done. In fact, he'd gone out of his way to help her feel comfortable. She just wasn't certain how much, or little, of her feelings she should express.

Craig looked up from his bookwork. He saw Sunny storming forward and Billie hesitating just inside the door. "Afternoon, ladies."

"Hello, darling."

"Sunny . . ." Craig turned his attention back to the papers on his desk. "How've you been?"

"How nice of you to ask. I'll tell Justin. He misses you."

"And I, him. Justin's a . . . an unusual young man," Craig said without raising his head. He'd worked hard to befriend the boy, and still wasn't sure he'd succeeded.

He looked up, over Sunny's shoulder. "Come on in, Billie. Your crates are in the corner." *Please, come in,* he mentally entreated. *Save me.*

Billie walked uncertainly into the room. Her confidence increased when he looked at her with such warmth and encouragement.

Sunny seethed as the other woman came forward. Brazen upstart. Just who did she think she was, to try to take Sunny Turnbow's man? She followed Billie over to the boxes. "What're those?"

Billie pried open the lid on the first crate. Books, slates, and pencils were stacked to the top.

Sunny harrumphed. "What're you goin' to do with all that?"

"Billie's startin' a school." Craig came over and put his arm possessively around her shoulders. "Already has seven kids, and even a few adults, signed up to start in a few weeks."

"Well! Now, why am I not surprised. Little Miss Perfect's on a real crusade to better the community."

"Look, Sunny . . ." Craig removed his arm from around Billie and took hold of Sunny's elbow. None too gently, he led her toward the door. "If you just came in to say hello, I appreciate it. Tell Justin I'll see him soon."

Sunny yanked her arm from his grasp. Standing on tiptoe, she peered back at Billie. "Good to see you, too, honey."

Billie inclined her head, frowning at the too-sweet tone in the older woman's voice. The hair on the back of her neck stood on end.

After Craig closed the door behind Sunny, he returned to Billie's side and gave her a hug. "Don't let her upset you, Angel."

"She doesn't. I think I understand a little about how she feels." The natural way he'd come to her and the sweetness of his gesture filled her heart to overflowing. She gave him a shy smile.

"You do? How?"

"She feels threatened. And she's jealous. Either one of those two emotions could cause a woman to behave irrationally."

"Maybe." He rested his chin on the top of her head and hooded his eyes. Had Miss Billie been jealous, too? Because of him? His chest constricted. He damned sure hoped so. Releasing her, he hunched his shoulders and added slyly, "But if she's behaving that way because of me, she has no good reason. There's never been anythin' between us."

Billie mentally shouted with joy, but visibly merely raised an eyebrow. "I don't think she sees it that way."

Anxious to get off the subject of Sunny Turnbow, he picked up a book from the crate. "Are these what you wanted?"

She nodded, grateful that he'd changed the subject.

"Good. Have you given any more thought as to whether you want to use the building next door?"

"It just depends on how high the rent will be."

"Last I heard, he was thinking about donating it."

"You mean we wouldn't have to pay anything?"

He shook his head.

She grinned and threw her arms around his neck, then just as suddenly backed up, frowning. "No. It wouldn't be right."

"What are you talking about?" Of course it would be right. Just the suggestion had earned him a hug. "Why not?"

"Because . . ." How could she explain her feelings about accepting charity—of any kind? Especially for something so important. After all, she had her own money now.

Craig gripped her shoulders and forced her to look at him. "This isn't a private business you're starting. It's a school. It's for the whole town. Don't most cities provide sites and build schools without it costing the teachers anything?"

"Yes. But—"

"Maybe this man can afford it, and wants to contribute a little something to the community. At least until the town votes to build a real school."

She tilted her head and studied his face. "You. You own the building."

He opened his mouth to argue, saw the look in her eyes, and shrugged. Before he realized what she was doing, she reached up and kissed him on the mouth. It happened so suddenly, he had to touch his tingling lips to believe it.

Such a sweet, unselfish gesture he'd made. "Thank you." It wasn't enough, but it was all she could think to say. She cleared her throat, glancing around for an excuse to prolong her visit. "I'm worried about Joe Smith. No one seems to have seen him lately."

"I keep hearing talk that he's working a claim on the other side of the creek."

"Oh, good." She scuffed her toe on the floor.

"I'm sure he'll come back around before long." How could he make her stay longer? There were so many things he wanted to say, to do—mainly just hold her in his arms. They'd both been so busy since that stormy, glorious afternoon at the ranch that they'd had little opportunity to be alone or to talk—especially about what was happening between them. He took a step forward but glanced toward the open door and the crowded street. No, the office wasn't a good place.

"Uh . . . I'll have someone take those crates next door so they'll be there when you're ready for them."

She smiled. "Thank you." She looked at him, but he

was staring out the window. "Well, I've got to get back . . . I guess." She wanted to put her arms around him and hold him forever. Wanted to tell him she loved him.

"See you tonight." He was so damned confused. He didn't want her to walk out the door. Wanted to keep her by his side today and always. But he couldn't. He'd fought and clawed so long to make something of himself that he didn't know how to make room in his life for a woman. Not even Billie Glenn.

Billie trudged morosely down the street, paying little attention to where she was going. It was so muggy and humid after the rains that she felt smothered. A wagon passed too closely, splattering her with mud. She moved farther away from the road, but continued her meandering, thinking about fate and wondering over the events that might have precipitated her flight from her past. A flight that landed her in Alder Gulch.

She had to remember. Had to put the pieces of her life together before she could make plans for her future.

Just ahead, to her left, someone was hammering on a false-front building constructed of wood and canvas. As she neared, she recognized Dr. Timothy Andrews. He was nailing a sign to a post and she stopped to read what it said. It was his name, with the initials "M.D." burned into the short plank.

When he saw her, the doctor called out, "Miss Billie, looks like you're walking much better."

Smiling, she answered, "Yes. Yes, I am." In fact, she hadn't even thought about her ankle that morning. Other than feeling a few twinges, she barely limped at all. "Evidently you decided to stay and open a practice."

He grinned. "After I talked to you, I got to thinking about it, and noticed all of the families moving into town. I may not be much of a miner, but I *am* a pretty fair doctor. Or *was.*" His eyes misted. "And I am needed."

"I'll say you are. I'm so glad you changed your mind."

He ducked his head. "Thanks to you."

"Oh, no. Eventually, whether it was Alder Gulch, or some other place, you would've gone back to your medicine."

"Maybe. Maybe not. But you made me see what was important. I do thank you for that."

"My pleasure." She felt heat crawling up her neck. "At least now there's a place to go when someone needs help."

"Yep. The door's open."

She waved and wandered on toward the emporium, actually taking the time to look now as she walked. Dr. Andrews was right. There were more new businesses opening every day. Good, solid structures were being built. Alder Gulch was quickly becoming a real town.

And she was a part of it. Was beginning to feel like she belonged, and that she could make a good life for herself here. Whenever she thought of St. Louis, she didn't think of it as *home*. Home was . . . in Craig Rawlins's arms.

All at once, her steps faltered. Goose bumps pricked her flesh. Sensing someone watching, she looked hastily around but saw nothing out of the ordinary. Everyone seemed in a hurry to get wherever they were going. Nary a soul glanced in her direction.

A stronger blast than usual from the hillside vibrated the ground. She inhaled deeply, relieved that she must have just sensed the explosion. There was nothing to be afraid of.

Several nights later, the emporium was again filled. Billie was proud of how well the place was coming along. The interior walls had been decorated with an ecru-and-rose brocade. Beige linen napkins adorned new tablecloths. And Anna had added doughnuts and crullers to the fare offered at the bar.

Men sat and read the latest paper and discussed, or argued, the war, politics, mining inventions, and home. The air hung thick with cigar smoke and the aromas of spilled liquor and coffee. She breathed deeply. It was the smell of success.

The only disappointing note to the evening was that Craig was gone—again. The second stagecoach of the day on the busy route running between Salt Lake City and Alder Gulch had been stopped and robbed. Over forty thousand dollars in gold dust had been stolen. After extensively briefing the Swenson brothers, Craig had reluctantly joined the Vigilance Committee. She had hated to see him leave. Though things couldn't be going better, she had an eerie feeling. Something was about to happen.

Mentally chiding herself, she collected a chip from a short, rotund man who immediately squashed the toes on her good foot. She fared little better with the next two men and was hobbling toward a chair during an orchestra break when the hair on the back of her neck stood on end.

She darted glances around the dance floor, but no one appeared to have noticed anything untoward. Taking hold of the back of a chair, she looked to see if Lucky needed help at the bar.

Her gaze passed over, then came back to a pair of faded brown eyes that darkened with recognition. Her heart froze. The man was very stocky and maybe a couple of inches taller than her own five feet and seven inches. Shaggy dark-brown hair stuck out from beneath his black hat. His round face changed expressions quickly, from surprise, to disbelief, to . . . something she couldn't read.

Perspiration beaded her flesh. He stepped up to her. A light-headed sensation caused her to sway.

"Wilhelmina, what are you doing here? Father and I have been worried sick."

Chapter Twenty-two

Billie's legs refused to support her. She sank into the chair. Her ears rang so loudly, she shook her head.

Samuel. Her stepbrother. Here. In Alder Gulch. Why?

"Wilhelmina?"

She shuddered and looked up. He stood directly in front of her, blocking any means of escape. So many emotions rioted through her that she couldn't sort through them all.

Her fingernails dug into her palms. She forced her eyes to meet his. "H-Hello, Sam." How strange. She hadn't noticed how close-set his eyes were before. Why, the narrow bridge of his nose barely fit between them.

Samuel made a tsking noise with his tongue. "Why did you run away? Thanks to you, poor Father's health is ruined. You should have come to us. *We* would have helped you."

The soft drip of his voice turned Billie's stomach. Every time he said her name, Wilhelmina, shivers raced down her spine. And then she realized he'd told her she should have gone to *them*. *They* would've helped her. Did Samuel know what had caused her to leave St. Louis?

She reached toward him, frowned, and snatched her hand back. Her eyes pleaded for answers as she looked at him. "Why, Sam? Why did I leave? Do you know?"

He cocked his head and studied her through slitted eyes. "You don't know?"

She shook her head. "I—I've ... lost some of my memory."

His expression shifted.

Billie suddenly felt a hand on her shoulder. She jumped and snapped her head around. "Oh, Pearl. Thank goodness." And behind Pearl was Anna.

"This fella giving you trouble?"

Billie clasped her hand over Pearl's. "N-no. Th-this is my step ... brother, Sam. Samuel Jones."

"Samuel Jones *Glenn,*" he corrected.

She closed her eyes, trying to remember. Yes, her father had gone through the formalities of legally adopting Sam, but it had been after she'd gone to finishing school. She didn't know many of the particulars, only that everyone had seemed so happy then. Now, why had she thought *seemed?* Her temples began to throb. Why couldn't she remember?

Pearl grimaced and gently extracted her fingers from Billie's grasp. She curled and straightened them to make sure her hand hadn't been broken. Her eyes narrowed on Samuel. "Did you just get into town?"

He backed up a step. "I've been here a couple of days. Why?"

Billie stiffened. The man she'd seen riding through town the afternoon she and Craig had come back from seeing the filly ... It must have been Sam. And she hadn't recognized him. Or had she not wanted to?

Pearl shrugged. "No reason. Just thought you would've come to see your sister before now, is all." She glanced over to Anna, who'd stepped in closer to Billie. There was something about Samuel Jones Glenn's beady eyes and too-cheerful features that she didn't trust. Even Billie was visibly shaken. Why? The man was *family.*

"I didn't know Wilhelmina was here. Saw her for the first time a few minutes ago."

ANGEL'S KISS   339

A deep sigh sounded through Billie's tight lips. Somehow, it was a relief to know he hadn't followed her,
hadn't been searching for her.

Anna asked him, "What ya gonna do here? File a
claim?"

He chuckled.

Billie shivered.

"Who'd want to *work* when the gold can be plucked
so easily from the man who's already mined it?"

Pearl's lips curled. "Then I take it you're a gambler?"

Molly and Falling Water joined them, having only
gotten in on the last of Samuel's statement. Falling Water was the only one who recognized the practicality of
his words.

Samuel patted his bulging vest pocket. "That's right,
sweetheart."

Black shadows flitted in and out of Billie's mind. Yes,
Sam had always been a gambler. She recalled many
evenings when her father had waited up and Sam had
come home drunk and complaining about being
cheated. He hadn't been such a good gambler then.

The orchestra began to play. Anna announced that
Billie would be sitting out, resting her foot. Within minutes, the girls were all drawn away. Pearl was the last to
leave, and she looked at Billie questioningly. "You going
to be all right?"

Billie hesitated, scolded herself for acting so perversely, and nodded.

When they were alone again, Samuel asked, "What're
you doing in a place like this, little sister?"

She sighed. He'd called her "little sister" when they
were younger and she'd always been so proud to have
a handsome older brother. She'd been the envy of all
the girls at school and many had cajoled her until she'd
invited them home with her on special occasions.

It hurt to think he might not be so proud of *her* anymore.

"*This place* happens to have been my idea. I'm a partner in its operation."

His eyes narrowed even more as his brows drew together. "Well, well. Who would've thought?"

Billie felt more and more uncomfortable beneath his probing gaze. She reached up to touch the necklace, which was hidden beneath her high-necked collar.

Samuel saw the gesture and was about to say something when the doors to the saloon slammed open. A man shouted, "There's a bunch of riders comin' in. Looks like someone's been kilt!" The doors "thwapped" again as he quickly left.

Billie's heart leapt into her throat, them plummeted to her toes. Craig? He'd gone with the committee. Had something happened? Had he been hurt?

Please, God, she prayed, *let him be all right.*

Rising unsteadily to her feet, she barely glanced at her stepbrother. "Excuse me, Sam. I have to go."

"But—"

She kept walking, following the stream of men who poured through the doors and into the street. All she could see was the sluggish movement of shapes and shadows. Then she heard the creak of saddle leather, plodding hooves, and muttered voices.

Through the blackness she distinguished a spot of white. As it came closer, she recognized Craig's stallion. As the riders drew abreast of the emporium and the light spilled through the door and window, she caught a glimpse of Craig's face and gasped.

She'd never seen him look so haggard and worn. The lines on his face appeared to be gashes. His hat was pulled so low she couldn't see his eyes, but his grim lips told her all she needed to know. Something had happened out there. Something horrible.

And then she saw a set of reins dangling from his limp right hand. She followed the line of leather straps back to an extra horse carrying a tarp-wrapped body.

A man standing in front of her stepped over and lifted

the tarp. When he turned around, he choked, "It's Joe. Joe Smith."

Oaths were spat. The noise level of the crowd rose. One man hollered, "What happened ta Joe? Did ya git them danged owlhoots what done it?"

Men raised their fists.

"Let's go git the dirty bastards."

"String 'em up."

"Hey!" yelled the man who'd identified the body. "Joe ain't been shot. His neck's broke."

Deathly silence covered the crowd.

Someone cleared his throat.

The merchant, Ike, spoke up. "It was an accident. We were looking for anyone carrying a suspicious amount of gold . . ."

Eduardo Crespin cursed. "I seen Joe this morning. He was on his way to City of Salt Lake. His gold go to bank and family. The gold he carry was his."

Craig dismounted and tied both horses to the rail. "That's what I told them. Only it was too late. By the time I got there, Joe was dead."

The men were speechless. Craig pushed his way through and disappeared into the emporium. Billie weaved between the men and followed him. Lucky and the girls were the only ones left inside, and they stood in the doorway where they could hear what was happening in the street.

Molly pointed toward the kitchen. Billie nodded and hurried her steps. When she entered the room, Craig stood with his back to her, staring . . . seemingly at nothing. He held Joe's cornet in his hand, his knuckles white with tension.

"Craig?" she whispered. When he didn't acknowledge her, she walked closer and put her hand on his arm. He flinched, but it seemed more from surprise than displeasure at her touch.

All at once, he turned, engulfing her in his arms. She felt his body tremble and hugged him to her. She'd never felt so helpless. What should she do? What could she say?

Strong, stalwart, always-in-control Craig Rawlins had turned to her, deeply affected by a friend's death. Gunshots and the undertaker's wagon might be common occurrences in Alder Gulch, but Craig would never take a man's death casually.

Her heart ached to ease his pain all the more because she loved him.

"Have you seen a man hanged?" His voice was deep and scratchy.

She gulped. "N-no."

"Good . . . I've seen three."

Billie waited. When he didn't explain, she questioned, "Three? When?"

"Two last week, and Joe."

"Ah-h-h." Now she knew why he'd looked so drawn and sad the time she'd seen him riding into town with the other members of the Vigilance Committee. The Committee. "Can you quit the Committee?"

"No!" He raised his head, gave her a squeeze, and stepped away. "We're all in this for the long haul."

Rubbing the back of his neck, he paced the length of the room. "There's no civil law for two hundred miles. If we citizens don't do something, there'll be no community to protect."

"Yes, but—"

"I was one of the first ones who mentioned forming some sort of group to take matters into our own hands. I'm as responsible as anyone—more so, when mistakes are made."

"You would've stopped them if you'd known."

He nodded.

"So you can't blame yourself entirely. Your motives were for everyone's good."

"But Joe—"

"Was an accident. A terrible accident. What you have to do now is think of the stagecoach drivers, their passengers, your freight, the bank employees whose lives you're saving. Someone is always bound to get hurt. And many times it's the innocent. But to safeguard the town, who wouldn't take the risk?"

"I suppose . . ."

"Why do they hang all those men? Why can't they bring them in to be tried?"

He shook his head. "No civil law means no sheriff or marshal or peace officer of any kind. No judge. No jail. And it was decided by everyone concerned that the only way to deter the outlaws was to pursue them relentlessly until they paid the penalty of their crimes on the gallows." His lips quirked. "Not my words, but it gets the point across."

"Mob rule always eliminates choices." She spoke the words sadly, but without judgment or accusation.

"I feel like we're playing God with men's lives and I don't like it. But the men who formed the committee are decent, hard-working, honest men. They're only doing what they have to do to protect their families and their businesses."

"You truly believe that."

"Hell, yes."

"So . . ." She walked around until she looked him square in the eyes. "Regret, grieve, and then forgive yourself."

"I wish it were that easy." He hunched his shoulders. "And what about Big John and Bobby? Joe's was just another death I couldn't prevent."

She swallowed. "Death is never easy and should never be taken lightly, ever. But you must go forward. Remember them, find a way to make their deaths count for something, and move on."

He reached for her and hugged her to him. She closed her eyes and savored the moment. She prayed she'd been a help, had said something to ease his mind.

"Thank you, Angel." He kissed the top of her head.

"I didn't do anything."

"You listened . . . Really listened. I've never been able to talk to anyone like I can talk to you."

She chuckled, but choked. "I feel the same way."

An emotion so soul-consuming he couldn't describe it, welled in his chest. His arms tightened. His mouth swooped down and captured hers. Whether her lips were already parted in an attempt to talk, or whether they opened under his sudden assault, he'd never know. All he *did* know was that he was able to plunge his tongue into her sweet, moist mouth and explore her softness to his heart's content.

Billie didn't know if it was the confusion she still felt after her encounter with Sam and then the emotional turmoil of trying to help Craig face his demons, but she felt as if his hard arms and warm body were a haven of safety, that this man offered her the promise of security and peace of mind. He made her feel whole, memories or no, and that by having him in her life, she'd find the courage to face whatever trials lay ahead. She'd been right before—home was in his arms.

And so she returned his embrace. Tasted and felt the exquisite softness of his mouth. It was good to be free, for just a moment, to allow herself to indulge her fantasies and desires, to give of herself in a way she'd never given before, by offering comfort and love.

Craig held on to her and soaked in her responses. If only he could cherish her forever. But though he welcomed these few moments, he knew better than to expect anything so wonderful.

Having never had the steadying influence of a father, or even a mother, who loved him, he had no way to measure the depth of her feelings. But no woman had ever made him feel so wonderful, so happy, so complete.

He'd never thought about being *happy*. She added a special kind of joy to his life—and he liked it.

"Say, Mr. Rawlins, we're gonna take Joe up to Boot Hill— Oops! Sorry." Lucky stumbled to a stop, his face beet red at the sight of Craig and Billie kissing.

The bartender's voice had grown stronger as he approached, but the embracing couple had been too engrossed with each other to notice. And even when they'd been caught, Craig was reluctant to let her go.

Billie, under no such dilemma, jerked away red-faced, and quickly smoothed her hair and bodice. The motions were wasted, however, as Lucky had turned away and was awkwardly tiptoeing out of sight.

Suddenly, her hands fluttered to her sides. She looked from Lucky's back to Craig, whose warm brownish eyes had never left her, and smiled. The smile turned into a chuckle. Soon Craig's deep rumble joined in and they laughed.

Hearing the merriment, Lucky turned back around. Hesitantly, he walked into the kitchen. "Really," he said, spreading his hands, "I'm sorry. Shoulda called out."

"It's all right, Lucky. No harm done, was there, Miss Billie?" Craig winked.

She shook her head, but couldn't stop the heat suffusing her face.

"What were you saying about Joe?"

"There's a coffin down at the undertaker's. We were thinkin' we'd go ahead and take Joe up to Boot Hill. Some of the boys are up diggin' the grave right now."

Craig hunched his shoulders. "Well, I reckon since everyone's already gathered, it wouldn't be a bad idea." He circled the table as he resumed pacing. "Does anyone know how to contact his family?"

Lucky frowned. "I'll check with Eduardo. He might know."

"Joe's saddlebags are hangin' over my saddle horn. Why don't you bring them in and we'll see if there's anything worth saving."

Lucky nodded. "Be right back."

While he was gone, Craig went around to stand in front of Billie. He traced her lips with his index finger. "You weren't embarrassed for him to see me kissing you, were you?"

She shook her head. Embarrassed? A little. That someone should see that they cared for each other. No. In fact, she was proud that a man like Craig found her appealing. She didn't care if the whole world knew.

"Here it is!" Lucky called loudly. He poked his head in first, saw that the pair weren't embracing, and walked on over to drop the bags on the table.

Craig untied the strings on one bag. He opened the flap and his eyes widened. It was stuffed with leather pouches. Taking one out, he spread the drawstring. Then, with Billie and Lucky looking on, he poured out dust and nuggets that appeared to be very high quality. He ran his hands into the bag, but found nothing besides more pouches.

The process was repeated on the other side. This time, along with pouches, he found a Bible and a packet of letters.

"Poor fella," Lucky admonished. "Wonder how much family he had?"

Craig decided against opening the packet and lifted the cover on the Bible. "I'll be damned. His name really *was* Joe Smith. Looks like there's a mother, a sister, and a married brother. We can send them the gold and let them know there's a claim if anyone wants to work it, or sell it."

"Yeah. The boys will like that."

Craig squeezed Billie's arm. "You want to go to a funeral, or would you rather stay here?"

Affronted, she informed him, "Mr. Smith was an employee and a friend. Certainly I'll go."

Craig managed a grin. "Of course."

The entire Empty Barrel contingent made the trek to Boot Hill. From the number of people crowded around, it appeared all of Alder Gulch had turned out to see Joe Smith put to rest. There were a few angry mutters and rumbles of discontent, but most of the men had accepted the death as the horrible mistake it was.

Since there was no preacher, everyone stood around

until Eduardo Crespin, Ben Hanshaw, and Jack Dawkins came forward. Eduardo cleared his throat. "Joe
Smith . . ." He remembered his sombrero and slid it off
his head to hang down his back. "Joe Smith was an
hombre bueno. He go to good place." He quickly
stepped back. Dick had brought his fiddle and began to
play. Since Joe supported the South, in a wonderfully
clear tenor voice, Ben sang the song, "Dixie."

Billie held her breath, waiting for half the mourners
to go for the other half's throats. But nothing happened.
Almost everyone joined in.

On the way back to town, Craig grabbed Billie's hand
and continued to hold it the entire way. Billie felt the
tingle in her fingers clear to the center of her being.
What magic had Craig Rawlins worked?

A short time later, the emporium was in full swing
again. Though it was late, to keep his mind off Joe, Big
John, and Bobby, Craig busied himself mixing gin and
pine, a drink that had to soak for two hours.

Lucky nudged his elbow. "Did Miss Billie tell you
'bout her brother comin' to town?"

Preoccupied, Craig shook his head and took a customer's order. Brother? He poured a jigger of whiskey.
That's right, she'd said she remembered her father and
brother.

During the next break, Pearl sidled up to the bar.
Craig glanced at her briefly, but continued cutting two
splinters from the heart of a green pine.

"Hear about Samuel Glenn comin' in to see Billie?"

"Lucky mentioned it." He concentrated on putting
the splinters into a quart decanter and filling it with Old
Tom gin.

Pearl frowned and looked for Lucky, but he was at
the other end of the bar pouring glasses of punch.
"What do you think?"

"About the brother?" He shrugged, distracted by his own thoughts. "Don't know. Didn't see him."

"But—"

Hands filled with empty bottles, he looked up. "Did something happen?"

"Well . . . no."

"What did he do?"

"Nothing, I guess. He left. But—"

"Then maybe I'll get to meet him the next time he comes in." Taking the bottles downstairs to the cellar, he realized he did happen to think it curious Billie hadn't mentioned her brother. And that Pearl seemed so suspicious of the man.

Upstairs, Pearl crossed her arms over her breasts and pursed her lips when Craig turned his back on her. Men! If you weren't talking about money, whiskey, or women, they weren't any more interested in what you had to say than a worn-out old rooster facing two dozen young hens.

Around ten o'clock the next evening, Craig was busy behind the bar, but while he worked, he surreptitiously watched Billie. She was acting strangely—continually looking over her shoulder, jumping whenever anyone came close. And during the breaks, she sat where she could watch the door.

Something was bothering her, and he was determined to find out what at his first opportunity.

The doors swung open and several men tromped inside. All had learned the rules and cleaned up—except one. Craig had never seen the man before. He was of average height and stockily built with dark hair and brown eyes that didn't linger long on any one place— *shifty* was the word that came to his mind. The fellow's shirt, vest, and trousers were unkempt and looked like he'd worn them for weeks.

Glancing to his left, Craig saw that Lucky was busy

and decided to handle the stranger himself. He stepped into the man's path as he headed toward the dance floor. "Hold up, stranger. It appears you don't know the rules around here."

Samuel sneered and tried to push past the impertinent bartender. "Look, *partner*, rules in this dump don't apply to me." He drew himself up and said importantly, "My sister owns the joint."

Craig stiffened. An awful feeling settled over him. Why hadn't he paid more attention to Lucky and Pearl last night? His eyes narrowed. "Sister?"

Samuel curled his lips and pointed toward the dance floor. "That's her. Wearing the emeralds." He eyed the tall man up and down, "If you work here, you should know her. Wilhelmina Glenn."

"And you say she's your sister?" Damn it, he should've made it a point to ask Billie about her brother. But then she sure as hell hadn't gone to any trouble to mention the fellow to *him*. Why?

Samuel brushed a layer of dust off his vest. The residue sifted onto Craig's polished boots. "*Step*sister." He scowled and gave the saloon a critical once-over. "Always knew she was a slut at heart."

That did it. Craig hadn't liked the man since he'd laid eyes on him. Now he grabbed the brother's shirt just at the base of his throat. "And what does that make you, you sonofa—"

A hand touched his arm just as he drew it back. He whipped his head around to find Billie standing beside him, her eyes a sad pale green as she stared at the man claiming to be her brother.

"You can let him go now," she said huskily, and watched as Craig reluctantly did so. Then, keeping her gaze directed at her brother, she said, "Hello, Sam." A cold chill shook her as his hard, glittering eyes stared back at her. She hadn't heard what had been said between the two men, but could tell they were both very angry.

"This . . . fellow . . . says he's your brother. Says he doesn't have to follow the rules and clean up before coming in." Craig spat, missing the closest spitoon by four inches. He didn't care. He'd wipe it up with this bastard's behind in another two seconds.

Billie took a deep breath and really looked at her stepbrother. He was wearing the same clothes he'd had on the other night and it didn't appear he'd washed or shaved since. He was also missing the bulge in his vest pocket and his confident air. He must be on another losing streak. That wasn't her problem.

She blinked and wondered when she'd become so uncharitable. Then, suddenly, she realized both men were staring at her, as if expecting her to say something.

"Well, are you going to let him stay, lookin' like that?" What he really meant was, *Are you going to back me up, brother or no?*

Samuel grinned cockily. "Of course—"

"Of course *not,*" she stated emphatically. "I'm sorry, Sam, but you have to leave."

Samuel's face flushed brick red.

Craig gave Billie a mental pat on the back.

Billie stood ashen as a cold campfire as Craig maneuvered Sam toward the door.

Samuel peered back at Billie. "Wilhelmina, stop him. You and I, we have to talk." His parting words grew dimmer. "I gotta have that necklace."

She heard. Her face contorted. She reached up and grasped one of the stones. It was hard and cold, matching the way her heart sat hard and cold in her breast. Suddenly, she swayed. The necklace. Sam. What was it about the two together that she should know? *They will keep you safe.* Dark shapes fluttered about her head. She raised her arms to ward them off.

Craig dusted his hands off after tossing the smart-mouthed stepbrother out of the place, and hurried back inside. He had a feeling in his gut that something was going on in Billie's head. The look in her eyes had him worried.

Damn. Sure enough, there she was—swaying, her arms thrown over her head as if she were warding off blows.

And then she screamed. A scream that raced chills down his spine.

Chapter Twenty-three

The first eerie shriek brought the commotion in the emporium to an abrupt halt. Silence settled over the room like a shroud. There wasn't a hardened heart that didn't melt a little at the sight of Craig Rawlins scooping the lady into his arms as if she were the most valuable possession in his world.

Pearl and Anna and Molly and Falling Water all rushed over to him as he strode with his now-limp burden toward the stairs.

"What's wrong with her?" Pearl shouted, struggling to keep up with him.

"What kin we do, Mr. Rawlins?" Molly asked, staring helplessly at the woman who'd done so much to improve her own life.

"I'll come with you," Anna announced, and started up the stairway.

Craig stopped and turned to the concerned women. He nodded at the crowded room and the worried men in the orchestra. "The most important thing you can do, for Billie's sake, is to keep everything running smoothly." He looked directly at Anna and then toward the bar where Lucky was coming around the counter. "Tell Lucky he's in charge tonight and you all do anythin' you can to help him."

When they hesitated, he assured them, "If I need help, I'll call. You have my word."

Once they'd agreed, he headed up the stairs. He'd just reached the hallway when he heard the first strains of music and imperceptively nodded.

Billie's door stood ajar. Thinking nothing of it, he pushed through and carried her over to the bed. He was busily loosening the laces down the front of her dress when he heard a soft click and turned to find the door was shut.

He jerked to his feet. Damn! Rushing to the door, he threw it open. Danny was just peeping from his room, rubbing his eyes.

"Danny, did you see anyone just now?"

"Naw, but I reckoned I heard somethin'. Someone jest runned by, goin' that a way."

Craig looked to the end of the hall and saw the curtains fluttering. Whoever it was must have come in and left through the window. He walked down and peered outside, but the alley was empty. After closing the window, he went back to Danny and rubbed the boy's shoulder. "You can go back to sleep now, son. Everything's all right." At least it would be after he had a long talk with the guards who were coming on duty soon.

Danny yawned and went back inside his room. Craig rushed on to Billie's room and breathed a sigh of relief that she still lay where he'd left her. If nothing else had gone right tonight, he'd surprised whoever had been waiting for her. Thank God.

He knelt on the floor, took hold of her hand, and stared at her frowning features. She was so vulnerable and at the mercy of . . . All at once everything came together. The gunshot. The cord across the stairs. And now the prowler. Someone was after *Billie*.

He squeezed her fingers and brushed a lock of hair from her cheek. Why? What could this sweet, kind, loving woman have done to make someone want to harm—possibly even kill—her?

Billie moaned. *She was in the library, all dressed up in her new green gown, waiting for her father. It was to be a special din-*

ner. She was leaving her teaching position and coming home to work with her father and stepbrother at the freight company. She was so excited.

The door opened. But instead of her father, Samuel staggered in. He was drunk. She could smell him all the way across the room. When he saw her, he sneered and called her ugly names.

"Billie! Billie, wake up." Craig grasped her hand more tightly as her head twisted back and forth on the pillow.

Ugly names. Names she'd never heard before and some she had. She backed up as he came closer. He was angry. Had thought she was out of the way when he'd talked their father into sending her to school. He'd even used good money to pay the schoolmaster to hire her.

Now she was going to ruin everything. Once again she would be the center of their father's world. She would be the one Thomas Glenn loved, not Samuel. She would inherit everything. Not Samuel.

He grabbed her. His nails dug into her flesh. She screamed. He laughed and tore at her beautiful gown. Yelling, he told her he was in control. From now on, she would do everything he said.

And then he tripped her. She fell to the floor. He came down on top of her. His foul breath smothered her. His weight held her helpless. She screamed. He slapped her. Again. Dear Lord, her wonderful stepbrother, whom she loved and looked up to and admired.

Sam! How can you do this to me? I love you! I love you.

No! His fingers were between her legs. He touched her in places he shouldn't touch her. It hurt.

The door flew open. Her father towered above them. His lips moved. Condemnation and disappointment flared in his eyes. Sam got up. Pointed at her. Her father shook. Shook so badly that when he looked at her, he was stricken with a sharp pain.

His heart! He staggered from the room. Her fault. All her fault. Never knew. Never knew of Sam's hate and jealousy.

Sam's face. Next to hers. No! He yanked her up and dug something from his pocket. Green. Emeralds. The necklace. She was a slut. She was cold, no good. No one would love her. She deserved expensive trinkets. He clasped it around her neck. He shook her and sneered, "They will keep you safe."

"Oh, Lord. No!"

Craig caught her free hand when she grabbed the necklace. He crawled onto the bed and held her as she fought and screamed her anguish. A droplet of water fell onto her chest. Craig was the one who cried.

A short time later, Craig had just dozed off when he felt Billie's legs shifting beneath his. He opened his eyes and found her face turned toward him. She'd been watching him.

"How're you feeling?"

She shifted again until she lay on her side, facing him. "Like a wet rag."

"What happened, Angel?" He brushed the backs of his fingers across her pale cheek.

"I remembered."

He thought of the silent battle she'd waged while he held her on the bed. It must be some story. All he asked, though, was, "Everything?"

She nodded.

He said nothing. If she wanted to tell him, she would. But he gathered her closer, needing to hold her. She did not resist. His chest ached with an emotion he couldn't describe.

"It was Sam."

"Excuse me?" He pushed his head back so he could see her face.

"Sam is the reason I left St. Louis."

Samuel Glenn was a dead man. At the first opportunity, Craig would deal with the cur. He'd see if the scum was brave enough to face a *man*.

Craig swallowed down his rage before asking calmly, "And your father?"

"I don't know," she sniffed. "He has a bad heart.

From what I recalled, he might have had an attack that
night. I might have k-killed him."

"Now, how could you have done that?" He clicked
his tongue.

She hiccuped. "By breaking his heart. By being a
huge disappointment." She told him then most of what
she'd remembered, making certain to mention the ex-
cruciating expression in her father's eyes.

"Are you sure he wasn't looking at Samuel?"

She shook her head. "No, but . . ." She didn't want to
think about it any longer.

Craig couldn't believe that a man who'd entered a
room and saw his daughter being attacked would think
the less of *her*. It didn't make sense. And as wrenching
an experience as Billie had had, she could have misun-
derstood.

"And the necklace? What about it?"

Automatically grasping a green stone, she told him all
she knew.

"Do you want me to take it off for you?"

"N-no!" Her fingers wrapped tightly around an emerald. "It—it's kept me going. Whenever I've wanted to
let the darkness swallow me, I'd hold on to the necklace.
I can't . . . won't give it up."

"It was your own strength and perseverance that got
you through. Not a damned necklace."

"I don't care." Her lower lip trembled. As much as
she'd like to believe him, she just couldn't. Not yet.

He quit pressing her. Sooner or later, she'd figure
things out on her own. "So, now what?"

"Nothing's changed."

"*Everything's* changed!" he insisted. "You don't have
that void looming behind you. You know what happened and why. You can get on with your life." And go
back to St. Louis, he thought sadly.

And because she now had an opportunity to recover
some of her confidence and poise, he didn't mention the
intruder. She didn't need any more to worry about.

"Right now, I'd just like to go on with the emporium and the school, if that's all right. If I didn't make too big a fool of myself tonight."

His chest expanded on an inhaled breath of relief. "Of course you didn't. And you can do anything you please." *Thank you, Lord.* He wanted more time with her, to delve deeper into his feelings, and hers. She had managed to make him reevaluate several of his decisions. He was amazed, curious, and determined to see what else was up the unsuspecting sleeve of fate.

Her nose brushed his neck when she nodded. "It's what I want for now."

"And your father?" He felt like a mynah bird, repeating himself over and over.

"I-I'll either find out from S-Sam, or send a telegram. If he's dead . . ."

He leaned up and gave her shoulder a shake. "You stay away from your stepbrother. You hear me?" He waited until she'd looked at him with rounded eyes and nodded her head. "Let me find out about your father." He relaxed his grip and bent to tenderly press his lips to her forehead. "We'll deal with the answer together."

She leaned back and gazed hopefully into his eyes. "Do you think there's a chance?"

"Definitely."

"What makes you so sure?"

"If he wasn't alive, your stepbrother would still be in St. Louis, gambling away whatever fortune your family possesses."

She hadn't thought about that. Just what *was* Sam doing in Alder Gulch? Was his purpose really to fleece the miners? The more she thought about it, the more probable it sounded.

"It would be a wonderful birthday present to find out he was alive and well . . ." she whispered.

He tilted his head. Birthday? When? But he didn't question her. He had ways of finding out. Wouldn't it be a nice surprise if they threw her a party? It would be the last thing she'd expect. And would be good for her. She needed some happiness, and the evidence that she was surrounded by real friends.

He kissed her eyelids closed. "Stay here and get some sleep. I'd better go back down."

"Thank you." She reached out and stopped him. "I'd never have gotten through that alone." And his kindness was just another rung on the ladder of reasons she cared for him so deeply.

"I'm glad I was able to help."

"D-do you have to go?"

He surely didn't want to. But, "Yes. Everyone in the saloon saw me bring you up here. I wouldn't want to completely ruin your reputation."

"What reputation?" she laughed a little hysterically. "I'm afraid women who work in dance emporiums are frowned upon anyway."

He shrugged. "There's not a person in this town who doesn't know what a decent, good person you are." Except for the one trying to kill her . . . and her stepbrother.

"Harrumph!"

"It's true."

"Whatever." She forced a yawn. "Didn't you say you needed to go downstairs?"

"Trying to get rid of me now?"

She nodded.

Hell would freeze over first. He grinned and kissed her on the cheek. "I'll check on you later."

"Is that a promise?" She sucked in her breath. She hadn't meant to say that out loud.

"You bet it is."

After the door closed behind him, she touched her fingers to her cheek, relishing the feel of his touch.

And then all trace of humor or fantasy evaporated. She stared up at the rafters, thinking back over the events that had caused her to run away from her home and the family she loved. Tears streamed steadily from the corners of her eyes and soaked into the hair at her temples.

After the orchestra announced, "Last dance, gentlemen," Craig instructed Lucky that as soon as the customers were gone and the doors closed, everyone was to gather in the kitchen.

Once Lucky and the four girls and the orchestra members had wandered in and settled into chairs around the table, Craig stood and cleared his throat.

"Billie remembered a few things about her past tonight. One of them was that her stepbrother is a no-good sonofa— gun." He inclined his head to the ladies. "I've given his description to all of the guards, but if any of you see him come in when I'm not around, look after Billie, all right?"

"I can't believe you thought you had to ask," an affronted Pearl huffed.

"What about if we just don't let him in, period?"

"I've thought of that, too, Lucky. But you know how busy it can get. We can't watch everyone. And I'd rather he contact her out in the open where we can watch him."

Some of the group shifted, ready to go home.

"That's not quite all." He told them about the intruder he'd scared from her room.

"Mebbe it was that Samuel gent," Molly offered. "Reckon we should—"

"No. He wasn't around when someone took that shot at us, or tied the cord across the stairs."

Anna scooted forward in her chair. "Danny keeps sayin' he hears somethin' in the hall at night. I been jest tellin' him to shush." Her eyes were wide, frightened. "Guess I shoulda believed him."

"Now don't go getting all upset. If I thought there was a danger to you girls, I wouldn't let you stay here. I've already spoken to the guards that come on duty after the emporium closes, and have hired more men to keep watch during the day. You should be well protected now."

That seemed to settle them down somewhat.

"And one last thing . . ." He waited until he had everyone's attention again. "Billie has a birthday soon. I'm goin' to wire some friends in St. Louis and do a little digging. When I find out the date, are any of you up to having a party?"

Even the musicians were enthusiastic. Ben thought he knew a piccolo player that might be interested in taking Joe Smith's place, since the man with the guitar had already left town.

"This is going to be a surprise, so don't mention anything to Billie. We'll get together again after I hear from St. Louis and make some plans."

Everyone discussed ideas for a while longer, until one by one they drifted home or upstairs. Finally, it was just Craig and Lucky.

"You're really worried about Miss Billie, aren't ya?"

Craig sighed. "Yes. I can't for the life of me figure out who'd want to hurt her."

"What would you say if I moved my things into the cellar and stayed here at night? That way I can keep a close eye on her . . . and Anna and Danny, too."

Holding out his hand, Craig said, "Thanks, Lucky." The two men shook. Then he added, "I'd feel a hell of a lot better if I could just hog-tie Billie and make sure she stayed in a safe place."

About half an hour later, Craig kept his promise, quietly opening Billie's door. He walked to the bed, where moonlight shone through the open window, illuminating dried tearstains on her face. She was such a lovely creature . . . The thought of something happening to her . . . of her suddenly being snatched from his life . . .

His fists clenched. To harm her, they'd have to go through him.

She still wore her dress. He hadn't unlaced her bodice very far and her breathing appeared labored. She had to be uncomfortable. With sweaty palms, he went back to the door and looked down the hall. When he'd come upstairs, there'd been a light under every door. Now they were all dark. Hmmm! He was left to his own devices.

Taking a deep breath, he softly closed the door and went back to her bed. A grin curved his lips. It was a lousy job, but someone had to do it.

His groin quickened as he remembered every silken inch of her luscious body. With trembling hands, he finished unbuttoning the dress.

"Billie? Wake up, Angel, and help me get you out of this contraption."

Billie blinked her eyes open. She sighed and held out her arms. "You came back."

Craig's throat suddenly went dry as a desert wind in June. Her eyes were filled with trust, and a vulnerability that shot directly to his heart. " 'Course," he croaked. "Told you I would. Now come on and raise up."

Once he'd removed the dress, and pulled her blanket up over her shoulders, he stood uncertainly. He wanted nothing more in the world than to crawl into that bed and love her like she deserved to be loved, but . . . She'd been through so much. He glanced toward the door.

Wide-eyed, Billie rose on her elbow. The blanket slid down, seductively displaying the rounded tops of her breasts through her lacy camisole. "You aren't leaving, are you?" Her voice quavered with alarm.

When she reached toward him, he threw his hat on the chair. "Hell, no." Peeling down to his drawers, he slipped in beside her so quickly that the bedstead creaked under the added weight.

Billie snuggled against him. Because of her earlier emotional turmoil, she turned to the person she knew best—her friend, her confidant, her lover. She couldn't go to sleep with bad memories clouding her mind. She needed to make new memories, wonderful memories, with the man of her dreams.

"Billie, I—"

"Sh-h-h." She slid her leg between his and raised her upper body onto his chest. Her lips whispered teasingly against his mouth, "Love me, Craig. Please, just love me."

Growling deep in his throat, he wrapped his arms around her, cuddling her breasts into the soft cushion of hair matting his chest. Then he trailed his hand down the pliant length of her body, from the soft underside of a firm breast, along her rib cage and small waist, over a flaring hip to her smooth, slender thigh.

He nibbled her lower lip and urged her mouth open to plumb the honeyed recess. Her tongue met his eagerly, thrusting and parrying until their bodies strained to get even closer. What little clothing remained, became too great a barrier. Garments sailed from beneath the blanket. Naked, wanting and needing, they stared into each other's eyes.

Craig opened his mouth, but before he could utter a word, Billie squirmed on top of him, straddling his hips with her thighs. She dipped her head, silencing him with a kiss full of passion and promise.

He slipped his fingers between her thighs, twining through her moist red-gold curls. His shaft throbbed with anticipation.

Billie instinctively rotated her hips, teasing and taunting the stiff male organ pulsing against her belly.

When she raised her upper body slightly, Craig took full advantage and filled his palms with her breasts. Gently squeezing the silken flesh, he circled her turgid nipples with his calloused thumbs, yet purposely avoided touching the sensitive buds.

Billie whimpered and took hold of his hands, forcing his palms over the hardened peaks.

Craig chuckled, lifted his head to take one of her nipples into his mouth and suckled greedily. He rolled the other between his thumb and forefingers, flicking the pebble-hard nubbin over and over with his nail.

Unable to bear the white-hot intensity of the heat igniting her lower belly, she moved her hips until his manhood nudged her nether lips.

Instantly, he cupped her buttocks and thrust deep inside her velvet sheath. Raising and lowering his hips, Craig exalted when the gold flecks in Billie's eyes sparked with fevered desire. Thrusting harder, his only aim was to give her the greatest pleasure possible.

Over and over he filled her. She felt his hardness slide to the center of her being and saw heaven. She'd never felt so warm and alive, so sure of herself. Her body spasmed. She dug her nails into his shoulders and met his lips with hers as he gallantly offered his mouth to muffle her cries.

They reached the pinnacle of release together, their bodies fused, minds filled with thoughts of the other. As their shudders gradually ceased, Craig pulled her down to rest, their damp bodies still joined and pulsing with the wondrous expression of their passion.

"Lord, Angel," Craig gasped. "I . . ." The emotions he felt for this woman boggled his mind. He wanted her—physically, of course, but it was more than just a sexual need. He wanted all of her. Her thoughts, her pleasure and pain, her . . . He swallowed. Her . . . love?

Billie yawned and shifted to his side. When their bodies parted, she felt a sense of deep loss, as if she'd lost a part of herself. Nuzzling her nose into the hollow of his neck, she sighed and whispered as she drifted off to sleep, "I love you, Craig Rawlins."

Craig's jaw spasmed. His hands froze on warm flesh. His entire body stiffened. He lay still as a dozing owl for several long, discomforting minutes, then very gingerly, so as not to awaken her, slipped to the edge of the bed. What did she expect from him? What *should* she ex-

364 *Judith Steel*

pect? At a complete loss, he did the only thing any self-respecting male would do in such a situation. He ran.

Billie stretched and kicked her bare toes from beneath the blanket. Opening her eyes, she stared out the window at the brilliant blue sky. She felt good. Better than she had in weeks. Although she still had her stepbrother to face, the haunting shadows were gone, as well as fear of the unknown.

Throwing the blanket back, she gasped, then quickly yanked it over her nakedness. Her startled gaze found her petticoats and underclothes discarded haphazardly about the room. All at once, memories flooded her. Soft, comforting memories. Of Craig Rawlins. Of the tender way he'd held her and made love to her.

After tucking the memories into a treasured corner of her mind, she got up from the bed, leisurely dressed, and walked into the hallway. She'd only taken a few steps when Danny suddenly rushed from Pearl's room and almost ran over her. His arms were filled with ribbons, his cheeks flushed pink, and his eyes danced with excitement.

"Good morning, Danny. What are you going to do with those beautiful ribbons?"

"I dunno." He shuffled his feet. "Ma wanted 'em. Gotta go."

She watched, openmouthed, as he took off like a shot, his feet clomping hurriedly down the stairs. Surely he hadn't thought she'd stopped him because she thought he was stealing the ribbon. No. But he'd sure looked guilty about something.

Following the boy into the kitchen, she stopped short when everyone in the room quit talking and turned to look at her.

Anna fluffed all the ribbons into a pile "M-mornin', Billie. How ya feelin'?"

"Fine. What are you all doing?" She glanced at the sewing articles piled on the table.

Pearl drew her over to the cabinet where there was a pan holding several cinnamon rolls. "We thought Falling Water needed another dress. Here," she shoved the still-warm pan into Billie's hands. "Eat these while they're still hot."

Molly began gathering up things. "Come on and sit down. We'll take this stuff up to Pearl's room to finish." She nodded toward the stairs. Soon, everyone had their arms full and were on their way out.

Billie's brows arched. "Just a minute and I'll help."

"Oh, no. You mustn't do that."

"Why not?" Anna had a rather wild expression in her eyes, Billie thought. "There's nothing else—"

"Danny! Uh, show Danny where Mr. Rawlins keeps them linen towels, would ya? An' Danny, ya kin show Miss Billie how ya learned to polish all that purty wood." With a sick smile, Anna ran after the other girls.

Danny slipped into a chair beside Billie. There was a long silence while he watched her eat a roll. He kicked his feet. Spun a spoon on the table. Finally, he asked, "Ya gonna eat all them rolls?"

Her lips twitched. "No. Help yourself." She watched him fidget, then pried, "What's going on? Why did everyone leave so quickly?"

He mumbled something around a huge bite of gooey cinnamon and sugar and sweet bread.

"What?"

"There you are, Danny. I was wonderin'— Oh, hello." Craig strode briskly into the kitchen, then hesitated. He'd been about to ask if the girls had everything they needed, and had seen Billie just in time.

She'd turned her warm, hazel eyes on him and he'd felt suddenly helpless. Eyes as large and soft as a doe's. Eyes he could drown in. Eyes that made him feel . . . trapped.

Tongue-tied and at a loss as to what to say to her, he stood awkwardly with his hands in his pockets.

"Good morning." His hesitation and stiffness hurt Billie. After all they'd shared last night, these were the last reactions she'd expected from him.

Danny used the moment of uncomfortable silence to escape. Mumbling a few more unintelligible words around a mouthful of cinnamon roll, he skipped merrily from the room.

"Anna asked me to show Danny where the linen towels were stacked. Do you—"

"Ah, finish your breakfast. I can do that."

And Craig was gone. The look of relief on his face when she'd given him an excuse to leave nearly tore out her heart. She daintily put down the remainder of the roll, calmly wiped her fingers on a napkin, then dropped her face into her hands.

What had happened? What had she done? What— She straightened. Sneering words she'd almost forgotten once again seared through her mind. *"No man wants a cold bitch. You're no good, Wilhelmina. No good."*

Craig was a man. Had a man's point of view. Was it possible he, too, blamed her for what had happened? If she'd just paid closer attention, had seen what was happening with Sam, that night might never have happened.

Yet, something good had come from the tragedy, she thought. If she hadn't left St. Louis, she would never have met Craig. Would never have found Alder Gulch. She really liked the raw, booming town. Had good friends here. Operated a profitable business. And most important, she had found her strength in Craig Rawlins.

She lifted her head and sighed. Craig had told her just last night he didn't believe her father blamed her. All she could hope for was that Craig had taken his own words to heart.

* * *

During the next few days, Billie tried not to let Craig's obvious avoidance of her keep her spirits down. She continued working on the schoolroom and unpacking the several crates of supplies.

She also noted that more people were moving into Alder Gulch each day. Lucky had mentioned that since Vicksburg had fallen during the first week of July, the Mississippi River was open for travel again—which meant the Union had all but won the War in the West. With the Union victorious at both Gettysburg and Vicksburg, Europe had reneged on its promised support for the South, and uprooted people were fleeing to California, Colorado, and Nevada. Naturally, she thought, news of rich gold strikes would lure a lot of them to Montana. No wonder every other face was that of a stranger.

Another thing that kept her mind in a dither was the fact that everyone in the emporium seemed to stop whatever they were doing whenever she approached. They made excuses and would quickly leave whatever room she was in. It had all started the night she'd regained her memory.

What were they thinking? She couldn't get anyone to stop and talk long enough to find out.

Craig was gone more and more with the Vigilance Committee, so she wasn't forced to constantly paste on a smile for his benefit. But she missed him. Kept watching the door for him to enter.

And it was while watching the door one evening that she saw Sam walk in. He spotted her immediately and hurried toward her.

Run. She had to run. But her feet were frozen. Her throat constricted. She couldn't even scream.

Chapter Twenty-four

Without preamble, Samuel Jones Glenn stopped in front of Billie and glared away the man whose dance chip she'd just taken.

"The necklace. Give it to me."

Billie backed up. "No."

"Damn it, I've got to have it." If he ever had any hope of returning to St. Louis and living through the day, he had to take back the heirloom. Damn the sniveling little coward whom he'd cheated it off of for running to Daddy and crying foul.

"Y-you gave it to me." Why she truly wanted to keep anything this man had clasped around her neck, she couldn't explain. But she just couldn't relinquish it.

"I didn't *give* it to you, you slut. I told you to—"

"You've been warned about coming here. You're not welcome." Lucky came up behind Samuel.

Suddenly, Pearl and Molly were on either side of Billie. Anna and Falling Water closed ranks behind them.

"You heard the man. Get out while you still can." Pearl emphasized her point by poking Samuel in the chest with her finger.

Molly looked at Anna and whispered, "Where's Mr. Rawlins? Outta town agin?"

Anna frowned and nodded.

Some of the customers listening to the confrontation began to gather around. Soon a wall of people separated Billie from Samuel. As he was pushed backward through the door, he yelled, "It's mine, slut. And I'll have it."

She clutched her hand around her neck, her fingers just brushing the emeralds. She turned her blurred gaze on her friends. "Th-thank you. Everyone. I—I—" She didn't know what to say. She'd never experienced an occasion where people had rallied around her. It was wonderful to think she hadn't had to face Sam alone.

Molly drew Billie toward the dance floor. "All right, y'all. Stop yore squawkin' an' let's dance."

The man whose chip Billie still held came to claim his dance. She forced herself to smile broadly and took his arm. He, like many to follow him, offered his protection to Billie. Several tried to coax the story behind the necklace from her, but she always managed to steer the conversation politely in another direction.

The gaiety of the evening seemed to increase with the hour. The girls actually seemed disappointed when the last dance was called.

Afterward, they sat in the kitchen and talked. Like the customers, her little family was curious about the necklace and Samuel. Anna, always the mother hen, directed the discussion away from Billie, who soon excused herself.

Molly went to the door and watched until she was certain Billie was safely in her room. Then she went back and plopped into her chair. "Reckon she knows?"

Anna shook her head. "Don't know how. An' she ain't said nuthin'."

"Words been spread all over town there's a party for Miss Billie tomorrow night," Pearl said. "And everyone's been threatened with their lives if they tell."

Falling Water sedately said, "She will be big surprise."

Molly clapped her hands with youthful exuberance. "I ain't never been ta no birthday party before. Ya gonna bake her a cake, Anna?"

Anna nodded. "First thing in the mornin'."

Pearl yawned and suggested, "If we want to be ready, we best call it a night."

Excitement shining in their eyes, concerns about Samuel Glenn unspoken on their lips, everyone retired.

Justin Turnbow found his mother in the mercantile the next afternoon. "Mother, did you hear—"

"Not now, Justin. I'm tryin' to pick out material for a dress. Don't you think this forest green is nice?" She spread out a fold of material and held it up next to her face.

"Yes, Mother, but—"

She turned her gaze on the proprietor. "I'll take eight yards."

Ike took the lustrous satin and put it on the counter to measure. "Anything else, Mrs. Turnbow?"

"Hmmmm . . ." She tapped her toe. "Maybe some white lace. And some of that pale-green twill."

Justin hovered over her shoulder until it appeared she'd decided on what she wanted. "Mother, there's a—"

"Hush, Justin. And some of that cotton. I need a new petticoat." She lifted her skirt just enough so that the merchant caught sight of her ankle.

He cleared his throat. "Yes, ma'am. Right away."

She whispered to Justin, "You have to know how to handle a man just right if you want things done quickly and to order."

Justin rolled his eyes.

"Now, what was it you were sayin'?"

"There's a party tonight. A big one. Over at the Empty Barrel," he rushed, in case she tried to interrupt again.

Her eyes narrowed. "The Empty Barrel? Tonight?"

Justin nodded.

"Where did you hear this? Why didn't you let me know right away?"

Ike ripped the material at eight yards. "It's been all over town for days, Mrs. Turnbow. Big surprise birthday party for Miss Billie. Everyone's going."

"Oh, well, yes. Of course they would." She drew her purse strings tight over her arm. "How much longer do you think that will take?"

"Ten minutes, by the time I measure the lace and twill and cotton."

"Would you mind terribly if I run an errand and come back in a few minutes?"

He shrugged. "Whatever suits you." Mrs. Turnbow was one customer from whom he never worried about collecting.

Sunny grabbed Justin's arm and hurried him from the store. "How'd you find out about this party?"

"Everyone was talking about it down at the stables."

"Were they invited, or what?"

Justin pulled his arm away from his mother, rubbing the imprint of her fingernails. "I don't know. Sounded mostly like folks from the saloon went around town telling everybody."

"Well, they didn't tell me."

"I didn't think you liked—"

"I don't. But they could've asked . . . I'll show them what happens when they slight Sunny Turnbow. That party will never happen."

"But, Mother, what are you going to do?"

Sunny smiled wickedly. "Just you wait and see."

Ben Hanshaw entered the saloon at seven-thirty that evening and looked around to see if Billie was present. When he saw she wasn't, he motioned Pearl to the door.

Pearl looked out and cursed until even Ben's ears turned red. "What's that friggin' sow think she's gonna prove?"

Ben flushed. "When one of the women grabbed me," he cleared his throat, "I was promised an hour I'd never forget, for free. All I had to do was go with her right then."

Another stream of oaths flooded from her lips. "If she thinks she's gonna get away with——"

Ben tapped her shoulder and pointed to the stairs. Billie was just descending.

Pearl pulled Ben away from the door. "My, my, Ben. Doesn't Miss Billie look nice tonight?"

Before either Billie or Ben could respond, Pearl took Billie's arm and turned her back toward the stairs. "But you know, your cheeks are a little pale. If I was you, I'd go up and do something about it right now."

Billie drew her brows together. "But——"

"Not much, mind you. Just a little."

As soon as Billie trudged reluctantly back to her room, Pearl rushed to the kitchen. Anna was putting the finishing touches on a cake and Molly and Danny were licking the icing bowl.

"We got trouble."

Everyone turned. Anna pursed her lips. "What kinda trouble?"

"Come look outside." Pearl led the way to the front of the saloon. "That damned Sunny Turnbow musta rounded up every whore in town. Ben says they're offering a free hour to the men what won't come to the party."

"That wide-hipped, big-titted hussy. I'll pull her dyed hair out till she's balder'n a snappin' turtle."

Pearl grinned. "That's a good one, Molly."

Molly preened. "Thanks."

Anna hissed, "What're we gonna do?"

Jack Dawkins burst through the door, breathing hard. "Hell, gettin' into this place's like runnin' a gauntlet of female artillery."

Molly pushed up her sleeves and hitched up the skirt of her cream silk dress. "I'm gonna go——"

"No!" Anna pointed frantically to the stairs. Billie and Falling Water descended, enjoying a one-way conversation. Billie was chatting merrily, apparently glad to find someone who didn't avoid talking with her. Falling Water was stoically silent and expressionless.

Danny, with globs of icing smeared on his cheeks, tugged on his mother's skirt. "What's goin' on, Ma?"

Grabbing a handkerchief from her pocket, Anna bent and quickly wiped her son's face. "Nothin'. An' don't ya fergit. Soon's we cut that cake, ya gotta march on up to bed. No arguin'."

"Aw . . . I know." He pushed his mother's hands away. "I always gotta miss the good stuff."

Ben quickly leaned forward and whispered, "Listen, I wouldn't do anything about . . ." he tilted his head toward the door, "that out there. When the gals stop a man, they gotta leave with them. Can't be many left. Mosta the fellas want to come pay their respects to Miss Billie. Those gals ain't gonna stop this party."

About that time, Eduardo and Lucky squeezed through the door. Both men's faces were as red as the dress Pearl was wearing. Eduardo cleared his throat and found an interesting crack in the floor to study. "Joseph Little Ears and his piccolo have, er . . . been delayed."

Molly giggled. Everyone looked at each other and chuckled. When Billie joined them, they made a concerted effort to move their group farther into the room so she wouldn't see outside.

Craig was the last to enter, just before time to open the emporium. He stopped inside the door, wiping his cheek in case some of Sunny's face junk had rubbed off. He'd spent ten minutes trying to force the woman and her "friends" to leave, but they hadn't budged. And he wasn't about to give in to Sunny's proposition. If the townspeople wanted to come, they'd come. He wasn't going to sleep with Sunny just to get the ladies in the barricade to go back to their "jobs."

Lucky rushed over to Craig. Looking over his shoulder to make sure Billie couldn't hear, he whispered, "They still out there, Mr. Rawlins?"

"Yep."

"Damn."

Craig folded his arms across his chest and glanced toward the dance floor where the girls were keeping Billie busy. "Does she know about this?"

"Not yet. And I don't think she suspects a thing."

Craig grinned, though his eyes became furtive when Billie darted a glance in his direction. She wore a raspberry-colored confection that made her look good enough to eat. Mentally shaking himself, he was still upset for letting things get so out of hand. It was all his fault that he'd misled her. He would not do it again.

But, damn it, when he looked at her, and she looked at him, like she was doing now, like a wingless angel in that prim frock, he couldn't seem to help himself. He had to go to her, to touch her, hold her. He wanted to make love to her so badly . . .

An overwhelming urge to run itched against the soles of his feet. He sighed. Already, the evening had taken a turn for the worse.

But it was her birthday. Surely he could conquer his alternately soaring and plummeting impulses for a few hours.

Billie knew that Craig had seen her but had darted his gaze away. He was acting so aloof. The backs of her eyes burned. Tears threatened to overflow at any moment. She inhaled deeply. Then again. She would not cry. Not now. Not tonight. Not ever. Not over Craig Rawlins.

Today was her birthday. She was twenty-six years old. Much too old to think a man like Craig would have more than a passing interest in her, anyway. Too old to believe in fairy tales and happy endings. She, of all people, should know better.

And today, she missed her father. He had always remembered and done something special to celebrate her birthday. She watched as they opened the doors. So, she'd celebrate secretly tonight. After all, she had a lot of things to be thankful for.

A few men wandered inside, but not nearly the number they'd been greeting on previous evenings. Billie noticed that Lucky wasn't even selling dance chips. And Danny was still downstairs. Customers came in and just sat down and visited. Now and then someone would look her way, then just as quickly avert his or her gaze.

A few of the businessmen and their wives came in. Her eyes widened. The men were bringing their wives?

The orchestra tuned their instruments. She began to pace. Why were they starting so late? And everyone had such silly expressions. What in the world was going on?

Jack Dawkins looked around the room. At a nod from Craig, he announced, "On three. One. Two. Three!"

Everyone shouted, "Happy birthday!"

Billie stood in stunned silence as the girls, then the orchestra and Lucky, then all of the townspeople, came up and wished her well. Danny was the first to point to a decorated table on the other side of the orchestra. "Look, Miss Billie, Ma made a cake. Don't it look good?"

Billie finally recovered enough to smile. And when she got started, she couldn't stop. "I can't believe it. How'd you all know?"

Everyone pointed to Craig.

He hunched his shoulders.

Her eyes devoured him. "Thank you. This is the nicest birthday I've ever had." A glimmer of hope welled in her chest. Surely a man who would go to this kind of trouble had to care a little. Didn't he?

"Here. The first piece goes to the birthday girl." Molly handed her a plate and fork.

Since there weren't enough plates and utensils to go around, only the ladies were given them. The men ate with their fingers, but didn't seem to mind the mess. Most of them hadn't had iced cake in years, if ever.

After they all had finished and Danny swept the floor,

Billie noticed an Indian with extremely ruddy features joining the orchestra. The others gave him a few hard looks, but when he pulled out his piccolo, they all struck up a beat.

"All hands round," Dick called.

No one moved. All eyes went to Billie and then to Craig.

Oh, no, she thought. They expected them to dance the first number together. Craig didn't want to, she could tell.

Craig figured out quickly what was expected. Evidently no one had noticed that the routine had changed the last few nights. Though he would like to protest, Billie's haunted face and sad eyes drew him like a moth to a flame. And that was just the way he felt as he walked toward her—that the minute he touched her, he would disintegrate in a puff of smoke.

But when he held her in his arms at last, and began to sway and step in time with the waltz, he was astounded to realize how good he felt to have her so close again. It felt . . . right for her to brush her body to his, to nestle into him, to . . .

All too soon the dance ended. He looked into her wary, confused eyes and was tempted to confess that he had no idea where to go from here. He wanted to ask if what she'd whispered that night was the truth, or if she—and he—had only been dreaming.

But before he could open his mouth, Lucky cut in. "My turn, boss. I can't miss the chance to dance with Miss Billie again."

Billie wanted to protest. She'd seen something in Craig's eyes. Something that she hoped to explore. But then she saw the line of men grinning and waiting to dance with her. Later. She'd have to talk to Craig later. Now, she felt honored that so many people were helping her celebrate the best birthday ever.

* * *

Justin peeked through the window and into the Empty Barrel Saloon. People were laughing and dancing. "The party's going on anyway, Mother."

Sunny cursed and grumbled to the three girls still standing in the street, "Might as well grab the next man and go on."

With so many men gravitating toward the sound of merriment, it didn't take long until she was alone. "Damn it, Justin, I was certain my plan would work. I asked favors from everyone I ever worked with."

"I guess folks like Miss Billie." Seeing his mother's quick scowl, he looked inside again. "There aren't that many people. You cut into their business."

"That's not good enough. I want to ruin her." Her lips curled. "I want to ruin them both."

"Doesn't sound as though you like those folks."

Sunny gasped at the voice coming from directly behind her. She spun and glowered at a dark-haired stranger. Between the light from the saloon and the moon, she eyed him up and down. He was nice-looking. Acted kind of gentlemanly, the way he tipped his hat and all.

She smiled and stepped close enough to rub her shoulder against his arm. "You new in town, handsome?"

He nodded and peered over Justin's shoulder through the window. He, too, remembered what day it was. "Looks like the queen bee's holding court."

Justin moved and leaned against the wall some feet away. His eyes narrowed on the stranger.

Sunny walked up and looked over the man's arm. "Who're you talkin' about?" she purred, and brushed sensuously against him.

"The woman in that dress the color of ripe berries." He spat. "She acts like she's royalty. But she isn't. And I ought to know."

Tilting her head, Sunny eyed the man curiously. "You

know our Miss Billie?" she drawled the name with contempt.

"Know her? She's my sister."

Sunny stepped back. "Sister?"

"Stepsister."

"Close enough. I'll be damned."

He strained his eyes, focusing on the emeralds sparkling around Billie's throat. "She's got something of mine. And I'm going to get it back."

Sunny stared at Craig. He pretended to mix drinks while he watched Little Miss Perfect. "She's got somethin' of mine, too."

Samuel pried himself away from the window. He heard the accusation in her voice and looked at Sunny more appreciatively. "Sounds like you and I have something in common."

Sunny batted her lashes. "I know a place where they serve good drinks."

Justin rolled his eyes.

Samuel offered his arm. She delicately took hold and he grinned. "If there's two things I like, they're a good drink and a beautiful woman to share it with."

"Ooohh, aren't you the sweet talker." She sashayed against him as they walked.

"You like men who give you compliments, do you?"

"Darlin'," Sunny purred, "I like a man who's interested in what I like."

Justin's eyes slitted as he watched his mother walk away. Then he rubbed his chin and looked back into the saloon. On a sudden impulse, he straightened his shoulders and strode confidently inside. The doors batted behind him. He scanned over the dance floor until he spotted Billie.

The music stopped. Between songs, he moved awkwardly to her side.

Billie was surprised to see Justin Turnbow, but happy, too. Though he was a bit strange, he'd been very kind to her the few days she'd spent in his home.

"Good evening, Justin. How are you?"

He ducked his head. "Fine."

"What are you doing here?"

"I—I just came to wish you a happy birthday ... And maybe dance with you."

She smiled. "How nice."

"Wh-where do you pay? I didn't see anyone when I came in."

She held out her hand. "There's one more number before the orchestra rests and they start giving out dance chips again. This first set was for a small party. Everyone's just been having fun. Come on." She pulled him onto the dance floor.

Justin found it difficult to concentrate on his steps and talk at the same time, but he tried. "Have you decided to stay in Alder Gulch?"

She nodded, tried to catch her breath, and puffed, "For a while." Looking into his face, she thought she saw a frown of regret. Why? But the expression was gone in an instant when he glanced at her briefly and smiled.

"Mr. Rawlins been treatin' you all right?"

She pursed her lips. What a strange question. But seeing who it came from, she sighed and answered, "Very well."

"There don't seem to be as many people here tonight as other nights. Has business been good?" he inquired.

"The emporium has been a real success," she told him with the smile of a proud proprietor.

Justin spun her in a tight circle, dipped, and spun her again.

Feeling slightly dizzy, she recouped quickly when the music stopped. She gulped in air. "Thank you. That was fun. Are you going to stay for a while?"

He saw Craig coming up from the cellar and shook his head. "I just wanted to wish you a happy birthday."

She put her hand on his arm and walked with him toward the door. "I appreciate your thoughtfulness. Come back sometime when we can talk."

Eyes hooded, he nodded and hurried on.

"Howdy, Just . . ." Craig let his words fade as the boy barely gave him a glance and a brief wave.

"What did he want?"

With a puzzled look on her face, Billie watched Justin leave. "To wish me a happy birthday."

"Oh." Sunny had probably sent him to see if she had succeeded in ruining the party. He was grateful she hadn't tried to come in. He wasn't anxious to face another go-round with Sunny tonight.

She stared at Craig's back and arms as he set down a cask of liquor and twisted it on end from side to side to maneuver it out of his and Lucky's way. Even beneath the starched cotton shirt, she could see the ripple of straining muscles and tendons. Beads of perspiration stood out on his brow and she had to clasp her hands together to keep from reaching out with her handkerchief and wiping them away.

But she did resist. Uneasily, she realized that he was nervous around her. What had happened to the camaraderie they'd once shared? His friendly caresses. Engaging grins. She missed the way he used to be and worried that his reaction now had something to do with Sam.

She bowed her head and returned to the dance floor. She didn't deserve a man like Craig. He had enough burdens. He didn't need hers.

She began to reconsider the answer she'd given to Justin's question about her plans. There were still a couple of weeks left on her agreement with Craig. At the end of that time, for her own peace of mind, she might have to leave Alder Gulch. She had come to love the man too much to feel his cold rejection every day.

From beneath lowered lashes, Craig surreptitiously cast glances at Billie's slumped back as she walked away. His fingers dug into the wooden cask so hard, he felt the

sting of splinters. It had been all he could do to keep
from grabbing her delicious body and devouring her
right there in front of God and all the men in Alder
Gulch. What on earth had the woman done to him?

He would have to hold himself in check. She deserved
better. She needed a man who could give her the life-
time of love and devotion he couldn't. He let the cask
thud to the floor. Damn his mother. Damn all the
women he'd ever known for taking and taking and
never giving in return.

If only Billie knew that from the help he'd been able
to provide her, he'd learned that he was far more emotionally crippled than she. But he was used to function-
ing in his own safe, cold world, and could never ask her
to share such a life.

He pried the splinter from his thumb with the sharp
tip of his knife. When he looked up again, he instinctively sought out Billie. She stood looking out a window.
The lanternlight was to her back and shimmered against
the sun-bleached strands of her hair. He sucked in his
breath as his thoughts were reinforced. An angel needed
someone pure and good. He could never meet those cri-
teria.

Billie shivered beneath the heat from his gaze. Why
was he watching her when— Suddenly, she decided she
had to know why he'd been acting so strangely. She had
to know *now*. Spinning, she headed determinedly toward
the bar.

Her toe caught on a warped board. She tripped and
fell to her knees. Glass shattered. She heard the sickening thud of a bullet hitting flesh. Fragments of the glass
bit into her back. Something hit her from behind and
forced her to the floor. Her head cracked against a chair
leg.

As her eyes clouded, she heard an anguished yell.

Chapter Twenty-five

"Billie!" Craig shouted. "Dear God, Billie!" He leapt over the counter and ran to her, throwing tables and chairs every which way. He stopped abruptly when he reached the spot where she'd fallen. Lucky lay on top of her, blood gushing from a wound in the back of his shoulder.

"Someone get the doctor. And hurry!"

He saw the girls standing near the stage, frightened, almost frozen in place. "Anna, over here! It's Lucky and Billie. They're both hurt."

The emporium burst into activity. Men came over to help Craig lift Lucky off Billie. Anna was there immediately, staunching the flow of blood from Lucky's back with pieces of her petticoat. Falling Water knelt to take a look at the wounds, then ran for the stairs.

Pearl and Molly pushed their way to where Craig was feeling Billie's arms and legs, looking for blood or some sign of injury.

"Did you see what happened? Did Billie get shot, too?" Pearl questioned, squatting down to run her hand down the back of Billie's head. "Poor thing."

Molly stood with her hands on her hips, looking out the window. "Only one shot. S'pose it got 'em both? Be durned good shootin'."

Pearl scowled. "Good shooting, my foot. It's—"

"I can't find anything wrong," Craig frantically interrupted. "Is she still unconscious?"

"Yep." Bending further over, she ran her hand under Billie's head to lift her face off the hard floor. "Uh-oh."

Molly came over to see and gasped. "Looks like she's got a goose egg on 'er noggin, don't it?"

"Ninny, goose eggs aren't that big. This is—"

"Shut up," Craig snapped. "If you can't do anythin' but argue . . ." He glanced at their stricken faces and bit his tongue. He knew exactly how they felt. He was worried, too.

"Sorry. I didn't mean that."

Molly ran to the counter and grabbed a towel. After dipping it in a bucket of water, she hurried back and began sponging the lump above Billie's temple.

"I don't think she was hit by the bullet," Craig surmised after finishing his inspection. "She must've hit her head when Lucky fell on top of her."

Pearl looked up at the soft swish of a skirt and saw Falling Water opening a leather bag. "What's that?"

The Indian girl knelt beside Billie. "Medicine."

Molly frowned. "Ahh-h-h . . ." The doors opened and she quickly glanced up. "Hold on, Fallin' Water, here's the doc."

Men pointed Timothy Andrews toward the side of the room. He took a look at both patients and went to Lucky first, ordering Craig to keep Billie still until he could get to her.

Falling Water narrowed her eyes at Molly and Pearl and removed several smaller bags from the pouch. "Need water."

Pearl darted a glance to the doctor, then looked to Molly, shrugged, and rose to fetch the bucket.

Billie moaned and tried to move her head. Craig lifted her up just enough that he could scoot under and cradle her in his lap.

"Sh-h-h, Angel. Hold still. You've been hurt."

"My—my . . . head . . ."

"Yore head's so durned hard, ya done broke a good chair. Know that?" Molly blinked rapidly to keep the moisture in her eyes from giving away just how scared she really was.

"It wasn't that good a chair," Pearl argued as she set the water next to Falling Water, "or it wouldn't have broke."

Craig looked into Billie's confused expression and smiled. At least Pearl and Molly were keeping her distracted.

Billie blinked, then winced. "What happened?"

"Some rowdies musta been shootin' in the street, an' a stray bullet come through the winder."

Pearl nodded at Molly's wisdom and plucked shards of glass from Billie's hair and skirt.

"I—I was standing there . . . turned . . . tripped. If I hadn't fallen . . ." She stopped. Her head hurt too badly to think about what could've happened.

Falling Water pushed in front of a scowling Molly, dipped her fingers into a pastelike substance, and spread it over the knot on Billie's head.

Molly straightened and spread her hands on her hips. "Reckon ya oughta let 'er do that, Mr. Rawlins?"

Craig gave Falling Water a grateful smile, then looked at Molly and nodded. "The Indians have been healing themselves for a long time. And I think we can trust Falling Water, don't you?"

"Well . . ."

"How's Miss Billie?" the doctor called.

"She's come to," Craig answered. "And she's getting some attention."

Dr. Andrews's eyes rounded when he saw Falling Water stir something into a glass and then hold it to Billie's lips, but he had to turn his attention back to his patient.

Billie made a face as she took several swallows of Falling Water's concoction. "Wh—what is that?"

"Balsamroot. For ache in head."

Arching a brow, Billie winced and said, "Thank you.

My head definitely aches." She lifted her hand, but Craig wouldn't let her touch the lump."

Molly pointed toward the paste. "An' what's that stuff?"

Falling Water gathered her bags and rose gracefully to her feet. "Yerba Santa. Help swelling. No pain."

Billie's gaze followed the Indian girl as she walked over to Dr. Andrews. Gingerly shifting her shoulders, Billie saw the doctor's hands moving swiftly as he worked over someone. "Who's that?"

Pearl, Molly, and Craig looked at one another, wondering if they should tell. But at that moment, Anna sobbed, "Lucky, you're gonna be all right, ya hear? Don't ya go an' die on me."

"Lucky . . ." Billie closed her eyes.

"Don't *you* go and start frettin'." Pearl wagged her finger at Billie. "He's going to be just fine."

Billie reopened her eyes and looked to Craig for confirmation.

He nodded. "I think he will be. The bullet hit the back of his shoulder, and the doctor got to it right away." To his surprise, he saw Andrews look up and speak to Falling Water just before he moved to make room for her to kneel by his side.

"Wh—where will he stay? He can't go back to his claim. Someone has to look after him." Her voice rose. "He can have my room. I'll—"

"Calm down, Angel. You'll sleep in your own bed. Lucky was plannin' on moving into the cellar, anyway. But for now, I'll make a pallet for him right here in the saloon. I can even stay and watch him if need be," Craig stated, leaving no room for argument. The fact was, he'd already decided to stay. He didn't believe for a minute the shot had been an accident. Like Billie said, if she hadn't tripped . . .

Until Lucky recovered, or Craig found the culprit, he wasn't about to leave Billie alone.

His hand trembled as he helped Pearl pick the glass

off Billie's dress. There were a few nicks in her arms
where the force of the shards had sliced her flesh. With
each new sign of injury, his rage mounted. He felt he
could explode into a million pieces himself from the
need to protect and defend her.

Suddenly, he felt a cool touch on his cheek. He jerked
his head and looked into Billie's huge, soft eyes.

"Thank you," she whispered.

He cleared his throat. "Lucky's a good man. We'll see
after him."

Molly and Pearl looked at each other and grinned.

Dr. Andrews came over and knelt beside Billie.
"How're you feeling?"

She looked at Falling Water, who'd followed the doctor over, and smiled. "Better. But my head still hurts."

He felt around the knot. "Yes, I imagine it does."

She grabbed his hand. "How's Lucky?"

"He lost a lot of blood, but the bullet went through
and didn't seem to damage any vital organs." Timothy
also smiled at the Bannock girl, and his eyes held profound respect. "Falling Water gave me something that
helped to stop the bleeding." He shook his head. "With
a few weeks rest, Lucky should be fine."

"Hot damn!" Molly covered her mouth and gazed
fearfully at Billie.

Billie grinned. "My sentiments exactly."

"And as far as you're concerned, stay in bed tonight
and tomorrow and see how you feel. Let me know if you
experience any dizziness or nausea."

"We will," Craig answered emphatically.

Pearl poked Molly in the ribs and mouthed, "Told
you."

Molly arched her brows, then mischievously asked
Billie, "Ya reckon ya kin make it up them stairs?"

"I'll carry her."

Before Billie could say a word, Craig had her scooped
into his arms.

Molly cocked her head and nodded imperceptively.

Dr. Andrews smiled and said, "I'll look in on you to-morrow," then turned, took Falling Water's elbow, and guided her back toward Lucky. "Tell me more about those herbs. Do they grow locally?"

Craig glanced toward Molly and Pearl and frowned at the sly grins curving their lips. "If you girls will come with me, we can bring back blankets to make Lucky's pallet."

"Sure thing, boss."

"Want one of us to stay with Miss Billie?"

Billie opened her mouth.

Topping the stairs, Craig hurriedly insisted, "I can sit with her a while before I relieve Anna with Lucky."

"Whatever ya say." Molly grinned impishly at Pearl behind Craig's back.

He laid the patient on her bed, then went with the two women to round up blankets. When he came back into the room, he stood awkwardly in the middle of the floor, hunching his shoulders as if trying to make a major decision.

"You don't have to stay with me," she said shortly. "I'm fine."

He looked into her pain-glazed eyes and at the dark circles surrounding them. "Sure. You're finer than frog fuzz split three ways."

"Well . . ." She tilted one side of her mouth. "Perhaps I'm not *that* fine."

He settled the chair close to the bed. "Promise me somethin'."

"What?" Warily, she noted the sudden seriousness of his expression.

"I want you to stay away from open windows and doorways. And don't leave the emporium unless I'm able to accompany you."

Her eyes rounded. "I'm not a prisoner."

"Promise!"

"Why?" She sensed there was something sinister lurking behind his demand.

He inhaled sharply. "Why? Because I think someone's tryin' to kill my partner."

"Someone's trying to kill your . . ." She repeated his words in a stunned tone. "Your partner? That's me!"

He gulped. "Ah . . . Yes."

She sighed and sank back on the pillow. She'd hoped he had wanted her promise because he cared for her as a woman. It would've been the perfect opportunity for him to say something—anything—about his feelings toward her. But all he was really concerned about was the emporium and the money and the hassle of replacing another partner. It was a cold thought, and only he could slake the chill.

"Billie?"

She turned her head toward him but just stared.

"You haven't promised."

"I promise," she said dully, and turned her head back. There was a cobweb in the corner and she focused on its intricate design. "Why? Why is someone supposedly trying to kill 'your partner'?"

Craig drew in a long breath. "I'm not sure."

Her eyes and temple began to throb from concentrating on the insect as it spun an addition onto the web. Her lids fluttered closed. She would *not* think of Craig, his unfounded suspicions, or her heartache. It only caused the pain in her head to intensify.

Craig propped his boots on the end of the bed. He had to keep his hands away from her or he would grab her up and hold on to her for the rest of his life. Deliberately, he raised his arms, linked his fingers, and placed his hands behind his head.

Tomorrow, first thing, he would intensify his investigation. He already had one suspect. Maybe two. For several reasons, he only hoped he was wrong.

The next morning Billie awoke to the sound of retreating footsteps. She opened her eyes, saw the bright

light, and winced. Her temple throbbed, but the pain
eased as she blinked several times.

"Anna? Is that you?"

Anna stopped abruptly and turned. "I'm sorry. Didn't
mean to wake ya."

"What time is it?" From the sunlight dappling the
floor, it had to be late.

"It's midmornin'. Danny's been in twice already. Ya
were sleepin' like the dead not to've heard 'im."

"How's Lucky?"

Anna collapsed into the vacant chair. "He's got a fever, but Falling Water mixed some herbs and Doc Andrews says he's gonna be fine once it breaks."

"Thank heavens."

"And Danny's been helpin' me feed 'im, an all."

Billie grinned. "You have quite a young man. You
should be real proud of him, Anna."

Clasping her hands in her lap, Anna ducked her
head. "I thank the Lord every day I still got 'im." A tear
rolled down her cheek.

Billie saw it and frowned. "What do you mean?"

"I near made a terrible mistake 'bout four months
ago." The tears rolled faster.

Concerned, Billie leaned forward. "It couldn't have
been that bad."

"I almost gave 'im away." She looked out the window
and into the heavens. "I almost gave my little boy
away." Sobs shook her thin frame.

Billie didn't know what to say.

"Things was so bad I couldn't . . . No one'd pay
to . . . We was hungry all the time. Only way I could
think to save my boy was to give 'im to some good
fam'ly. Someone who'd take good care of 'im, an' feed
'im and give 'im clean clothes fer helpin' with the
chores."

Reaching out, Billie took a hold of Anna's hand.

"But when it was time, when I was on the door-
step . . . I couldn't. I couldn't do it. We'd been through

so much together. An' if'n we starved, we'd do it together."

"Oh, Anna."

Anna looked up and squeezed Billie's hand. "My
Danny an' me, we thank the good Lord ever' day he
done sent ya to us."

Billie sniffed. "Now look what you've gone and done.
I've got to cry, too."

The two women looked into each other's watery eyes
and smiled.

Craig stepped out of Billie's doorway and leaned
against the hall wall. He'd been on his way to see if Billie was hungry when he heard the two ladies talking.
He'd stopped in his tracks. Hadn't meant to eavesdrop,
but had been unable to move.

Questions rioted in his mind. He thought back to the
day when he'd been eight years old and his mother had
placed his hand into that of a stranger.

Before then, his only memories were those of moving
from one brothel to another, of people pointing at him
and telling his mother they didn't want to see his face
downstairs.

Again the stranger's hand became his full focus. The
rough, calloused, hard-hitting hand.

Had his mother believed she was giving him a better
life by taking him to live with the farmer and his family?
She'd told him so many times how sorry she was, that
a brothel was no place for a child.

But there was no way he could ever know for sure
what she'd been thinking. His mother had died. She'd
never known that he'd been treated worse than one of
the farmer's mules, or that the pious man had never let
Craig forget his sinful upbringing. She hadn't known
he'd run away when he was twelve and had been on his
own ever since.

His fingers clenched into fists. Had he been wrong all

these years? Had her motives been good but her judgment of human beings poor? Had *he* misjudged *her?*

He blinked back the burning in his eyes. If that was true, he had a lot of thinking to do. His whole life could've been built on lies. Feeling the foundation beneath him quake, Craig walked unsteadily down the stairs and out the door.

Billie was disappointed when, after a half-hour battle with Pearl to win her right to journey downstairs, Craig wasn't there. Late as it was, he wasn't there. And stupid woman that she was, she could hardly wait to just feast her eyes on him.

A niggle of panic started deep in the pit of her stomach. She glanced quickly around the room and was relieved to see that the food and punch had already been set on the counter. Walking into the kitchen, she saw Lucky stretched out on a cot. Sitting on a chair that had been drawn up near the his head, she leaned over to see if he was awake.

"Evenin', Miss Billie," he said weakly.

"Hello, Lucky. I'm so sorry about this."

He slowly moved his head from side to side. "Why?"

"Mr. Rawlins," she gulped. It was strange to feel more comfortable putting thoughts of him at a distance. "He seems to think your bullet was meant for me."

"Yeah. He told me."

So, everyone had seen Craig but her. "In a way, I feel that your getting shot is my fault." She frowned, thinking Lucky was suddenly choking, but then she heard his gurgle of laughter.

"Just like ... woman. Take ... all ... credit."

"I beg your pardon?" What was he saying? That it *wasn't* her fault? Of course it was. If she hadn't moved ... A bolt of lightning struck her, or should have. Dear Lord, she would probably be dead, or lying on that cot instead of Lucky.

She felt a touch on her hand and looked into eyes that gleamed with new life.

"It's . . . good." He coughed.

She sniffed. "Good? Your getting shot?"

He nodded once.

"You're crazy."

He nodded again.

Her eyes narrowed.

"Crazy . . . in love."

She sat up, astounded, then sank back and smiled. "Anna?"

"Yeah."

She looked into the main room and saw Anna setting out slices of cinnamon bread. Every once in a while, she'd glance toward the kitchen.

"Does she feel the same?" It was a silly question, judging by the giddy grin on Anna's face.

He nodded a little less certainly. "Think . . . so."

She sighed. "Well, I'm glad something has gone right for a change."

He grimaced and pointed to her head.

She reached up and felt the lump. It had gone down some, but not a lot. "I'm all right. Just a little headache."

All at once she remembered the main reason she'd come to see Lucky. "Has Mr. Rawlins been in this evening?"

He shook his head.

Her lips turned down. Where could the man be? What would they do for a bartender if he didn't show up?

"Recipes . . . under counter."

"What?"

"You . . . mix . . ." His lids drooped. He blinked. His eyes closed.

Billie sat there, stunned speechless. Her? Mix drinks?

Pearl stuck her head around the jamb. "When you want to open?"

"It's time already?" She rubbed her temple, which had started to throb.

"Five minutes."

She forced herself out of the chair and ordered her feet to carry her to the bar. She searched through glasses and bottles and stirrers until she finally heard the rustle of paper. With a pounding heart, she pulled out several sheaves and read the names of drinks and how much of what to mix.

She also found a shaker, some chopped ice, and located other articles she might need. Then she quickly glanced over the labels on some of the bottles to get an idea of what looked like what.

Anna leaned over the counter and watched her. "How's Lucky?"

"All right."

"Oh . . . Good."

"Lucky's a nice man, isn't he?"

Anna nodded. "Wonderful."

"And he seems to like Danny."

Sighing, Anna said, "But no one'll ever be as great in Danny's eyes as Mr. Rawlins."

Still looking over the varieties of whiskeys, bourbons, cordials, and gin, Billie thought a second, then questioned, "That's not so bad, is it? A boy would be pretty fortunate to have two such good men to look up to."

"You might be right."

Suddenly, the doors swung open and Craig strolled into the room.

Billie thought she would faint with relief. "Where have you been? We were about to open and there was no one to tend the bar."

He shrugged and walked to where she'd placed the recipes.

She stood back and stared. His boots were scuffed, his trousers dusty. The usual spotless white shirt was wrinkled and stained. His vest hung open. He wore no tie. Reddish-brown stubble prickled his chin.

But his eyes were what worried her. He looked at her as if he'd never seen her before. He wouldn't hold her gaze. He seemed confused and disoriented. The confident, sometimes overbearing Craig Rawlins was missing.

"Sh-should we open now?" she asked.

His eyes hooded as he shrugged.

Pearl scowled, but walked over and pushed the doors open.

Men crowded inside.

Billie watched for a minute to make sure Craig had no trouble filling the drink orders. Then she surreptitiously cast glances in his direction as she headed toward the dance floor. Something truly unsettling must have happened to Craig. But what? What had happened to her stalwart, sturdy-as-a-rock partner?

Craig left immediately after the emporium closed. Nearing his house, he stopped at the top of the hill and looked down on the lights of the town. His gaze focused primarily, though, on the emporium. And, as always, his thoughts were of Billie.

Damn it, what kind of web had the woman woven around him? His whole life had turned upside down and it was all her fault. She was all he thought or dreamed about. With every breath of air he smelled her special scent. Her taste tantalized his lips. His fingers still tingled with the silky-soft feel of her skin. Closing his eyes, he pictured the seductive curve of her mouth when she smiled just for him.

"Aw ... Angel ..." he groaned. She'd slowly but surely chipped away the protective barrier guarding his heart. All that remained was a warm, pulsing organ whose beat rapidly increased at the mere sight and sound of her.

He was so confused. He hadn't been himself lately. Hell, he didn't even know who *he* was anymore. Some-

how, he had to sort through his feelings and make a few
decisions about which direction his life was headed.

Craig Rawlins was the topic of conversation around
the kitchen table back at the emporium.

Pearl kicked off her slippers and wriggled her toes.
"The boss was a real bear tonight. Never seen him
stompin' and growlin' to himself like that."

Lucky lifted his head off the cot. "Everything go all
right tonight? Mr. Rawlins needed me, didn't he?"

"Of course he needed you. But he handled everything
just fine," Billie assured the injured man.

Sitting in the chair by his side, Anna smoothed a lock
of hair from Lucky's damp forehead. "Don't ya worry
'bout nuthin', ya hear? We all pitched in to help. 'Specially Pearl."

Pearl's face flushed. "Cut that out. I didn't do no
more than anyone else."

Billie rubbed her aching forehead. "Yes, you did. You
all did."

Molly noted Billie's pale features and pretended to
yawn. "Don't know 'bout the rest o' you, but I'm plum
tuckered out." She got Pearl's attention and canted her
head toward Billie.

"Uh, me, too. Let's all call it a night."

Billie climbed to her feet, blinked, and looked around
the room. "Where's Falling Water?"

Molly snorted. "She an' that new doc had their nog-
gins together all night. No tellin' where they be."

Anna's expression brightened. "I'll wait down here till
she comes in an' make sure them doors is all locked up
tight."

Lucky grinned and squeezed her hand.

The next evening, Billie stood to the side of the window watching as a more congenial Craig Rawlins strode

down the street. She wished he didn't have to be a part of the Vigilance Committee anymore. There had been fewer wagon and stage holdups and no attempts at all lately on the bank or businesses. And after the incident with Joe Smith, Craig had talked the Committee into modifying the death penalty to only those outlaws whose guilt was actually proven. The others were warned to leave the county, or else. So far, none had returned.

Suddenly, she frowned. The hairs on the nape of her neck stood on end. She backed away from the window and rubbed her palms up and down her arms. When the doors opened, she jumped, then smiled at the man with the familiar gimping walk and salt-and-pepper beard.

"Buck."

The old man grinned. "Howdy, ma'am." His lively brown eyes roved over her appreciatively. "Looks like you've done right well for yourself."

She nodded, though sadly. "Yes, it *seems* so." Billie gave herself a mental shake. "What brings you here this evening?"

"I'm yore bartender."

"You are? Have you mixed drinks before?"

He lifted his chin and looked along the bridge of his thin, sharp nose at her. "Young lady, a man gets to be my age, ain't a whole lot he hasn't done."

Thoroughly chastised, she swept her arm toward the bar. "It's all yours. Good luck."

He went behind the bar and immediately helped himself to a handful of Anna's sugar cookies.

Wary after the incident by the window, she glanced cautiously around the room. Everything seemed normal enough—the Swenson brothers at their stations, the girls decked out in new full-skirted gowns designed to dazzle, the musicians playing in tune.

Lucky, much improved, sat in a chair and sold dance chips, just like Billie had done when her ankle was injured.

Any stranger looking the place over would have declared it a successful business, but she felt a strange premonition. Was it because Craig wasn't there? Was it his absence that made her feel her world would soon turn end over end?

She was glad to see the large crowd again. Pearl had broken down—rather eagerly—and told her about Sunny's attempt to draw away her customers. Thank heavens the men's defection had been short-lived.

Despite her initial fear, the evening progressed smoothly. She was beginning to relax about eleven-thirty when gunfire erupted down the street. Everyone rushed to the front of the emporium, looking through the window or out the doors.

Billie, too, was curious, but remembered her promise to Craig and remained near the back of the room. Several napkins had fallen to the floor and she bent to pick them up. When she started to rise, she felt that eerie sensation again—that prickly feeling warning of imminent danger.

She straightened slowly. Her eyes locked on a pair of scuffed brown knee boots that came to a stop just a foot away. The thick, heavily muscled legs and torso announced who it was seconds before she stood face-to-face with her stepbrother.

Chapter Twenty-six

Billie looked frantically around the room. Only Lucky remained. The others had pushed through the door and stood outside gawking. She started to yell, but the cold, round tip of a pistol barrel jammed into her throat.

"Hand it over, now."

Her mind screamed, "No!" all the while her trembling hands raised. She fumbled with the clasp, unable to get it free.

"Hurry," Samuel hissed.

"I—I'm . . ." She couldn't talk. Her throat hurt where the gun poked her skin.

"If you don't give it to me in two seconds, I'll pull this trigger."

"Hey, there," Lucky yelled, trying to get up. "Leave her alone."

"Shut up and sit still, crip, or my little stepsister dies."

Blood pounded in her temples. She prayed Lucky wouldn't move. The faster she hurried, the more clumsy she became.

A woman screamed.

Samuel darted a glance in that direction and cursed, shoving the gun deeper into Billie's throat. She choked and coughed, losing her grip on the stubborn clasp.

Suddenly Pearl was there, beating Samuel over the head with a newspaper. He ducked. Billie dodged clear. Molly instantly launched a spittoon at Samuel's head.

His gun went off but the bullet smacked harmlessly into the ceiling. Suddenly, the Swenson brothers, with their shotguns cocked, appeared on either side of Samuel.

He hissed, "I'm through asking, slut. Next time, I *take* it." With tobacco and who-knew-what-kind of spit dripping from his hat and shirt, he ran through the kitchen and out the back door.

Anna, who'd run to shield Lucky, asked, "Want us to follow him?"

Billi shook her head. "He's gone. At least for now." Taking a deep breath, she rubbed her tender throat and fingered the emeralds. They hadn't protected her.

Pearl scowled. "Honey, that damned necklace is going to get you killed someday."

Billie closed her eyes. Craig had told her the same thing not long after she arrived in Alder Gulch.

Samuel Jones Glenn stumbled up the steep path. His handsome face contorted with rage at the thought of being beaten by a bunch of whores. Women. They'd always gotten the best of him. For years, even his mother had harped on how lazy he was, that he'd never amount to anything.

But then she'd married Thomas Glenn, one of the wealthiest men in St. Louis. Samuel's fortunes improved considerably. He suddenly had money at his disposal and didn't have to do a thing to earn it but butter up the old man. And then Thomas had been stupid enough to adopt him. Samuel had even figured out an ingenious accident for his stepfather, but now Miss Billie had turned up.

He'd had it this time. No woman was going to outsmart Samuel Glenn again.

He stopped in front of the carved oak door and wiped spittle from his face with a handkerchief. When he was satisfied he was cleaned up enough, he knocked.

The door cracked open. He pushed past the Indian

servant and ordered, "Tell your mistress I'm here. Quickly."

The maid wrinkled her nose at the man's putrid odor, and gratefully left his presence to do as she was bade.

A few minutes later, Sunny walked into the parlor, tying the sash to her green silk robe. "Samuel, what brings you— Good grief! What happened to you? You smell worse than the trash heaps in town." She rushed forward when he started to sit on one of her expensive chairs. "No! Come out into the hall."

Samuel's eyes hooded. He walked over and closed the door, then leaned his back against it. Another woman ordering him around. And here he'd come to her for comfort. He grabbed her arm and yanked her against him. "I want you, Sunny."

She made a face. "Ugh! Not without a bath. I've never smelled—"

"You weren't listening. I want you. Now." He spoke clearly, slowly enunciating each word in a too-controlled manner.

Sunny winced when his fingernails dug deep into her flesh. "Ouch! You're hurtin' me."

He inhaled, enjoying the feeling of power. It was almost as heady as the night he'd had Wilhelmina in his grasp. That night his sister hadn't acted so high and mighty. She'd bowed to his demands. Just like Sunny Turnbow would—ultimately. She'd do everything and anything he asked—or ordered.

With both hands on her shoulders, he forced her down. The more she struggled, the better he liked it. "There. That's a good place for you. On your knees."

The fear welling into her dark eyes excited him. His blood flowed hot and heavy to his loins. "Open my pants."

Sunny shook her head.

"Do it," he growled, his fingers biting harder.

"No. Not like this. All I want—"

He raised one hand and slapped her. She would have

fallen back if he hadn't held on to her with his other hand.

"This is about what *I* want. Understand?"

Tears stung the red imprint on her cheek. She nodded.

"Unbutton me." He spread his legs and grinned as she released his engorged member. "Now kiss me."

Sunny groaned. "Please . . ."

"Yes, please." He put his hands over her ears and squeezed.

She gasped.

"Are you going to do as I say?"

She tried to nod, couldn't, and stammered, "Y-yes. Don't—don't hurt me." She swallowed, puckered her lips, and barely touched the tip of his manhood. She nearly gagged.

"You can do better than that. Do it like you did the night we first met." He leaned his head back and stared at the ceiling, his lips slack and rubbery.

"L-let's go up to b-bed. Like that night. This hurts," she whined, "and—"

"Shut up. Do it."

She crawled forward to ease the pressure on her neck. Her stomach roiled. He stank all over.

He popped his palms hard against her ears.

She screamed.

Pleasure shot through him. "Do it, whore!"

There was a light rap on the door.

Sunny's eyes rolled hopefully toward the portal.

He gradually increased the pressure of his hands.

She whimpered.

"Whoever it is, tell them to go away."

Having no doubt whatsoever that he would hurt her terribly if she didn't follow his orders, she called out, "It's all right, Lucy. Y-you can go on h-home now."

Except for Sunny's desperate gasps and Samuel's excited breaths, silence fell over the room. At last there was a faint shuffling and mumbled, "Yes, ma'am," from the other side of the door.

Sunny's hope was dashed with each receding footstep.

Samuel sighed and nudged her lips with his organ. "Do it. Now!"

Gulping, she closed her eyes and licked him from the thick, hairy base up to the slick, moist head. She did it over and over, imagining she was somewhere else, with someone else. She tried not to breathe the stink of him, then tried not to think at all.

He rotated his hips, pumping himself between her lips. "Take me in. All of me."

Her eyes narrowed. Her jaws spasmed.

"If you bite, you know what will happen."

Through the pain in her head, she nodded. Suddenly his grip tightened. He positioned himself and thrust so deep he hit the back of her throat. Nausea churned in her stomach. She gulped and choked.

"Suck, whore. Suck."

He held her head so tight that she had no recourse but to do as he commanded. She sucked as he moved his hips forward and back. Foward and back.

He spread his legs and grunted. Hot semen gushed into her mouth. With each movement, he shot more. She swallowed and swallowed. Tried to breathe. Couldn't get air. Just when she thought she would pass out, he released her. She sagged to the floor, gasping.

After dragging in several breaths, she rose to her hands and knees and began crawling to the door. A cruel laugh sounded behind her. She crawled faster.

Samuel grabbed the collar of her robe and lifted until she stood on her feet. Turning her around, he untied the sash and ran his hands over her shoulders and down her arms until the silk lay in a pool at her feet.

He grinned. All she wore were her drawers. "You must of been expecting me." He fondled a heavy ivory breast and tweaked her long nipple. "Funny how a whore's nipples are so big. Must be from the constant use."

She shrank back when he bent his head. His teeth grasped the tender bud in warning. She stood quietly while he nipped and nuzzled. Holding her thus, he reached down and slid his hands inside the band of her pantalettes. With a swift jerk, they slithered over her buttocks and down her legs.

Sunny cringed and smothered a moan of terror.

He moved closer.

His limp member began to stiffen. Swaying, she tried again to get away.

He grabbed her chin and held her until she looked at him with wide, frightened eyes. "That's right, whore. Look at me. We've got a long night ahead of us." His fingers twisted her hard nipple. "Think of the fun we're going to have."

Dawn was breaking when Justin Turnbow silently let himself into the house. Tiptoeing across the polished wood floor, he headed toward the stairs.

At this time of morning, his mother was usually dead to the world, but he wasn't taking any chances. If she ever found out what he'd been doing, she'd be very disappointed. And Justin couldn't stand to make his mother unhappy.

A noise from the parlor stopped him in his tracks. He tilted his head and listened. Something rustled. He heard a moan. Reaching into his jacket, he pulled out a derringer and moved slowly and quietly to the closed door.

Holding the knob in his free hand, he pressed his ear to the jamb and listened again. Another rustle. A soft moan. With the gun held ready, he shoved the door open and rushed inside. "Hold it right there. I've . . . Mother?"

"Justin?" Sunny attempted to cover her nakedness

with her robe, but the silk was shredded. She squinted.
Both eyes were almost swollen shut.

Justin grabbed a coverlet from the back of the sofa
and gently drew it over her bruised and battered body.
Tenderly gathering her in his arms, he rocked back and
forth. "Who? Who did this to you?"

Thursday afternoon, Billie had to leave the emporium. Though she hadn't forgotten her promise to
Craig, he was nowhere to be found and she wanted to
get away from the stuffy confines of the building. She
just needed some time to herself, time to think.

A short walk brought her to a large boulder near the
creek. Rain the previous evening had the water running
high and had washed away a lot of the refuse. She could
actually smell the freshness of the damp air.

With her elbows on her knees, she rested her chin on
the backs of her crossed hands and stared at the water
lapping and swirling over rounded pebbles. A myriad of
emotions waged war within her. She thought back over
the conversation she and the other girls had had after
closing last night.

Falling Water had apologetically announced that she
would be leaving at the end of the month—five more
days. Dr. Andrews had asked her to assist him in his
practice and she had accepted.

As if Falling Water's announcement was just a pre-
lude, Anna had flushed scarlet and told them Lucky had
asked her to marry him. Billie was thrilled and sad
and . . . envious.

As if thought could manifest a person, Anna appeared. Billie watched the woman pick her way over
puddles of water. At last she drew even with the boulder. Billie cocked her head and asked, "Are you here to
tell me what you couldn't last night?"

Anna paled, but nodded.

"You're quitting, too." It wasn't a question. Billie had

known that Lucky wouldn't want his wife to spend her evenings dancing in another man's arms. And Anna would want to get as far away from the reminders of her past as she could.

"I don't wanna let ya down, but—"

"Anna, you could never do that."

"But—"

Billie scowled and directed the conversation away from disappointments. "What are you going to do after you're married?"

Anna shrugged. "Don't know. Reckon we ain't made many plans."

"If you decide to work outside your house, I've got a suggestion." Her lips twitched. "That is, if you'd like to become wealthy and live in a huge home like Sunny Turnbow."

Anna laughed. "Who wouldn't. But . . . what is it? I'm warnin' ya, I'm through—"

"A bakery."

"Hmmmm." Leaning against the boulder, Anna watched the water rush by. "Reckon folks'd pay fer my cookin'?"

"You could count your money all the way to the bank. In fact, I'd be the first in line for your cinnamon rolls."

Anna tilted her head and looked at Billie from the corner of her eye. "Really?"

"Really."

"Reckon I'll give it some consideration."

"Good."

The two women chatted a few more minutes, then walked arm in arm back to town. Anna returned to the emporium to start supper. Billie headed for the mercantile. She'd seen a comb that would perfectly match the gray sateen gown she planned to wear that night.

She reached for the doorknob just as someone came out and bumped smack into her.

"I beg your . . . Sunny?"

The woman pulled the collar of her cloak more tightly around her throat and tugged the wide, floppy brim of her hat lower over her eyes. She hurriedly brushed past Billie.

That was strange, Billie thought. Sunny Turnbow going out of her way to avoid a confrontation? Something must be wrong.

"Sunny, wait." Billie caught up and grabbed the woman's arm. She peeked under the brim at the black-and-blue splotches discoloring the once-beautiful features. "What happened to you?" she whispered.

Sunny pulled away and hurried on, mumbling, "It's none of your concern."

For a moment, Billie hesitated. She looked across and up and down the street. She had that eerie feeling again, that someone, or something, sinister was watching her. But as swiftly as she'd felt the sensation, it was gone. Suppressing a shiver, she ran after Sunny.

"I won't let you go until you tell me what happened." No matter their differences, Sunny was suffering and Billie wanted to help if she could.

"Not here." Sunny's voice was raspy.

"Where?" Billie had to hurry to keep up, even though she had the longer legs.

"Come to my house."

Billie arched her brows at the sharply issued invitation, but tagged along anyway, her sympathy and curiosity running rampant.

Once inside the foyer, Sunny handed her cloak and hat to the Indian woman and led Billie past the parlor into a smaller sunlit sitting room. Sunny went directly to a bottle of bourbon and poured herself a large shot. Turning to her guest, she asked, "Want some?"

Billie shook her head, staring in shock at the marks that were now plainly visible. A shudder ricocheted down her spine. "Who did that to you?"

Sunny snorted. "Do you have to ask?"

Billie drew in her breath. "What do you mean?"

"Someone very close to you."

"Close?" The only person she could think of was . . . "Oh, no! Craig wouldn't—"

"Not Craig," the older woman snapped. "Sam— Samuel. Your precious brother."

All of the breath rushed from Billie's lungs as she collapsed into the nearest chair. A strong feeling of déjà vu stampeded over her.

"What's the matter?" Sunny sneered. "You don't act very surprised."

"I—I'm sorry to say, I'm not." She looked Sunny directly in the eyes. "And I'm so sorry for what he's done to you."

The sincerity in Billie's tone caused Sunny to glance away. "Are you trying to say he's done this before?"

"Once . . . that I know—" Billie's voice cracked.

Sunny whirled to stare, wide-eyed.

"Me," Billie confirmed.

Sunny refilled her glass and sat in the chair opposite Billie. "When?"

Billie shrugged. "It's a long story. More importantly, why did he hit *you?*"

"Oh, honey. He did more than just hit me."

Billie closed her eyes.

"That bastard . . ." Sunny's eyes misted. "H-he did things to me . . . no one . . . even in the worst cribs I ever worked . . . ever did."

Billie reached out and grabbed Sunny's hand and refused to let go, even when the other woman tried to draw away.

As if a dam suddenly burst, Sunny poured out the anguish of Samuel's rape.

Billie squeezed Sunny's fingers. Outrage boiled inside her that her own stepbrother was so brutal.

"But it was nothin' more than I deserved. Nothin'."

"What did you just say?" Billie couldn't believe her ears. She had to hear Sunny say the words again.

"I asked for it," she sniffed. "And he gave it to me."

"You can't be serious." Billie bolted to her feet.

Sunny wiped her eyes.

"Did you invite that ... that ... beast ... to rape you?"

"N-no."

"Of course you didn't. Did you politely ask him to beat you?"

"No."

"Then what makes you think you deserved to be beaten and raped?"

Sunny ducked her head. "We'd ... been together before. One time."

Billie rolled her eyes. "So? You evidently gave him permission once. Does that entitle him to come back and hurt you?"

"No!" Sunny stiffened her spine.

All at once Billie began to hear her own words. How could she blame herself for Sam's nature, or his violent attack. She'd been trying to convince Sunny that her stepbrother's actions were not Sunny's fault. Could Billie accept that his actions months ago in St. Louis hadn't been *her* fault?

"You see ... I like men. I like to—"

Billie patted Sunny's shoulder. "That's fine. What you like and what you do is your own private business. No one else's. But no one has the right to force something on you you don't want." She took a deep breath. "Sam has problems."

Sunny stared into Billie's eyes. In the next instant, the two women were holding on to each other, both sobbing their pain and frustration.

Neither saw a thin shadow slip through the house and out the back door.

Half an hour later, Billie charged down the main street of Alder Gulch, boldly looking into saloons and scouring the gambling dens. Rage flowed through her with such intensity that she gave no thought to fear or impropriety as she stuck her head inside each sleazy den of iniquity.

Eventually, she noticed that a familiar little man was following her. When she stopped to catch her breath, he stopped, too, and stood staring at her.

She studied him carefully and found nothing threatening about him. Finally, she asked, "Don't I know you? Haven't you been in my Grand Palace?"

The man frowned.

"I mean . . . the Empty Barrel."

He nodded.

She spread her arms. "Was there something you wanted?"

He nodded again.

When he just scuffed his feet in the dirt, she turned and started on. She didn't have the time to waste.

" 'Scuse me."

She sighed and turned around again. "Yes?" she said impatiently.

"You lookin' fer your brother?"

"He's not . . ." She snapped her jaws shut. Why waste her breath trying to explain the relationship between Sam and her. "Yes. Have you seen him?"

"Late last night." He quickly continued. "He left town early this morning."

"You wouldn't know where he is, would you?"

He rolled a chaw of tobacco around his mouth and spat. "Not exactly. All's I know is, during the wee hours this morning, he 'won' Tiny Benjamin's claim."

Billie understood the bitterness in the man's voice, the way he accentuated the word *won*. "He cheated Mr. . . . Benjamin, didn't he?"

He shrugged, but the scowl on his face voiced his suspicions.

"Well, thank you for letting me know." She felt the flush still heating her cheeks and said, "I guess I've been making quite a spectacle of myself."

He grinned, exposing two front teeth with a wide gap between them. "That's all right. We all kinda like ta look at ya, Miss Billie. Any way we can."

Her brows drew together.

He winked.

She realized he was teasing and smiled. She had to quit taking everything so personally. Her stepbrother had done that to her. It was another item on a long list of reasons to find him.

Would he come back to Alder Gulch? Or was he smart enough to know he'd gone too far this time?

The stones hanging around her neck suddenly burned her flesh. No, as long as she had the necklace, he would be back. And she could hardly wait to get her hands on him.

Lost in thought, she wandered slowly toward the emporium. She'd failed to pay close attention to the time. Now, through the doors and windows, she noticed lanterns being hit. She must have been at Sunny's longer than she'd realized. Was Anna holding dinner, waiting?

A large shadow suddenly blocked her path. Billie glanced up. With the light shining directly behind him, it was impossible to see the man's face. She stopped, holding her breath.

"Thought I warned you not to come out like this alone." Craig nearly strangled on his relief at having found her.

She nearly fainted with relief that Craig was back and had come looking for her.

"The saloon's going to open in an hour. Where've you been?" He clenched his hands into fists and fell into step beside her.

"I've been . . ." If she told him she'd been looking for Samuel, he'd want to know why, and she'd promised Sunny not to mention what had happened.

"You've been *what?*" He took hold of her arm and hurried her along. He had an uneasy feeling and kept watching the shadows and darkened doorways.

"Uhm, just walking and thinking." That was no lie. She'd done both all afternoon.

"Contemplating the troubles of the world?"

"No, just Alder Gulch. That's more than enough to worry about for me."

"Come up with any solutions?" A deathly silence enveloped the area. He glanced behind them.

"A few."

A sharp click from across the street broke the stillness.

"Aw, hell." Craig threw himself into Billie and rolled with her to the ground.

Billie yelped.

Craig grunted as the report from a gun echoed between the buildings. He shouted in her ear, "Damn it, woman. Now do you see why I warned you to stay inside?"

"But—" She wanted to tell him that she'd been on her way back when he'd confronted her and that, yes, she'd been aware of the danger. But she didn't say a word. Instead, she froze at the feel of something hot and sticky on his side.

Her jaws opened, but she couldn't force out a word. Finally, she squeaked, "Blood."

Chapter Twenty-seven

"You've been shot." Hysteria edged Billie's voice. She pushed Craig off her and squinted in the dim light to get a better look at his side. Her hands shook so badly that she hardly touched him for fear of causing him more pain.

Craig grabbed her hands and stilled them. "It's just a graze. What about you? Did you hurt your head again?"

"No. But you—"

"It's a long way from my heart. I'll be fine." He said it loud enough that the crowd gathering around began to disperse. And even as he thought about it, that very heart he'd mentioned pounded double time. He was holding her. Comforting her. What if he wasn't around someday to protect her? His heart literally ached with the fear of not being able to . . . *love* her.

Billie pulled her hands from his and scrambled to her feet. "The emporium's not far. Let's hurry. We need to stop the bleeding." Her eyes narrowed and she pushed him back down. "Wait." She bent and tore a strip of cloth from her petticoat, folded it, and pressed it against the wound. Then she made him hold his elbow against his side to keep it in place. "Now, we can hurry."

He couldn't hide his grin as she fussed and worried over him. It felt good, and he allowed her to herd him along until they reached the saloon. Just before they went inside, he stopped and turned her to face him. "Don't work tonight, or any night, until we find whoever's responsible for this nonsense. One of these times, they aren't goin' to miss."

She stared into his concerned, sincere features, secretly pleased and surprised by his adamant appeal. But hiding from reality never solved anything. She shook her head.

"Listen to me—"

She held a finger to his lips. "Please understand . . . I've been terrorized long enough. I won't hide and cower anymore." Most importantly, her self-confidence and pride were at stake.

Respect for Billie Glenn settled deep inside him. Yet foremost above his regard was fear—fear that her bravado would be her downfall. But how could he go against her wishes?

He knew what she'd secretly faced and conquered. He knew how far she'd come. She'd earned the right to decide what and who she must confront.

"Then will you at least stay inside?"

She nodded. "If I need to go out, I promise I'll find you first."

"Yeah? You've said that before."

"I'm sorry about this evening. Time just got away from me. It won't happen again." She looked at his blood-soaked shirt. Her eyes misted. Once again, because of her, someone she loved had been hurt. The responsibility was more than she could bear.

He sighed and put his good arm over her shoulder. Besides wanting to hold her close, he was getting tired and a little dizzy.

Feeling the brunt of his weight and sensing a weakness he would never admit, she quickly opened the door and guided him inside.

Pearl glanced up from helping Danny polish the counter and rushed to their sides. "My Gawd, when're you folks going to realize the war's being fought back East, not in the Empty Barrel?"

With his right arm in a sling, Lucky came from the kitchen. "The light's better in the kitchen. Take him back there."

Danny hovered anxiously, but stayed out of the way as the adults removed Craig's shirt.

"Reckon I oughta go get the doc?" the boy asked, upon seeing the long, bloody gash.

Lucky shook his head. "It doesn't look all that serious. I think we can take care of it, son."

Danny's eyes left Craig to study Lucky adoringly. Lucky felt his gaze and cast the boy a grin.

"Is Falling Water here?" Billie dipped a cloth into a basin of fresh water and cleaned the slash.

Craig winced.

"She's upstairs." Pearl tore a towel into strips.

"Danny? Would you mind asking her if she has something to put on Mr. Rawlins's wound before we bandage it?"

Danny nodded and ran from the room.

After Craig explained what had happened, Lucky looked at Billie. "I agree with Mr. Rawlins. It's not safe for you down here, especially since we don't know who's after you."

"Or why," Craig added menacingly.

She puffed out her chest, saw Craig's brows raise, flushed, and let out a breath before saying, "The same goes for the rest of you, apparently. Should we all turn out the lanterns and crawl beneath the beds? Then what about tomorrow? There's work to be done. Do we send someone else to do the errands and chores?"

Lucky and Craig looked at each other. Lucky shrugged. Craig arched his brows.

Danny skipped into the room, holding out a small leather pouch. "Miss Fallin' Water says to put this yarrow stuff on Mr. Rawlins."

"Thank you, Danny." Billie poured the powder into

her palm, then smeared it over Craig's wound, making sure it covered the entire gash. Pearl helped her tie the bandage around Craig's ribs.

"Well," Lucky sighed. "Since I couldn't talk anyone out of working tonight, guess I'd better get busy."

"I'll do Anna a favor and help you," Pearl grinned. "You know she thinks it's too soon for you to go back to work."

"Yep, and don't think Mr. Rawlins and I haven't noticed how you've taken over the place lately. If you're tryin' to get our jobs, forget it," he teased.

Danny grabbed at Lucky's hand and followed the bantering pair from the room.

Left alone with Craig, Billie shifted her feet and searched awkwardly for the pockets in her skirt.

Craig grabbed one of her hands before she could hide it and pulled her close. He sensuously examined each of her long fingers, then spread her palm against his chest.

The steady thud of his heart pulsed through her nerve endings and vibrated up her arm. Sparks burst into flames in the pit of her stomach. Her niplles throbbed. She ached between her thighs. She darted a glance to his heavy-lidded, seductive eyes and her heart leaped like a jackrabbit.

His breath tickled the lobe of her ear. She swayed toward him.

"The bandage is too tight, Angel. I can't breathe."

Breathe? Who needed air? Bandage? She blinked. Bandage too tight. Disappointment quieted the upheaval taking place in her body. She'd hoped he was going to kiss her. So, why hadn't he?

He rubbed her fingers along his uninjured side. His smooth, supple flesh ripped. She licked her lips and sighed.

He whispered against her neck, "Would you mind loosening the knot?" He fought back the quiver threatening his voice. He'd wracked his brain for an excuse to keep her with him for a few more minutes. To have a chance to talk to her alone. Now he was beginning to think the whole idea had been madness. Her sweet, delectable body was tormenting him beyond belief.

Billie almost cried from frustration. All he wanted from her was help with his bindings. Why had she expected anything else? He'd run from her like a buck during hunting season for the past week. She jerked her hand from his chest, though it was difficult to free her fingers from the mat of soft, curly hair. She shoved his good arm out of her way until she could reach the knot. Her knuckles brushed enticingly against his skin.

Craig gasped. His eyes leveled on the swells of her breasts. A lock of her hair curled against his cheek. He closed his eyes and groaned.

Billie's hands shook. "I'm sorry. I didn't mean to hurt you." She had to take her mind off thoughts of his gorgeous male body and pay attention to what she was doing.

"You didn't." He inhaled sharply, smelled the scent of pure woman, and shook his head. "I mean . . . not in the way you're thinkin'."

Her eyes rounded.

"Aw, hell." He pulled her onto his lap and kissed her until they both had to gasp for air. He threaded his fingers into the glossy hair on either side of her temples, kissed the fading bruise, then forced her to look into his eyes.

"No one is goin' to hurt you again, Angel. Not as long as I have a breath in my body." The force of his emotion constricted his throat. All at once the suspicion he'd been avoiding for weeks was confirmed. He'd fallen in love with this vibrant, wonderful woman. Love. He didn't know much about it, but had finally found someone for whom he was willing and able to learn.

She watched the conflict erupting and ebbing in his eyes. Such beautiful eyes. Eyes that told her more than she was afraid he'd ever dare to say. The tenderness of his embrace . . . The raspy timbre of his voice . . . They all told her he cared. Really cared. Her heart soared.

"Hey!" Molly called from the doorway. "There's a crowd out front. How long ya wanna keep 'em waiting'?"

Craig started to get up, but Billie pressed her bottom firmly into his lap to keep him seated. A deep blush burned her cheeks when she felt the evidence of his desire. She ignored her own leap of excitement and informed him, "No, you don't. You aren't going to do anything but rest."

"But—"

"But, nothing. Go up to my room and lie down. We can handle things down here." She glanced away. "And you'll be close enough that someone can check on you. In case you . . ." He kissed her hand. His lips nibbled her palm. A prairie fire scorched her insides.

"Who's goin' to check on me, Angel?"

"Uhm . . . Whoever . . ."

He licked each finger, tasted, suckled. "Who?"

"Oooohhh . . . I'll look in—"

"That's better."

He silenced further discussion with a kiss that curled her toes and left her reeling as she stood and stumbled from the kitchen. As for himself, he had to sit for a while. He'd had a startling revelation. And he was numb with shock.

Craig Rawlins in love. Who would've thought?

Craig had no idea how long he'd been asleep when he awakened amidst the sweet-smelling pillows and soft blankets on Billie's bed. The lantern was lit and turned low and Billie herself was slumped uncomfortably in the chair. He started to get up, felt a sharp pain in his side, and tried again a little less quickly.

Stiffly, he walked to the door and closed it, then strode quietly over to her. He stood looking down on the long, thick mass of loose hair curling wildly toward the floor and at the iridescence of her angelic features.

Emotions he had no words to describe filled his heart as he lifted her from the chair and carried her to the bed.

He felt a twinge in his side as he stretched out beside her. But it was nothing compared to his joy when she smiled in her sleep, whispered his name, and curled against him. Folding her in his arms, he marveled at the peace and contentment she brought to his soul. He wanted her in the most elemental of ways, but was more than happy to just hold her, cherish her, and dream of the future.

Was it possible? Had he reconciled his past misconceptions enough to love and live and enjoy a life with Miss Billie Glenn? He'd learned a lot from Danny and Anna and Pearl and Molly—and Billie. Things that had changed his feelings toward women in general and his mother in particular.

Some women, faced with circumstances beyond their control, were forced to do whatever it took to survive. It didn't make them a damn bit worse than any one else— maybe made them tougher, stronger.

Was it possible for him to start over with a new outlook on life? He damned sure hoped so.

The next day, Craig continued with his investigation, but could find no evidence to help solve the mystery of who was after Billie. Every once in a while he would favor his injured side and the urgency of the situation would bead his brow with sweat. If anything happened to her . . .

Meanwhile, Billie sat upstairs while the farmer's market wound down, alternately staring out her window and sewing feathers onto a new bonnet. A tap on the jamb turned her attention to the door.

Pearl walked in to see what Billie was doing. "That looks nice. You going to wear it this evening?"

"I thought I'd wear it to church tomorrow." She put in one last stitch and set the hat aside. "Are you going?"

Pearl shrugged. "I don't know. Never been one to go to church, even when I was little and the folks were alive."

Billie cocked her head. "You wouldn't have to go far."

"Yep. It was real nice of you to let that preacher use the saloo— emporium for his sermons."

"No one else offered him a place. With all of the families moving into town, I think it's important that Alder Gulch have a place to worship."

"Think more of the people will add to Mr. Rawlins's donation to build a real church?"

"I'm sure they will. After all, some of the ladies object to meeting in an . . ." Billie grinned, ". . . *emporium.* Even if it is the grandest place in town."

Pearl rolled her eyes. "Maybe I'll see what he's got to say, but right now I've got to go over to the school. Some of the fellas want to learn how to say *I adore you, Pearl,* in French."

Billie waved her away. "Have fun." She thought it nice, but unnecessary, that everyone seemed to think they had to check on her and tell her where they'd be if they left. She wasn't afraid.

About half an hour later she was mending a rip in a hem when she heard the pounding of horses' hooves and looked out the window. Craig and a large group of men were riding fast out of town. She jumped up and ran downstairs.

Lucky was carrying an armload of supplies Anna had just purchased from a farmer when Billie caught up and trailed him into the kitchen. "Do you know where Craig was going in such a hurry?"

Dropping lettuce, green beans, and corn onto the table, he said, "He's on his way out to his ranch. Seems someone sent a message that outlaws were goin' to raid his horses."

"Oh, no." She thought of all the new colts and fillies and her little "Angel."

Lucky patted her shoulder. "He can take care of himself. And that wound is healing real well."

She knew Lucky was right. Craig Rawlins was the most capable and resourceful man she'd ever known. But he also recklessly challenged danger. Anything could happen . . .

On the way back to her room, she purchased two apples from a family who were packing up what goods they hadn't sold. Everyone was leaving, so Danny and a couple of his new friends could sweep and dust before the emporium opened in another couple of hours.

She'd just started up the stairs when Molly called out, "Gotta run to the mercantile. Anythin' ya want?"

"I can't think of anything."

"See ya later."

Billie went on up to her room. Taking a bite of crunchy fruit, she gazed through the window to the street below. So many changes had taken place in the town during the past month. The holes in the street had been filled. A lot of the trash had been covered over and garbage was now being hauled to a site outside of town. Permanent buildings were being constructed and more women and children could be seen entering the stores.

The pounding stamps and dull booms that were the hearbeat of the mining community could still be felt and heard, but the residents had become so inured, they hardly seemed to notice.

"Billie? You all right?" Anna hesitantly stepped into the room.

Billie jumped, then nodded. "I was just noticing how Alder Gulch is growing."

"Yeah. It's somethin', ain't it?"

They both looked out the window, then at each other. "It's a little different than it was when we first met."

Anna nodded. She twined her fingers together. "Lucky's invited me an' Danny to supper at the boardin' house. An' if we go now, Danny'll still have time to do his chores."

Billie smiled at the girlish excitement glistening from Anna's eyes. The woman had blossomed with Lucky's attentiveness. And Danny now trailed after Lucky like an adoring puppy.

Anna suddenly beamed. "Jest think. I'm bein' taken out to dine. Don't have to cook, or nuthin'. But . . ." she added quickly, "there's fresh bread an' sliced ham on the table if ya git hungry."

"Thanks." Billie heard Danny calling his mother. "You better get going. They might decide to leave without you."

Anna batted her lashes and swished her hips on the way out. "I don't think so."

"Go on, anyway."

Billie's grin faded as, a few minutes later, she watched Anna, Lucky, and Danny walk down the street. Although it was nothing she'd given much thought to, she'd always assumed she would one day marry and have a family. But she'd gone and fallen in love with a man who didn't show the slightest interest in commitment or the word "forever."

Sometimes she wondered if the hands fate dealt made sense. There certainly seemed to be no rhyme or reason to the events that had transpired in her life recently; except that she felt she'd grown to be a stronger, more independent individual. She certainly couldn't complain about that, could she?

All at once she noticed the long shadows in the street and realized it was only an hour or so until the emporium would open. The apple had tasted good, but Anna's ham and bread held a sudden appeal.

Halfway down the stairs, her steps slowed, then stopped altogether. The large room was dim and deathly quiet. Where was everyone? Ooops. She remembered now. They had all had things to do. She was alone.

For heaven's sake, she scolded. Hadn't she just commended herself for becoming stronger and more independent? There was nothing to be afraid of. She'd walked down the stairs and to the kitchen a hundred times without mishap. It was ridiculous to suddenly become a worrywart.

Taking a deep breath, she descended the remaining steps and marched boldly to the kitchen doorway. See? Nothing to it. With a deep sigh, she entered the smaller room, only to stumble to an abrupt halt.

Sitting at the table, eating her food, was Samuel Jones Glenn.

Craig and the members of the Committee pulled their horses to a stop outside the barn. Dust swirled and sifted away on the wind. He looked all around, but could see no sign of trouble. Horses stood at the rails of their corrals, nostrils flared, whickering at the new arrivals.

Ezekiel walked from the first stall and out the barn door. "Afternoon, suh. Yo needs more hosses at the stable?"

Craig ignored the question and asked his own. "Have you had any trouble here, Ezekiel? Or any of the hands at the camps?"

"No, suh." He frowned and shook his head. "Ever'thin's jest fine. Why?"

A tremor raced up Craig's spine. It suddenly dawned on him that the warning had been a ruse to get him out of town. Out of town and away from the emporium.

Billie! Dear Lord!

Be reasonable, his common sense said. *Calm down.* She wasn't alone. In another hour the orchestra and the Swensons would be there. She was fine.

But the hairs on the back of his neck continued to tingle. He had a gut instinct that Billie was in danger.

"Ezekiel, bring that bay gelding. I need to trade horses." While he exchanged his saddle to the bay, he explained his fears to the others and told them to follow as best they could since there weren't enough horses for everyone to ride a fresh mount.

As he galloped from the headquarters, he heard Ezekiel's warning. "Be careful, suh. Watch your back."

"It's about time you came down, little sister." Samuel licked ham from his fingers. "I don't like to be kept waiting."

She considered turning and running from the room, but immediately rejected the notion. She was through running and hiding. She could—and would—face Sam and rid herself of her demons—or demon.

"If you didn't sneak around like a mangy coyote, you might not have to wait." She took another step forward, but then stopped.

"Well, well . . ." He suddenly produced a thin-bladed knife and began cleaning under his nails. "If that isn't a pot calling a kettle black. A whore and a mangy coyote. Quite the pair, aren't we?"

"I used to think we were," she commented sadly.

"Are you going to give it to me, or do I have to take it? I will, you know."

She didn't pretend not to know what he wanted. And when she reached up to touch the emeralds, they didn't provide the reassuring comfort she'd come to expect. Instead, she looked into her stepbrother's pale, cold eyes and shivered.

"Don't worry about the necklace, Miss Billie. He won't need it where he's goin'."

Samuel and Billie both jumped at the sound of the high-pitched voice coming from just inside the back door.

"Justin? Wh-what are you doing? Put the gun away. It might go off and hurt someone."

Justin's lips parted in a thin, cruel grin. "Yes, I know."

"Look here, boy," Samuel complained, rising to his feet. He inconspicuously lowered his knife. "The 'lady' and I are talking business. Take your toy and go play somewhere else."

Sweet, strange Justin Turnbow cursed words she'd never heard before. Billie's insides chilled. He cocked his pistol and ordered Samuel to sit down. She was even more shocked when her stepbrother blanched and obeyed.

"Wh-what do you want?" There had to be some logical explanation for Justin's behavior.

Justin shook his head. "It's not what I *want,* Miss Billie. I hope you understand. It's what I have to do."

"I'm afraid I don't understand. Why don't you put away the gun and we can talk about this."

He waved the gun barrel first toward Samuel and then Billie. "It's much too late for that. I have no other choice but to kill you."

Billie's breath caught. She choked out, "You c-can't be serious. Y-you—"

"Oh, but I'm very serious. My mother won't be happy again until you're both gone."

Billie swallowed a mouthful of bile. His mother. In the space of two seconds she thought back to the times when his eyes had been fixated on Sunny. Everything he'd said or done concerned his mother.

Samuel shifted in his seat. "Look, kid, I don't think you know your mother—"

"Shut up!" Justin screamed. He took a menacing step toward Samuel, waving the pistol. "You hurt my mother. Hurt her bad. And you, more than anyone, must pay." He kept the gun pointed at Samuel, but looked at Billie. In a very calm and rational voice he explained, "I like you, Miss Billie. I really don't want to kill you. But Mother won't love me again until you're gone. She loves Mr. Rawlins and she's been very upset since you came to Alder Gulch. No one can come between Mother and him."

Billie held out her hands. "But Justin, you know we are business partners. And we're friends."

"Of course," he continued, lost in his own thoughts, "I can't let Mr. Rawlins have her, either. I'll feel bad about him, too. But no one comes between Mother and I. No one."

Her eyes rounded with the dawning of a horrible truth. A sickening wave of nausea swept over her as Billie sagged against a cabinet. It took several tries before she forced her voice to work. "J-Justin . . . Did you . . ." She cleared her throat. "Did you . . . Mr. Turnbow . . . Bob Rawlins . . . My accidents?"

He waved the gun again and began to pace. "Those men . . . They weren't nice to me. They tried to turn Mother against me. Said I should be put away someplace." He turned wild eyes on Billie.

She shrank back.

"I had to do something," he shouted, his high voice suddenly deep and angry. Then he blinked. The contorted muscles in his face relaxed and he was once more rational. "Mother loves me, you know. Only me."

Samuel stood, glaring defiantly down the wavering barrel. His fingers tightened around the knife hidden at the side of his leg. "There's no need for this, kid. Sunny—"

At the sound of his mother's name from the hated man's lips, Justin again snapped out of control. "Sit! Sit down. I'll shoot!" He jumped up and down with nervous excitement. "And you . . ." He darted a quick look at Billie. "I tried to scare you away. You said you wouldn't stay." His voice rose to a shrill crescendo.

Realizing the boy was working himself into a frenzy, Billie edged toward the middle of the shelf and a bottle of brandy. She risked a glance at Samuel and saw that he was watching her. He imperceptively nodded and started to rise from his chair, drawing Justin's complete attention.

Billie grabbed the bottle. She threw it at the gun.

Samuel kicked the chair out of his way and brought up the knife. He lunged for Justin.

The back door crashed open. Craig rushed into the

middle of the fray. Seeing Justin and Samuel wrestling for the weapon, indecision caused him to hesitate. A gun fired. The struggling pair seemed wrapped in a cocoon of suspended time. A knife dropped and clattered. Slowly, Samuel Glenn sank to the floor.

Billie screamed. Blood gushed from her stepbrother's chest. His eyes sought hers just as he collapsed. The hatred he directed her way in that split second propelled her backward.

"Justin, what're you doin'? You got the bastard." Craig stared at the smoking barrel pointed at his chest.

Craig's voice penetrated Billie's horror. She glanced up to find Justin holding the gun on Craig. Her heart stopped. Craig had no way of knowing Justin's intentions. He wouldn't know that the boy had plans to kill him, too.

That knowledge galvanized her into action. Growling low in her throat, she ran at Justin. He swiveled and fired.

Billie flinched as the bullet stung the top of her shoulder, but it didn't stop her momentum. She careened into Justin before he could recock the pistol.

"What the hell?" Craig stood stunned. He couldn't believe Justin had shot Billie. Or that Billie now had the boy on the floor and was wrestling for the gun. All at once he realized Justin must not have been there to protect Billie.

Two strides carried him to the twisting, grappling pair. When Billie rolled to the top of the heap, he grabbed her around the waist and set her kicking, flailing body aside. Next, he slapped the gun from Justin's hand. A solid left hook to the jaw put the youngster down.

Footsteps pounded through the saloon. Lucky and both Swensons rushed into the kitchen, guns drawn. Muscles quaking and voice shaking, Billie told them about Justin and the terrible things he'd done.

Lucky found a length of twine to bind Justin's hands before he came to.

Billie then stumbled over to stand beside Samuel. His lids fluttered. She jumped back. "He's alive."

"What do you want to do with him?" Craig could muster no charity for Samuel Jones Glenn. The man had harmed Billie. He deserved whatever pain he suffered.

Pearl stepped through the doorway. "You can take him to my room."

Billie closed her eyes and timorously touched the necklace. "No. He was my brother. Put him in my bed." Sighing, she raised her eyelids and whispered, "He needs a doctor."

Lucky looked to Craig, who nodded.

Billie watched as Samuel was carried from the room, then she ran to Craig. She threw her arms around him and sniffed loudly.

Craig enfolded her against him and nuzzled his nose in her hair. His eyes fell on a dark-red blotch on the top of her shoulder. He sucked in his breath. "Angel, you're hurt." Setting her away so he could get a better look, he pulled the shoulder of her dress down. The wound barely marred her beautiful, creamy skin, but fury shot through him at the thought of what could have been a tragedy.

Billie had forgotten about the bullet grazing her. "I—I was so afraid . . ." she sobbed.

He pulled her into his arms again, savoring the feel of her. "He can't hurt you, now, Angel. I'll—"

"No. I was afraid Justin would k-kill *you.*"

He was speechless. She had risked her life for him. Had taken the bullet aimed at him. His gut churned. He crushed her against him.

"I l-love you," she whispered. She had to say it. She'd come close to losing him just now, and couldn't bear the thought that he might have died and not known how deeply she cared.

He stiffened. This time she wasn't half asleep. She knew exactly what she was saying. His throat clogged. Despite his numerous gigantic flaws, she really loved him. Dear God. What better way to prove it than to give her life for his.

The breath was squeezed from Billie's lungs. She

thought he was going to crack her ribs, but refused to tell him to stop. She gripped him tighter, hoping and praying his reaction to her declaration was in his actions and not in his lack of a reply.

"Angel, I—"

"Miss Billie? Miss Billie?" Danny ran into the room, his eyes round as saucers. "That man upstairs, he's askin' fer ya."

She gulped. "I'll be right there." Glancing expectantly at Craig, Billie waited for him to continue. Her stomach knotted. *Hurry. Say something. Anything.*

Perspiration popped out on Craig's forehead. His palms tingled. But when he saw Anna and Molly coming up behind Danny, he shook his head. This wasn't the time. When he said the words she needed to hear, it would be in some private place with no fear of interruptions. He wanted no misunderstandings.

He cleared his throat and looked into her flashing eyes. "I'll go with you, if you like."

She closed her eyes and swallowed down her keen disappointment. It was her own fault. Why did she continue to anticipate the unthinkable? She left herself open for rejection.

"Uhm . . . no. I'd rather go alone." She spun and stalked from the kitchen.

Craig sucked in his breath. She'd looked so . . . so . . . disheartened. But then, she was going to see her stepbrother. That would be a chore for any rational person.

Molly came up to Craig. "Mr. Rawlins, there be a gent out front what says he wants to see ya."

His eyes never left Billie as she dejectedly walked across the dance floor and dragged herself up the stairs. Rubbing the back of his neck, he asked, "Did he give you his name?"

Molly nodded. "I think ya best come see."

Chapter Twenty-eight

Dr. Andrews met Billie just outside her bedroom door. He wiped his bloody hands on a towel and looked her squarely in the eyes. "Is that man a relative?"

She nodded and looked at the still form on her bed. "Is—is he d-dead?"

"Not yet. But he won't last long." He shook his head. "I'm sorry. There was nothing I could do."

She squeezed the doctor's arm and slowly entered the room. Each step that carried her closer to *him* was fraught with conflicting emotions. Love—for the jovial brother he'd been when she was a young girl. Fear—from the cold, heartless man he'd become. Sorrow—for the helpless soul dying on her bed. Compassion—because he was still her stepbrother, still family, no matter what he'd done.

Timothy followed her inside. "He passed out just after asking for you. Here." He placed a bottle in her hand. "When he comes to again, he'll be in pain. Give him what laudanum he needs until . . ."

She nodded. "Thank you. Should I stay . . . Uhm . . . How long . . ."

He gently patted her shoulder, saw the bloodstain, and probed through the material of her blouse until he saw that it wasn't serious. He reached in his bag and put some ointment on the shallow flesh wound.

"I can't be sure how long he has. Stomach injuries

can be unpredictable. But if you want to talk to him while he's rational, I'd suggest you stay and take your chances."

After the doctor left, she pulled the chair near the bed and sat down. Her stepbrother looked almost peaceful lying there asleep, boyish and innocent. Why? She'd loved him so much. Why had he changed? What had happened to turn a young man with the world at his fingertips into a greedy, uncaring monster?

Tears for a wasted soul trickled down her cheeks. Samuel Jones Glenn. What had happened to the Sam who'd once cared for her?

Craig poured his guest a shot of bourbon. "There you go, sir. I'll—"

"Justin! Where's Justin?" Sunny Turnbow yelled as she charged through the doors. "Craig, what have you done with my son?"

"Excuse me a minute, sir."

Craig pointed to the guard's chair where he and Lucky had bound the despondent boy.

She hurried over and knelt by Justin's side, running her fingers through his thin, ruffled hair and peering helplessly into his lifeless eyes. "Justin . . . Justin, what have you done?"

When her son just sat there, head drooping, registering no response, she turned accusing eyes on Craig.

He held up his hands and shrugged. "He's been like that ever since the fight ended."

"What happened?" Her breath hissed shakily through her teeth as she placed her hand on Justin's shoulder.

Craig told her everything and shook his head. "It sounds like Justin is obsessed with you, Sunny. He's sick."

"What are you goin' to do with him?" She fussed with Justin's shirt, straightening the shoulders, refastening the buttons.

"All I can do is turn him over to the commit—"

"No!" She scrambled to her feet and grabbed Craig's shirt. "You can't do that. They'll hang him. You know they will."

He drew in a deep breath. "He killed Big John and Bobby. And he tried to kill Billie. There's nothing else I can do."

"Yes." She gnawed the inside of her lip. "Yes, there is."

"Then you tell me."

She gulped and begged, "Let me take him. Now." She tilted her face close to his. "I know a place . . . a place where I can take him. He'll be locked up, but he'll get help. And never harm anyone again. I promise." She crumpled Craig's shirt in her fists. "Please! Please don't let them hang my son." She collapsed against Craig, sobbing piteously.

Craig was torn. He'd made a vow to Bobby. To keep that vow he'd have to let the Committee have the boy. On the other hand, Sunny had already lost John Turnbow. Should any mother suffer the loss of her son if she wasn't forced to? No. And Craig wouldn't be responsible for that. Justin would hurt no one else if he was locked away. Besides, the obsessive Sunny would also be removed from Craig's life—his and Billie's.

He splayed his hands on his hips. "How long will it take you to get him out of town?"

"I—I can go right away. We'll just take what we need for now and send for the rest later. You . . . Would you see to selling the house and arranging for my money to be deposited in another bank once we're settled?" She swiped a tear from her cheek.

He nodded. "Of course."

She went back to Justin. He didn't acknowledge that he knew she was there. "My poor baby."

Craig stared at the obviously tormented young man and the distraught woman. As hard as he tried, he couldn't summon the hatred he thought he'd feel upon catching his cousin's murderer.

He glanced over to the older gentleman swallowing the last of his drink. As the man started toward the stairway, Craig knew he owed his own change of heart to the lady upstairs. The woman he loved.

A grin curved his lips. It was getting easier to think the word. He just hoped he'd be able to *say* it with the right amount of conviction when the time came.

Something fluttered against Billie's chest. She snapped her eyes open. Samuel was awake and reaching for the necklace. She blinked the blurriness from her tired eyes and scooted back. Samuel licked his lips. "Th-they're . . . mine," he croaked. "Give . . . me."

Her chest ached as she stared into his rheumy, hate-filled eyes. She'd expected him to wake up and apologize or ask her forgiveness or to try to make things right between them before he died. She was once again sadly mistaken.

With shaking hands, she decided to give him what he wanted. As her fingers found the clasp, she thought of everything she'd been through wearing the emeralds. They had been her protection. They had been her reminder of the past when she didn't know she had one. Her entire life had changed when he'd fastened them around her neck.

The necklace also represented a lie. The truth behind them had been meaningless.

Her vision blurred as she held the emeralds out to him, but there was a strength in her purpose that had been missing for a long time.

His trembling hand rose, fingers groping.

"Stop. That necklace is going back to its rightful owner."

Billie spun around. Her eyes rounded. "Father."

Samuel's throat gurgled. His fingers curled into a fist

as Billie's hand dropped, pulling the necklace out of his reach.

Thomas Glenn strode to his adopted son's bedside and looked into Samuel's glazed brown eyes.

Samuel's lips moved. His body contorted. He gasped one time. Suddenly, his eyes rolled and his head lolled to the side. His hand remained fisted. A final gesture of defiance.

Billie's lips trembled. She slowly rose to her feet. Gazing at the gray-haired man staring at her stepbrother, she whispered again, "Father?"

Thomas turned from Samuel's body and never blinked before wrapping his daughter in an unsteady embrace. "Oh, baby. I was so afraid I wouldn't get here in time."

"Wh-what?"

"I'd just traced a shipment of school supplies to your name, and the town of Alder Gulch, when I received a telegram from your young man. And when my detectives told me they'd followed Samuel to a mining camp called Alder Gulch ... I was afraid I'd lost you again."

Wiping a tear from her cheek, she pulled back so she could see his face. "You were looking for me?"

"Of course." His shoulders slumped. "You didn't think I would try to find you?"

She shook her head.

His mouth dropped open. He placed a hand over his heart in utter disbelief. "I don't understand, daughter. Have I done something to hurt you that badly?"

"I ... when you came into the library and s-saw what I'd done ..." She choked and ducked her head, unwilling to see the disgust in his eyes again.

"What *you'd* done!" he bellowed. "What nonsense are you babbling? Why would you think I thought you'd done something wrong?"

She gasped for breath. "Th-the look in your eyes. The disgust ... And the way you left. You couldn't look at me."

"My God. I was shocked, stunned, to think that a boy I'd raised as my own could do something so vile to his sister . . . my daughter. I couldn't breathe and knew I didn't have the strength to stop him myself. I went into the street and called for help." He closed his eyes. "When I came back with the constable, you were gone. Samuel had passed out on the sofa and could tell me nothing. I was frantic. My doctor said I suffered a mild heart attack, so my efforts to find you were delayed."

Billie backed up and fell into the chair. Behind her father, she saw Craig leaning against the jamb, arms crossed over his broad chest, watching, listening.

Then once again she sought her father's face. "I thought you blamed me. Thought you—"

"I love you, my darling daughter." He bent over and took her cold hands into his wrinkled ones. "You were always—will always—be the light of my life. I blamed myself for not recognizing Samuel's vicious nature. He could have . . ." He coughed. "You could have . . ."

She rose and embraced her father. "I'm sorry. I shouldn't have run away. But something . . . in my mind . . ."

Thomas kissed her forehead and patted her shoulder. "Your young man explained everything before I came here. I'm the one who's sorry. So very sorry. And I'll make it all up to you when we get back to St. Louis."

Frowning, Craig pushed away from the wall and strode into the room. "I'm sorry to intrude, but I think we'd better have the Swenson brothers come up and take him," he nodded toward the body, "to the undertaker."

Thomas nodded and turned Billie around so she wouldn't have to look at Samuel again.

"Where do you want him buried?" Craig asked.

Billie watched as pain settled in her father's features. "Why don't we put him in Boot Hill."

Thomas considered taking his son back to St. Louis, but looked into his daughter's haunted eyes. "That will be fine." He also took the necklace dangling limply from her fingers. "But this I'll return to the young fellow Samuel cheated."

Her lips compressed into a tight line. She took her father's free hand and squeezed his fingers. "Sam was good once. We'll try to remember those times."

Craig placed his arm possessively around her shoulders. "Are you all right?"

She nodded, unable to find the words to describe how she really felt. At the top of the stairs, she finally looked into his eyes. "You sent for my father."

He felt an unfamiliar warmth invade his cheeks. "It finally dawned on me that I'd heard of the Glenns from St. Louis. Your father and I have done business together for some time, but never met. I telegraphed, but he was already close to finding you."

Thomas followed them down. "Don't sell yourself short, young fella. If it had taken me even another day, I might have been too late. I'm extremely grateful. If there's ever anything I can do . . ."

Craig arched a brow. "You can give me permission to take your daughter to supper."

"Done." Thomas grinned.

A little man who'd been standing at the counter came over and stared at the emerald necklace in Thomas Glenn's hand. The man put his arm as high up on Thomas's shoulder as he could reach and turned back toward the bar. "So he stole a necklace, did he? Let me buy ya dinner and I'll tell ya about my claim."

Billie watched her father being led away and started to protest Craig's high-handed behavior.

Craig sensed her hesitation. "You haven't eaten, have you?"

She recalled the ham and bread Anna had left. "No, but the emporium—"

"Will run smoothly without us. And Tiny said your father can bunk with him at the boardinghouse."

Billie's eyes rounded. Tiny Benjamin. Now she remembered where she'd seen the little man. He'd been the one who'd told her about Samuel's cheating a miner out of a claim—his claim.

Craig hunched his shoulders and narrowed his eyes at her. "Now, what other excuse can I find an answer for?"

A mischievous gleam brightened her eyes. "What about—I'm exhausted and want to go up and rest?"

"You had a corpse in your bed. You'd have to wash the blankets."

A shiver raced up her spine. It would be hard to walk back into the bedroom. She licked her lips. "You win. This time."

Billie took Craig's arm as they walked away from Mrs. Timms's boardinghouse. "Thank you for bringing me here. I needed to get away from the emporium."

"I'm glad we weren't too late."

"Me, too. But . . . shouldn't we be getting back now?"

He stopped her with a quick kiss on the lips.

She sputtered, but didn't argue when he walked her toward a section of the town she'd never seen before. At last, her curiosity got the best of her. "Where are we going?"

"We need to talk—alone—and can't do that at the saloon."

"Emporium."

"Whatever." He stifled a grin, hoping she wouldn't become suspicious. She was in for a real surprise tomorrow, and he could hardly wait to see her face when she saw the new sign.

She paused when she saw a log cabin directly ahead. A welcoming lantern burned in a large front window. "Whose house is this?"

He assisted her up two steps and across a narrow porch. After opening the door, he stepped back so she could precede him inside. As she brushed past, he said quietly, "I built the cabin myself."

She stopped just inside the door. The interior was much the same as that of the ranch house, with a large fireplace and throw rugs to cover the wood floors. But here, the furniture was plush and padded and very comfortable and cozy looking.

"It's lovely."

He slid his hands into his pockets and rocked back on his heels. "You think so?"

"Uh-huh."

"Well . . . Sit down. Would you like something to drink?"

"No thank you. I'm fine." But once she'd sat on the long sofa, she twined her fingers together beneath a concealing fold of her skirt.

"Me, too." He plunked onto the opposite end of the couch.

They sat quietly, only their eyes moving as they cast nervous glances around the room.

All at once, Craig blurted, "Don't go."

"I beg your pardon?"

"To St. Louis. Don't go."

"But I—"

"You still have a little time left on our agreement."

"I know."

"I'm going to hold you to it."

"Of course." She watched the lines around his eyes and mouth deepen, wondering why he was suddenly so tense. What made him think she'd renege on their business deal? "What gave you the idea I'd be going to St. Louis?"

"Your father mentioned it this evening. I just thought—"

"I've never gone back on my word."

He fidgeted and scooted closer. "I didn't mean to sound as though I thought you would." He cleared his throat. "I just don't think you should leave."

"Why?" Her pulse accelerated. What was he really

trying to say? She watched a muscle twitch in his jaw
and also moved closer.

"I . . . you've done a good job at the salo— emporium. You've made a lot of friends. I just don't think you
should leave." Damn it, he'd said that a thousand times.
Why couldn't he bring himself to tell her what he was
really thinking? That she was beautiful and wonderful
and that he didn't know how he could go on without
her. She'd twisted him around her little finger and . . .
he liked it.

She pursed her lips. "I do like it here."

"And you still have the school to finish."

She nodded. "And the church."

Her enthusiasm urged him closer. His knee touched
hers. "They need you here."

"They?"

"They . . . we . . . I'd like you to be a permanent res-
ident."

Her palms tingled. "Why?" She could see in his eyes
that there was something else he wanted to say. Her
heart thumped crazily against her breast. Was she going
to have to drag it out of him? Her elbow brushed his
side. She was aware of the contact all the way to the pit
of her stomach.

"I, uh . . . just told you." He shifted uneasily. His
thigh nestled next to her hip.

"Anyone could've done what I have. Could go on
from where I leave off." And she truly believed that. She
refused to think she was anyone special—except maybe
to him.

Craig grabbed her hands, forcing her to quit rubbing
her fingers together. When he lifted his head to look
into her eyes, her breath caressed his cheek.

"Angel, if anyone in Alder Gulch could've accom-
plished what you have, don't you think it would've been
done already?"

She shrugged. "Timing is everything." Her shoulder

rubbed up and down his chest. Air seemed to evaporate from the room.

"You don't give yourself enough credit." His nose touched her cheek. She smelled like summer flowers and woman. He touched her lower lip and her lips parted on a soft sigh. She looked like a woman waiting to be kissed. Timing was everything.

"Aw, hell." All of the things he'd been fighting to say escaped his mind. He gathered her in his arms, bent his head, and kissed her with all of the emotion he had yet to put into words. Slowly, he grazed his lips tantalizingly over hers, outlining her teeth with his tongue, coaxing her mouth open to explore her soft, sweet flesh.

Billie melted against him. She'd begun to wonder if he would ever kiss her again. Didn't know if she'd be able to survive without feeling his firm lips and hard body next to hers again. Yet, she hated leaving herself open to this kind of torture. Craig deserved a strong woman, a woman who wouldn't make the terrible mistakes she had and perhaps risk ruining his future. She didn't trust herself to be able to do the things he'd expect from a partner—or a wife.

But as long as he was offering another wondrous kiss, she could hardly refuse. If she did finally leave Alder Gulch, she would be able to take some wonderful memories with her.

With a soundless moan, she twined her tongue with his. She tasted coffee, whiskey, and man. She delved into his mouth, molded her body to his—teasing, inviting . . .

Craig felt as if his lungs were filled with fire when he broke the kiss. When she'd passionately returned his embrace, his response had been drawn from his soul. If angels kissed like that . . . His arms tightened as he breathed deeply and rasped, "I've never wanted anyone as much as I want you. You fill my dreams and every waking thought."

"I—I want you, too." She waited to feel a rush of

shame for so wantonly expressing her feelings, but it never came. Instead, she felt Craig's gentle fingers caress her cheek and jaw and neck. A faint whimper sounded from her throat as she boldly returned each exploring touch. His smooth flesh rippled over muscles as hard as iron. Fascinated, she wanted to feel every inch of him.

When her words finally penetrated his passion-drugged mind, he lifted his head and stared into gold-flecked green-brown eyes that reminded him of a regal forest. "You don't understand," he drawled huskily.

She shushed him by tenderly placing her index finger on his lips. Nodding, she told him, "Oh, but I think I do." Lifting his hand from her shoulder, she turned her head and kissed his palm, seductively trailing her tongue over the flesh her lips had just caressed.

Craig shuddered. "Are you sure, Angel? You really want me."

His uncertainty warmed her soul. "Yes. Kiss me."

His lips curved sensuously against hers. "Yes, ma'am."

She didn't know how her chest could possibly contain her heart as it swelled to overflowing with love for Craig Rawlins.

Craig melded his mouth with hers. White-hot flames scorched through him. At last he lifted his head, gazed wonderingly into her flushed features, then stood shakily, his heart in his hand as he extended it to her.

Panic rioted through Billie, but she looked into his eyes and saw his vulnerability. With a deep breath, she placed her hand, and her trust, in his strong, capable grasp.

He swept her into his arms before she had a chance to change her mind. Carrying her, he strode swiftly into his bedroom and laid her in the center of a huge feather mattress covered with colorful quilts. He sank beside her, adoring her with his eyes as his fingers fumbled with buttons and stays.

Billie smiled shyly and tugged his shirt from the waistband of his trousers. She got up on her knees to tug it over his head and marveled at the sudden surge of power that flowed through her when he groaned and they collapsed side by side.

She saw the question in his eyes as her hands fluttered over his chest. Was he daring her to continue undressing him? In brazen response, her fingers inched slowly down his hard, flat stomach, teasing the narrow strip of wiry hair that disappeared beneath his waistband.

Her hands trembled over the first button, flinching each time the muscles under her knuckles quivered. Unsure if she could really carry through, she looked helplessly into his warm, blue-green eyes. Big mistake. Desire flared and consumed her as his gaze scorched every bare inch of her body.

Another groan erupted from Craig's taut lips when she looked at him, so vulnerable and filled with need. He managed to give her a reassuring smile, though he felt as if he would explode into a thousand molten pieces.

At last, between the two of them, they freed him from his trousers, removed his boots, and then sank back, holding each other, bare flesh gliding against bare flesh.

"You're so soft," he whispered into her ear as he smoothed his hand down her belly and over her hip.

Her throat thickened. "So are you." She wanted to briefly close her eyes, to take a moment to savor the feel, taste, and smell of him, but couldn't take her eyes off his male perfection. He was all hard muscle and long bones and . . . all man.

As he slid his manhood between their bodies, she swallowed. He felt soft as silk. Warm with life. She wrapped him in her moist palm.

"Angel . . ." He kissed her eyes, the tip of her nose, each corner of her mouth, then trailed his tongue down her neck and chest until he reached the firm mound of a breast. He teased and tickled, working his way toward the cherry-hued aureole. The bud of her nipple puckered and hardened before his eyes, beckoning his touch.

Billie squirmed with impatience. Her nipples burned with sensation as even a faint puff of breath sent tingles shooting through the core of her body. Aching need filled her with a pulsing coil of heat.

When his warm mouth engulfed her nipple, she thought she would explode with each suckling pull. Thought she might die from the pleasure of the pain. Her legs spread. His lifted himself over her. His fingers massaged her belly and moved lower . . . lower.

Breath hissed from her lungs when he touched her there. His finger slipped through the moistness.

Craig moaned into her mouth as he kissed her, thrusting his tongue in and out, in and out until she joined him in the mating dance. Gently, slowly, he eased his finger out of her.

Her hips followed the motion, trying to maintain the contact to ease the sudden emptiness. And then he was there, melding her body with his. Instinct took control as Billie strained upward, seeking what he promised to give, giving more in return.

A feral growl vibrated his thraot. With a sharp thrust of his hips, he made her his. Only his.

She couldn't get close enough to him, literally tried to crawl inside his skin. She moved her hips in a rhythm counter to his. Felt a tightness in her belly that coiled and coiled until she had to clamp her teeth into her lower lip to keep from screaming as she attempted to pull him into herself. Pinpoints of light sparked behind her eyelids. She held on to Craig as explosion after explosion vibrated her body.

Craig thrust over and over taking her as far as her body could go. He gasped and filled her one last time, pumping his seed into her greedy womb. Her muscles clamped around him, draining him of everything he had, except his all-consuming love. Billie Glenn. There'd never been a woman like her—would never be another. He rolled to his side and cradled her to him in trembling arms.

Their bodies still joined, he brushed damp tendrils of hair from her cheeks. He felt like he'd come home. For the first time in his life, he'd found a place where he belonged.

Placing a finger beneath her chin, he turned her face to his and waited until she opened her eyes. With what he knew had to be a silly grin, he whispered, "I love you, Billie Glenn."

Billie stiffened. "You love me?" She had to hear him say the words again, just to be sure she didn't dream them.

He grinned and laved the throbbing pulse at the base of her neck. "Is that so hard to believe?"

"I . . ." Her heart thundered in her chest. Tears burned the corners of her eyes.

He kissed her mouth closed. "Don't say anything yet. I have something I want to give you." He rolled away so he could open a drawer on the bedside table and grinned when her body rolled with him, as if she never wanted to let him go. His throat tightened. He hoped she would always feel that devoted.

When he turned back, he slipped his hands behind her neck and clasped together the ends of a necklace.

Billie gasped when she felt something cool brush her throat. She bent her neck and gazed in awed wonder at the delicate workmanship of a gold chain adorned with tiny chunks of raw gold. A tear trickled down her cheek as she realized the significance of his gesture. "I—it's lovely."

He whispered, "Think of it as a sign of renewal as I pledge my love and promise to honor and protect you for the rest of our lives."

She swallowed, feeling the polished texture of the imperfect stones. Imperfect but beautiful. Imperfect, and a symbol of all that was dear to her. Imperfect. As she was imperfect. But oh so valuable. Her heart blossomed.

Producing a dainty but worn gold band, he took a deep breath and said, "It belonged to my mother, who said it belonged to her mother." He had no idea if it was true, but he now believed because he wanted to. "I love you, Billie Glenn. I'd be honored if you would be my wife."

Her gaping jaw snapped shut. She croaked, "Are you sure you want *me?*" It seemed natural to repeat his own words.

"Yes, Angel. Hell, yes."

She looked into Craig's loving eyes. He'd put his very soul at risk in offering her the ring. "Y-yes."

He'd been holding his breath so long, his ears buzzed. "What?"

"Yes. I love you. And want more than anything to marry you."

He whooped with joy, smothered her in a hug, and sealed their bond with a kiss.

Epilogue

The rocking chair creaked and groaned beneath the weight of two people as they sat on the front porch of the ranch house watching the yearlings cavort in the pasture. A red-and-white filly whinnied, reared, and pawed the air as if in greeting.

"Look at Angel. Isn't she beautiful?"

Craig Rawlins had eyes only for his wife. "She certainly is."

Billie ducked her head when he playfully nipped her ear. "Stop that. I'll spill my lemonade." But she mischievously grinned and stroked his inner thigh.

He growled and snuggled his nose into her neck. "You don't regret movin' to the ranch, do you?"

"Of course not. I love it." Her eyes narrowed as she set down her glass. "You don't regret selling the Grand Palace, do you?"

"Not at all. I think Lucky'll do better with it than we did." He lightly brushed the back of his hand across her bodice and smiled with satisfaction as her nipples hardened.

Billie shivered with pleasure. "I'm so glad he kept Pearl as manager. She'll do a wonderful job."

"Yep." Thoughts of what he'd like to be doing with his wife distracted him from the conversation.

She flushed and darted her tongue along her lower lip. "Uhmm, would it be all right to see if Molly could make me another dress? I'm already outgrowing this one."

Chuckling, he ran his hand over her extended belly. "We better hurry. Ever since Ike offered her the back room in the mercantile to do her sewing, she hasn't even had time to come visit."

"Anna, either. Between Danny and the bakery, she's so busy she can hardly get away."

He sighed contentedly and leaned back in the rocker. He twined his fingers with hers and drew them to his lips, where he gently kissed the backs of her hands.

"I'm glad everyone seems happy. I'd feel guilty as hell if we were the only ones."

Billie eyed her husband's relaxed features a little worriedly. "Speaking of busy and working, what are you doing, staying home so often? How come you aren't in town doing business and starting new enterprises?"

He turned one of her hands loose and waved his arm, indicating the surrounding barn, corrals, and pastures. "This is a thriving business right here. Look at all of the horses that need to be bred, raised, broken, and trained."

"You have Ezekiel for that."

"Yes, and since your father sent a good man to oversee Glenn-Rawlins Freight, I'll have all the more time to spend with my lovely bride and soon-to-be new daughter."

"Son."

"Whatever."

She traced his lips with her thumb. "But you've always been so concerned with having the best and earning the most . . . I worry that you won't be happy."

He kissed her soundly, then groaning, gathered her into his arms and carried her inside, all the while ducking her playful swats.

After sitting her on the bearskin rug in front of the blazing fire, he gracefully eased down beside her and swept a lock of red-gold hair behind her ear. "Thanks to you, I've discovered more important priorities than just making money."

She trailed her fingers up the inside of his trouser leg. Her breath caught when she felt the degree of his arousal. Even when she was as big and clumsy as a milk cow, he still wanted her.

A tear of pure joy trickled down her cheek as she leaned over and puckered her lips. "Don't just sit there, partner. Kiss me."

"Yes, ma'am."

Author's Note

Virginia City's Vigilance Committee was formed December 23, 1863. Twenty-four men signed and adopted detailed regulations and bylaws. They had no law enforcement or jails within two hundred miles, and decided the only practical punishment for serious crimes was—death.

By February 3, 1864, the Committee had hanged twenty-two outlaws and road agents. Dozens of others were scared out of the county.

A People's Court was soon established to try future offenders by judge and jury.

Please forgive my using fictional license to turn back the dates of history several months for the expediency of my story.